THE PARATWA

Christopher Hinz

A TOM DOHERTY ASSOCIATES BOOK
NEW YORK

THE PARATWA

Copyright © 1991 by Christopher Hinz

Cover art by Kevin Murphy

A Tor Book
Published by Tom Doherty Associates, Inc.
175 Fifth Avenue
New York, N.Y. 10010

Tor Books on the World-Wide Web:
http://www.tor.com

Tor® is a registered trademark of Tom Doherty Associates, Inc.

ISBN: 0-812-53093-4

First Tor edition: December 1995

Printed in the United States of America

0 9 8 7 6 5 4 3 2 1

Also by Christopher Hinz

Liege-Killer
Anachronisms
Ash Ock

This one is for
Earl Hinz and Pam Reynolds

—from *The Rigors*, by Meridian

It was the time of our emergence. It was the time of the first coming, when the Earth was still vital and the Ash Ock were fresh as today's memory; in retrospect, a fragile era, but one where life itself seemed aglow with all manner of possibility, where we Paratwa felt destined to rule the Earth, to rule the stars. It was a time when each of us sizzled under the spell of our own unique simultaneities, relishing the genetic fates that had cast our souls into two bodies instead of one. It was a time when our binary spirits seemed molded by the essence of some primordial ubiquity, our bodies glazed to perfection, our minds burnished by the hands of an immortal poet.

It was a time of the Ash Ock, the royal Caste—those five unique creations whose sphere of influence exploded outward from that secret jungle complex deep in the Brazilian rain forest, enveloping the world, uniting us, directing our disparate Paratwa breeds into a swarm of binary elegance that, for those brief fragile years, seemed unstoppable.

It was a time of innocence. It was a time that could not last.

Some of us began to perceive the underlying dynamics of Ash Ock power, to comprehend their subtle manipulations, to hear the distinctive growls of five exquisite motors beneath five exquisite hoods. The mirror that the Ash Ock had held before each of us, which had reflected only our virtues, splintered under the roar of those engines; our worship of their godlike prowess yielded to mere admiration, appreciative yet tempered by the knowledge that those of the royal Caste remained mortal, despite their incredible magic. And that magic, partially swollen by our own needs and desires, gave birth to a child swaddled in the robes of scientific superiority. The poet departed, never to return.

It was a time of terrible betrayal.

As the Star-Edge fleet—under the clandestine guidance of Theophrastus—prepared to escape from an Earth drowning under the fury of the Apocalypse, some of us began to learn the real secrets of the Ash Ock. And that juncture marked the beginning of a cynicism that spread through our ranks with the swiftness of a biological plague. By the time the Star-Edge fleet had cleared the boundaries of the solar system, Sappho and Theophrastus were almost faced with open revolt, for many of the Paratwa had trouble adjusting to the indignity of these ultimate truths.

But Ash Ock patience helped all of us persevere. The crisis passed. An even greater vista of conceptualization was now open to us, and we were invited to perceive the universe from new and dizzying heights. Most of us lost our cynicism. Those few who did not kept their doubts to themselves.

Theophrastus proclaimed: "Never forget that you represent the vanguard of the second coming."

"And never forget that you serve the *true* Paratwa," *Sappho added.* "Your lives now intertwine with the destiny of the chosen."

History texts were subtly altered; the roles of the other three Ash Ock—Codrus, Aristotle, and Empedocles—were lessened to those of supporting players.

Codrus was really the first of the royal Caste to fall from Ash Ock grace. His tways, like the tways of Empedocles, were of mixed sexes—male and female. Even in those early days, when we were still emerging from the landscape of humans, when Theophrastus had not yet infiltrated the Star-Edge project, bending it to his own designs, Sappho had begun to suggest—subtly—that dual-gendered Paratwa were inherently flawed. For a while, even I fell for her elegant craftiness, though eventually I came to see such illogic as a refraction of my own male/male prejudice.

Still, I understood some of Sappho's negativity toward the others of her breed. Codrus often displayed the most blatant weaknesses, misconstruing Ash Ock formulations for precise truths, falling into that intellectual trap of regarding the mind as the ruler of the body. Those facets of reality that Codrus failed to grasp became DATA to be processed, information that simply remained undigested by his networks. Eventually, Codrus's inability to fathom the depths led Sappho to regard him like the child of her royal family, his tways forever loyal and anxious to please, yet his monarchial consciousness incapable of reaching its destined maturity. He was ultimately precluded from all Ash Ock intricacies, and it was arranged that he be left behind when the Star-Edge fleet departed. Until his death at the hands of the Costeaus, centuries later, Codrus remained blissfully ignorant, a true intellectual pauper.

Aristotle, for a time, also remained unaware of the greater concerns, although Aristotle's ignorance was not of his own making, for in many ways, he was the equal of Sappho: shrewd and cunning, with a natural aptitude for the intricate methodology of politics. Aristotle's male/male interlace seemed to know—instinctively—how to utilize others to amplify his own desires; he played the human race as a preinformation-age grandmaster played chess.

In the earliest years of Ash Ock ascendancy, I was the servant of Aristotle, and I grew to admire and respect the sophistication of his agile mind. For a time, I actually came to like him, especially after he had introduced me to Empedocles, youngest of the five, male/female tways whose infectious lust for all manner of experience rivaled even my own. In truth, I loved those years that we spent training Empedocles, helping to mold our young warrior into an elegant bastion of Ash Ock authority, ready to assume his place in the sphere of the royal Caste, to become the champion of all of Earth's Paratwa.

And for a time in those early years, I even doubted Sappho's wisdom in keeping Aristotle—and thus Empedocles—ignorant of the greater reality. In Codrus's case, I understood. But I felt that Aristotle and Empedocles should be given full access to Sappho's knowledge—the secret knowledge—which at that time she shared only with Theophrastus and a few trusted lieutenants: Gol-Gosonia, myself, a handful of others.

Eventually, however, I came to see that Sappho was correct in keeping Aristotle in the dark, for that monarch's plans within plans began rivaling the complexity of even her own intrigues. The simple fact was: Aristotle was too much like Sappho. There could be but one ruler, and

Sappho—by virtue of birthright alone—would be sole proprietress of our destiny.

Nevertheless, the day when I betrayed Aristotle—and doomed Empedocles in the bargain—remains the most regretted day of my life.

Gillian felt eager for another fight. The darkness of Sirak-Brath seemed an ideal place for one.

He followed Buff and the smuggler through the alley separating a pair of low-tech industries—a nuke breeder and a manufacturer of organic soak-dye—the dank passage cutting between the towering buildings like a thin wafer sliced from a monstrous loaf. From the wet floor of the alley, the dirty vacu-formed walls—slabs of reinforced plastic veneered in ancient brickface—soared over two hundred feet up into the night sky. Shadowy forms interconnected the two buildings: a plethora of structural support shafts, conduits, and soggy flexpipes. There were no windows.

A sliver of pale, yellowish gray light was exposed at the peaks of the artificial canyon, and that illuminated snippet should have revealed the distant slabs of the Colony's cosmishield glass, and beyond, the darkness of space. But the thirty-eight-mile-long orbiting cylinder had managed, over the two and a half centuries of its existence, to acquire one of pre-Apocalyptic Earth's nastier habits: air pollution. During peak manufacturing periods, the smog became so dense that Sirak-Brath's atmospheric circulators could not remove it faster than it was being generated.

Buff turned to the smuggler. "How much farther?"

In the dim light of the alley, she was the shorter and thinner of the two figures. Weeks of hiding out with Gillian in a Costeau exercise cone had enabled Buff to shed nearly fifty pounds. She remained stocky, but there was little fat; upper arms bulged with muscle, and her legs now boasted a strength and agility that she had never known at her former weight.

The smuggler grunted. His name was Impleton, and he pointed ahead and whispered words that seemed to dissolve in the dense air, even as Gillian leaned forward, straining to hear. But Buff had understood; the black Costeau's firm nod provided assurance that Impleton's response gave no cause for alarm.

Gillian's last visit to Sirak-Brath had been over half a century ago, and tonight's smog seemed much worse than any he remembered from that first sojourn, in 2307. Back then, the periodic onslaughts of dirty air had not seemed so conspicuous, the haze so impenetrable. He would have expected that during his fifty-six years of stasis sleep, legitimate technical improvements would have contributed to making the air invisible again.

But despite the imminent threat of the returning Paratwa starships—a threat whose closing horizon lately had spawned bitter tensions throughout the populace of the Irryan Colonies—day-to-day scientific and technical advancements were still under the control of E-Tech, the powerful institution whose tenets essentially served to limit the degree of change. E-Tech's two-and-a-half-century-old ideal—to prevent wild permutations in the social structure, like those that had decimated the Earth during the Apocalypse of 2099—made it difficult for a Colony to alter the status quo. Sirak-Brath's smog served to illustrate the downside of E-Tech's otherwise noble cause.

Sirak-Brath had other problems as well. It was popularly considered to be the black sheep of the Irryan Colonies—the cylinder denizens of the other two hundred and sixteen orbiting space islands could point to with disdain. No matter how bad your home Colony might be in a particular respect, Sirak-Brath was probably worse. The industrial cylinder boasted the highest crime rates, the dirtiest streets, and the most consistently corruptible politicians. Many non-mainstreamed Costeaus, black marketeers, and high-tech smugglers called it home.

The alley began to curve to the left, and a soft breeze

brought an oppressive odor of untreated sludge. Gillian glanced over his shoulder, saw the pale remaining light from the side street, nearly two blocks away, slowly compress into nothingness, and the heavy barred gate, through which Impleton had led them into this service corridor, disappear. Now, only the smog-reflected light from above remained to guide their footsteps.

Gillian closed his eyes, listened to the night: the dull omnipresent hum of heavy machinery, distant sirens of local patroller or E-Tech Security vehicles en route to fresh crime sites, their own footsteps, flapping across the wet pavement, an occasional echo of a human voice, amplified to prominence by the acoustic qualities of this artificial canyon. Sounds that were recognizable aspects of Sirak-Brath. Sounds that carried no threat of danger.

But there was still time.

The alley continued its steady curve to the left, on a sweeping tangent, until finally they were walking perpendicular to their original direction. Fresh bright light appeared up ahead; the canyon walls peeled back to reveal a cul de sac where nuke breeder joined organic soak-dye manufacturer, their common bulkhead a monolithic eruption of greasy pipes and spiraling twill tubes. It was power distribution machinery combined with an overworked pollution control grid. The entire conglomeration had been designed to serve both industries and probably others as well, whose sterns would be butting against the far side of the towering mech-wall.

Buff and Impleton became crisp silhouettes as they headed into the light, the fresh illumination provided by a series of globed lamps positioned ten feet above the dank floor. Buff's hairless pate, cosmetically scarred by a series of twisting blue and red lines—the deliberate handiwork of luminescent crayons—began to shine. In the daytime, the black Costeau often wore a hat, but when a Colony's mirrors rotated into darkness, she exposed her shaved skull and the shiny photoluminescent streaks.

Blue lines and red lines, crisscrossing the crown of her head, all freshly painted each morning, as important to Buff as any other aspect of her daily grooming. Blue lines and red lines, each bound by the faint perimeter of her natural hairline, each glowing, like a nest of wet snakes. Buff was of the clan of the Cerniglias, but the painted streaks remained universal Costeau symbols. Blue for mourning. Red for vengeance. With Costeaus, the two colors often went together.

Buff had painted herself every morning for nearly a month and vowed to continue the ritual until she found the Paratwa assassin—the one who had been terrorizing the Irryan Colonies for the past five months. The one whose tripartite self—*three* discrete physical bodies controlled by a solitary, telepathically interlaced consciousness—remained unique among known Paratwa breeds. The one whose brutal massacres, throughout the orbiting cylinders, had been linked to the imminent return of the Paratwa starships.

The one who had killed her friend Martha.

Impleton—fat, pale-skinned, wearing a knee-length pink corselet coat—craned his neck and muttered something to Buff. She paused at the entrance to the bottleneck, waited for Gillian to catch up.

"He says Faquod's not here yet."

Gillian went hyper alert. Senses, normally diluted by a wide range of environmental stimuli, focused; muscles prepped for instantaneous response. His tongue slithered along the tiny rubber pads attached to his bicuspids and molars—the activation circuitry for the hidden crescent web hardware strapped around his waist. One snap of the jaw and the defensive field would ignite, form a near-invisible sheath along the front and rear contours of his six-foot frame, a barrier capable of deflecting projectile and energy weapons alike. And hidden in the sleeve covering his right forearm, gripped securely in a slip-wrist holster, lay a pale egg with a tiny needle protruding from one end.

His Cohe wand: a device infinitely rare and highly illegal, the original weapon of the Paratwa assassins from the days before the decimation of Earth, over two-and-a-half centuries ago. The Cohe was devilish to control, requiring years of training to become proficient in its more subtle capabilities. But once mastered, it was a weapon that bore no equal.

Impleton sucked in his gut and said loudly, "Faquod, he will be along shortly."

Two other figures were poised in the bottleneck. To Gillian's right, a well-groomed man with a sawed-off beard leaned against the wall, one hand tucked under his black coat. And across the alley, seated on a four-foot-high ledge, was a blond-haired muscle boy, grinning like a scuddie. The youth was stripped to the waist. Bulging pectorals bore tattoos of ancient motorized cycles and the cryptic phrase, *I'm a Harley in Heat*, was printed neatly above his navel.

Buff scowled. "You said he'd be waiting here for us."

The smuggler rolled his eyes. "Faquod, he does as he pleases."

The muscle boy laughed. Gillian approached the youth while casually scanning the mech-wall, already fairly certain of what he would find on it. He was not disappointed.

About twenty feet up, squeezed amid the filthy spirals of relay tubes and monstrous conduits, sat a hunched figure with a thruster rifle. It was a fairly good hiding place, though not good enough to escape Gillian's detection. Although he had met Impleton only yesterday, their brief encounter had provided enough raw data to establish a psych profile of the swarthy black marketeer. Gillian had known that bold deceit would be Impleton's fashion; the presence of an armed backup, out of sight, fit the smuggler's profile like a glove.

Impleton licked his lips. "These high-tech playthings you desire . . . Faquod, he says that they are not easy to come by. Faquod says they will not be cheap."

Gillian halted two paces away from the grinning muscle boy and leaned over the four-foot ledge that the tattooed smuggler sat upon. On the other side of the wall, a vertical drop plunged fifteen feet into a plodding river of sludge covered by a fine-meshed net. The harsh odor of untreated sewage, far more potent than it had been in the alley, assailed his nostrils. Gillian suspected that the open sewage channel was illegal.

"Very expensive," continued Impleton, his fat cheeks squirming as if his mouth were stuffed with unchewed food.

"Faquod—he will want at least half the money in advance, I am sure."

"You told us that already," Buff replied calmly.

"You have the money?"

"Not with us, of course." Buff sighed. "You don't think we're that foolish, do you?"

Gillian leaned against the ledge and relaxed his muscles, body poised for action. He was now fairly certain that Impleton was lying. *Faquod's not coming. We've been set up for a knockdown. They're planning to rob us. Maybe kill us as well.* He found himself secretly smiling as he began to consider ways to extend the duration of the upcoming fight. It was important for him to be able to relish every moment.

The smuggler with the black coat and sawed-off beard carefully withdrew a small thruster from his pocket. He made no threatening gestures, keeping the weapon aimed at the ground.

Impleton yawned. "My men . . . they're very excitable. I told them they would be paid tonight. I hope they will not be disappointed."

"Yeah," agreed Buff, with a sharp glance at Gillian, "I certainly hope no one gets pissed."

The fat smuggler stroked his chin. "I think that maybe you have some of the money, anyway. Down payment money. Sign of good faith. You give it to us. We give it to Faquod."

Buff scowled. "You bring Faquod. Then we'll talk about money."

Impleton's pudgy face attempted a smile. "Your way . . . it is not good for business. Faquod . . . he likes to know that there is trust, that there is openness."

Gillian felt his chest begin to tingle—the onslaught of the familiar desperate excitement that now directly preceded his fights. Buff referred to his eagerness for confrontation—for violence—as "full-body hard-on," and she was probably not far from the truth. Over the past month, his increasing desire to engage in combat had developed strange sexual overtones. Fighting had mutated into a distinct mode of self-expression; violence and lust had become intertwined.

But Gillian knew that at its core, the fighting remained a

way for him to keep his turbulent inner forces at bay, a way to temporarily relieve the tremendous mental/emotional pressure that relentlessly strove to devolve his consciousness. He fought not only because it felt good but because it helped to maintain his sanity.

He turned to Buff. "We're wasting our time. These scuddies have been lying to us. I don't think they're smart enough even to know Faquod."

Impleton sneered. "Not smart? Smarter than you, maybe. Smart enough not to wander into an alley with strangers, maybe."

Gillian let out a harsh laugh, heard it echo up the canyon walls, heard his own heart beating with excitement, with the urgency of wild desire. A fresh assault of malodorous sewage drifted up from the sludge river. He inhaled deeply. The odor should have repulsed him, should have carried with it a hundred connotations: childhood naughtiness, genetically determined distaste, a manifest of internal responses, learned and innate. But it smelled good. The whole night smelled good.

He spun to face Impleton. "You're right. You should never allow yourself to be alone with strangers. It's not smart. It's not safe."

The smuggler with the sawed-off beard raised his thruster and pointed it at Buff. She held up her hands, pleading restraint.

"Look," she said softly, "we really don't want any trouble." She glared at Gillian. "We just want to meet Faquod."

"Then you pay," said Impleton. "Meeting Faquod . . . that is a privilege."

Gillian pointed his finger at the muscle boy, four feet away. "Can this ignor fight? Whenever I see someone like this, I'm reminded of the value of contraceptives. If his parents had only known."

"Oh shit," muttered Buff.

Muscle boy lost his smile. Saw-beard tightened his grip on the thruster and glanced at Impleton, waiting for orders. Impleton's mouth squirmed. The fat smuggler released a loud belch.

The belch was a signal. Muscle boy hopped down from the ledge and took a step toward Gillian. "I'm going to—"

His words ended in a choking gasp as Gillian's right foot lashed out, slammed into his belly. Muscle boy doubled over in pain.

Saw-beard pivoted, aimed his thruster at Gillian. He was far too late. Gillian, biting down hard, ignited his defensive web, heard the near-invisible crescents—front and rear—hum softly as they came to life. Saw-beard fired. Gillian, braced against the ledge, was hit by the discrete blast of energy, feeling it as a gentle nudge against his front crescent.

A single-tube thruster, thought Gillian. *A one-second recharge interval before it can be used again.*

All the time in the world.

Gillian flexed his right wrist and compressed his knuckles, launching the Cohe wand from its slip-wrist holster into his waiting palm. He squeezed the egg.

The twisting black beam whipped up the side of the mech-wall, the leading fifteen to twenty inches of the hot particle stream disintegrating everything in its path, the remainder of the beam merely a trail of harmless light. The fourth smuggler, perched twenty feet above the alley, screamed as twill tubes, relays, and conduits exploded, showering him beneath a mix of hot liquids and pressurized gases. Live wires arced; the alley's gloom vanished in a sizzling display of electrical madness. The smuggler—along with a melange of exploding flares—was jolted from the mech-wall, his arms flailing wildly, thruster rifle flying from his grasp, his crescent web turning the color of red wine as it soared to full power, trying to neutralize the thrashing high-voltage cables.

The smuggler was still in midair when Gillian twisted his wrist and turned the Cohe's deadly energy on Saw-beard. For an instant, the black beam seemed to coil in upon itself, lancing into an expanding spiral as it hurtled high into the air. Gillian squeezed the egg harder and jerked his wrist; the Cohe's deadly energy stream performed a U-turn, plunged toward the ground. Saw-beard opened his mouth in astonishment as the Cohe's devastating energy sliced off the barrel of his thruster.

Gillian released pressure on the egg-shaped wand. The black beam vanished just as the plummeting smuggler slammed onto the floor of the alley.

Muscle boy, still clutching his guts, reached into his pants pocket. Gillian jerked forward, extended his left foot through the weak side portal of his web, and slammed his heel into muscle boy's chest. The tattooed smuggler grunted hard, collapsed to his knees.

Get up, Gillian urged, feeling the excitement race through his body, unrestrained, as if his inner skin were being tickled, as if there were feathers in his bloodstream. His breath came in short intense gasps and he could feel tremendous waves of heat coursing up and down his chest. Full-body flush. Full-body hard-on.

"Cohe wand," whispered Impleton, the words echoing his fright. Buff grabbed the smuggler by the neck and yanked him forward so violently that he fell to his knees.

Saw-beard dropped the useless remnant of his weapon and backed away, his eyes wide with fear. The man from the mech-wall remained prone on the floor of the alley, moaning softly.

Gillian stared at muscle boy. "Get up!" He slithered into a combat crouch, turned sideways toward the tattooed smuggler, ready to lash out with hand or foot through the web's portals.

Muscle boy raised his head. A defeated face met Gillian's. Hard contours had been transformed into quivering patches of fear, humiliation. There was no more fight left in him. Eyes like those of a beaten puppy stared up at Gillian, begging forgiveness.

"No!" Gillian screamed, lunging forward, grabbing muscle boy's ankle and elbow, lifting the terrified smuggler overhead. With one violent twist, he sent him cartwheeling over the ledge. Muscle boy's shriek lasted until the youth plowed into the net-covered sludge river, fifteen feet below. There was a loud muffled splash, and then steaming gray geysers sprayed Gillian, bringing with them fresh wafts of the foul odor.

Gillian felt cheated; the fight had ended too soon. His left sleeve was damp with sludge, and he rammed the garment against his nostrils, sucked in the odor, wanting it to over-power him, hoping sensory overload would occupy conscious-ness, take his mind away from the reality of his damaged psyche. But the smell was a poor substitute for the cathartic power of violence. In a rage, he started toward Impleton.

The fat smuggler was on his knees, quaking in fear, his head pivoting wildly between Gillian and Buff. "Won't tell what I saw!" he pleaded. "Please . . . won't tell—"

Gillian grabbed the front of Impleton's coat and rubbed the protruding needle of his Cohe into the thick flesh of Impleton's neck.

"Won't tell," repeated the terrified smuggler, his voice dropping to a whisper, his eyes blinking like a set of short-circuiting status lights.

"Let's talk about Faquod," suggested Buff.

Impleton, with an overly vigorous nod of his head, man-aged to scratch himself on the needle of the Cohe.

"Oww!" he screamed.

"Calm down," ordered Buff. "And maybe you'll survive this night."

"Faquod," urged Gillian. "Where is he?"

The smuggler's lips began to quiver, uncontrollably, until finally the words exploded from his mouth.

"You're a Paratwa!" His eyes panned back and forth be-tween Gillian and Buff. "You're tways!"

Buff laughed. "And you're a shitpile with maggots for neu-rons! Now talk! We want to find Faquod!"

Ten feet away, Saw-beard started to inch forward. Gillian glared at him. It was enough of a warning. Saw-beard froze in midstride.

"Don't want to die," whimpered Impleton.

"Faquod!" shouted Buff. "Where is he?"

Gillian pressed the Cohe's needle tip deep into a fold of flesh on the smuggler's neck, until it almost broke the skin.

"Fin Whirl in centersky," babbled Impleton. "Fin Whirl—tomorrow night. Faquod—he is always there. He never misses it."

Gillian glanced at Buff. "You know where this place is?"

"Yeah, I know where Fin Whirl is." A deep frown settled

on her face. "Where else?" she asked Impleton. "Where else can we find him?"

"Don't know," whispered Impleton, his eyes begging. "It's truth! Fin Whirl—that's all I know."

Gillian leaned down, pressed his mouth against the smuggler's ear. "If you're lying, I'll come back for you. I'll slice off your head and put it in my trophy case."

"Fin Whirl," cried the smuggler. "It's truth—I swear!"

"Fin Whirl's a big place," pressed Buff. "Where exactly?"

"He has a private booth—BS-four."

Gillian believed him. He nodded to Buff, and she laid her palm on Impleton's forehead. The smuggler jerked once. His eyes glazed over, and he fell forward into her arms, unconscious. She let him slide off her body onto the damp paving and opened her palm, exposing the tiny white neuropad attached to the skin. She crooked her finger at Saw-beard.

He came quickly, almost eagerly, obviously finding a few hours of deep sleep via synaptic scrambling preferable to any further encounter with Gillian's Cohe wand.

"You may as well be comfortable," suggested Buff, pointing to Impleton's prone form. Saw-beard sat down beside his partner and rested the back of his head on Impleton's ample gut. Buff gave a quick touch with the neuropad. Saw-beard's eyes glazed over as he entered induced sleep.

"Let's go," said Gillian.

They began to jog up the alley, around the bend, retracing their path, toward the huge gate that Impleton had keyed open for them, toward the sanctuary of the street. Their boots splashed against puddles, spraying the canyon walls with the foul conglomeration of liquids, like twin-rotored boats leaving overlapping wakes.

"What's Fin Whirl?" asked Gillian, picking up the pace. It felt good to run hard, run fast, keep the body stimulated.

"I don't think you should go there," said Buff, the distaste in her voice easily discernible.

"We have to."

Buff did not reply. She was a Costeau, and she would do what was necessary. They had been partners for over a month now, ever since that Venus Cluster debacle in Irrya.

Their near-fatal encounter with Slasher and Shooter—two tways of the vicious tripartite assassin who had been ravaging the Colonies—had provided a commonality of cause. Buff needed to avenge the death of her friend Martha; Gillian needed to keep his inner turbulence under control.

"What's Fin Whirl?" he repeated.

"It's a place where games are played . . . dangerous games." She paused. "I don't think you should go there."

They reached the end of the alley, jogged to a halt in front of the massive service gate. Gillian found the control panel on the left wall, pressed the button. Silently, the gate slid open.

They emerged onto the narrow side street, deserted except for an old man seated on a stoop across the way, his head encased in a metallic shroud—a ree-fee—a self-powered programmable holo, providing a sensual experience as rich as the wearer's darkest fantasies. The man was muttering to himself:

"Now, silky—onto the floor. Onto your knees. Give us what we've been asking for. Ground it, silky. Ground it good. Make it earth, silky. Make it wet as the world. . . ."

Behind them, the gate closed automatically. They headed quickly up the street toward one of the main boulevards, three blocks away, to a place where Sirak-Brath began to lose its shadows, where its fantasies became accessible to all.

"Is Fin Whirl an entertainment complex?" probed Gillian. "A fantasy club?"

"It's no fantasy. It's very real."

"But a place of enjoyment, nonetheless?"

Buff grimaced. "I don't think you should go there."

The message decoded itself. On screen, the weird blending of darting icons—spheres, triangles, bubbling spirals—erupted into words and sentences.

PERPS A WHITE MALE AND BLACK FEMALE. NO POSITIVE ID, BUT WEAPON USED ON SMUGGLERS DEFINITELY A COHE WAND. INTERVIEW WITH INJURED SMUGGLER SUGGESTS THAT MALE DISPLAYED EAGERNESS FOR CONFLICT. PERPS WERE OSTENSIBLY TRYING TO CONTACT A HIGH-TECH WEAPONS DEALER NAMED FAQUOD. PROBABILITY EXTREMELY HIGH THAT PERPS WERE GILLIAN AND BUFF.

The lion of Alexander scanned the intelligence report a second time, then turned off the monitor, an action that automatically sent the Sirak-Brath report into the obscurity of the Costeaus' secret files. Not that secrecy seemed so important in this instance. The lion had a feeling that Gillian's actions would soon be discussed throughout the cylinders. No one had seen a Cohe wand used in over fifty years.

He recalled Gillian's parting words, weeks ago.

"If something should happen to me, Jerem . . . if I should become someone—something—that you no longer recognize as Gillian . . . and you're sure that I can't be brought back . . . send your Costeaus out to find me."

To bring you back? the lion had asked.

"No. Not to bring me back."

Gillian's meaning had seemed clear: *before I become something monstrous, uncontrollable—before my monarch, Empedocles, becomes master of this body—kill me.* At least that was how the lion understood it.

Was it time to obey Gillian's wishes?

The lion rose from his seat and slipped an arm around his waist, kneaded his palm across an aching muscle in the lumbar vertebrae. It was an old injury, acquired in youth, stirred to prominence by the ravages of late adulthood. He wished his wife was here right now; Mela was an expert masseuse, but she remained in the Alexanders' home cylinder—the Colony of Den—with some of their children and grandchildren. Den was one of the three so-called new colonies, all Costeau places that had been admitted to the Irryan federation in the past twenty years under the auspices of the mainstreaming movement.

I am Jerem Marth, the lion of Alexander. I am sixty-eight years old, and today I am feeling my age. He would have liked nothing better than to hop on a shuttle and make the short journey home. But duty demanded his presence here.

He marched from the communications room, down a long wide hallway, and out the back door of the A-frame, into his small secluded garden at the rear of the house, where wildly sprouting azul rosebushes in twenty-six shades of blue encircled a genetically stunted white birch. Overhead, the great green forest, dominated by soaring pines, rose up and vanished into the heavily clouded skies of Irrya. It was the gloomiest day the lion could recall in many a month: damp and cool, with sharp gusts sweeping down from the cylinder's central core, lacing the tall trees, showering the ground with fresh pine needles. Perhaps his aching muscle had been stimulated by the morning's abnormal ecospheric conditions.

Irrya's weather programmers, despite a wealth of opposition, had fought a hard political battle to make today gloomy, as per their complex schedule, formulated months in advance. That schedule indicated to them that the sociopsychological well-being of the populace required periodic alterations in the status quo. Despite notable opposition, the weather programmers had been most insistent that the local Irryan government not hinder today's onslaught of unpleasant skies.

Local freelancers had been covering the spirited debate. Fine weather advocates remained in the majority, most of them virulently opposed to sun blotting. Even though the Irryan Governor herself had publicly reasoned that today's shrouded skies had been the only such atmospheric alteration in the past two and a half months, her statements had failed to win the majority. The fine weather advocates demanded the continuation of the Irryan norm—seventy-two degrees, low humidity, near-cloudless skies.

In these times of impending crisis, they argued, *Irrya, our seat of intercolonial government, needs the consistency of pure undaunted sunshine in order to function at its highest level. This is not the time to go mucking around with the weather, not with the Ash Ock servant, Meridian, soon to arrive in the Colonies, harbinger to the as-yet-undetected fleet of return-*

ing Paratwa starships. For all we know, our 217 cylinders are about to be invaded and conquered by our ancient enemy.

But another faction in the weather struggle argued just as vocally that a little change in day-to-day routine was good for the soul, that some overcast skies might serve to remind people that their ancestors on the planet had been forced to live without any potent forms of weather control throughout most of Earth's history. The pro-change advocates also suggested that too many days of perfect weather could lull people everywhere into false feelings of immunity. Some of them were even lobbying for more extreme atmospheric alterations, such as thunderstorms.

The lion recalled a memory from childhood: a T-storm in his home Colony of Lamalan, he and his mother huddled on their front porch, watching a pair of figures creep along their neighbor's yard. That had been Jerem Marth's introduction to the creatures who had forever altered his life. On the day of *that* thunderstorm, he had met two men who were not really two men. He had encountered his first Paratwa.

The lion knelt beside one of the bushes, checked for tiny pinch bugs on the underside of the azul roses—one of Irrya's unique, difficult-to-eliminate, garden pests. With his other hand, he continued to knead the aching muscle in his lower back.

A sigh escaped him. As Nick had pointed out weeks ago, people everywhere seemed to be focusing more and more on negligible issues in order to avoid the one that scared them the most: the imminent return of the Paratwa starships. The intercolonial entertainment index had reached an all-time high; everyone sought escape, however nebulous and temporary, from the grim reality that a race of violent creatures, who might just possess enough technology to destroy the Colonies, were on their way back. Clubs and taverns everywhere were jammed; touring dramusicals were opening to record runs. For the astute businessperson—for the citizen capable of ignoring the threat of future decimation—it was a time of great profit potential. In the field of public diversions, new fortunes were being made every day.

The lion realized that the majority of the Irryan populace

did not truly believe that the state of the weather was an important issue. But many of the billion-plus colonists seemed unable to deal directly with the return of the Paratwa. The reality of it filled them with inexpressible dread, and arguing about the weather served as a catharsis for those hidden feelings. The lion only could hope that if and when a day of true crisis was upon them, people would maintain sight of the pertinent issues.

And if that day ever did come, the lion hoped it would be under sunny skies.

He found himself chuckling heartily, amused by his own contradictions. So much for his sharp analysis of the weather debate.

A Costeau guard, with thruster rifle slung over his shoulder, emerged from the house, searching for his leader. The young guard glanced around suspiciously, obviously scanning the surrounding forests for some indication of what was causing the lion of Alexander, Chief of the United Clans, acknowledged head of the entire Costeau population, to laugh aloud. When the guard realized that they were alone, he cleared his throat.

"Sir, I have Doyle Blumhaven for you."

The lion felt the last remnant of joy slip from his face. Doyle Blumhaven was one of the few people capable of doing that to him.

He sighed. "Bring a monitor outside. I'll speak to our esteemed Councillor right here." And never mind the weather.

The guard shook his head. "No, sir, he's not on screen. He's here, at the retreat."

Doyle Blumhaven? Here in the flesh? E-Tech's Director rarely left his offices in the main governmental district, some thirty miles to the south. And as far as the lion knew, Blumhaven had never before been to the clan of Alexander's private preserve. Although they were both Councillors of Irrya, the lion could not imagine what had motivated Blumhaven to enter the unofficial heartland of the Costeaus.

He nodded to the guard and then made his way around the stone path that encircled the large A-frame. Near the front of the house sat Doyle Blumhaven, at one of the lawn tables, on a slightly elevated ridge of groomed albino grass. He wore a conservative blue suit, expertly cut to deemphasize his heavy frame. A servant had already brought a tray of refreshments and Blumhaven was munching contentedly on pita bread stuffed with mashed flounder.

At the sight of the lion, a tight smile crept across the Councillor's pudgy face. "Terrible weather, isn't it?"

"Most upsetting."

Blumhaven licked a crumb from his upper lip. "Councillor, this retreat is a marvelous place. You and your Costeaus should be most proud."

"We are," replied the lion, perceiving the E-Tech Councillor's words as a reminder that Costeaus were different from other Colonists. Despite the great inroads made to mainstream the Costeau population, the walls of prejudice still existed. To the lion's way of thinking, Doyle Blumhaven remained a living example of subtle bigotry.

At least they don't call us pirates anymore, he mused, recalling the once-common nickname for Costeaus, a nickname that the mainstreaming movement had worked hard to eliminate from intercolonial vocabularies. *Of course, deep down, we still think of ourselves as pirates.* It was an identity that even the most mainstreamed Costeaus still clung to, long after they had given up their clan odorant bags and assumed the soothing smells of proper culture.

Blumhaven finished the pita bread and reached for a pitcher of cognac tea. "It's just a shame that my visit cannot be under more pleasant circumstances." He glanced upward at the darkening skies.

Before the lion could respond, another guard emerged from the house. The guard handed the lion a printed message. The lion read it silently, then sat down at the table, directly across from Blumhaven.

"Doyle, my security people report that you have brought with you a speck camera and some tracking gear. I'm afraid that it's our policy to discourage active surveillance gear here at the retreat."

Blumhaven shrugged, then reached under his coat. The guard leaned forward, anticipating being handed the devices, but Blumhaven quickly snaked his hand across the table and deposited the two small rectangular units in the lion's palm. A spark of static electricity jumped between the devices.

"Sorry," muttered Blumhaven. "These damn things are always giving me shocks. I carry them only because my Security people insist."

"Of course," said the lion, handing the devices to the guard, who whisked them back into the house. "Your equipment will be returned to you at the main parking lot when you depart," he offered, not satisfied by Blumhaven's explanation of why such devices had been brought here. Still, Doyle's reasons were probably innocuous. *Perhaps he feels the need to protect himself amid this haven for pirates.*

"Foolish of me," said the E-Tech Councillor. "I wasn't thinking. I didn't even stop to consider that your retreat would be under such tight security."

"Of course. And now, Doyle, just what are these unpleasant circumstances that have prompted your visit?"

Blumhaven set down his drink. "Recently, a special audit of the E-Tech stasis vaults uncovered a discrepancy. It seems that the stasis capsule that was supposed to contain Gillian and Nick was switched with another capsule. A bit of chicanery, I'm afraid. We can't seem to locate the Gillian/Nick stasis capsule anywhere."

The lion remained silent.

"And last night, of course, a man used a Cohe wand in Sirak-Brath, and with a great degree of expertise, according to witnesses. Since the killers responsible for the Order of the Birch massacres have never employed that particular weapon, and since Gillian is known to be an expert with the Cohe, E-Tech was wondering if Gillian—and Nick—could have been awakened from their stasis sleep?"

"It certainly sounds possible."

Blumhaven gave a forced chuckle. "Yes ... very possible. And if so, that means that there is quite possibly a traitor in the E-Tech vaults—a highly skilled programmer with confidential access to the E-Tech stasis vaults, and probably the data archives as well.

"Since it is well known that the lion of Alexander has been

an advocate for awakening these two men from stasis, E-Tech was wondering if you—or any of your Costeaus—might have some knowledge of these troubling events?"

The lion smiled grimly. *Do you think I'm a complete idiot? Do you think I'm going to admit that Inez Hernandez, Adam Lu Sang from the data vaults, and myself conspired to awaken the Paratwa hunters from their fifty-six year sleep?*

Blumhaven, seeing that no answer was forthcoming, continued. "Since you personally knew Gillian a long time ago, our people believe that he might try to contact you." The Councillor licked his lips. "Could this have occurred already?"

"If Gillian were to contact me, I'm afraid such a meeting would be held in the strictest confidence."

A flash of anger distorted Blumhaven's baby fat cheeks. "This is a most serious matter . . . a *criminal* matter. And for your own benefit, I might say that political suicide is not an attractive thing to witness. If you know something about Gillian and Nick, I would strongly suggest that you come out with it right now. It will only be a matter of time before we identify the traitor in the E-Tech vaults who arranged for the awakening, and that person will bear the full brunt of E-Tech prosecution. Doubtlessly, to save his own skin, this person will implicate any fellow conspirators.

"I might add that since E-Tech determined the identity of one of the perpetrators who escaped from the Venus Cluster massacre—a Costeau named Buff Boscondo—we have been diligently trying to identify her male companion. We now believe that this male could have been Gillian. Since this Boscondo woman, who boasts quite a history of unproven criminal activities, has been known to associate with the clan of Alexander—*your* clan . . ." Blumhaven trailed off with a meaningful shrug.

The lion stared upward, into the great bubbling patches of gray-green mist that marred the seventy-mile-long capitol cylinder. Directly overhead, where the cosmishield glass should have been providing this sector's primary light source, the mirrored image of the sun was totally hidden behind swiftly churning cloud banks.

A day of programmed obscurity.

"Doyle," he said quietly, "if E-Tech should learn anything new regarding these affairs, I would appreciate being kept informed."

Blumhaven stiffened. "I can assure that you will be kept abreast of current developments."

The lion stood up. "Is there anything else that we need to discuss?"

"Nothing that can't wait until the next Council meeting," replied Blumhaven, slowly lifting his bulk from the chair.

The lion walked him toward the path leading to the main parking lot beyond the woods. "Anything new on the Order of the Birch massacres?" quizzed the lion, knowing that this remained a sore spot with Blumhaven. E-Tech Security still seemed totally impotent in dealing with the continuing killings. There had been two new massacres in the last week alone, bringing the total number to eleven.

"We have some leads," muttered Blumhaven. "Since the Venus Cluster killings—since we first learned that it is probably a Paratwa assassin we are dealing with—we have been making steady progress."

Steady progress, thought the lion, a misnomer for *we've learned nothing new*. And Blumhaven obviously did not realize that the lion had been the one responsible for leaking the information that the Order of the Birch killers was indeed a singular Paratwa. The lion remained angry that the Council had voted—over his own and Inez Hernandez's objections—to withhold that information; publicly, E-Tech Security continued to proclaim that the killers probably were *not* a Paratwa, although increasing numbers of freelancer reports disputed those assertions.

Of course, the lion recognized that he was just as manipulative with information as Blumhaven. The E-Tech Director and the rest of the Council still did not know that the assassin they were dealing with was a tripartite, composed of *three* tways instead of the normal two. Nick, ever one to hoard information, had felt it best that they keep that little tidbit to themselves, at least for the time being.

The lion halted at the edge of the woodland. "Good-bye, Doyle."

Blumhaven's tone softened. He almost sounded polite. "Please give some added consideration to what we have discussed. Your political future must certainly be more important to you than a misguided friendship."

"It's not," said the lion. Blumhaven stared at him for a long moment, then turned and marched up the winding path through the pines. The lion waited until Doyle had vanished from sight before heading back to the house. Nick stood waiting for him just inside the door.

The lion shook his head. "Our little conspiracy is being uncovered."

"I was listening," said the midget, leaping up onto the lawn table. "I'm not surprised that Blumhaven's finding things out, but I'm real curious about why he felt he had to come down here and tell you what he knows."

The lion nodded. "A bit strange."

"At any rate, if he had any hard evidence, he would have used it. So he's still guessing."

"But not for long, I'd suppose. Is Adam still trying to penetrate E-Tech Security?"

"Yeah," said Nick. "I guess we'd better warn him that things are getting edgy. Tell him to back off a bit ... at least from E-Tech Security. But I don't want our efforts against the sunsetter to be hindered."

The lion scowled. "Adam could be in great danger—"

"We're *all* in great danger, Jerem, so it's almost an irrelevant point. Besides, in the last couple of weeks we've been developing a closer understanding of the relationship between the sunsetter and Freebird. Adam is convinced—and I'm beginning to agree with him—that Freebird is protecting the sunsetter from harm solely because that is the best method for a computer program of its nature to thwart its own destruction by the sunsetter. By acting as the sunsetter's guardian angel, Freebird stays one step ahead of it.

"We're also beginning to suspect that the sunsetter's primary reason for destroying all of those ancient programs in the first place was to drive Freebird out into the open."

"Freebird is the sunsetter's actual prey?"

"It sure as hell is looking that way. There's a very strange relationship between these two programs. I hate to anthropomorphize, but the more we learn about Freebird and the sunsetter, the more I feel that we're dealing with a pair of ancient enemies, long at war with each other."

The lion gazed at a genetically altered peach tree near the corner of the house, its rainbow elephant leaves flopping in the soft winds. A faint smell of dead fish assailed him: the unique identifying brand of the clan of Alexander, still worn by many of the Costeaus at this retreat in small odorant bags fastened to their waist belts.

He turned back to Nick. "I suppose even if I ordered you and Adam to abstain from your efforts for a while, it wouldn't do any good."

Nick grinned. "Hell, Jerem, we're computer hawks. Neither rain nor sleet nor snow nor Paratwa will keep us from our appointed rounds. But relax—I'll tell Adam to be extra careful from here on out."

"I do not think that I will be able to do much relaxing in the weeks to come."

Nick gazed up at the brooding skies. "Yeah . . . the storm's a-coming."

Susan Quint, at a state of consciousness somewhere between the dusk and the darkness—on the rim of the dreamtime—believed in her own immortality.

It was a feeling totally consistent with her new-found body-thought, her hyperenhanced awareness of self, the completeness of existing freely in one place at one time: her intellect a true focusing and amplification of base emotions—

anger, fear, joy, sorrow—those raw natural feelings complementing the deeper urges of the physical self.

I am a force existing discretely within a matrix of other forces. I am a human being alive within the larger world.

Susan pulled back from the dreamtime, allowed logical thought to disengage slightly from the undammed flow of mind/emotion/body, allowed herself to perceive her own nature from a distance, like a winding river glimpsed from a steep hill. Now she could see her vision of immortality through the unencumbered apparatus of digital conception, as a human mimicking the actions of a computer. Far above the river of her own soul, she could analyze the interconnections among the three distinct states of consciousness. From that vantage point, she conceived of immortality as it truly was, not as some mythological state enabling a person to live forever, but as the free, totally unencumbered flow between the distinct facets of her own self: mind/emotion/body. Within the realm of the creature known as Susan Quint, she could move in any direction; the river brooked no bounds. She could swim to any inlet, bask on any bank, dive beneath the deepest stretches of water without mortal fear of drowning in whirlpools of childhood pain.

Yet she could see clearly those places where she was again a child, trying to understand her parents' bizarre behavior, trying to attain a stability within a home that—at times— offered little more than a dark sanctuary against the more dimly understood dangers of the real world. Now Susan could apply the logic of intellect to that portion of her life. Now she could understand how her parents' fanatic religious devotion to the Church of the Trust had driven them insane, and how that insanity had created the wellsprings for much of the unpleasantness in her life. The greatest turbulence had occurred during Susan's eleventh year, when her mother and father had committed suicide.

She would never again forget the pain.

I am my body-thought. I have access to the entire tapestry of my past; all my triumphs, all my grief. I am immortal. I contain eternity.

"Where are you?" challenged a voice.

Susan, with one impossibly fast motion, dove from that

conceptual vantage point, high above that river of her life, back into the roaring clarity of pure body-thought. In the relatively spacious midcompartment of their shuttle, she whirled to face the voice.

Simultaneously: jaws chomped together, activating her crescent web. Hands slid effortlessly into the side pouches of her flakjak, whipped out two small knives, energizing them via skin galvanics and palm pressure.

Multicolored beams leaped from their hilts, tripling in length as she charged forward, her arms extended outside the crescent web's protective aura: standard attack-posture for a fighter armed with flash daggers.

Beside Timmy stood the familiar target grid. Susan spun sideways, chopped five times with her right arm, pivoted one-eighty degrees, leaped sideways, then thrust her left flash dagger straight at the profile of the dummy's narrow head. The makeshift quintain, crudely cut from a baffle plate of titanium alloy, shredded into half a dozen pieces. Susan's final thrust burned through the left earlobe of the now-unsupported head; gravity sent the pieces crashing to the deck.

Her proctor's eyes widened with obvious pleasure; Timmy's massive body seemed to quiver, the folds of fat dancing in an ecstasy of satisfaction. "Dead center." He chortled, gazing serenely at his handiwork, the pieces of which now littered the floor of the shuttle's midcompartment.

"I'm glad you're impressed," said Susan, deenergizing the twin daggers and replacing them in the flakjak's specially designed slip pockets. She maintained the invisible crescent web in its active mode, however, continuing to protect her body from front and rear attack. Some days, Timmy was full of tricks; it would not do to release her defenses just yet.

He smiled openly. "You made it look easy. Your piercing technique with the daggers is excellent, but don't get trapped into using the blades in that specialized way. At four of your last five sessions, your death-blow was delivered with a thrust."

She shrugged. "It felt right. I assumed this was an enemy with an active web. It would be far more difficult to slash through the crescent's weak side portals than to administer the blade as I did."

Timmy chewed on that for a moment. Then: "Soon you'll be ready for moving targets."

"I can't wait." She edged her way over to one of the mid-compartment's windows, making sure that she kept Timmy in peripheral view.

"Where are we?" she asked. They were flying very low across the surface of the planet, probably less than six hundred feet above the ravaged terrain. Damaged buildings, most of them two- and three-story concrete structures, stood along the edges of trash-strewn highways. Everything was whipping by extremely fast; Timmy had the shuttle on automatic, was keeping them at low altitude to lessen their chances of being spotted by ground-based E-Tech scanners.

Timmy glanced out the window. "We're over some small city in the Carolinas, I imagine. Very soon, we'll be heading out over the Atlantic, then down across Cuba. We'll stay over water as much as possible for the remainder of the flight."

Susan nodded, not really knowing where those places were. Earth geography was an arcane subject, to say the least.

"Are you sure we won't be spotted?" Those buildings rushing by below them . . . even though this town was obviously abandoned like everything else on the planet, there was always the possibility that E-Tech ground crews might be in the area.

"Don't worry," said Timmy, smiling one of his cryptic smiles. "Our flight plan avoids all known E-Tech bases. Should we be visually spotted by any stray work crews, chances are we'll be mistaken for Costeaus. And this shuttle boasts highly sophisticated radar and scan deflection gear. Even if someone locks onto us, they won't be able to track us very far."

Susan kept staring out the window, thinking about how different this day had turned out to be. They had left the Ontario Cloister early this morning, heading out onto the beach for their so-called daily walk, which was actually nothing more than an excuse for getting out of sight of the encampment so that Susan could be given her latest regimen of training. But this morning they had continued to walk along the dark sand, farther than they had ever gone before. The long low buildings of the Cloister had disappeared from sight and even the towering red atmospheric revivifier, one of two that loomed over this protected region of the planet, had eventually vanished behind a tumultuous series of hills.

Moving inland, they had come to the remains of a small town. Nestled at the foot of a steep rise, inset into a mountain, was an artificial cavern, probably once used for industrial storage.

Timmy, procuring a key from his backpack, had proceeded to input several sequences into the codelock. Ancient machinery groaned to life, and the thick door slid open. Susan, bursting with curiosity, followed her proctor into the warehouse.

The shuttle rested serenely in the middle of the huge building. Covered with dust, and enshrouded by layers of cobwebs—eerie testament to one of the few Earth creatures who had managed to survive and adapt to the nuclear/biological Apocalypse—the small craft's airlock opened to Timmy's sequencer.

"We're leaving the Cloister?" she asked.

"Yes. For good."

A short wade through strings of cobwebs and then into the airlock, the craft automatically coming to life as they entered its domain. With Timmy in the pilot's seat, the main vertical landing jets had grimaced, then roared to full power, spreading flame and smoke across the floor of the warehouse, dissolving all vision. And then Susan felt the vessel rise, crack through the vaulted ceiling as if it were an eggshell, rise triumphantly over the dead town, ascend into the smogged skies of upper New York state.

And at that moment, Susan had recalled Timmy's words from several weeks ago, on the fateful day when he had awakened her true consciousness after twenty-six years—a lifetime—of pain-induced slumber.

A journey beyond your dreams, he had said.

"Beyond my dreams," she whispered.

"What?"

She turned away from the window to face him again.

"Nothing." She bit down a second time on her molars, deactivated the crescent web. She was getting better and better at reading Timmy's moods. She could tell that there would be no trickery today, no unscrupulous surprises to test her reflexes, to push her body-thought toward its ultimate state. Wherever and whatever that might be.

He sat down on one of the bunks, stared at her curiously. "You don't seem to ask me as many questions of late. Don't you care where we're going? Don't you want to know what Timmy, great manipulator of your life, has in store for you next? Don't you wonder why I've been training you with flash daggers, the second deadliest hand weapon ever devised?"

"Second deadliest?"

"Yes. For those able to discriminate, the Cohe wand is the weapon of choice."

"Then why not train one of those with me?" She refused to consider that he did not have one. Timmy seemed to have access to *everything*.

He shook his head. "Proper utilization of the Cohe must begin at a very young age. You are too old."

Susan smiled. Being called old at twenty-six, by a man who had been around for about three centuries, was a novel experience.

"What about the Order of the Birch assassin? Why would Slasher be using daggers instead of a Cohe?"

"Flexibility of function, perhaps. And it is possible for certain weapons to complement one another, in tandem forming gestalts even more potent than Cohes."

"Slasher and Shooter—you believe they're a Paratwa, don't you?"

"Yes. They are aspects of one. I am quite certain."

She frowned. "But you have nothing to do with the actions of this Paratwa?"

"No, Susan. And this is not the first time you have asked me that question."

"Call me suspicious," she said with a grin. "So it was just coincidence that brought me to Honshu Colony on the day of that massacre."

"I certainly did not plan it. Whether the assassin arranged for you to be there remains to be seen."

"I keep thinking about that massacre, about looking into the face of that one tway and *knowing* that we knew each other. But I still can't figure it out. I still have no idea where I know him from." She watched Timmy's face carefully, searching for some indication that he might know more about the Order of the Birch killer than he was letting on. But his eyes revealed nothing.

She let out a bored sigh. "When will we get where we're going?"

"It will be a few more hours. Do you want me to satisfy your curiosity?"

"No, I can wait. I like surprises."

"You surprise *me*, Susan. Your general lack of curiosity over these past weeks has been nothing short of astounding. I keep expecting you to challenge me, perhaps even attempt to alter the course that I have set for us."

"How can I alter your course if I don't know where we're going?"

Timmy chuckled. "That is a strange logic loop."

"Only if you're on the outside looking in," she stated confidently.

"If it pleases you to be kept in the dark, so be it."

"Pleasure has nothing to do with it."

Now it was Timmy's turn to frown. "What do you mean?"

"You're leading me somewhere. To a place, a time . . ." She hesitated, struggling to contain strange fragments of emotion within the limiting range of words. "One thing I'm certain of: you're leading me toward pain."

"We all travel toward pain," he said quietly.

"When you were a Paratwa—when you were still a complete Ash Ock—did you ever use assassins? Send them out to kill innocent people?"

"I sent them out to kill."

"Did it ever bother you?"

"No."

She turned away to stare out the window again. "You're

going to send me out to kill someday. That's why you've been training me with the daggers."

"Yes, Susan."

No. You're lying. Sometimes she could tell when he was being untruthful. There was purpose behind his weapons training, but it had little to do with turning Susan into a skilled assassin. It was something else. Something that defied such an easy description.

But she knew she was right about the pain. *I'm going to suffer.*

Timmy wiggled his fat form up out of the bunk. "It should be obvious that as your training intensifies, my influence over you will wane. When the time comes, I shall merely make suggestions. When the time comes, you will make your own choices."

"Maybe I'll turn on you?"

"Perhaps."

"Maybe I'll kill you."

His left eye—the real one—squinted at her, as if it were trying to close itself against a wetting of tears.

"Perhaps you'll kill me," he said.

She turned her back to him. "Nothing scares you. Not even death."

"I have already died, Susan. Don't you understand that yet?" A touch of anger sharpened his tone. "When I was whole, when I was the Ash Ock Paratwa, Aristotle, when I was the *other*, I feared nothing. It was not until my first tway was destroyed, until I entered that pit of agony and loss, that I began to understand the true nature of fear.

"And then came the long days of misery, the inner torture as my monarch Aristotle sought to coalesce with my surviving tway. Agony, Susan. Agony beyond words." His voice faded.

"Finally, my tway could hold out no longer. He gave in, surrendered his distinctiveness, allowed the melding of tway and monarch into one being, one creature, untroubled by the raging storms of disparity. I could go anywhere and do anything, but I could never again be truly alive. Aristotle is gone. His tways are gone. Only Timmy remains."

He sounded as if he were going to start crying.

"I'm sorry," she said.

For a while, there was silence between them. Susan listened to the gentle roar of the shuttle's main engines, and her thoughts turned back to what her life had been like in the Colonies. She had been a progress inspector for La Gloria de la Ciencia. She had always kept herself very busy. She had traveled from place to place—one cylinder to another, one lover to another. It had all seemed so very important. It had all been so very meaningless.

No . . . not completely meaningless.

Aunt Inez, her closest living relative, had been real. Aunt Inez had been a true friend.

I wonder if she thinks I'm still alive?

When Timmy spoke again, his voice was hard, controlled. "There is no going back, Susan. What I once was no longer exists. I am dead, Susan. Never forget that."

A chill went through her. Outside, the shuttle broke from the Carolina shoreline, glided over the serene blue waters of the Atlantic Ocean.

"I will never forget," she promised.

FIN WHIRL.

The sign, in the shape of a small gazebo, rested on silver struts high above the buildings, between a Victorian S&M club and a four-story pseudo-Germanic beer hall. Behind the sign, in this semideserted alley, a few hundred yards east of the infamous Zell Strip, an eight-foot wide tube rose up into the darkness and vanished into Sirak-Brath's smogged skies. This entrance to Fin Whirl, like most others, was a pneumatic cylinder. Elevators fed people in and out of the actual complex, situated in centersky, some two miles overhead.

The sign looked ancient, a ruby red set of mismatched letters crammed into the perimeter of the latticework pavilion, the whole mass actually composed of natural fluorescent drip particles, which continuously fell like lava from the sign's outermost ring, puddling on the pavement near the plain steel door between the buildings. Gillian had seen such signs before, on Earth, during the pre-Apocalypse, in places like Rio and New York and Tokyo. Alone among the Colonies of Irrya, Sirak-Brath stood like a sentinel of the past, a dazzling icon of a world that once was.

"I don't know you." The doorperson, a seven-foot-four Japanese wearing the garb of a nineteenth-century American lumberjack, challenged them. He parted his lips in an imitation of a smile, unsheathed a broomhose from his belt, and began sweeping the puddled drip particles back toward an input shaft beside the entrance. The lavalike mass was instantly sucked through a set of pressurized hoses, reformulated into the sign's outer ring. "Can't let you in if I don't know you."

Buff smiled tightly. "Then allow us to introduce ourselves—"

"Names don't matter," interrupted the giant. "Can't go in unless I know you."

"You could pretend," suggested Buff, while Gillian drew a wad of cash cards from his money belt.

The giant shook his head. "I don't know you well enough to accept a bribe."

Buff snorted. "Well now, you seem to be making things real complicated. You're not going to force us to travel to one of the main entrances, are you? We can get into Fin Whirl from another sector, you know."

"But you came here," the giant pointed out.

Gillian said, "We like privacy. This entrance is a bit more discreet."

The doorperson shrugged. "I only let special people in this way."

"We're the most special people you could imagine," Buff assured him.

The giant finished sweeping up the mass of drip particles, reattached the broomhose to a hook on his belt. "All right—give me your hands, palms up."

Gillian shrugged and extended his arms. Buff did the same.

The giant alternated his attention from hand to hand, running his surprisingly dainty hands across their digits, probing with his fingertips, pressing his thumb firmly into the soft flesh of their palms. Finally he released them and stepped back a pace. He turned to Buff.

"You're a Costeau."

She sighed. "Good guess."

"Not just a guess," insisted the giant. He turned to Gillian, gazing oddly at him for what seemed to be a long time. Gillian matched his stare.

"Are you armed?" the giant asked.

"Yes."

"Weapons should be left here."

"I don't think so," countered Gillian, keeping his tone free of challenge.

The giant stepped back another pace and folded his massive arms across his chest. He nodded to Buff. "You can go in. Your friend . . . him I'm not sure about."

"We're together," said Buff.

Gillian found himself getting angry. "What is it you want?" Disturbing urges ascended; irrational desires to fight this giant, to allow himself to be drawn down into a mode where violence was the only situational response, where physical struggle could be utilized to help control his raging inner world. Full-body flush. Full-body hard-on.

Buff, reading his agitation, spoke quickly. "Faquod—we're here to see Faquod."

The giant broke eye contact with Gillian. For a moment, he seemed to hesitate. Then: "All right. Make it two hundred cash cards, and you're both in."

Gillian withdrew the money from his belt and handed it to the giant, who carefully counted it before moving from their path. The door slid open. They entered the vator and strapped themselves into a pair of acceleration couches.

"Upside or Downside?" asked the giant.

Buff signaled thumbs-up. The giant fingered a control, preparing to close the door. But before he pressed the button, he turned to Gillian.

"Your hands . . . be very careful. You have hands that

could destroy the fabric of all they touch. They are not natural. They are the hands of chaos."

The door slammed shut. A jolly mechvoice emoted a five-second countdown, and then Gillian and Buff were squashed into their seats for the few brief—but rigorous—seconds it took for the vator to ascend the two miles to Sirak-Brath's centersky.

Gillian ignored the powerful G-forces, the whistling screech of the high-speed transport; his mind swirled with the giant's words. *The hands of chaos*. Deep inside, he could feel the presence of Empedocles pressing against consciousness, seeking the eruption of the whelm: the forced interlace that would bring them together. He acknowledged a moment of ancient pain.

Catharine, how I miss you.

The gentle intertwining, the subtle melding of two consciousnesses into one; never again could the interlace occur naturally. Catharine was gone. Death had sullied the purity of the process. If the whelm came now, it would more closely mimic the destructive conflagration of two tectonic plates grinding together, attempting to occupy the same space at the same time.

The hands of chaos.

The vator jerked to a halt. "That was a lotta fun," snarled Buff, rubbing her chest. "First it's games with a psychic monster, then we get our bodies squashed in a speed vator."

"You complain a lot these days."

"Extra yes, I complain a lot! You know, being with you is not exactly easy. You have a funny habit of bringing out the worst in people."

"I avoided physical conflict with our friend down there."

Buff grunted, unfastened the acceleration straps, and floated free of the couch. She grabbed a side rail to right herself, then oriented her weightless body in line with glowing green arrows on the inside of the door. The portal opened and they used the side rail to float/walk out into Fin Whirl, into a maelstrom of shrieking humanity.

"I got ten-event upside spillseeker champions!" shouted a young man, barely an adolescent, rushing at them. He thrust a packet of bubbling holos toward Gillian's face. "Two hundred bytes for the lot. No transitionals. If you got a licensed rep, we can do business without cards!"

Gillian gazed at the strange holos, which seemed to be constantly melting into one another, reemerging in new and altered abstractions. Each depicted a particular Fin Whirl player, wearing full protection gear: brightly colored shieldware, arm gauntlets, transparent helmets with an array of wires attached to their hip-mounted jetpaks. The holos spoke; male and female players took turns announcing themselves with such names as Murky Sumoza, Blockbuster Giga-Quad, Slim-Trim Three, Jefferson Airplane.

"No thanks," muttered Buff, shoving the young hawker out of their way.

"This is a collector's set!" he cried, suddenly whining like a little boy. "I gotta sell. *I gotta sell!*"

An older man, possibly the youth's father, grabbed the hawker by the back of the neck and yanked him through the open door of the vator.

Gillian followed Buff through the crowd, surprised that his feet—and everyone else's, for that matter—remained on the floor. Here in this centersky zero-G environment, where the Colony's spin rate was effectively canceled out, he should have been falling free. But although they remained essentially weightless, an odd downward pull biased their footsteps toward the deck.

He recalled Nick mentioning that the Colonies now possessed a technique for inducing, on a small scale, artificial gravitational proclivity, via sophisticated combinations of cohesive energy fields and mass-controlled airjet streams—ultra-high-tech stuff, unknown even in the days of the pre-Apocalypse. The Irryan Colonies *had* managed to advance some technologies—albeit a very few—beyond the glorious epitome of the late twenty-first century.

Fin Whirl's management obviously recognized the benefits of keeping people glued to the floor, rather than allowing such a crowd to ramble wildly in three dimensions. Best to put limits on pandemonium; best to keep chaos at bay.

An abrupt fury overwhelmed Gillian, and he began shoving his way through the crowd, pushing people out of his path, ramming passersby with his elbows, deeply hoping that someone would take offense, challenge his arrogance, push back.

Buff grabbed his arm. "Jesus, Gillian! Calm down. We're here to see Faquod, remember?"

He drew deep breaths, forced his body to adopt the soothing rhythms of composure, forced placidity to wash over the rage. In the innermost reaches of consciousness, he had the feeling that Empedocles was laughing at him, perhaps amused by his constant struggle.

How many times had the fury come over him in these weeks since he and Buff had parted with Nick and the lion? How many fights had he initiated?

First, there had been those days hiding out with some of Buff's clanspeople, the Cerniglias, and their daily visits to that exercise cone, attached to the small Costeau cylinder by one-way umbilicals. The 2G-plus power workouts had given Gillian the opportunity to meet many other Costeaus who enjoyed the rigors of hand-to-hand combat in an ecosphere where everyone weighed twice as much as normal. Gillian had relished those days, those intense confrontations in the ring, punishing his body and the bodies of his opponents, beating all comers, fighting until he was so tired that he simply fell asleep on the mats, fighting until even Empedocles's endless scrutinizing was circumvented, until his monarch's omnipresence dissolved into the barest ghost of a dream.

And then, in the alley, with Impleton and his men. A short fight but satisfying in that it had temporarily purged Gillian of his pain and fury, temporarily neutralized his monarch.

I need to engage in eternal combat. As insane as that idea sounded, it seemed the only real solution for his existence, the only logical method of maintaining himself as a discrete consciousness. The only way to keep chaos at a distance.

His hands began to shake, and he balled them into fists, crushed them against his sides, willed himself not to lash out at some innocent passerby. He followed Buff across the packed floor, toward the tunnels leading to the arena. They jostled for position, spearing their way through the mad crush of humanity that funneled toward the ramps leading to Fin Whirl's inner sanctum.

Wave upon wave of people: pro-gamblers, silkies, and smugglers; addicts of scud and ree-fee, chemfreaks and demortified coke drinkers. There were Costeaus, both mainstreamed and freestyle, the latter filling the air with the stench from numerous odorant bags, a melange of foul smells representing dozens of clans. There were marked criminals, with bright red libbers attached to their foreheads, the implanted electrodes not only signaling their whereabouts to parole officers but pulsing their brains when synaptically monitored antisocial urges reached danger levels. And there were outsiders galore: tourists and thrill-seekers and wide-eyed weekenders who came for excitement, an alteration in their routines, a panacea for their boredom, any state of mind that might amplify or enhance the inherent dullness of their structured existences.

Like Rio, thought Gillian. *Like Tokyo.* The crowd in Fin Whirl reminded him of those places, and the other great lost cities of the Earth, where humans mixed in seemingly senseless arrangements; where those who understood the nature of their environments walked amid those whose comprehension remained dim, limited. In practical terms, Fin Whirl was a place where scam artists and hustlers of all manner and description flowed in the same stream as the uninitiated. Fin Whirl was a place where the not-so-honest could diligently soak the not-so-poor. It was a true gambler's heaven.

Gillian sensed something else: the particular mixture of the streetwise and the ignorant in Fin Whirl mimicked the ratios found on Earth during the final days. And Fin Whirl was, in fact, probably a fair microcosm of intercolonial society. It seemed to Gillian as if more and more intercolonial citizens seemed unable to interpret correctly and fathom the symbols underlying their very environments. Like the inhabitants of late twenty-first-century Earth, the colonists of Irrya increasingly walked in the shadows, living at the mercy of those who fully understood the distinctions between darkness and light.

At the mercy of the Paratwa. At the mercy of the Ash Ock.

The world, Aristotle had once proclaimed, *is made up of those who understand their own depths and those who do not. And the balance between those two ever-changing factions determines the state of the culture, determines whether there is war or peace, whether there is freedom or slavery, whether a civilization reaches for the stars or descends into the polygenetic barbarity of its own past.*

A faint shudder raced up Gillian's spine. *The Colonies of Irrya are doomed. They've become victims, waiting to be vanquished. There is no real hope left.*

And with that shudder came the living icon that was Empedocles. And Gillian, for a brief moment, was able to perceive the mental pollution that was brought on by his monarch, the poison that Empedocles leaked into Gillian's mind, overwhelming his thoughts with a toxic blend of defeat and failure, slowly eroding Gillian's will, pushing him toward acceptance of the inevitable: the whelm.

Bring us together, urged Empedocles. *Unite our souls. Now— before it is too late.*

"No!" snapped Gillian, gritting his teeth.

Buff took off her cap, exposing her shaved skull with its photoluminescent streaks, the blue and red lines, the Costeau symbols of mourning and vengeance. "Talking to *him* again?"

"Yes."

"Who dressed you this morning?"

Gillian smiled; grim thoughts trickled back into the depths. "Don't worry, I'm still in charge of clothing decisions. Besides, I don't think Empedocles would have picked the garb of an ICN banker." He reached down and fingered the four ends of his double tie. "This is far too stylish for my monarch. He was never much of a dresser. He could never decide if he liked the male or the female look."

"Yeah, I know some boys and girls who have that problem."

Gillian realized something else. His clothing should have marked him as a tourist, an outsider, a potential victim for the shadow walkers here in Fin Whirl. But the hustlers seemed to ignore him, and he sensed that it was more than just Buff's presence that spared him as a potential mark.

They look at me, and they know that I'm one of them.

He thought about the palm-reading giant at the entrance. What had motivated the giant to challenge them? What did it matter what entrance a person used to enter Fin Whirl? Did the giant ascribe it as a personal mission of some sort? Did his odd method of selectivity provide a sense of satisfaction? Did the giant come across others who possessed the hands of chaos?

Buff leaned over and whispered, "I think we've got company."

Gillian instantly nestled his body against hers; a natural combat instinct to prevent separation during a sudden onslaught of violence. In this kind of crowd, tight back-to-back fighting techniques would be demanded.

His lust for confrontation returned—full-body hard-on, as strong as ever. Muscles twitched, hungry for the nourishment of action. He wiggled his right wrist, felt the lump of the Cohe wand nestled safely in the slip wrist holster beneath his wide-sleeved jacket. The shadow of Empedocles crept back into awareness.

"Now don't get your cock up," warned Buff. "I don't think anything's going to happen here. But I'm pretty sure we're being watched and followed."

"By whom?"

"I'm not sure—not exactly. There're two of them, I think. Maybe three. Trailing us at a distance. I spotted them when we got off the vator. I don't think they're intercolonial—certainly not E-Tech Security. Probably not local patrollers, either. The good folks who run Fin Whirl pay extremely large fees—*taxes*, they are called—to the Sirak-Brath authorities to make sure that this place is not overrun by police. Of course, they could be patrollers, working on a special investigation."

"Looking for us," said Gillian.

"Yeah, maybe. We are getting a bit popular lately, what with you and your nasty black beam terrorizing poor innocent smugglers."

Gillian grunted.

"But if these guys are official," continued the Costeau, "I think there'd be more of them—a half dozen, probably. When patrollers do come to Fin Whirl, they usually come in force."

"Faquod's people?" wondered Gillian. "By now, he must have gotten the word that we're looking for him."

"Yeah," agreed Buff. "And you did sort of dropkick Impleton and company. For all we know, that gang *could* have been Faquod's best friends."

"I doubt it."

They reached the nearest tunnel and were almost crushed as hundreds of bodies tried to plunge through the constricting portal at the same time. The shaft gently angled upward for a short distance, and then the pressure of the crowd abruptly relented and they were plopped out into the main grandstands encircling Fin Whirl's Upside arena, into a fusillade of noise and light. The high-tech gravitational bias seemed to increase; Gillian experienced the odd sensation that, below the knees, he was walking through a 1G environment, while the rest of his body remained weightless.

The grandstands were almost full, crammed with five or six thousand spectators/bettors, separated from the basketball-court size playing field by a ring of twenty-five-foot-high transparent glass barriers, which looked like thinner versions of the massive cosmishield glass slabs that protected the Colonies' sun sectors. On the field itself, six players were lining up for the next game.

Huge billboards, made up of thousands of genetically modified captive cockroaches, floated overhead. Using power processors, the billboards' controllers stimulated the shells of certain roaches into intense states of multicolored photoluminescence, aligning the bugs into tiny channels on the surface of the billboard, effectively spelling out a variety of messages. The technology was familiar to Gillian. Adbug aesthetics had been inordinately popular during the mid- to late-twenty-first century, despite vehement opposition by insect rights organizations.

The billboards provided gambling odds for the upcoming game as well as counted down the time remaining before betting ceased. Bettor booths ringed the cosmishield wall and each one had a line of at least twenty people. Most of the individuals were screaming and cursing at one another; those in the back of the line were the most vocal, desperate to place wagers in time for the upcoming round.

"C'mon," urged Buff, leading Gillian up a steeper ramp between two of the grandstands, which were named Blake and Shelley. They reached the top, where the expensive private penthouse booths overhung the regular spectator sections. Each penthouse was rectangular, about thirty feet wide, and fronted with a solid sheet of mirrored glass. Booth BS-four was the third one on their left. They halted before it and gazed at their reflections.

"We're here to see Faquod," announced Buff.

A corner panel seemed to quiver, and then a doorway appeared, exposing a short flight of stairs. Gillian followed Buff up into the booth, turning at the last minute to stare at the two men poised on the ramp thirty feet below them. The duo, seeing that they had been spotted, quickly turned around to face the playing field. Gillian smiled. It was an amateurish attempt to throw off suspicion. Maybe the pair were from the authorities after all.

But just as Gillian was about to turn back into the booth, he caught a glimpse of a third man, poised on a landing about a dozen steps below the other two. The man looked straight at Gillian, smiled warmly, and waved his hand in apparent recognition. Gillian had no idea who he was. The door closed before he could consider an appropriate response.

Faquod's domain was a study in luxury. Its height-adjustable sofas were pristine examples of art deco elegance, and the amusement grid and refreshment console, connected by a graceful curving arch, bore a fragility that seemed alien to Sirak-Brath. Twin lavatory doors, quaintly discriminatory, had wavy black and silver stripes. The diagonal pattern was disrupted only by the oversized handles: one shaped like a limp penis, the other like a sagging breast.

Faquod slouched alone on the massive central sofa, gazing out over the arena, where the burning of roaches' shells indicated that less than a minute remained before the next game. In person, the smuggler did not look very threatening. Este Faquod was tall and skinny, with pale chocolate skin, curly gray hair, and eyes that expressed terminal boredom.

The other occupants of the booth were a pair of beautiful redheaded women, who looked to be in their early twenties. Twins, obviously, but for a moment, Gillian did not appreciate just how close they were. Then he spotted the plastic swatch of artificial skin connecting them, shoulder to shoulder. Siamese by design. The twins sat in front of the amusement grid, playing some sort of two-dimensional screen game featuring burial and revivification under severe arctic conditions.

Faquod laughed, a low unrestrained chuckle which sent a faint chill through Gillian. Reemul the liege-killer had possessed a similar laugh.

"Attention getters, yes, my little redheads certainly are. Yes. They were born separate, but I told them that if they were willing to be surgically connected, and remain Siamese for one year, that I would give them one of my Pocono speed slope teams and enough start-up money to make a serious run at next year's championship. Yes. They've two months to go."

"Crazy ladies," muttered Buff.

Faquod rose. "Yes. Buff, I haven't seen you for a time. Word has come to me that you seek new toys. Things on the technological order of the salene. Yes?"

Buff nodded. "We're willing to pay, Faquod. You set the terms." She glanced at the bonded redheads. "In cash, of course."

"Cash. Yes." The smuggler rose from the sofa. "Do you have money riding on the game?"

Gillian gazed through the transparent wall, down into the arena. A whistle blared and the six players, each atop a circular skateboard, triggered their jetpaks and accelerated toward the center of the field.

Buff shook her head. "We're not here to bet."

Faquod turned to Gillian. "How about you, Cohe wand man. Are you a bettor?"

Gillian tensed.

Faquod grinned at him, then ambled over to the edge of the window-wall. Down on the field, the first two players made contact, their shielded bodies clipping each other with tremendous force. The first player, a tall female in scarlet colors, ducked low, transferred the force of the collision into a change of direction, maintaining her balance and rocketing away from the crash. But the second player, in royal blue, had no such luck—or skill. He lost control, fell forward; the propulsion from his jetpak, which could not be turned off without forfeiting the game, changed direction, went from horizontal to vertical, launching his near-weightless body some thirty feet into the air. He flailed his arms, desperately trying to regain balance, but his random gesticulations only served to send him tumbling end over end. In slow motion, he crash-landed on the dirt at the edge of the field, sending a cloud of red dust swirling into the air. Shaken, the player scampered to his hands and knees and crawled to the sidelines. A roar of approval went up from the crowd, their overall delight tempered by booing from some quarters—bettors, no doubt, who had chosen the royal blue whirler as their champion.

"Want to see what that looked like Downside?" asked Faquod, not waiting for an answer, but pointing his wiggling finger at an overhead com. A small section of the window faded into the contours of a video screen. The camera angle displayed a replay of the initial game contact, but from the perspective of Downside: the mirror-image near-identical stadium that lay beneath their feet.

Each player Upside had his Downside counterpart: a figure in similar attire and colors, yet without jetpaks. Downsiders were incapable of any independent mobility with respect to the playing field, although they could move their upper torsos and arms. Each Downsider's boots were attached to a skateboard just like his Upside double, but the Downsider's board remained aligned, via powerful induction beams, to the Upsider's board, essentially traveling at the same speed and in the same direction. The Fin Whirl playing field was, in essence, a huge mirror: where the Upsider went, his Downsider "image" followed.

Gillian watched, fascinated, as the Downsider version of the opening collision played itself out on Faquod's screen. The red player again kept her balance; the blue player hurtled high into the air, his trajectory mimicking the arc taken by his luckless Upside analogue.

"Yes," said Faquod, looking pleased. "Sometimes, you know, the Downside counteraction is *not* identical. Sometimes the Downsider manages to slightly alter the nature of the game, perhaps leaning a few extra inches in one direction, perhaps slamming into another player—an event that occurs Upside as a near miss. And should the Downsider knock down a player, that player's Upside counterpart is automatically disqualified."

"Interesting," said Gillian.

"Yes. Two types of bettors, you know. Those who play Upside, who prefer to match their purses to the skill and daring of the individual athlete. Then there are those who play Downside." Faquod smiled. "Two different styles of personalities, actually: those who prefer a game based mostly on skill versus those whose taste runs to a game based primarily on chance."

Buff shrugged. "This is all very fascinating, Faquod, but we're here about weapons, and we sort of have the feeling that we shouldn't stay in one place for too long." She pointed down to the two men who stood on the landing. The pair were pretending to follow the game, but they kept casting furtive glances up at Faquod's booth. "We have silent partners."

"Do you know who they are?" asked Faquod, in a tone that suggested *he* did.

Buff shrugged.

"They are freelancers from FL-Sixteen," announced the smuggler. "Their assignment is Fin Whirl. They must have recognized you."

Buff frowned. "I don't see how they could recognize us so easily. Both of us had facial alterations, done just last week—"

"Descriptions were provided to them earlier today. Impleton sold his tale of encounter with you and Cohe wand man to the freelancers. Yes. Freelancers pay well for information. I'm told that Impleton made quite a profit on the deal.

"And now that the freelancers know your identity, it won't be long before E-Tech Security and the local patrollers find out as well. In fact, I'd say there's a possibility that the authorities have already been alerted to your presence here. Throughout Sirak-Brath, you have managed to inform a great number of people that you are searching for me. A priest from C of the T even came to my *home* this morning, seeking to make contact with Cohe wand man."

"A priest?" wondered Gillian. He pointed to the third man, who stood below the others. "Is that him by any chance?"

Faquod stared for a moment. "Yes, that is him. Perhaps he got here by following the freelancers?"

Gillian did not reply. *A priest from the Church of the Trust, looking for me? Why?*

Buff coughed. "All the more reason for us to go about our business and then get the hell out of here. Yes, Faquod?"

The smuggler shrugged.

"We're looking for another salene. Plus a couple of those fancy little three-tube thrusters. And if you have any other new weapons available—"

Faquod waved his hand. "Yes. Nice toys. All illegal. All hard to come by. All very—"

"Expensive," concluded Buff. "You can save the shitline, Faquod. I know—business is tough. You're not making much of a profit anywhere. Life is difficult. Taxes are killing you." She sighed. "So how much for two of these thrusters and another salene?"

"More money than you have, unfortunately."

"That sounds a bit too expensive," Buff quipped. "How about fifty thousand for—"

Faquod held up his hand, pleading silence. "Buff, we cannot do business. Yes. I am sorry. You and Cohe wand man, are, at the present time . . . how shall I put it? . . . bad risks? There are too many people looking for you. It is too dangerous for me to sell you *anything*. You are unacceptable bets."

"Whirl crap!" snapped Buff. "You can arrange it so no one would know."

"My booth could be under hostile surveillance at this very moment. The patrollers could be watching. Even E-Tech Security. Both of you could be arrested the instant you leave here."

"We won't be arrested," promised Gillian.

Faquod grinned. "Yes, Cohe wand man, it would take a great deal to arrest you, I am sure. But the fact remains: we cannot do business, not now. Perhaps in a few weeks. When things are calmer." The smuggler paused. "There is, of course, the possibility that I could arrange to have you visit one of my professional compatriots. Yes. I am not the only one who deals in these toys."

Buff scowled. "That would be most generous of you, Faquod. Could this be your week for good deeds? Or is it possible that you want something in return for such information?"

"I do wish a small favor, actually. The simplest of things."

"You want my Cohe wand," concluded Gillian.

The smuggler yawned and stretched out on the sofa. He looked like a cat extending to its full length.

"Yes. Not to keep, of course. Just to borrow. Let's say for one week. A mere seven days. Surely, Cohe wand man, you can survive without your little toy for that length of time. In return, I will put you in touch with a supplier of high-tech playthings. Yes. I will even guarantee that he charges you reasonable rates."

"You can't duplicate the Cohe wand," Gillian pointed out. "It's been tried before. The wetware batteries, the manufacturing techniques—they're long lost."

Faquod, still stretched out on the sofa, rolled over onto his stomach. Gillian had the feeling he was going to start purring.

"I am aware of such difficulties. But new-tech is always happening. Yes. Possibilities can become probabilities, theories can become designs. What do you say to my proposal, Cohe wand man?"

"No."

Faquod smiled and shrugged. "A preordained answer. Warriors are not easily separated from their weapons."

Buff stared coldly at the smuggler. "I hope you're not going to hold this against us, Faquod."

"Business, Buff. Yes? Vendettas are reserved for personal affronts. Which leads me to ask: how is your search going for Martha's killer?"

Buff rubbed her palm across her shaved head, as if physically touching the crisscrossing blue and red lines made it easier to answer. "No luck."

"Indeed. Last week, if I recall, the Order of the Birch assassins struck that transport facility in Kawala Port, Big Tunisia. Sixty dead, wasn't it?"

Buff grimaced. "We'll find him. And when we do, the bastard's going down. Count on it, Faquod. This assassin's going to pay for what he did to Martha."

The smuggler chuckled. "Righteousness, Buff. Yes. Admirable. But I note you said *bastard*, not bastards—you refer to this creature in the singular. Does that mean you believe the freelancer stories? That these Order of the Birch massacres are being done by a *single* Paratwa assassin?"

"I wouldn't bet against it."

"How sure are you?"

Buff hesitated, looked at Gillian. He shrugged. There was no reason *not* to tell the smuggler what they knew.

"It's a tripartite assassin, composed of *three* tways." Gillian went on to explain what they had deduced about the killer. When he finished, Faquod looked genuinely pleased.

"And you, Cohe wand man, you also were once of the binary spirit. Yes. You're the one from fifty-six years ago, the one who destroyed Reemul the Jeek."

Gillian raised his eyebrows.

"I have contacts in E-Tech Security," explained Faquod. "They tell me that they can't seem to locate the stasis capsule you and your midget friend were sleeping in. They're beginning to think you're awake. On the loose. They are very worried."

Gillian shook his head. "When Meridian and the rest of the Paratwa return, I'm going to be the least of their concerns."

Faquod laughed.

Buff raised her eyebrows. "You're not worried about the starships?"

"Worried about what? Business will change—old fortunes will disappear, new ones will come into existence. Yes. The return of the Paratwa presents both inconvenience and opportunity."

Buff muttered, "I think things are going to get a lot worse than all that."

"She's right," said Gillian. "I wouldn't underestimate the

changes that might occur. This is the Ash Ock, Faquod. It won't simply be an exchange of taxation authorities."

The Siamese redheads, giggling with delight, stood up. Carefully, they turned to face their master.

"Este!" said the first. "We beat our old score!"

The second grinned mischievously. "Don't you think we should be rewarded?" She threw him a kiss.

"Yes. Rewarded." The smuggler rubbed his belly. "I would like to discuss the changing political structure with you all day, but I'm afraid other duties must take precedence. It is time for you to leave. Good-bye, Buff—may your vendetta be bloody." He turned to Gillian. "I'm glad we could meet, Cohe wand man. Someday, perhaps, when the immediacy of the moment is less hostile, I would like to see you in action, down on the field. You would make a formidable Upside whirler. But then again, perhaps such a game would not prove attractive to one who plays for real. Yes?"

Faquod opened the door for them. Without another word, Gillian and Buff left the booth.

"Well," grumbled Buff, as they headed back down the stairs between the sections of the grandstand, "now what the hell do we do?"

Gillian pointed openly to the two freelancers, who were still trying to pretend that their interest was in the game. "Let's go down and challenge that pair to a fight."

"Very funny."

"Who says I'm joking?"

Buff gripped his arm securely. "I've got a better idea. Let's go get a room and have sex again."

"I'd rather fight."

Buff sighed. "Yeah, Faquod can really put a person in an extra foul mood."

A few steps below the freelancers, the mysterious priest caught their eye. He began smiling and waving at them.

"Should we?" asked Buff.

"Why not?"

As they passed the two freelancers, Gillian observed that both wore high-laced transparent plastic boots with mismatched argyle socks, one of this year's hottest fashion concepts. He also noted that they stood pressed tightly against each other, so close that one man's right boot was pressed against the other man's left boot. Gillian smiled.

He snapped his wrist, launched the Cohe wand into his palm. A gentle squeeze of the egg . . . a sharp flick of the wrist . . .

The black beam flashed for only an instant, curling between the freelancers' legs, the incinerating tip of energy lancing across their boots, melting the two pieces of adjacent plastic into one mass. Their boots sizzled. A waft of oily smoke rose.

"Hey!" shouted the closest freelancer, staring down at his smoking boot. His eyes widened with fear as Gillian leaned over and whispered in his ear.

"Don't follow us anymore, okay."

The second freelancer, not realizing exactly what had happened, saw the plume rising from his feet and jerked sideways in panic. But his right boot was now completely fused to his partner's left one. Both men lost their balance at the same instant, fell backward onto the landing. A wreath of spectators, not knowing what had actually happened, roared with laughter. The freelancers cursed and tried to tear apart their cojoined feet.

"Cute," muttered Buff. "A Cohe wand in front of five thousand people."

"No one noticed."

"Yeah, well let's get the hell out of here anyway, okay?"

"In a minute."

The priest appeared to be in his mid-forties. He had long dark hair, speckled with gray, and a well-kept beard. His right hand clutched a small suitcase. He smiled as they approached.

Gillian said, "I understand that you've been looking for us."

"True, but now that I've found you, I must admit to being somewhat fearful. My boots . . . they are of genuine restored leather. I hope they will not be damaged by your wand."

Gillian frowned. "What do you want?"

"My name is Lester Mon Dama, and I have been sent to

find you and deliver a message." He sighed. "I've been trying to track you down for weeks now, ever since my master learned that you and the Czar were awakened."

"The Czar?"

"Yes, the Czar—your partner, Nick. During the pre-Apocalypse, you know, he was known as the Czar."

"I don't know what you're talking about."

The priest shrugged and leaned forward, whispering. "I'm afraid that you do. Your name is Gillian, and you are the surviving tway of the Ash Ock Paratwa Empedocles."

Gillian scowled. Buff put a hand under her coat, preparing to unsheathe a weapon.

Lester Mon Dama raised his hand. "Please, you have nothing to fear from me. I am simply a messenger."

"Then give your message," demanded Gillian.

The priest opened his suitcase and withdrew a small data brick from beneath an antique telephone directory. The faded yellow cover was labeled BELL ATLANTIC.

"I've a weakness for twentieth-century telephonic materials," said Lester Mon Dama, smiling apologetically. "I've been collecting this sort of thing since I was a boy."

"Whatever keeps you out of trouble," muttered Buff.

The priest continued. "It is understandable that you may not have heard of the Czar. That name was known only to the ruling Ash Ock—Sappho, Theophrastus, Codrus, and Aristotle—and their minions. But there is another name that I believe you will know." He paused. "Does Jalka trigger any memories?"

Gillian's mouth almost dropped open. Inside, Empedocles erupted into turmoil; monarchial thoughts burned across Gillian's awareness like tracers from a geo cannon.

Jalka!

It was a name only Gillian and his monarch could know, a name learned ages ago, in the pre-Apocalypse, before the Earth had been reduced to a near-barren wasteland. Gillian and Catharine had still been children, maybe seven years old, still in training at the Ash Ock's secret camp in the Brazilian rain forests. One day, their Ash Ock proctor, Aristotle, had called them into the deep privacy of a training den. There,

Aristotle had revealed the secret name of one of his own tways: Jalka.

Aristotle had sworn them to secrecy. *Jalka* was never to be uttered, never written, anywhere, even in the presence of Aristotle himself. *Jalka* was to be their absolute secret, known only to Aristotle and Empedocles—and their four composite tways.

At the time, Gillian and Catharine had not deduced their teacher's deeper intentions, but they had been suitably impressed by his grave manner and had vowed to keep the name secret. And Gillian knew that neither he nor Catharine—nor Empedocles—had ever broken that vow. Months after the event, Catharine had come to a conclusion about their proctor's intentions.

Jalka is our password, she proudly announced. *If we have to contact Aristotle secretly someday, or he us, then we use that word. And Aristotle probably has other passwords linking him with other Paratwa.*

Gillian understood then, but he did not understand now. Jalka was a tway of Aristotle, but Aristotle's tways had perished during the final days. Jalka had been dead for over a quarter of a millennium.

Inside, Gillian sensed Empedocles withdrawing, deep into the recesses of his mind, shearing the links between their shared consciousnesses, pulling back until he became simply a dark blur of thoughts on the perimeter of awareness. Gillian's monarch was as deeply disturbed by the revelation as *he* was and probably desired time alone—as separate from Gillian as possible—to consider the extraordinary ramifications of this priest's revelation.

And when Empedocles retreated, Gillian felt instantly calmer. His muscles relaxed and his cauldron of emotions fell below the boiling point. He thought about how truly wonderful it would feel to be forever free of his Ash Ock monarch, to be able to live always as a single solitary creature.

Lester Mon Dama appeared to be waiting for Gillian to say something. When no response was forthcoming, the priest gingerly—so as not to arouse the now-wrathful looking Buff—handed the data brick to Gillian.

"This is from Jalka, my master. It will lead you to him."

A loud roar filled the arena. They turned to the playing field. Three whirlers had collided; two of them lay on the ground, unmoving, apparently knocked unconscious by the force of the crash.

The priest said, "I must go now. I have been away from my parish for quite some time, and in these days of increasing troubles, the Trust requires my renewed attention."

Buff grabbed his arm. "I'm sure the Trust can survive for a little while yet without you. For all we know, you've just handed us a bomb."

A weary smile crossed Lester Mon Dama's face. "If my master desired your deaths, then you would already be dead." He turned to Gillian. "You know Jalka. You know his power."

Gillian nodded slowly. "Buff, let him go."

Scowling, she released the priest's arm.

"Jalka is in a hurry," said the priest. "The package—please open it as soon as possible." Turning, Lester Mon Dama made his way down the stairs and disappeared into the crowd.

"So who the hell is this Jalka?" quizzed Buff, glancing back at the two freelancers, who had finally managed to remove their melted communal boot.

"An old friend," answered Gillian. *And one who can't possibly be alive.*

Corelli-Paul Ghandi wondered how he would die.

He sat in Colette's favored zephyr chair, on the top floor of their three-story Pocono chalet, on the fully enclosed veranda overlooking Speed Slope Fourteen. The near-invisible web of the zephyr, a body-shaping fountain of powerful airjets, nestled his body with a cradling mother's security, its hesitant touch and gentle cries of melodic protest providing an equilibrium as indulgent as flesh. But the zephyr seemed to be blessed with an even greater symmetry than flesh; as the chair held him in its structured balance, persistently redefining the interface of body and air, Ghandi fell into the illusion that he was seated on nothing at all. Deeper senses decreed that a barrier remained a barrier, that the zephyr was as real as the sprawling picture window that fronted this floor of the chalet, separating inner warmth from the chill of outside air.

Will I die quickly?

The zephyr whined as he leaned slightly forward; pinpoint streams of air rippled across his back as the chair reacted to a rhythmic set of spasms lancing up his spine. Colette claimed that the zephyr was the most comfortable seat ever designed. Could Ghandi dispute her?

His thoughts returned to a day, maybe five years ago, when Colette had asked him to update his will. He was to change the prime beneficiary from Colette, his wife of two decades, to CPG Corporation. Colette's stated reason had been that in the event of Ghandi's death, his personal finances should flow directly back into the corporation, where they could be redistributed most effectively, where the least amount of legal wrangling would need to take place. A minor readjustment.

Was she planning my death even then? For Colette, the tway of an Ash Ock, with a lifespan upwards of half a millennium, five years hardly constituted advance preparation. Five years was nothing for a Paratwa of the royal Caste, whose complex plans for conquering the Irryan Colonies may have been initially conceived over two hundred and fifty years ago.

Ghandi shook his hand and hunched forward, allowed the zephyr's airjets to contribute to his forward motion, lift him upright. *I'm being paranoid. I'm attaching significance to an event that was more likely nothing more than what was stated—a minor readjustment.*

And the words of Sappho, uttered weeks ago, seemed to lend credence to his irrationality.

We must provide our enemy with a suitable shadow to chase. You will be that shadow, Corelli-Paul. It is you who will be called upon to make the great sacrifice, to become the public scapegoat.

Throughout history, most public scapegoats were more useful alive than dead.

He touched the tiny band encircling his wrist, felt *twelve-fifty-seven* enter awareness as the chrono's field pulsed the time into his neural circuits. The chrono was circuitously new—just one of a number of high-tech luxury items that CPG's subsidiaries were reintroducing into the vast marketplace of the Irryan Colonies. At the present rate of reinnovation, only a few more decades would have to pass before the cylinders theoretically ascended to that epitome of technological accomplishment that had strobed the waning years of the twenty-first century. Of course, reaching the wild heights of the pre-Apocalyptics assumed that the Irryan Colonies would not follow their ancestors down a similar path of self-destruction.

Ghandi drew a sharp breath. *Twelve-fifty-seven—only a few minutes to go.* Colette has asked Ghandi to be present in the chalet at one o'clock. To meet a visitor. To take part in an important event.

Is she going to kill me today?

In the back of his neck, the familiar twitches began anew—the silent shriek of the microbes—his body's way of protesting the split in his life, between the way it was and the way that he secretly—in the throes of dreamtime—wanted it to be.

I've betrayed the human race. Twenty-five years ago, I fell in love with Colette, tway of Sappho. I sold my future to the Paratwa. And there is no turning back.

Would his death be a quick one, at the hands of Colette? A dagger in the night, perhaps? Or something more subtle, like a male-specific poison, vaginally introduced during intercourse, in the manner of the Roki Katill, that crazed sisterhood of twenty-first-century prostitutes whose worldwide mandate to decimate the male of the species had, for a brief period, led to a statistically relevant increase in monogamous relationships.

Or maybe Colette would not do the actual deed. Perhaps killing Ghandi, her lover and partner for a quarter of a century, would prove too torturous, too arduous a task. She did, after all, love him; his murder would not be a rejection or betrayal of their close personal relationship but rather a grim recognition of an altered reality. Colette's tway, the other half of the Ash Ock Sappho, would soon be returning from the stars. And a ménage à trois between Ghandi and the tways of a Paratwa simply did not seem practical.

The microbes reached their familiar threshold of agitation, then polarized into the dark energy of a shiver that bolted the length of Ghandi's spine.

Maybe Colette will allow the maniac to kill me. The maniac— Calvin the Ash Nar—the one-of-a kind tripartite assassin, hater of most things human. Calvin would certainly carry out any execution with great relish. Especially Ghandi's.

Or perhaps it would be Meridian, Jeek assassin, errand boy for the royal Caste, who would soon arrive in the Colonies to address the Council of Irrya and provide them with the ultimatum that was expected to force their surrender.

There was no way out. No hope remained.

He sighed abruptly, realizing that he had temporarily overloaded consciousness with a crushing myriad of possibilities for his own termination. Even with the end drawing near, even with disparate events beginning to coalesce and centuries-old Paratwa plans beginning to yield the genetically bred binaries their ultimate victory, a respite was needed.

The last twenty-five years have been pretty good, he reasoned. Having Colette as a lover, being wealthy beyond his childhood dreams, being the ostensible head of CPG, fifth largest corporation in the Colonies—those were tangible rewards.

But he recognized the rationalization for what it was.

I could kill myself.

He drew a fragile breath and moved closer to the window, stared down across the snow-covered hillside to the bleak gray road far below the level of the chalet, to the side of the small garage where the treaded snowrovers were housed. There, in front of a small permanent snowdrift, varying only in depth as Pocono's weather crept through its slight seasonal variations, lay a faint depression, signifying the existence of a helix core.

Ghandi watched the spot carefully, his attention increasingly focused, waiting with an expectation far beyond the consequence of what was to occur, almost managing to convince himself that something of great importance was destined to take place.

The wind picked up; the side of the garage served to channel the swift breeze, intensifying the eddies. The faint depression in the snow erupted to life; a swirl of newly fallen flakes abruptly levitated into a six-foot-high double helix—a near-perfect imitation of the DNA signature. The helix held its shape for only a few seconds before disintegrating into a graceful swirl of dreamy white puffs.

Ghandi pulled back from the window. Pocono's helixes were a frequent oddity, occurring throughout the leisure Colony. Researchers claimed that Pocono's odd windshapes were caused by a combination of the Coriolis effect—induced by the Colony's rotation, the presence of powerful ground-level air currents—common to most cylinders, and the proximity of the tubular speed slopes. Some of the more romantically inclined tourists tended to believe that the double helixes represented the vibrant struggle of the Colony itself to attain organic integrity. Life from the lifeless.

A hot seismic shudder lanced up Ghandi's spine: an echo of his microbe dance, straining to reach some distant epiphany. He rubbed the back of his sleeve across his forehead, wiped away beads of fresh sweat. *I can't kill myself. I wouldn't know how to do such a thing.*

And Colette knew that as well. She knew Ghandi was a survivor, had known it that very first day when he had entered her shuttle, in the dead city of Denver, Colorado, twenty-five years ago. Colette would never have chosen a lover/partner who displayed the weakness of one who would forfeit his own life. The tway of an Ash Ock would never permit a human to exist that far beyond her control.

Sounds from the adjacent storage room. Footsteps.

Ghandi turned away from the window, stared through the open door into the smaller chamber, into the stairwell. Colette came first, hips swaggering beneath the folds of a pleated lemon skirt. She strode purposefully across the anteroom, a secret smile framed by her perfect oval face, golden curls ensconced by the transparent sheen of an electrostatic cap. Behind her, panting from exertion, trod Doyle Blumhaven.

Colette shimmered through the open doorway, halted, slapped her palms against her narrow waist, then began to wiggle her butt rhythmically; like a hermit dancer with limbic implants, regurgitating private symphonies from random synaptic activity. Blumhaven, his thick chest sucking down air, obviously straining from the exertion of three flights of stairs, glared solemnly at Colette's coquettish display.

Colette laughed. "A female!" she urged, arresting her swivels, grinding to a stop. "I could get you one, Doyle. A genuine female of the species homo sapiens. It would be something different for you. A challenge—a new semiotic referent." She laughed again. "Life's far too short to place limits on experimentation."

Blumhaven, scowling, continued to suck air.

"How about a fifty-fifty?" goaded Colette. "A constructed herm with an extendable penis in the vaginal canal. A pleasant surprise for your tongue."

"Disgusting," managed Doyle, even as a flicker of excitement played across his face.

Colette giggled and turned to Ghandi, licking her lips, playfully, seductively. He restrained an urge to embrace her, sweep her off her feet, carry her to the bedroom, allow her to drive the microbes into retreat, banish his pain to netherlands free of self-corruption.

She clapped her hands. "Corelli-Paul, lover of loves— Doyle has brought us wonderful news." Her aquamarine eyes seemed to dance across Ghandi's face, like the eyes of a child trying to study all aspects of a thing simultaneously to comprehend its reality. Ghandi repressed a shiver.

"Doyle's news is so important that I urged him to come here directly, deconstruct the relevancies in person, so that we might address ramifications within a more intimate environment."

Ghandi did not understand, but he remained silent. Usually, scrambled telecommunications sufficed for their frequent contacts with the E-Tech Director, since E-Tech's own official policies served to discourage—if not *prohibit*—Blumhaven from private socializing with corporate citizens over whom his organization served as watchdog. And in this particular instance, it was even more important to maintain distance. Doyle Blumhaven had, after all, been bought and paid for by Colette more than two decades ago.

His wife read his concern. Her smile faded to a mock sigh. "Doyle, I believe my husband feels anxious about your presence here."

Blumhaven bobbed his head. "Nothing to worry about, Corelli-Paul. I took ample precautions. My itinerary has me visiting Pocono's history library, seven miles away. I told my security people to take the afternoon off, enjoy some of Pocono's sights, and I entered the library alone." Jowls twisted; a tiny smile emerged from between the thick red cheeks. Ghandi was sure that Doyle had put on some extra pounds since their last face-to-face encounter, months ago, at an import restrictions conference in Flying Detroit.

"I bundled myself into a hooded parka," continued Blumhaven. "I drove a snowrover—a one-shot rental—and parked it nearly half a mile away from here, in one of those crowded elevated lots that overlook this Speed Slope. And I walked from there. Quite a hike up to your chalet."

"Quite a hike," agreed Ghandi, glancing at Colette, wanting her expression to provide answers. *Why ask him to come here? Why risk a face-to-face meeting?*

Colette revealed nothing. "Ah, yes, Corelli-Paul, Doyle has wonderful news. Utilizing his own resources, he has managed to track down the traitor in the E-Tech vaults, the one who probably awakened Gillian and the Czar."

Ghandi reached toward the control panel beside the huge picture window, intending to clench the glass.

"No," said Colette firmly. "Let us continue to enjoy the view, Corelli-Paul. I doubt if anyone can see us."

Ghandi shrugged and allowed his hand to drop away from the shading controls. She was probably right. Pocono's permanent cloud cover, combined with the chalet's sensor field—a plethora of antisurveillance devices—seemed to ensure their privacy. The enclosed veranda *was* visible from the opposite bank of the suspended speed slope, some sixty feet away. But today happened to be the one day this month that the slope was closed for reicing of the winding trough's upper entrails. No jetpak skiers would scream the tube.

She plans everything, thought Ghandi. A chill swept across his shoulders.

Blumhaven's gaze wandered across the small veranda, obviously searching for a place to sit. But no chairs slid from the walls or spiraled out of slice grooves on the thickly carpeted floor. Sensors refused to acknowledge his presence.

And the veranda itself remained bare of stable furnishings. Only a pair of nineteenth-century polished silver spittoons placed in opposite corners disturbed the room's simple rectangular geometry. They were antiques acquired by Ghandi several years ago during a particularly virulent purchasing spree in the weird sunless streets of Bangkok Colony. He could no longer recall what had prompted his interest in the cuspidors.

Blumhaven squinted as he took notice of the faint disturbance of air in front of the picture window. Intrigued, he raised a curious eyebrow toward Colette. But she just smiled at him, offering no explanation for the illusory presence of the zephyr.

The Councillor, concluding that sitting was not an option, cleared his throat.

"The name of the traitor is Adam Lu Sang. He's a young programmer with high-level clearance in the vaults. A born troublemaker. Always contradicting his superiors, that sort of thing. Anyway, he's the one, no doubt about it. Adam Lu Sang is the only programmer who could have possibly arranged for the switching of that stasis capsule containing Gillian and Nick. After weeks of cross-checking and candid interviews with everyone who has full access to the vaults, my operatives have determined that Lu Sang is our boy."

Colette's smile remained in place, but it suddenly metamorphosed into an unreal caricature, drained of emotional significance, a form without substance. "Do you have actual proof?"

"This Lu Sang's too clever to leave us anything so clean as a hard-evidence trail in the computer net. But he's not quite as sharp when it comes to physical movements. Apparently, he's never realized that E-Tech Security routinely operates spot surveillance checks on all of our high-level programmers. And one of those surveillance checks revealed that Adam, within days of the period when we suspect the stasis capsule switch was actually made, changed his itinerary and rather furtively tramped off to Irrya's northern extremes."

"The lion's retreat," murmured Ghandi.

"Precisely," said Blumhaven.

Colette moved to the window, gazed up at the winding speed slope, at the twenty-foot-wide banked ice trough suspended by delicate cables disappearing into Pocono's slate skies. The cables were ultimately hinged to a reinforced nexus in the gravity-free core of centersky, miles overhead.

She said, "It's going to snow."

Blumhaven shook his head. "I don't think so. I was listening to the forecast on the way over. The programmers have nothing on the schedule until the end of the week. . . ."

His voice drifted away as the first flakes began to fall. Oversize crystals rapidly blossomed into a cascading series of white sheets, plastering the window, blotting the view.

Ghandi turned to Blumhaven. "Why did it take you so long to learn of this Adam Lu Sang's visit to the lion of Alexander? It seems to me that your Security people should have been pretty suspicious when they found out that this programmer was secretly visiting an Irryan Councillor."

The E-Tech Director shrugged. "Nearly everyone—even high-level programmers—occasionally tend to commit acts that could be construed as suspicious. But it was not until we cross-referenced departments—studied Lu Sang's movements in conjunction with his other deeds—that his visit to the Alexanders' retreat took on true significance."

Cross-referenced departments? True significance? Ghandi scowled, thinking that Colette's latest appraisal of E-Tech was doubtlessly correct: after years of Doyle's mindless leadership, the regulatory organization had mutated into a bureaucracy of immense proportions, with interdepartmental communications obscenely handicapped.

His wife turned away from the window. The barest trace of annoyance now colored her tone. "And how about *your* Security precautions, Doyle. I hate to review this, but can you be absolutely certain that your own current movements are not under surveillance by your own Security division?"

"Impossible," uttered Blumhaven, with the conviction of a political candidate.

"What about the Edward Huromonus action/probe?"

"I would know if I was under surveillance," insisted Blumhaven.

Colette sighed.

"I was *not* followed. I'm certain of it."

Again, Ghandi wondered why Colette had insisted on a face-to-face gathering.

Her tone softened. "Adam Lu Sang ... he was probably one of the first programmers to dispute our cover story about the origin of the sunsetter, that built-in terminators were responsible for the data decimation."

"Yes," said Blumhaven. "From the beginning, Lu Sang believed that there was a sunsetter in the archives. Which brings up another matter, Colette. When are you going to call off this sunsetter? If you recall, our original arrangement called for your program to remove itself from the archives following the specific data decimation of a number of old programs— the ones that you claimed could someday threaten CPG's monopoly on a number of high-tech products—"

"Change of plans," interrupted Colette. She turned back to the window, stared out into the raging storm. "Doyle, did you know that Pocono's weather has never been fully controllable? Cold temperature maintenance, combined with a heavy moisture base, occasionally exhibits properties of its own. The result is periodic random behavior—a price that one pays for dealing with an exotic system."

Blumhaven frowned. "You mean that sometimes it snows by itself?"

"Yes. That is what I mean. And once in a great while, an exotic system actually begins to get out of control. Chaos occurs. And often the only way to regain control is to amplify the very distortions that are creating the randomness within the system. Sometimes you must allow the noise to overwhelm the music, or permit forty days and forty nights of rain, or pull out the rods and permit the fissionable mass to achieve nuclear glory. Sometimes you must do these things to elevate the system to a new plateau—cause a new stasis to be achieved so that fresh lines of control can be created."

Blumhaven continued to frown. "Do you want Adam Lu Sang . . . do you want something to happen to him?"

Colette chuckled. "Delicately put, dear Doyle. Yes. I want something to happen to Adam Lu Sang. In fact, in a very short time, I am going to have a handwritten message delivered to our young programmer—a beautiful forgery, with the lion of Alexanders' own DNA prints included for authenticity's sake. This message will instruct Adam to go *immediately* to the lion's retreat. It will warn him not to attempt any contact with the lion, either through the computer net or via regular com channels. This message will command Lu Sang to take extraordinary precautions to ensure that he is not followed. The very tone of the note will suggest great urgency, great secrecy." Colette paused. "You did manage to acquire the lion's DNA signature during your visit."

Blumhaven's eyes widened with understanding. He nodded and withdrew a tiny data brick from under his jacket. "Here's the lion's prints, plus what fragments of the retreat's security profile I was able to obtain before the devices were confiscated."

"Excellent," murmured Colette, slipping the brick into a fold pocket of her skirt. "Was the lion suspicious?"

"Not unduly so. When I handed him the surveillance units, he gave no indication that he thought the static spark was anything more than the reactive field of highly charged sensors. I'm certain he never suspected that the units—in tandem—were acquiring cellular specimens. And when the lion's security officer returned the units to me a short time later, I double-checked them immediately, as you instructed. They had not been tampered with."

"And you retrieved the data from the surveillance devices as I asked? And then destroyed the units?"

"Yes," said Blumhaven, with a thoughtful nod. "But I'm still curious, Colette. Where did you get such devices? I did a basic scan of the archives, and I could not locate anything more than references to such hardware. And the prototypes that were mentioned were lost ages ago, during the Apocalypse."

"Black-market offerings," Colette lied. "From Sirak-Brath."

Ghandi knew that the majority of CPG's high-tech playthings had a far more esoteric origin: Theophrastus, the Ash Ock technological wizard. But Blumhaven could not know that. The E-Tech Councillor remained a mere fragment of the whole, an almost wholly unconscious element within the intricate tangle of Ash Ock schemes. Blumhaven was unaware of Colette's true nature, blind to the real goals of the deadly sunsetter, oblivious that his actions were leading the Paratwa toward ultimate victory.

Unconsciousness as a way of life, thought Ghandi. Doyle Blumhaven did not realize just how lucky he was.

The Councillor's face darkened at the mention of the Sirak-Brath underground. "In the future, Colette, may I suggest that you exercise extreme caution when dealing with those black marketeers? Edward Huromonus's action/probe has specifically targeted them as the prime generators of E-Tech corruption."

"Indeed," said Colette, smiling faintly. "And Edward Huromonus has certainly turned out to be an enemy of formidable proportions."

"The problem with Huromonus," muttered Blumhaven, "is that he doesn't know where to draw the line. He's even begun to dig into *my* personal finances."

"Rash of him."

Doyle shook his head. "I may have been a fool for putting Huromonus in charge of this action/probe. The man has no sense of restraint."

Colette laughed bitterly. "Restraint! Rich, Doyle, rich indeed! Restraint—the word conjures images of someone who would deliberately bind his own hands prior to a fistfight. I ask you now, Doyle, as I've asked you in the past: did you truly think that this Edward Huromonus was the sort of man who would place limitations upon such an investigation? Did you truly believe that you would remain above his scrutiny?"

"I needed the action/probe to look good," argued Blumhaven. "You *know* that. You can't imagine the battering that E-Tech's been taking over these past few years. Why, half the populace was beginning to believe that the organization is totally corrupt! And those damned freelancers—they crucify us every chance they get! I'd have cut my own throat if I'd permitted another whitewash."

For a moment Colette stood silently, her gaze wandering across Doyle Blumhaven's face with that same chilling intensity that she had earlier displayed toward Ghandi. "You did manage to set up the raid without complications?"

Blumhaven nodded. "The raid will take place according to your plans."

"And your E-Tech Security force knows that it will be rendezvousing with the other car?"

Blumhaven scowled. "Yes . . . but I still don't understand why the ICN has to be involved—"

"The ICN will be there to act as neutral observers," Colette turned toward the door and clapped her hands three times in rapid succession.

With a sharpness of movement that took Ghandi's breath away, two figures slipped into the room. Two males—twins— each garbed in translucent chiffon gowns, naked underneath, their hands hidden behind their backs, their gowns clasped by identical crystal brooches shaped like spiders, with each of the eight legs of the arachnids terminating in a phosphorescent emerald.

Blumhaven's gaze fell immediately to their crotches, to engorged cocks pressing up through narrow slits in the silken material, protruding like weapons. The Councillor's pudgy face seemed to ripple, forming a patchwork quilt of desire, unreserved, unself-conscious, untainted by the presence of Ghandi and his wife.

"All things considered," said Colette, "you've done well, Doyle. The scales have tipped in your favor. Huromonus was a mistake, but Adam Lu Sang has more than compensated for your error." Her voice fell to a whisper. "Reward yourself for your efforts. Feast . . . until your body achieves its own repose."

Ghandi, swallowing a spasm of fear, willed himself to take a step backward. He could not. Muscles seemed frozen.

The twins with the ramrod penises had names, Ky and Jy, but they remained aspects of the one, the Ash Nar, two-thirds of Calvin, the murderous tripartite Paratwa.

Blumhaven leaned forward, dropped to his knees, slithered up to the tways, took hold of a stiff cock in each hand, rubbed his face against the delicate fabric that caressed their hips. Colette touched the wall control; now the window glass clenched, mutating rapidly from clarity to opaqueness.

Slowly, the Ash Nar twins raised their arms above their heads. Ky opened his palm, revealing a compressed cube: a smart tarp. Four hands, working in concert, effortlessly and silently unveiled the ethereal fabric until it formed a tent shadowing the E-Tech Councillor.

Blumhaven did not notice the activity above him. His attention shifted to the left, to Jy, to the tway's waiting penis. Doyle's lips, on the verge of attachment, quivered; his tongue sampled air.

Run, Doyle! thought Ghandi, selfishly, knowing that he did not really care about Blumhaven's life but desperate to escape being a witness, escape another jolting inner quake of the microbes, the externalized turmoil of his endless inner struggle.

"A devouring fever," murmured Colette.

From the stairwell in the anteroom, a beam of harsh black light snaked through the doorway, circled the veranda twice, then whipped around Doyle Blumhaven's throat like a noose. The Councillor's eyes bulged wide; for a timeless instant, his cheeks quivered, baby fat flesh parading into tantrum as the body realized it had been cheated of all rewards.

Ky and Jy released the tarp. It fell onto the Councillor just when the black beam crushed inward, garroting Blumhaven, instantaneously severing his spinal column and neck muscles. The tarp, now sensor-driven, enveloped Blumhaven's decapitated head and torso, neatly interlocking itself around his feet. Two hundred-plus pounds of enshrouded animal matter spilled to the floor.

Ky and Jy, in tandem, and without touching themselves, ejaculated, spraying the bodybag as it rolled onto the carpet. Semen coalesced in odd little splotches on the still quivering corpse, forming mushy tears that ran down between folds of fabric.

It took another few seconds for the Councillor's disjointed systems to achieve entropy. Blumhaven's leg kicked once and then the body was still.

Ghandi's muscles unlocked. He managed a feeble step backward, toward the massive pane of the shrouded window.

"Well done," praised Colette.

Ghandi swallowed, finding his voice. "Why . . . why Blumhaven?"

"Necessary," she replied, as if that one word of explanation totally sufficed.

Ky and Jy slipped their spent cocks back into their chiffon gowns, then knelt on both sides of Blumhaven and heaved the bodybag to chest height. A moment later, the third tway, Calvin himself, namesake of the trio, slithered through the door. He wore white leotards, heavy black boots, and a baggy green blouse imprinted with twentieth-century cartoon figures, each deformed into various alphabet caricatures. In his right palm rested the telltale egg-shaped weapon—the Cohe wand—its needle shaft protruding like an ancient antenna, poised to receive.

"Dump the body in-Colony," ordered Colette. "Be as ceremonious as you like." She faced the taller tway. "Are you certain Blumhaven was not followed?"

Tway Calvin grinned and raised his left hand. Holotronic letters, green as the emerald spider broaches worn by his other tways, glistened into razor-sharp words inches above his fingertips.

OUR LATE ASSOCIATE WAS NOT FOLLOWED. I TRACKED HIM CAREFULLY. Calvin lowered his hand and carefully replaced the Cohe wand in the slip wrist holster beneath his sleeve.

"You've done well, Calvin. In fact, excellence has marked your efforts over the past few weeks."

Tway Calvin's cheeks boiled into a smile. Ky and Jy, holding the bodybag, began to hop up and down, as if facial expressions alone could not express their pleasure. A loose floorboard squeaked.

"Latest status of the skygene infections?" asked Colette.

Calvin extended his hand. POSITIVE INFECTIONS NOW CONFIRMED IN ALL BUT TWELVE COLONIES. IF YOU WISH, I COULD DISPOSE OF THE REMAINING COURIERS IN ONE LAST MASSACRE.

Colette gave a thoughtful nod. "I suppose that at this point, the methodology of courier destruction is no longer of great consequence. You may use your own discretion."

Ky and Jy stomped wildly. Staring at the two sets of legs, Ghandi was reminded of a video he had once seen of a wild Earth stallion desperate to escape its corral.

LONG LIVE THE ORDER OF THE BIRCH, ordained Calvin's fingers. His smile bloomed.

Colette turned to Ghandi. "My love, you surprise me. I would have thought that it was obvious that Doyle was becoming too great a liability."

"I hadn't realized," Ghandi heard himself mumble.

"Yes. I see." She smiled warmly. "At any rate, if we've been reading E-Tech's internal politics correctly, Edward Huromonus will most likely be appointed as the temporary Director of the organization. He is far more rational than Doyle was. Once Meridian's ultimatum is presented to the Council, Huromonus will likely be swayed into accepting the most logical solution to the dilemma. The Colonies will be ours."

One of Calvin's tways chuckled as the trio steered the bodybag through the doorway and into the stairwell. Ghandi and Colette were left alone on the veranda.

She moved to the control panel beside the window, clenched the glass back into its transparent mode. The storm had abated; only stray bullets of white remained to waffle the skies. She gazed silently into the grayness.

Ghandi stared at her profile, grimly wondering if she had merged with her other half, become Sappho. The eyes of Colette's Ash Ock monarch would reflect a light that did not originate in this room; the eyes of Sappho would reveal a presence that seemed utterly alien.

But when she spoke, Ghandi's anticipation—his dread—melted away. She remained Colette.

"Come to the bedroom, my love. I desire you."
"I desire you," he echoed.

"Anything new on Blumhaven?" asked Nick.

The lion sat down, squeezing himself into a narrow space between the midget and a towering set of molded equipment racks. This spare bedroom, in the A-frame house at the retreat, seemed smaller to the lion each time he entered it. Nick and Adam Lu Sang acquired new computer gadgetry with the devotion of climate-conscious squirrels.

"No real updates," answered the lion. "He's been missing for almost a full day now, but about the only thing that E-Tech seems willing to admit is that he entered that history library in Pocono after telling his Security people to take the afternoon off. When his chauffeur came to pick him up at the library a few hours later—as instructed—Blumhaven was gone. E-Tech is still considering whether or not to close the cylinder—put Pocono Colony under martial law."

"Considering?" grunted Nick. "Assholes. They should have closed every terminal the instant they learned that their boss man had disappeared."

"You're probably right."

Nick's fingers pecked at the keyboard; a small input screen displayed a long sequence of alphanumeric characters. On a large monitor, immediately above, cottony puffs emerged from a dreamy blue sky. It was the signature of Freebird, the strange rescue program that continued to hinder Nick and Adam's efforts to thwart the data-destroying sunsetter.

"If I were going to place bets," said the midget, pulling back from the terminal with a scowl, "I'd make two wagers. One is that Blumhaven's the victim of foul play—"

"E-Tech is beginning to suspect as much."

"—and two is that very soon now, short of a minor miracle, this goddamned sunsetter is going to kick the living shit out of Freebird."

"There's nothing at all you can do?"

"Adam and I see only one possibility. Assuming that we're right—that Freebird is indeed the sunsetter's primary target, that this entire twenty-two-year assault upon the archives has been accomplished to drive Freebird out into the open so that it can be destroyed—then we have to figure out a way to protect Freebird. We have to offer the rescue program a haven and somehow convince Freebird to *enter* that haven. This is not going to be easy, especially since Adam and I now agree that Freebird's pre-Apocalyptic."

"You're sure?"

"Yeah, pretty sure. The program's got a real pristine feel to it. Like Pop-Tarts, straight out of their wrappers."

The lion refrained from uttering a bewildered: *Pop-Tarts?*—thus sparing himself from Nick's trademark response: *Never mind.* In recent days, the lion tried to allow the midget's delicious tidbits of twenty- and twenty-first-century history to burst forth without comment.

"Freebird," continued Nick, "probably dates from somewhere between 2090 and 2097, the final year when most of the archives were originally transferred from the planet to the Colonies. Which means that its mommy is long gone."

"You once told me that the archives were thoroughly detoxed before they were transferred up from Earth."

"Yeah, as thoroughly as we knew how. Obviously, this program got through."

"So its controller is long dead," mused the lion. "We're dealing with a fully automated program."

"Yep. And that means that a purely emotional appeal will likely be ignored. We can't just say to Freebird: 'Gosh, come into my computer net and you'll be cozy and safe.' If its mommy were around, such a tactic might work, provided we could get its mommy to trust us on human terms. But dealing strictly with a logic-driven program?" Nick shrugged. "I figure that we gotta make a real intellectual appeal. Either that, or we make him an offer he can't refuse."

"An offer he can't refuse?"

"Never mind."

The lion sighed and got up from the console. "What about your IRS 1991 program? The other day, Adam mentioned that the two of you may have a new theory as to why Freebird first made itself known at the exact moment your assault program attacked the sunsetter."

Excitement flashed across Nick's face. "Yeah, and if we're right, Freebird could prove even more important to us than we first imagined. Adam and I think that the sunsetter, simultaneously faced with *two* new programs—IRS *and* Freebird—elected to make an emergency run home to its mommy, for updated instructions. And I'd be willing to bet a shitload of cash that Freebird was counting on *exactly* that reaction. When the sunsetter headed home to tell mommy about these strange new programs, Freebird was ready. Freebird *followed* the sunsetter to its check-in terminal. A simple but brilliant strategy."

"Then Freebird knows who's running the sunsetter."

"Yep—or at least it knows the sunsetter's primary check-in location. And since we're already assuming—with a fair degree of certainty—that the sunsetter's mommy is the same person or persons responsible for the Order of the Birch massacres . . ."

"Aşh Ock," concluded the lion, realizing that this provided added spin to their already palpable suspicions. "And if you're correct, Freebird could lead us straight to the Paratwa—at least to the ones we know must already be in the Colonies."

"Bingo."

"So you have to find a way not only to protect Freebird from destruction by the sunsetter, but also to pierce its defenses and get to its primary data."

"Yeah. First we gotta persuade Freebird to enter our bedroom. After that, we work on getting its clothes off."

"Make her an offer she can't refuse?" suggested the lion.

Nick grinned. "Now you're catching on."

The lion took a step toward the door. "By the way, Inez Hernandez called. She just learned through some contacts that a pair of FL-Sixteen freelancers spotted Gillian and Buff in Sirak-Brath yesterday, at a sporting arena called Fin Whirl. They met a smuggler named Este Faquod, a known dealer in high-tech weaponry."

"Interesting," said Nick, sounding bored. He turned back to one of the keyboards and started typing again.

The lion fell silent. These days, when it came to discussions involving Gillian, the lion sensed that a brooding pain still plagued the midget. No matter how much Nick tried to deny it, shrapnel from the last violent encounter between the former friends had left a deep gash. And the wound showed no signs of healing.

Two gifted cripples, he thought, using one of Nick's own analogies. Once, Gillian and Nick had been bound together by a twisted amalgam of needs. And now . . .

"Does Inez have any new leads on Venus Cluster ownership?" asked Nick.

"Nothing. The ICN is still being as stubborn as ever."

"That's too bad. I thought that by this time maybe—"

The door slid open. A Costeau guard entered, his thruster rifle held in the ready position. "Sir, there's a commotion outside. Buff Boscondo. She just arrived. She's drawn weapons and refuses to relinquish them. She demands your presence."

They followed the guard to the front of the house. Outside, in the stark triplicated sunlight of a cloudless Irryan midday, Buff sat casually at the lawn table on the elevated ridge of albino grass. She had a thruster in one hand and the salene in the other. Her weapons were pointed at two Costeaus who stood before her. Another pair of guards crouched below the ridge, behind Buff, their rifles sighted at the back of her head.

The lion raised his eyebrows. "There is a problem?"

Buff plopped her feet lazily across another chair and leaned back. "Nothing but a slight misunderstanding, I hope. I came here for a peaceful visit and *boom*—my clan brothers"—she waved her thruster arm at the surrounding guards—"demand that I surrender my weapons."

"A new policy," the lion explained. "Our security precautions have become more stringent since the last time you were in the retreat. You should have been stopped at the gate."

"Yeah, well there were some old friends of mine doing guard duty. *They* trust me." She glared at the two guards.

"Intentions do not matter," chided the lion. "You are violating security—"

"I can see that. But the problem is, my own *personal* security precautions have also undergone some changes." She gazed coldly at the Costeau guards. "I don't give up my weapons. You might say that I ascribe to this policy with something on the order of religious fervor."

Spare me from fervor, thought the lion.

Nick grinned at her. "You've lost weight and you've had a facial. And what an interesting hairdo. I don't believe I've ever seen a tie-dyed scalp before."

Buff chuckled and ran the butt of the salene across her shaved skull. The photoluminescent array of crisscrossing stripes rippled across the tight black skin. "Colorful, huh?"

"Buff," ordered the lion, "put away your guns."

"I will if *they* will."

The lion sighed and motioned to the guards. The Costeaus lowered their rifles. Buff slipped her weapons under her open leather jacket, then raised her hands, palms up. "See. Totally defenseless."

"We're happy campers now," said Nick, smiling serenely at the guards. They did not smile back.

"You came alone?" asked the lion.

"What you see is what you get."

"Gillian?"

"He's all right. Let me rephrase that. He's as right as he ever is, which means that he's just about as whacked out as the last time you saw him." She hesitated; a dark scowl crossed her face. "Gillian sent me back here. Something happened. Yesterday, a man—a priest from the Church of the Trust—caught up with us. Lester Mon Dama was his name. He had a message for Gillian, a data brick, from someone called Jalka."

Buff waited to see if the names elicited any response. When the lion and Nick remained silent, she continued.

"This Jalka—whoever he is, Gillian knows him. There was a definite reaction."

Nick frowned. "What sort of reaction?"

"It scared the hell out of Gillian."

Jalka. The lion could recall neither a face nor any data to fit the name. He turned to Nick.

"Rings no bells here," offered the midget, keeping his attention on Buff. "And Gillian asked you to come back to the retreat?"

"Uh-huh. And it was pretty strange. I mean, Gillian's not exactly most stable person to begin with, but after the encounter with this priest, he got downright weird. We went to a hotel and he sat cross-legged on the bed for about two hours, barely moving, not saying a word, ignoring my attempts to start a conversation. Finally, he snapped out of it. He asked me to leave him alone for a while. He said that he wanted to access the data brick in private.

"So I went for a walk. When I returned about an hour later, Gillian was gone. There was a written message on the bed." Buff withdrew a crumpled paper from a jacket pocket and handed it the lion. He read it aloud.

The pressure never yields. Being more than one and less than one—simultaneously—is like living within a cracked sphere. And every day, fractures grow larger, threatening to shatter my life into fragments. I want to fight and destroy. I want to be fought, be destroyed. The hands of chaos cannot be denied.

I am going away. Perhaps I am going home, to a place that I do not know and a time that I do not comprehend. Only Jalka has the answers now.

There is a good chance that you will never see me again. Give this message to the lion. And tell Nick that the madness of reason should have never been so cruel as to tear apart a good friendship.

The lion drew a deep breath. "It's signed 'Gillian.' "

"Son of a bitch," murmured Nick.

The lion was not absolutely certain, but it looked as if a sharp grimace of pain had flashed briefly across the midget's face. Had Nick seen, momentarily, the true extent of what he had lost? Had he realized that the parameters of a real friendship could never be totally deconstructed by endless tangents of denial? If Nick *had* seen, *had* realized, then there was a chance that the chasm between the former friends could again be crossed.

But only if Gillian returned. And the message indicated the improbability of such an event.

The lion crumpled the note and threw it on the table in front of Nick.

"Hell of a goodbye," said Buff.

Nick folded his arms across his chest and stared at the crumpled shred of paper. "Did Gillian say anything else about this Jalka? Anything at all?"

"Not a word."

The lion turned to one of the guards. "Lester Mon Dama—this priest from the Church of the Trust. I want you to access every available network. Contact all of our private sources. I want a complete profile of this man, and I want to know where he is. And likewise, find out about this Jalka."

The guard nodded and jogged into the house.

"I'll make a wager," offered Buff. "I'll bet that you'll find no trace of Lester Mon Dama, that he'll have conveniently disappeared."

The lion, without knowing precisely why, knew that Buff's hypothesis would be proven correct.

Four hours later, they were back out on the elevated ridge. Late afternoon sunlight, still triplicated but far less intense than earlier, had begun its staged alteration into the soft reds and ambers of early evening. At the upper and lower edges of each cosmishield strip, subtle bands of violet appeared, outlining the muted glows, giving horizontal definition to the sunsettia: that ancient earthly art form that still attracted virtuosos from the ranks of intercolonial sky programmers.

The lion was reading a report on Lester Mon Dama from a hand terminal, which included the facts that the priest had missed his last two Church appointments and that his acquaintances had not seen him for several days.

"Too bad I had no takers on that wager," muttered Buff. "Might have been profitable."

Nick, standing atop a lawn chair, gazed over the lion's

shoulder at the small readout. "Yeah, that's the problem with a sure bet. Can't ever find any suckers."

The lion frowned. "It says here that Lester Mon Dama had some serious problems twenty-four years ago. There was an accident involving three Church of the Trust obstetricians. They were killed in his car. Prosecutors considered bringing manslaughter charges against the priest—"

He trailed off as three Costeaus emerged from the A-frame and raced toward them.

"Adam Lu Sang is here," announced the first man, a towering black named Vilakoz, who served as the retreat's daytime security chief. "He's just entered the main lot."

What now? wondered the lion.

A few minutes later, the young computer hawk came into view along the stone-coated path which wound its way down through the pines from the parking lot. He gave a hearty wave.

The lion frowned. "Didn't you tell Adam not to risk coming here anymore?"

"Sure did," drawled the midget. "This better be good news."

"Why do I get the feeling it's not?" wondered Buff.

The path terminated just below the slightly elevated ridge where they stood. The slender gaunt-cheeked programmer ascended the albino-grass knoll in three quick leaps.

"Here I am."

"Here you are," said Nick.

"What's going on, Adam?" asked the lion.

The E-Tech programmer's face drooped; epicanthic folds became more prominent, highlighting his Oriental ancestry. "You sent *me* the message."

"What message?"

Adam handed the lion a tiny flotsam brick, a metal chip encoded with a personalized communique. The lion passed it to Vilakoz. The security chief quickly procured an ingress from his utility belt and snapped the brick onto its scanner.

"It's dated today," announced Vilakoz. " 'To Adam Lu Sang: vital that you come to the retreat immediately.' Those last five words are emphasized. 'Do not utilize the network.

Do not utilize com channels of any sort, including coded ones. Desperately important that you heed this message to the letter. Take all necessary precautions to ensure that you are not followed. Our collective safety depends upon your actions. Do not delay.' "

Vilakoz hesitated for a moment, then faced the lion. "Sir, the message appears to have been written in your cursive, then transferred onto the flotsam. And it appears authentic. Your DNA prints are encoded, along with the seal of the lion of Alexander."

"I made sure it was validated," insisted Adam, looking more worried by the moment.

The lion shook his head grimly. "It's a forgery. I sent no message."

"Oh shit," muttered Buff. "Why do I get the feeling that I picked the wrong day for a visit?"

"Bad timing," agreed Nick.

An urgent beeper wailed to life on the security chief's belt. They all turned to Vilakoz.

He switched to speaker and cranked the volume. Another Costeau's voice filled the air.

"This is Majis at the main gate. E-Tech Security's here— three carloads of them. They have warrants—all kinds. Search and Seizure, Judicial Confiscation, Unspecified Arrest—the works. They say that they're prepared to use force if I don't let them through."

"Let them pass," ordered the lion. He faced one of the rifle-wielding guards. "Take Nick, Adam, and Buff inside. Hide them."

Adam shook his head. "I'm sorry ... I should have been more careful—"

"It's not your fault," said Nick.

"Go!" snapped the lion. "Quickly!"

The guard turned to obey but froze as a vigorous roar blossomed from the south. A small jet flashed into view, skimming a mere fifty feet above the tree line.

"E-Tech Security assault craft," announced Vilakoz, speaking into his com.

With a deafening shriek, the jet braked to a near-instantaneous halt, directly over their heads. From the grimy black undercarriage, less than a hundred feet above them, heat baffles snapped downward; vertical engines flared to life, stabilizing the craft. Babelmutes—stringy tendrils of noise-absorbent flux—fell from the underbelly, flapping in the jet's own wind, killing the worst of the engine noise.

A stern, amplified voice, almost as deafening as the un-muted turbines had been, echoed across the clearing. The surrounding trees reverberated with tonal harmonics, making it seem as if the words originated from the soaring pines instead of the bowels of the jet.

"Do not move. You are being tracked. Iso-seeks are fully armed. To those persons bearing weapons, please set them on the ground and take three steps backward."

The four Costeau guards reacted in typical fashion. They aimed their rifles at the hovering jet.

Nick muttered, "We can't be arrested."

The lion knew that if he gave the signal, his guards would open fire on the craft. He also knew that thrusters against an armed jet bearing isolation targeting systems was suicidal. And starting a war against E-Tech would be the height of dementia.

"Weapons down," commanded the lion. The Costeaus reluctantly obeyed.

Buff smiled grimly at Vilakoz. "I've still got a salene under my jacket. What do your people have that they're not showing?"

Vilakoz faced the lion, directing his words at the grass to discourage audio scanners. "Sir, our systems have targeted the craft. The jet can be taken out."

The lion shook his head. "That is *not* an option. Our strategy will be restrained cooperation, Vilakoz. Is that clearly understood?"

Vilakoz nodded.

A line of three vehicles came into view, bouncing down the stony path, their all-terrain tires kicking up fierce sprays of rocks and rubble. The first two cars, black-and-gold striped, bearing E-Tech insignias, screeched to a halt at the foot of the grassy knoll. The third vehicle, lower in profile than the others, and boasting the white-on-white shadow logo of the ICN, stopped about a hundred feet away from the ridge.

"What's the ICN doing here?" wondered Nick.

"Neutral observers," the lion deduced. "They've come to make sure that the amenities are followed, that E-Tech acts with propriety toward a Councillor of Irrya."

Doors on the black-and-gold cruisers slid back; four uniformed officers hopped from each vehicle. In pairs, they dropped into combat crouches, surrounding the ridge. When they were positioned, a ninth figure, a short pot-bellied man dressed in a drab olive suit, emerged from the second car. A row of tiny black pimples on his lower lip revealed the presence of a multi-source transceiver. The lion noticed that he had only four fingers on each hand: the little digits were missing.

"Uh-oh," whispered Buff.

"Buff Boscondo!" exclaimed the pot-bellied man. "Plasma necropsy specialist from La Gloria de la Ciencia, isn't it? But then again, that was last month's disguise. Today you are simply Buff Boscondo, loyal Costeau." He smiled as he ascended the knoll. "That's a very interesting hairstyle. I don't believe I've ever seen anything quite like it."

"That's what they all say."

"Allow me to introduce myself to your friends, Buff. I am Inspector Xornakoff. From E-Tech Security, if that fact is not already apparent." He approached the lion and handed him an ingress. The lion activated the unit and began scanning its multiple pages of documents.

"Warrants, sir," explained Xornakoff. "They fully detail the extent of our authority here, as well as carefully outline the degree of disruption that you might expect from this unfortunate but necessary intrusion. It is E-Tech's profound hope that a mutually cooperative effort will lead to a peaceful consummation." The Inspector paused. "I know that you have other armed security personnel on the grounds and within the house. I also have the distinct feeling that even with jet support, our small force would be no match for a determined resistance. Naturally, it is our sincere hope that any impulsive acts can be avoided."

"We will not start a fight," promised the lion, his eyes still scanning the ingress but privately wondering just how many more E-Tech Security units were being held in reserve. That the retreat was completely surrounded was a foregone conclusion, but Xornakoff—or whoever had arranged the raid—was obviously no fool. He had kept the point force deliberately small and then openly declared that his officers were probably outmatched. Smart and subtle reasoning: the raid had been planned by people who understood Costeau psychology.

"I notice," said the lion, "that these documents are all notarized—with today's date—by the Director of E-Tech. Since it my understanding that your Director, Doyle Blumhaven, is still missing—"

"Missing since yesterday," supplied Xornakoff. "Sir, your meaning is well taken. Actually, these documents all bear *in absentia* authorizations, made by an acting committee of high-level officials. After certain information came into our hands a short time ago, this ad hoc committee issued us the warrants."

The lion continued to scan the documents, grimly aware that Adam's arrival had triggered the raid. *A complete setup. Adam's security must have been compromised.* Not surprisingly, Adam Lu Sang headed the list of those who were specified on the arrest warrants.

And three other names were listed as well.

Xornakoff seemed to be following the lion's thoughts. "Let's see—we have Adam Lu Sang and Buff Boscondo." He pointed to the midget. "And you must be the one they call Nick."

"Nah, but I can see where you'd get us mixed up. Actually, I'm Lawrence Arabia, the lion's Jesuit instructor. I just dropped over for a cup of tea."

Xornakoff smiled. "A sense of humor. Yes, that fits the description. At any rate, the three of you are under arrest."

Nick shrugged. Adam Lu Sang swallowed nervously. Buff glared at the closest set of E-Tech officers.

"That makes three out of a possible four," said the Inspector, turning back to the lion. "And now, sir, if you would be so good as to produce the last individual, a major portion of this unpleasantness will be behind us. I need the man who usually goes by the name of Gillian." Xornakoff paused. "At least that is the moniker he uses when he is not impersonating technical specialists."

"Gillian is not here."

"Indeed. We will, of course, have to verify that assertion. Do we have your permission to begin searching the house and grounds?"

"You don't need my permission," the lion replied coldly.

"No, sir, I do not. But again, E-Tech desires this matter to be expedited with as little disruption as necessary. I do understand the difficulties you must be facing right now, and, believe it or not, I do sympathize with your emotions. But if you can see clear to grant your fullest cooperation, I can assure you that our search will be conducted with as much dignity as possible." The Inspector let his gaze wander across the entire gathering. "You have my absolute word on this."

The lion perceived a solemn truth on Xornakoff's face, and he noted how several of the Costeau guards began to relax. The man projected a blatant honesty, cleanly and without compromise. The lion wondered how someone as open as Xornakoff had managed to reach the relatively high rank of Inspector within Doyle Blumhaven's spirit-crushing bureaucracy.

He realized he was being unfair. Stereotyping remained a sin on both sides; Costeaus, whether mainstream or hard-line, tended to engage in the same sort of prejudicial behavior that they criticized Colonials for. E-Tech as a whole could not be totally dismissed because of the misguided actions of its leadership.

The lion found himself a bit surprised at his own objectivity, considering the circumstances. "Conduct your search," he said.

The tip of Xornakoff's tongue flicked across one of the raised pimples pasted to his lower lip. Instantly, four of the eight surrounding officers scampered toward the house. Vilakoz mumbled a command into his own transceiver, doubtlessly reiterating to the Costeaus in the house that the coming intrusion was fully authorized by the lion. Vilakoz did not look happy.

Nick wagged a finger at the ICN car, which still remained a hundred feet away from the ridge, its occupants hidden behind smoked windows. "How about them? If they're observers, they sure as hell should go along into the house to do some firsthand observing."

Xornakoff nodded to the lion. "Is that your wish?"

"It is."

The Inspector raised his hand and signaled toward the car.

They waited expectantly, but the doors of the ICN vehicle failed to open. Xornakoff signaled a second time.

No response.

The Inspector frowned; his tongue flicked across another of his lip dots. "You men in the ICN car—have you been following this conversation? Your presence is requested inside the house."

The white car just sat there, a silent presence on the albino grass, and the lion was suddenly reminded of one of those beach paladins, found on the leisure Colony of Aegean—a floating organic shroud—a semitranslucent membrane protecting sunbathers from ultraviolet overexposure, camouflaging its own existence by mimicking the background.

"How many people in that car?" demanded Nick.

"Two," answered the Inspector.

A strange expression appeared on the midget's face. Slowly, grimly, he turned to face Xornakoff, so that his back was to the car. "Before today, you never met the occupants of that vehicle, right? You simply received orders that the ICN would be sending observers."

"That's correct," said the Inspector, still frowning. "Two men. They rendezvoused with us—"

"Get off the ridge!" hollered Nick. "It's an ambush!"

The roof of the ICN vehicle snapped open. A strange glassy sphere, attached to a thick shaft, rose from the body of the car, flowering into a weird bouquet of gleaming silver spikes.

"Run!" yelled Buff, diving across the lawn table, tackling

the lion, sending their bodies tumbling down the embankment, away from the car.

The lion saw a flash of blue heavens, a whirl of treetops. And then coils of silver light were lancing skyward from the ICN vehicle to the hovering E-Tech assault craft.

The jet shrieked. Metal twisted, folded in upon itself, as if the entire craft were being smashed between megalithic rocks, grinding it to rubble. Golden flames leaped from the underbelly—vital fluids being squeezed from its deepest cavities—and then pieces of twisted remains, unrecognizable as technological procreation, tumbled *upward*, away from the sunlit albino field, falling into the sky, a sprawling mass of debris, impossibly ignorant of the cylinder's gravitational polarity.

—And then the lion's breath was knocked out of him as he slammed into the packed soil at the base of the knoll. He shook his head to clear his senses, wondering if his eyes could be trusted, wondering if what he had seen had actually taken place.

"C'mon!" yelled Buff, grabbing his arm, yanking him to his feet. They stumbled toward the house, managed only two faltering steps before the very air seemed to change in quality, became stale and dry, sucked free of all moisture, stripped of its cohesiveness. The lion started to turn around.

The ridge exploded.

He saw figures enveloped in a blinding white light, lifted into the air, thrown end over end, away from the knoll, tumbling like freefall circus charlies but battered lifeless by the force of the blast. And the lion did not understand what crisis-driven subconscious process made the determination, but he knew, in that instant of piercing light, that one of the flying corpses belonged to Adam Lu Sang.

The blast radius expanded, enveloped them, catapulting him forward, and he hit the ground head first, somersaulted violently into a large blue rosebush at the base of the A-frame, below a window. Thorns slashed through the fabric of his thin shirt, ripping into his back.

Buff, oozing blood from a gash below her chin, whipped

out her thruster and fired into the window. Slab glass disintegrated, raining them with shards.

"Up!" she hissed, grabbing the lion by the elbow and propeling him through the opening. They half-dove, half-scrambled over the glass-strewn sill and tumbled into the day room.

A Costeau guard, her rifle unslung, leaped in from the hallway, took one quick look at Buff and the lion, activated her crescent web, and charged toward the window.

"Get down!" hollered the lion and Buff simultaneously.

The warning came an instant too late. From outside, something hit the guard's front crescent with the force of a geo cannon. Scarlet tracers streamed from her web as she was picked up and hurled backward at deadly velocity, straight into an acrylic painting of Aaron, the lion's adoptive father. The painting and the wallboard behind it exploded, pulverized by the force of the collision.

"Jesus Christ!" yelled Buff.

The guard was gone. Only a splintered hole in the wall—a huge leering eye, stood on end—remained.

The lion shoved Buff forward. On their hands and knees, keeping below the level of the window, they clamored like terrified puppies toward the hallway entrance.

Two more guards, crouching low, appeared in the doorway. They reached down, dragged Buff and the lion out into the corridor. Another explosion shook the house. Small ceiling panels, torn loose, crashed onto the carpet.

"We think it's Paratwa," cried Buff. "Two tways, maybe three. It'll be coming into the house."

The lion dragged himself upright, tried to ignore a sizzling pain coursing through his knees. "Let's go!"

Buff turned to him. "Are you wearing a web?"

"No."

She yanked him in close to her, snapped her jaws down. Front and rear crescents ignited. The air hummed; dust from the dislodged tiles sparkled as motes danced away from the activated energy field.

"Stay tight against me," ordered Buff. "My web should protect us both."

The lion said nothing. The Costeau in the day room also had been wearing a web.

Sounds of a new commotion emanated from the front of the house. The two guards whirled, raised their thrusters. A trio of figures came hurtling around the corner.

It was Vilakoz, the retreat's security chief. And one of the E-Tech officers, now weaponless and clutching a bloodied shoulder. And behind them, barely visible, cursing and limping at breakneck speed: Nick.

"Faster!" urged the midget. "This ain't a goddamn scout jamboree!"

At the opposite end of the corridor, thirty-five feet away, a door slid open. Four thrusters and a salene were instantly aimed into the open portal.

"Hold!" shouted Vilakoz.

Another Costeau—a young girl, barely a teen—came out of the room, walking slowly. She was not wearing a web. Her head was lowered. All her attention was focused on the digital readout of the rhythm detector strapped across her waist.

"This way," she said softly, her sweet preadolescent voice seeming to suggest that nothing unusual was taking place.

"Go!" ordered Vilakoz, hustling Nick in front of him, shielding their backs with his own rear crescent.

En masse, they raced down the hallway, their crescent webs ejecting shafts of red lightning as multiple defensive fields interacted, furiously protesting the cramped conglomeration of bodies.

They followed the young girl through the portal and into one of the guest bedrooms. Beyond the bed and dresser lay another door. The girl, still gazing at the rhythm detector's readout, hesitated, then spun to face the wall adjacent to the second entrance.

"Something's coming at us—this direction—very fast—definitely organic—about three seconds away."

"Get ready," ordered Vilakoz, crouching low, aiming his thruster at the bare wall.

Buff and the other two Costeaus raised their weapons. The lion felt a shudder race through him. *Not since childhood have I been so scared! Not since . . .*

"It passed overhead," announced the girl, spinning around and flipping the rhythm detector up closer to her face. "Right over the house. A jetpak rider maybe. I don't know—"

The sound of explosions—like grenades being detonated in rapid sequence—came from somewhere outside.

"Go!" shouted Vilakoz, pointing toward the second entrance.

The girl nodded, raced toward the door. But she came to another sudden stop, right in front of the portal. "Another signal—"

The door blew inward, knocking the girl backward onto the bed. A fierce orange light, bright as the sun, spilled into the room, like a cauldron of deadly fire dumped from some ancient rampart.

The air gleamed, crackled, as the orange light leaped up at them from all sides. Crescent webs hissed, emitted puffs of fiery brown smoke, then became completely visible, metamorphosing into miniature cascades, darkly tinted, like waterfalls of molasses.

Something came through the door—a dancing figurine, a smear of jerky movements. Through the blur of Buff's web, the lion could just make out the shafts of flickering light clutched in the creature's fists.

Flash daggers, thought the lion, recalling descriptions of the deadly weapons used by the tway known as Slasher.

The creature leaped at them. Cartoon blades reached out, doubling in length, cutting through the distorted crescent webs of the two Costeau guards as if the protective fields were not there. The guards went down, their chests carved open, huge globs of blood spilling onto the floor.

Someone screamed: "Webs aren't working!"

Thruster fire erupted from behind the lion, nailing the creature. But the blasts merely altered the tway's direction slightly; the creature seemed to frolic with the thruster blows, twisting its body to avoid direct hits, offsetting the drubbing force of thruster energies in a mad dance of counterpoint rhythms.

Such speed! the lion thought, images of movement registering too fast to comprehend fully.

Cartoon daggers assumed new axes. The E-Tech guard with the injured shoulder screamed as twin scalpels of color lopped off his arms. The young Costeau girl hurtled from the bed and threw herself at the creature, the rhythm detector held in front of her—shield and weapon.

"No," the lion heard himself whisper.

A flash dagger lanced downward, plunging through the boxy rhythm detector in a burst of scarlet flame, continued its forward drive straight into the girl's temple, directly above the left eye.

The girl seemed to release a loud sigh, like the disappointed utterance of a child denied some precious thing.

Noise—agony—erupting inside the lion's head, enveloping him, as if mad dogs were barking directly into his eardrum.

Buff had fired her salene.

The weapon's wavering sheet of white light spilled onto the tway, outlining it's crescent web, and for a stark instant, the creature froze. Conflicting energies dueled as the disruptive expulsion from the salene sought to decoalesce the polarized field of Slasher's defensive web.

"This way," yelled Vilakoz, grabbing the lion by the shoulder and yanking him back toward the hallway door. A tremor passed through the lion as his body slipped through the murky brown cascade—water without wetness—of Buff's now-useless crescent web.

Slasher's own web neutralized the effects of the salene. White fire melted away. The tway spun toward the lion, hurtled forward. Buff leaped into its path.

"C'mon, fucker!" she screamed, deactivating the useless remnants of her own web, lunging forward, thruster wailing. At point blank range, she blasted the creature's front crescent. Discrete packets of energy battered the tway, shoved it backward through the open portal. Buff charged after it.

And then the lion was out in the first hallway again, with Vilakoz at his side. A fresh set of explosions came from somewhere outside the house. The corridor was empty.

"Where's Nick?"

Vilakoz shook his head. "I think he was—"

"Right here!" yelled the midget, hurtling through the doorway ten steps behind them.

The lion pointed to another portal, still closed. "Through there! We can get to the back of the house—"

The left side partition, to their rear, collapsed inward. A rolling mass of wallboard and assorted rubble billowed into the hall, trapping Nick on the other side. The midget screamed, then disappeared beneath a thundering cloud of debris.

A car had driven through the wall. It had E-Tech markings.

A door slid open. "Get in," ordered a man's voice.

The lion glanced at Vilakoz. The security chief, with thruster extended, rammed his massive body into the vehicle. The lion hesitated, peering down the hallway for some signs of Nick. Nothing. The hallway was completely blocked.

"Get in!" hollered the voice, more desperate this time.

The lion leaped into the front seat, pinching Vilakoz between himself and the driver.

"Hang on," screeched the tall E-Tech sergeant. A deep gash across his forehead leaked tiny rivulets of blood, down between his eyes, along his nose, to the corners of his mouth, where the red tears coagulated in dark clusters.

With the three of them jammed in the front seat, the door snapped shut. The sergeant reversed the engines, backed out through the devastated day room, through a massive opening where an outer wall had once stood, into sunlight and destruction.

"Somebody's going to pay," muttered Vilakoz.

"Believe it," said the sergeant, brake-locking the car's left side wheels. The vehicle spun around. The sergeant rammed the accelerator and pinched a control stud on the wraparound dash. Blue flames—uncorralled fires from the car's auxiliary rocket engines—rose from beneath the vehicle, licking at the windows. Shrieking, the car raced across the white grass toward the stony path. The lion was pressed into the thick cushions.

An undulating shriek—above and behind them. The lion

managed to twist his head around and stare out through the rear window.

A black jetpak—a prone rider enclosed by maneuverable rocket tubes—raced out of the northern sky, scant feet above the tree line, arcs of pulsating gray lightning rippling beneath the rider's body as if he were some ancient water surfer skimming across waves of his own making. He was heading straight for them.

The lion instinctively ducked low in the front seat. The jetpak rider shot directly overhead.

"Spirit of Ari," muttered Vilakoz, as shafts of lightning gouged huge chunks of dirt from the field immediately in front of them. The E-Tech sergeant swerved the car to the right and cut the rocket engines. The vehicle raced over a small rise and up onto the stony path just as the bizarre jetpak rider vanished into a swath between towering pines at the southern edge of the retreat.

The car was now moving parallel to the distant house. The lion stared out the side window and bore witness to the true devastation of the attack.

The A-frame was a twisted shambles, pockmarked with monstrous holes—including the one they had driven through—and emitting wafts of gray smoke that curled up into the afternoon sky, disappearing into the brightness. *Fading embers,* thought the lion, acknowledging a desperate sadness rising from within, an omniscient force tunneling beneath his rage, fear, and pain, adding greater depth to the horror while it simultaneously subtracted potency from his very spirit.

Never before had he felt such a sense of loss. Never before had he been bruised by the knowledge of such defeat.

And he knew that one Paratwa had done this.

The knoll where they had stood only moments ago had been stripped clean; human beings and albino grass, lawn chairs and table gone, the earth blotted, ravaged. Beside the elevated ridge, the remains of the two E-Tech cars lay up-ended, shattered hulks of black and gold, minor monuments to technological achievement. Crisp geysers of tangerine flame spouted from portions of the surrounding forests; pines yielded their needles in consummations of oily smoke until they became serrated spears, poised for futile jousts against an indifferent sky.

A few figures still moved in the clearing, but they appeared to be dazed and wretched, wandering like the lost children of Apocalyptic Earth, the last generation who had been unable to escape to the Colonies and who had slowly perished in the radiation and plague-scarred cities, the final victims of a planet's madness.

The lion had seen authentic videos from those ancient times. He knew.

One Paratwa.

The E-Tech sergeant abruptly wrenched the car to the left. They leaped from the path, cut through a cluster of youthful oaks, and screeched to a halt in a thicket of vines overgrowing a white birch. *Unmolested woodland,* the lion found himself thinking, and wondering, in the same instant, why they had stopped.

Dread came over him.

There were only two E-Tech cars and they're both back there in the clearing, destroyed. Where did this car come from? How could it have gotten into the retreat so fast?

"Please allow me to introduce myself," said the sergeant, turning to them with bared teeth. A repugnant smile began at his mouth, slithered up across his cheekbones. All traces of human emotion vanished from the sergeant's face. The gash on his forehead took on a remote quality, an air of fabrication.

Vilakoz, sitting in the middle, tried to raise his thruster.

Too late.

The sergeant's fist came up with blinding speed, an energized attack gauntlet brimming with sparks, juiced to maximum power. Vilakoz caught the gauntlet in the face, directly below the nose. The security chief's head snapped back against the headrest, then crashed forward. He was unconscious even before his jaw slammed into the dashboard.

The door opened. The lion was shoved from the vehicle, onto his back, onto cool moist earth, and then the creature was somehow out of the car, and propping himself on the lion's stomach before the lion could even think to move.

Gauntletted fingers closed around his throat, squeezed. The creature's other hand rammed itself into the lion's mouth and for one petrifying moment, the lion feared that the tway's probing digits were going to snake their way down his throat. He stifled an urge to gag.

"Jerem Marth, lion of Alexander, Councillor of Irrya," certified the creature, speaking calmly but in an odd cadence that somehow suggested it did not often use the complexity of speech. "I believe that I have your attention."

The tway lifted the lion's head and wagged it up and down, providing an affirmative answer to his own question.

"Jerem Marth, it is said that you've been helping that foul remnant of Empedocles, the one who calls itself Gillian. They say that once, long ago, you even enabled Gillian to destroy Reemul."

I'm going to die. With the gauntlet crushing his neck and the creature's other hand jammed between his teeth, fingers almost to the back of his throat, the lion could barely breathe. He thought about not being able to see his wife and children once again. He wondered where Gillian was.

"Jerem Marth—good news. It is your lucky day. You are to be listed as a survivor of a Paratwa attack." The tway sighed. "Personally, I would prefer to kill you. But politics being what it is, there are reasons that you be permitted to continue processing oxygen."

The tway smiled and released the gauntlet from his throat. The lion gasped. His chest heaved, sucking air through his nostrils. His mouth remained an almost completely blocked canal, filled with the creature's gloved fingers. The lion wanted to bite down, crush through those fingers, but something told him that such an action would prove to be a terrible mistake.

His lips quivered. *This creature—it plans everything.* Contingencies existed for all situations, against all tactical responses.

The lion knew his reasoning was sound, but he also knew that such rationalizations burned from the hot fires of cowardice. *I want to live.*

"You are afraid. That is good. Your fear will help you to remember the importance of what I am about to show you."

The tway held up his left palm. Sharp green letters—some

sort of holo display—clustered in the air above the creature's fingertips. "This is a message from Sappho."

Sixteen words. A simple transmittal. The lion read it once, knew that it would remain engraved in his memory for the rest of his life.

Letters faded. Fingers retreated from the lion's mouth. And then the tway was on its feet, racing toward the car.

"Have a nice day," it offered, grinning as it hopped into the vehicle. The door closed. The car backed up, then accelerated southward, into another overgrown thicket. Branches quivered. The car disappeared.

For a long time, the lion did not move. When he finally stood up, his heels sunk into a puddle of gooey mud.

What hope do we have? He recalled a conversation with Nick, weeks ago. They had talked about what they would do if the Paratwa conquered the Colonies. They had talked about never surrendering.

He wondered if Nick were still alive.

I am sixty-eight years old, and I want to live.

The thought shamed him.

Tumescent patches of gray and white whipped across the shuttle's flight deck windows, obliterating the forward view. Not just clouds, thought Gillian, but radioactive, biologically poisoned smog as well. They blew together, the natural married to the unnatural in ceremonial rectitude, fathering this perversion of an atmosphere that had been Earth's legacy for over two-and-a-half centuries. The residue of humanity's greatest accomplishments wedded to the very spirit of Gaia. An unholy alliance, scattering its tainted children to the winds, surrounding the globe, decimating all that had once thrived.

Gillian felt his palms tighten on the armrests of the acceleration couch. He sat in the pilot's seat, but he was not flying the shuttle. He had needed merely to insert Jalka's data brick into the craft's navcom and then sit back, relax, and enjoy the view while automatic sequences guided the vessel out of Sirak-Brath's orbital control.

The data brick had given Gillian access to an opulent bank account, supplying enough money not only for the shuttle rental but for the ridiculously huge deposit that the smuggler had insisted upon after Gillian had requested the vessel *sans crew*. Even then, the smuggler had remained uneasy about the deal, voicing his suspicions that Gillian might not return with his vessel: "This craft has great sentimental value to me," the smuggler had said at last, his hushed voice curling into maudlin imagery, as if he were discussing a lost lover. "I simply could not bear the thought of losing it."

Gillian had asked the man whether he was also sentimental about insurance payouts.

The smuggler had liked that, and a wall had been breached. Chuckling, the man had shown Gillian the layout of the vessel, and after assuring himself that his new renter could indeed pilot such a craft, had departed, reasonably contented. Gillian had been tempted to urge the smuggler to get a head start on the lengthy insurance claim process. But there had been no sense in pressing his luck.

Besides, maybe I will be coming back.

He doubted it.

Outside, the gray and white continued to swirl.

Sit back and relax, Gillian urged himself. *Enjoy the view.*

But such ancient codicils for pleasurable flight no longer carried any meaning for him. *I no longer know how to relax.* And there was no view.

Hours ago, there had at least been something to look at: the sun, the crisp beauty of the cylinders floating in the vacuum, cold and peaceful, like perfect glittering icicles snapped from their roots, motionless, as if they had been captured by some photographer in the instant of their fall. And as the early hours of the flight had passed, those mirrored icicles—the Colonies of Irrya—had compressed, shrinking into a compact mass, assuming inconsequential proportions within the vast blackness.

And then they were gone, and the shuttle was unfolding its earthly wings, plummeting into the density of atmosphere, on a spiraling descent toward the secret destination contained in Jalka's data brick. Perceptible references had vanished into the plodding smog/clouds, the cankerous gray and white of a polluted world.

Yet despite visual evidence to the contrary, the atmospheric poison levels were actually the lowest they had been in the past two hundred and fifty years. The present mixture of smog and cloud might appear just as vapid, but the relationship of natural atmospheric cover to human-created pollutants had changed drastically. Nick had pointed out the phenomenon to Gillian several weeks ago, and current data from the shuttle's external scanners augmented the midget's interpretation.

"The planet is finally healing itself," Nick had announced one morning, not long after their latest stasis reawakening. "The pollution levels are diminishing; significant changes are occurring almost weekly. E-Tech claims credit, insisting that its long-range 'Ecospheric Turnaround' projects are responsible. But E-Tech's role has not been consequential enough to create the kind of changes that are taking place. I believe we're witnessing a natural process. The Earth is coming back on its own."

If Gillian had faith in omens, he would have taken that as a good sign.

And he found himself wondering—yet again—if Nick were still alive.

The attack upon the lion of Alexander's Irryan retreat had occurred only hours ago. Gillian had picked up the freelancer report on the shuttle's monitoring system.

"A brutal massacre of terrifying proportions," the FL-Sixteen freelancer had growled. "A vicious attempt to rip into the very heart of the Costeaus! An act of cold-blooded villainy by stormtroopers straight from the gates of hell!" Freelancer Karl Zork was a bear of a man with a zigzag red beard and a delivery styled to overwhelm.

Zork had raged on for several minutes, but he had offered little real news other than the fact that there had been a massacre and that the lion of Alexander had been one of the few survivors. Names of the dead had not yet been released.

Nick could have been at the retreat. And Buff, delivering my message. And Adam Lu Sang. And Inez Hernandez. Maybe they're all dead. Maybe the lion was the only one to escape.

Gillian did not want to know.

Following the initial report, he had turned off the monitor and disengaged the emergency call system. There would be no more reports from those distant icicles. Despite a continuing urge to learn about survivors—Nick and Buff especially—he had made the decision and would stand by it.

Only Jalka mattered now.

Since yesterday, since the run-in with the priest, Gillian had been consciously denigrating his time spent in the Colonies, trying to reduce the importance of all former liaisons. Someday, if he lived, he would likely pay the price for such self-repression; an eventual surrender, perhaps, to bitter nostalgia. Or worse.

But from the moment the priest had uttered the secret name of Gillian's former master, he had been struck by an overwhelming urge to stand again before a tway of Aristotle. Long suppressed desires had surfaced; Ash Ock memories had washed up on the shores of consciousness, depositing refuse from a past that could no longer be ignored.

Only Jalka mattered now. Even Empedocles seemed to recognize that truth.

Although Gillian's monarch continued to grow in strength, driving the two of them forward with relentless determination, driving them toward that ultimate fate which Gillian could not bring himself to accept: the abomination of the permanent whelm—tway and monarch fused together in a complete surrender of personalities, consciousness grotesquely interlaced, like the clouds and smog, like the gray and white; even though that horizon drew closer, Empedocles had become less intrusive since their encounter with the priest. Gillian sensed that his monarch also believed that Jalka might know of a way to help.

Jalka had to have the answers.

That was truly what drove Gillian now, the desperate hope that Aristotle could suggest a way for himself and Empedocles to live in peace, to live distinctly; an end to monarchial lust for the synthesis of personalities.

If it can be done, Jalka will know how.

Outside, the sky abruptly wilted; relentless flows of gray and white dissolved into the deeper blue of calm ocean, unfolding endlessly from horizon to horizon.

He checked the altimeter: three thousand feet and dropping fast. The acceleration couch's autostraps curled across his chest and thighs. A quick glance at the navcom indicated that the shuttle was about two hundred and twenty-five miles northeast of the Brazilian seaport city of Fortaleza, just south of the equator.

Eighteen hundred feet over the water now, and still descending fast. Gillian punched up a coordinate reference grid, wondering if there were some tiny island out here.

Nothing. No land masses. Only ocean, and fairly deep ocean at that—three thousand-plus feet throughout the entire grid.

A thousand feet above the water now, a wall of liquid rising to meet the shuttle. His thoughts churned: *Am I going to be smashed against the sea? Was Jalka's message just an elaborate ruse?*

Six hundred feet. Too close. Decision time.

He typed the disengage command into the navcom keyboard, tried to free the unit from its domination by Jalka's software.

No response. The navcom refused to disengage. Jalka's data brick must have launched its own override tracers into the system.

Navcoms possessed safeguards against such sophisticated software, ways for a vessel's pilot manually to override the entire system. But Gillian knew that it would take at least ten or fifteen seconds to accomplish such an override and regain control of the ship.

He did not have that much time. The ship was less than two hundred and fifty feet above the water. In about three seconds, he would plow into the ocean at a thirty-degree angle.

The acceleration couch's emergency system was triggered. Restraint clamps tightened across his arms. Hydropads bubbled up from the seat's interior, curling into his groin, his armpits, the back of his neck, providing extra cushioning against the immense G-forces sure to be generated by the impact. He forced himself to relax, knowing that he had a far greater chance of survival if the couch's smart sensors were allowed to regulate body motion.

Suddenly the engines cut off. Retros fired, braking the shuttle, quickly reducing his airspeed to less than one hundred and twenty miles per hour.

Seventy miles per hour. Thirty-five.

A quiver went through the ship as the vertical landing jets erupted, blasting the tranquil surface of the sea with full-powered streams of fiery exhaust. Wild ripples spread out from the vessel, disturbing the ocean's stillness, forming an ever-widening perimeter of resonance.

The forward acceleration indicator fell to zero. The shuttle settled effortlessly onto the surface of the Atlantic Ocean. Vertical landing jets shut down. Sensors freed his body from the couch and he stood up and leaned against the window frame and gazed out at the rippling sea.

What now?

The shuttle continued to rock gently for another few moments, then became perfectly still as internal gyros achieved stability, balancing the craft on the plane of liquid as easily as if it were resting on the solidity of shuttleport remac. Waves lost their momentum, dissipated. Slowly, the ocean returned to its calm state.

Gillian turned to the scanners, hoping that they would display a nearby micro-island, something new perhaps, a volcanic upthrusting, something not listed within this vessel's navcom. But there were no signs of land. He set the scanner range to maximum, checked the surrounding airspace for another incoming craft. Nothing.

And suddenly, heavy mists poured over the vessel.

The fog seemed to lift itself out of the very water, as if the surface of the ocean had mutated into a sheet of dry ice, releasing great billowing clouds, murky specters, expanding and merging into one another until there was nothing left to see through the flight deck windows except an endless wall of gun-metal gray. Gillian was not overly familiar with the planet's current ecosystems, but he suspected that whatever was occurring was not a natural phenomenon.

The ship tilted slightly to starboard, then righted itself. On the control panel, a sensor blinked, calling his attention to the external audio scanners. He touched the stud.

The sounds were like nothing he had ever heard before.

A rhythmic dance of liquid in motion, pouring, dripping, as if the shuttle had become centered amid dozens of waterfalls. Scanners began outputting impossible data. If the equipment could be trusted, a solid mass was rising from the water on all sides of his ship. Something huge, with leading edges like serrated lances, as if the ocean were being pierced by a hundred irregular monoliths, each one already a hundred feet high and continuing to rise, monster harpoons, cascading torrents of salinated liquid down their sides. Spears from the depths, each creating its own seemingly endless waterfall, as if the sea were being pumped up from within each one, infinitely recycling, keeping the lances wetted, oiled by the ocean.

Like a ring of teeth. Like the gaping mouth of some nightmarish sea creature.

But the scanners gave no indication of organic presence. And Gillian suspected that the massive spears must represent the upper portion of a mechanical construct of incredible proportions.

The teeth were high over the shuttle now, hundreds of feet above the ocean surface. They began to bend toward the center, close in upon one another, preparing to swallow his shuttle as if it were an insignificant bit of the ocean's flotsam. Grinding and slithering sounds now filled the flight deck as the ring of teeth sawed into one another. Soft and hard noises seemed to be combined, as if this monstrous thing were somehow both organic *and* mechanical.

Abruptly, the sounds ended. Outside illumination disappeared entirely; viewports became darker than the blackness of deep space, where at least the pinpoint glitter of distant stars existed to temper the void, provide a relationship between what was inside and what was outside. But now there was no outside. Now the only light emanated from within.

Gillian found himself recalling a story told to him in childhood, perhaps by Aristotle, perhaps by one of the Ash Ock scientists who had created the royal Caste. It had been the tale of an ancient mariner who had been swallowed whole. Swallowed by a whale.

This is no whale, he reasoned. *This is ...*

Sensors erupted into a tantrum of throbbing cries, warning him that the shuttle was now being drawn beneath the surface of the Atlantic, trapped within the closed jaws of this monster, this whale, this thing that now sought to return to the depths from where it had come. And Gillian felt something strange at the edge of awareness—something new, something old—a kind of feeling that he had not experienced since the early years of childhood, a sensation of unbridled awe at the very strangeness of the world.

Empedocles felt it too. His monarch seemed to exhale a breath of wonder, a neural discharge that tickled Gillian's spine, a dragon of pure feeling cascading down their common backbone, like water rushing over an upthrust spear.

"What do you think it is?" Gillian asked, vaguely aware that he was speaking aloud.

Empedocles's reply came as another wave of tactile impressions, breaking across their shoulders, running down their arms; a torrential downpour, soaking skin, muscle, and bone, as invigorating as a spring rain.

We'll find out soon enough.

Gillian could not say whether that last thought came from himself or from his monarch.

—from *The Rigors*, by Meridian

Shortly before one of my tways was scheduled to depart, I was summoned to an inner chamber of the Biodyssey. Over the past few days, I had been attempting to prepare myself emotionally for the reality of my upcoming separation; internal tension levels were running high. Weird dreams plagued my rest periods, fantasies of what it would be like to exist as a solitary creation, a unit that could not be separated. I dreamed of humans. I dreamed of Gillian.

I had never before been disassociated for more than a few days. But this time my tways would be forced to tolerate several months of physical solitude: one would remain aboard the Biodyssey, the other would make the advance journey to the Irryan Colonies. I did not know how I would endure the extended deprivation of body-to-body contact. In fact, I was a bit surprised—and relieved—that my turmoil manifested itself only through these odd dreams. One might have expected nightmares.

The place to which I was summoned had been designed as a standard interface chamber. My side of the wall consisted of a small darkened amphitheater. Beyond the translucent partition, which was constantly in motion as if swept by invisible breezes, lay the Os/Ka/Loq portion of the room. Although the wavering interface barrier permitted me to see only dark blurs on the other side, the partition freely allowed the passage of sound.

There were seven of them over there, all tways from different Paratwa, or so it seemed. They were braying and cackling and producing a rich cacophony of noise that I assumed to be conversation, though one could never be quite sure. The Os/Ka/Loq were capable of a nearly infinite variety of sounds, utilized for a nearly infinite variety of reasons, and I was certainly no expert in tonal translations. Nevertheless, I had acquired some proficiency over these many years, at least in terms of recognizing the repetitive signature patterns of particular individuals. The creature on

*the right was definitely Sappho's twap—Colette's other half. Two of the
others I recognized as well, mainly via their distinct olfactory airs, which
also permeated and penetrated the interface. Their Os/Ka/Loq names
were unpronounceable, so I had assigned them my own derivative nomenclatures: Thyme and Rhubarb.*

*The com panel in front of my two seats ignited; the sparkling green
letters of a holotronic interpreter took shape in the air as the Os/Ka/Loq
brought me into their discussion. It turned out to be a forceful debate.*

*The topic was all too familiar. I repressed twin sighs, assumed poses
suggesting keen interest, and watched as their braying and cackling was
reformed into modest English sentences.*

*Thyme: INDIVIDUALITY HAS PERVERTED SAPPHO. SHE
LEADS DUALITY OF LIFE. SAPPHO LOSES SIGHT.*

*Rhubarb: COLONIAL DESTRUCTION NOT DESIRABLE
NOW. COLONIAL DESTRUCTION DESIRABLE THEN.*

*Third Os/Ka/Loq from the left: THEN CANNOT BE
CHANGED. ONLY NOW CAN BE CHANGED. MUST FOCUS
ON PRESENT, NOT PAST.*

*I knew that the interpreter was capable of providing only basic frac-
tional segments of their complex and multihued thought patterns. Rich
subtleties were being excised, nonverbal expressions indiscriminately ignored by the machine's limited expressionism. To suggest that Os/Ka/
Loq "language" did not translate well was to be guilty of wild
braggadocio.*

*The twap of Sappho responded to the attack with habitual aplomb.
NECESSARY LIMITATIONS OF EARTHLY ENVIRONS.
KASCHT REEKS OF THE LACKING.*

Rhubarb: FACT KNOWN. EXCUSE UNACCEPTABLE.

Sappho: EXPLAIN/ENLIGHTEN.

*Rhubarb: SUCCESS/FAILURE HINGED ON IDENTICAL
AXIS.*

*It was an oft-repeated phrase, and one whose precise meaning re-
mained vague. As near as I could ascertain, when an Os/Ka/Loq accused a brethren of hinging success and failure on the same axis, it was
tantamount to calling him/her a mindless bastard.*

*Sappho rose to the occasion. SKYGENE INFECTIONS SERVE
TO GUARANTEE PREMEDITATED STRUCTURE OF VIC-
TORY.*

Thyme released a particularly hideous bray. NO GUARANTEE POSSIBLE.

Rhubarb: COLONIAL DESTRUCTION NOT DESIRABLE NOW. COLONIAL DESTRUCTION DESIRABLE THEN.

The tway on the far left moved. Behind the screen, there was a blur of motion as this heretofore silent Os/Ka/Loq repositioned himself/herself in the center of the seven shadowy figures. For several minutes, I sat in a vacuum of dead silence, waiting patiently, hiding my boredom.

Eventually, this newly centered tway spoke.

AN ERROR IN JUDGMENT HAS MUTATED. TWO-AND-ONE-HALF EARTH CENTURIES HAVE PASSED. OUR CUMULATIVE OS/KA/LOQ COMMITMENTS NOW TOTAL NEARLY THREE AND ONE HALF EARTH CENTURIES.

There was no mistaking the interpreter's clarity: this tway was deliberately shaping its thoughts for my benefit. He/she desired my complete understanding.

INDIVIDUALITY MAY HAVE TRULY PERVERTED SAPPHO. SHE MAY LEAD A DUALITY OF LIFE. IF THIS EVENT HAS OCCURRED, THE SIDE EFFECTS MAY ALTER OUR DESIRED OUTCOME.

Sappho obviously did not agree. INCORRECT ASSESSMENT. SKYGENE INFECTIONS COUPLED WITH RAPID RESEEDING OF PLANETARY SURFACE COUPLED WITH POLITICAL PRESSURE WILL YIELD CONQUEST. HUMANS ARE HANDICAPPED WHEN FACED WITH COMPLEX ACCELERATED EVENTS.

The center tway was not impressed. IF THERE IS FAILURE, YOU WILL SUFFER COMPLETE DISINCORPORATION.

They all became silent again for a time. I knew what disincorporation was. For the Os/Ka/Loq, it was a fate considered worse than death.

Sappho finally responded to the threat, as best as she could. DISINCORPORATION WILL NOT BE NECESSARY.

The Os/Ka/Loq in the center moved forward, closer to the translucent partition. Something resembling a tentacle extruded itself from the creature's body. The tentacle sprayed the wall. Thick globules of some pasty fluid trickled to the floor. I was unable to ascertain whether the Os/Ka/Loq was blowing its nose or reacting to Sappho's optimism.

The lion of Alexander wished to stop pondering his betrayal. He had grown tired of running yesterday's events across a field of conscience that offered no sympathy.

It's done. I must not dwell upon it. I must forget.

He could not.

Here in this twenty-sided chamber, within this shrine where the Council of Irrya would soon be meeting, the lion sat alone, enclosed within the lush familiarity of the seat he had tenured for the past two years. Walls, gilded in leather and boasting exquisitely rare pre-Apocalyptic paintings, seemed more unreal than he could ever recall. Insubstantial, they were, like holos with the beams deliberately misaligned, as if his very surroundings were attempting to mimic the works of the great 3D artists of pre-Apocalyptic Earth, the trans-impressionists, who light-stroked vibrant chromas with the wild passion of disengaged intellect.

The lion shook his head, tried to wash away his sense of unreality. *This room is real. There are no holos. The vaulted ceiling, lost in darkness, is a substantial thing. The prism chandelier that hangs from the darkness is real. The pale golden light that reflects up from this polished table is real.*

As real as holos. As real as imitations of stimulated light.

Yesterday's tragedy had created this metamorphosis, this dreamlike state that forced the lion to be a detached observer, witnessing his life from a perspective once removed from consciousness. Intellectually, the reasons for his metamorphosis seemed clear: an overwhelming cacophony of shame had transcended the parameters of bearable feeling.

The shame of wanting to survive.

I should have spit in its face.

But the Paratwa assassin had forced him to the edge of

nothingness, where life held inconceivably great value. For those few brief and terrifying moments, the lion had desired the continuation of his own existence more than anything else in the universe. He would have said and done anything to ensure that the assassin spared his life.

Again, he recalled that pivotal event of fifty-six years ago, when he and his mother had faced certain death at the hands of the liege-killer, when Gillian and Reemul had danced their final dance—lightning eurhythmics—weapons firing with inhuman speed, Paratwa warriors in the heat of death battle.

The lion had always known that he had drawn great strength from that childhood event. His actions in helping Gillian defeat the liege-killer had provided a reservoir of power, a streaming inner force that was always there, always available to be tapped when needed. For bravery in the face of certain doom, the twelve-year-old Jerem Marth had been granted a clarity of will remarkable even among the Costeaus. And that clarity had led him into a life of grand accomplishments. He had become the lion of the Alexanders; he had become Chief of the United Clans and a Councillor of Irrya.

And yesterday I betrayed all of those roles. Yesterday I became a coward.

Anger mushroomed. He raised his fist and smashed it down on the table.

Damn that creature! And damn me for my cowardice!

And he knew that until the full brunt of his shame could be felt, only this disjointed emotional catharsis could occur. Shame into anger. Humiliation turned inside out. And the repression of pristine feelings, keeping him one step removed from the flow of substantiality, a victim of the *élan vital* instead of an aspect of its current.

He thought: *Is this what it's really like for Gillian? Is he forever banned from feeling the depth of his own true self? Is he trapped outside a sphere of forbidden emotions, condemned to live beyond the grounding sanctity of real feeling?*

The lion acknowledged an altered sense of shame in comparing himself with Gillian. *If he is forced to live like this all of the time, then what right do I have to complain?*

His fist ascended, brimming with new fury. *Every right, damn it!*

Propriety spared the table another blow; the chamber's massive black door opened. Three figures entered the room.

Inez Hernandez came toward him. "Are you all right?"

"Yes."

She looked older, somehow, more somber; another victim, perhaps, of excessive emotional repression. Or perhaps it was just that today Inez wore no bacterial skin toners, no fluff earrings, no trace of makeup of any sort. A plain charcoal suit, elegantly cut, complemented her pageboy bundle of black hair.

A few days ago, Inez had staged a funeral service for her niece. Susan Quint had been missing for over a month now—another suspected victim of the rampaging Paratwa assassin. Even though Susan's body had not been found, the lion also believed that she had been hunted down and murdered by the creature, following its failure to kill her during the Honshu terminal massacre. Still, the lion had urged Inez to postpone the exigency of formal rites. There was always the possibility, however remote, that Susan would turn up.

But Inez had not been swayed by his judgment. *Best to get it over with,* she had insisted. *Best to put Susan's life behind me. These days, there are more important concerns.*

He had not been able to dispute such logic.

Inez took a seat, as did her two companions.

"Council of Irrya, September 13, 2363," uttered Maria Losef, Council President, Director of the Intercolonial Credit Net. "Confidential database, standard access," she continued, for the benefit of the chamber's electronic recorders.

The lion, hearing that cold unyielding voice, felt a fresh swell of anger. He glared across the table at her, hoping to elicit some sort of response, but Losef ignored his malice the way she ignored everything else. Ice blue eyes moved past him, continued scanning the chamber with all the pretensions of a twenty-first century mind-shunted clone. Yet beneath the blond fringe of her DI haircut, Losef bore a sincere and remarkably agile intelligence. The more brazen freelancers suggested that it was perhaps not a *human* intelligence, but that bothered the "ice dyke" no more than their frequent innuendos intimating that her sexual encounters took place within holo simulations of medieval torture.

She was as hard as the hardest of Costeaus, and the lion respected such raw strength. But Maria Losef was also a major dictator of ICN policy. The Credit Net had been hindering all investigations into discovering who controlled the corporation known as Venus Cluster, where Gillian, Buff, and Martha had encountered the two vicious tways of the tripartite assassin. Losef simply would not divulge the information. Never mind the fact that with such data they might be able to track down the crazed Paratwa assassin who had now struck a dozen times in the past five months. Losef insisted that releasing such information violated ICN policy. ICN policy was the glue that kept the Colonies' complex trade network from falling apart; therefore, the ownership and control of Venus Cluster would remain a secret.

Madness.

The third figure was a tall twig of a man, with a somber face, piercing green eyes, and a chin that sharpened into a gray-speckled goatee. Wiry tendrils of dark hair, pulled into a severe ponytail, contrasted sharply with his facial growth; it was as if two distinct genetic lines fought for control of his countenance.

He was E-Tech's freshly appointed acting director and, thus, today's representative to the Council of Irrya. Prior to assuming Doyle Blumhaven's office, he had been head of the specially formed action/probe assigned to investigate E-Tech corruption.

His name was Edward Huromonus. The freelancers called him "Crazy Eddie."

He sat next to Losef and turned to the lion. "I extend my condolences."

The lion nodded.

"Any word on Blumhaven?" asked Losef.

Huromonus shook his head. "Doyle is still missing. Foul play is suspected. I will provide a formal report before this meeting ends."

"Very well," said Losef. "First order of business will be a discussion of the twelfth known Birch attack."

Inez said, "We should no longer infer that these attacks have anything to do with the Order of the Birch. The Alexanders' retreat was attacked by a tripartite assassin. It seems obvious that this creature—and its rulers—have dropped their smokescreen. The recent actions of this assassin no longer allude to political terrorism traceable to the Order of the Birch. We are, plainly and simply, dealing with Paratwa."

"Any new word on survivors?" asked Huromonus.

"I'm a survivor," said the lion, feeling the anger gestating just beneath the surface, knowing that he had to keep it in, knowing that brutal logic was needed now. "My security chief, Vilakoz, survived. The tway who tricked us into its vehicle calmly drove the car to the E-Tech Security checkpoint outside the retreat." The lion paused. "That tway even helped real E-Tech Security officers load the unconscious Vilakoz into a medvan."

"Unmitigated boldness," commented Huromonus. He stared at the lion for a long moment before turning to his monitor. His fingers flashed across the keyboard used to maintain two-way communication with E-Tech headquarters. Although Irryan Council meetings were usually considered closed-door sessions, each Councillor was permitted to maintain data links with respective departmental entities.

Inez started to say something when the small sharp-edged pentagon in the center of table came to life. A quintet of identical swirling screens exposed the ruggedly handsome face of Jon Van Ostrand, Supreme Commander of the Intercolonial Guardians, and the fifth Councillor of Irrya.

"Sorry I'm late," announced Van Ostrand. "We had a minor problem with a nuclear warhead aboard one of our attack ships."

Inez hunched forward, instantly concerned. La Gloria de la Ciencia was responsible for building most of the defense net's nuclear arsenal. "Another construction defect?"

"No, we solved the last of those problems months ago. This event was simply a matter of human error. A minicrisis, but one that was fortuitously resolved."

Van Ostrand's words originated from millions of miles away, instantaneously transmitted via the FTL, the invention purportedly designed by Theophrastus of the Ash Ock and captured from Codrus fifty-six years ago. The semiorganic transmitter was actually located far below street level of the Irryan Capitol building; this pentagon merely served as a remote unit.

All superluminal FTLs operated in linked pairs. One such pair bonded Van Ostrand with the Council chambers. Aboard the Guardian Commander's op-base satellite, one-half of a completely different FTL—the one taken from the Ash Ock and used as a prototype for this model—silently resonated in step with *its* companion. And the other half of *that* FTL was presumed to be located aboard one of the returning Paratwa starships.

Van Ostrand's op-base, beyond the orbit of Jupiter, served as the nerve center for the Colonies' huge defense network. Well over two million Guardians patrolled the outer regions of the system, waiting in their nuclear-armed attack ships, defense satellites, and support colonies, poised to repel the invasion that had been anticipated for over half a century.

But since yesterday, the lion's already grave doubts about their ability to repel an invasion had grown deeper. In fact, he no longer believed that the Colonies of Irrya possessed the power to resist the returning Paratwa.

We're going to be conquered. It was a defeatist attitude—he recognized it as such—but the idea continued to cling to awareness, finding refuge there, bolstered by the schism emerging from his own cowardice.

"Jon," began Inez, "we were talking about yesterday's massacre. I was just about to ask the lion whether he believes that Adam Lu Sang was the target of this attack?"

The lion shook his head. "Adam was merely the trigger for the massacre. Obviously, his security was breached." He gazed at Huromonus. "The E-Tech archives must have been compromised. Someone found out that Adam was working on tracking down the sunsetter. This person—or persons—leaked that information to the Paratwa. The tripartite assassin was set loose."

"I read your formal report," said Huromonus, still typing. "According to you and your co-conspirators—Inez, Nick, and Gillian—at least one Paratwa leader, presumably the Ash Ock Sappho, is already within the Colonies."

"Evidence suggests that conclusion."

Huromonus stopped typing and faced the lion. "E-Tech is not sure whether to honor Adam Lu Sang as a hero or prosecute him as a traitor."

"He's dead," stated the lion. "If all the facts were known, I believe most people would consider his actions selfless and heroic."

"Perhaps," said Huromonus. "Still, many matters concerned with Adam's traitorous archival activities need to be resolved. Lu Sang's violation of his security oath and his flagrant distribution of classified data have created extensive repercussions. Even such tangents as the commencement of death benefits to his family need to be addressed. . . ."

Inez sighed. "What's the point? I strongly suggest that now—*especially* now—is not the time to persecute a slain man."

"Prosecution" corrected Huromonus, "naturally would be *in absentia*. But your objections are duly noted." He paused. "I should also point out that under the Irryan constitution and E-Tech charter, the activities of both you and the lion are subject to legal action."

Losef jumped in. "I propose that any such legal actions be postponed until the Council has dealt with the more pressing issues of the day."

On the FTL screens, Van Ostrand looked noticeably relieved.

"Agreed," said Huromonus.

The lion knew that no one wanted to engage in an interagency dispute that had the potential of ripping apart the Council. If there were any hope whatsoever of defeating the Paratwa, they had to maintain, at least for the immediate future, a common front.

"Losef," began Van Ostrand, "could we discuss the technology that was used during this massacre? We received the reports, but my people here are extremely concerned about some of the weapons apparently utilized by this Paratwa assassin. Any additional ideas that might be generated via a rehash might well save lives." The Guardian Commander did not need to add that he and his troops could very well be the first lives thus saved.

"No objections here," said Losef.

Inez cleared her throat and accessed her own monitor. "La Gloria de la Ciencia has been collating all available data, from the lion's people and from the two E-Tech officers who also survived the attack. The recollections from one of those injured survivors, an Inspector Xornakoff, were particularly incisive.

"We appear to be dealing with several applications of unknown technology. First and foremost, there was the devastating weapon that destroyed the E-Tech assault craft. 'A glassy sphere attached to a thick shaft that rose out of the ICN-disguised vehicle'—those are Inspector Xornakoff's words. This sphere apparently produced coils of silvery light that, when they touched the body of the assault craft, caused an implosion, followed immediately by a gravitational anomaly. The crushed remains of the assault craft were hurtled upward opposite normal-G expectations. The major pieces of the destroyed craft quickly entered a rapidly decaying orbit within Irray's centersky. Hub control captured these fragments and transferred them to one of La Gloria de la Ciencia's research facilities.

"Examination of the remains has shown a molecular breakdown—of unknown origin—affecting nearly all of the plastics and metals within the vessel. However, the bodies of the crew exhibited no such molecular deterioration—they died because of the incredible stresses inherent in the implosion. This factor suggests that the weapon was designed for use against nonorganic materials."

Van Ostrand frowned. "I've never heard of such a weapon. Are there any known pre-Apocalytic prototypes?"

Huromonus shook his head. "Preliminary checks of the archives have thus far located no corollaries. Naturally, it's possible that such data once existed and never survived the

Apocalypse. Or, the sunsetter may have wiped out all traces of this weapon."

"About this sunsetter," posed Van Ostrand. "Is there any possibility that the *real* goal of this mysterious data destroyer is to infiltrate our defense network? And not the archives, as has been assumed?"

"An interesting theory," replied the lion, "but one that we have pretty much dismissed."

Inez agreed. "Adam Lu Sang and Nick looked into that possibility very early on, but they ruled it out as too complex for even the sunsetter to accomplish. The sunsetter is capable of decimating specific programs, even duplicate programs within the same system, but there is no way for it to permanently destroy, for instance, a particular program within your defense network. If it wiped out such data, you could simply replace the data after cleansing the system. The sunsetter's great destructive capabilities within the archives arise from the fact that many of those programs are *irreplaceable*."

"Granted that what you're saying is true," continued Van Ostrand, "would it not be possible for this sunsetter to, at least temporarily, paralyze the operation of our defense network at a critical juncture?"

"Yes," admitted Inez, "I suppose that's possible."

The lion shook his head. "But Nick and Adam considered such a scenario unlikely. As is stated in my formal report, the sunsetter seems to be irrevocably attuned to hunting down and destroying this one particular ancient program: Freebird. All of its actions to date point to a search-and-destroy mission aimed at wiping out this Freebird."

"For reasons that are not yet comprehended," said Van Ostrand.

"Correct."

Huromonus added, "Since my action/probe confirmed what Adam Lu Sang knew from the beginning—that there was a sunsetter loose in the archives—we have turned up some disturbing irregularities in the network, dating back to a period some twenty-two years ago. That is when we believe the sunsetter was first allowed to penetrate the archives."

"How?" asked Van Ostrand.

"We don't know."

Inez said, "There are rumors . . . that Doyle Blumhaven is suspected of being involved with the original inputting of this sunsetter."

Huromonus shrugged. "We investigate many rumors. But until substantial evidence is uncovered, we will let the freelancers handle such allegations."

It had to be Blumhaven, thought the lion. Huromonus must also suspect that Doyle was involved, although he obviously was not yet ready to make such knowledge public. Nevertheless: *if Doyle had something to do with inputting the sunsetter, then that means he is in league with the Paratwa. Did they kill him too? Did the Paratwa make Doyle disappear in the same manner that Susan Quint was made to vanish?*

Inez cleared her throat. "Getting back to the technology utilized by the assassin, we believe that the explosion on the ridge in front of the house was the result of traditional rocket-launched explosives. A geo cannon sprocketed with vapor grenades is our best guess. It was likely mounted along the underframe of the attack vehicle. Several Costeaus who were wearing active crescent webs were also believed to have been killed by this weapon. A geo cannon is one of the few artillery weapons known to be able to blast through a defensive web."

"Why wasn't this ICN vehicle scanned when it entered your retreat?" asked Van Ostrand, with just the faintest trace of accusation in his voice. "You have state-of-the-art tracking gear."

The lion sighed. More than any of them, Van Ostrand—the militarist—longed to find fault with the methodology of their defenses. *He wasn't there at the retreat. He doesn't understand.*

"The vehicle *was* scanned," the lion answered calmly. "Absolutely nothing unusual was detected."

Van Ostrand frowned. "So it appears that we are also confronted by superior screening devices."

"That's correct," said Inez. "Also in this regard, the Paratwa apparently possess a crescent web nullifier more powerful than our own salene. When this nullifier was activated, all active webs, within an area of unknown parameters, were deactivated. By comparison, our own salene is capable only of temporarily interrupting an energy field."

"So they're ahead of us there, as well," murmured Van Ostrand.

"It would appear so," said Inez. "And although our salene—used against one of the tways by Buff Boscondo—did disrupt the assassin's web, it did so only momentarily. The tway was quickly able to neutralize the salene's discharge."

Huromonus turned to the lion. "This Costeau—this Buff—I am curious as to where she procured her salene. E-Tech still lists that device as a fully restricted item. As yet, only a few special E-Tech Security units possess them."

The lion sighed. "As I understand it, the prototype has been available on the Sirak-Brath black market for quite some time."

"I suppose that fact should not surprise me," replied Huromonus, "given the extent of E-Tech corruption that my people have thus far uncovered."

Van Ostrand arched his eyebrows. "This Buff Boscondo—did she survive the attack?"

The lion stared at the far wall. "We found her in the A-frame, in what was left of one of the rooms. Buff had been killed in a particularly gruesome manner. She was slain by the tway known as Slasher, literally chopped to pieces by flash daggers."

"I see," muttered Van Ostrand.

Inez explained. "Buff had been with Gillian and Martha during the Venus Cluster incident. At the retreat massacre, none of the other close-combat victims bore such severe injuries. Buff's wounds would indicate that the Paratwa bore an extreme personal grudge."

Beneath the table, out of sight, the lion balled his hands into fists.

"What about Gillian," probed Van Ostrand. "There's still no sign of him?"

"We don't know where Gillian is," the lion truthfully admitted. He said nothing about Buff's final message regarding the mysterious Jalka and the Church of the Trust priest.

"And this Nick . . . was he gravely injured?"

Initially, the lion had wanted to divulge the entire truth to the Council, explain how they had dug the midget out from under the collapsed wall, how surprised they had been to learn that he had suffered only minor injuries. But Nick had insisted that some deceits be maintained.

"Nick was transported to one of our hospitals back in Den," said the lion. "He is still in a coma."

Edward Huromonus frowned but remained silent.

Inez continued. "Other technology utilized by the assassin includes some sort of electromagnetic device—described as 'gray lightning'—that appeared beneath the tway who was outfitted in the jetpak. This 'gray lightning' device appears to have been both offensive and defensive, able to protect the jetpak rider as well as serve as a ravaging assault weapon.

"Finally, there was the assault car itself, which, during the heat of the battle, managed to alter its shape and colorings, changing from a low-slung standard-issue ICN vehicle into an E-Tech cruiser. The pre-Apocalyptics dabbled in this sort of technology, although the archives"—she turned to Huromonus—"do not appear to list direct antecedents."

Huromonus nodded. "We're still searching."

"Transformers," suggested Van Ostrand. "I remember hearing that term once. I believe that is what the pre-Apocalyptics used to call these shape-changers."

"Thank you," said Huromonus, typing the word into his terminal. "We'll reference 'transformers' in our search grid."

"And there was absolutely no trace of this vehicle after the attack?" asked Van Ostrand.

"Apparently," said Huromonus, "the tway in the assault car managed to escape during the massive turmoil following the attack."

"And what happened to the other two tways?" asked Van Ostrand, looking more incredulous by the moment. "How did *they* escape?"

"The one in the jetpak landed in the woods and apparently walked right through our lines." Huromonus shrugged. "The third tway, Slasher . . . we believe he rendezvoused with the assault car."

An angry scowl distorted Van Ostrand's face. "You had

hundreds of your security personnel surrounding that Preserve!"

Inez shook her head. "Jon, you seem to be searching for a culprit here—someone to blame. But please don't judge this incident through too narrow an eye. This creature has struck the Colonies twelve times that we know of. And with the exception of the Venus Cluster incident, we have not been able to even remotely hinder its actions." Her knuckles skimmed along the edge of the table, like an ancient set of bearings unleashed from their journal box, rolling out of control. "Now I understand why the pre-Apocalyptics tried so hard to wipe them out."

"They're superior to human beings," interjected the lion.

"True, in certain limited respects," granted Van Ostrand. "They're faster—"

"Superior," insisted the lion, aware that this tack would produce nothing but argument. But he seemed unable to control himself.

"The Paratwa *are* superior to human beings; that's the real reason the pre-Apocalyptics attempted a controlled genocide of them. Every last one of them was to be destroyed, even the ones who essentially did nothing to harm humans. But racially, we were scared of them. They represented an interspecies competition the likes of which modern humans never had to face. The Paratwa had to be totally and utterly destroyed. It was the only way for us to feel secure."

Van Ostrand smirked. "That's an interpretation usually reserved for those who turn their backs on a fight."

He doesn't understand, thought the lion, even while wondering whether his own recent cowardice was influencing his views.

No, it's more than just my own feelings. The Paratwa are superior to us. That's a simple truth, but one that has remained unexamined within the collective consciousness of the human race for over three centuries. We can't truly face that reality, so we rationalize. We tell ourselves that we're the best there is, but we're not. We created a species that was better.

"This is a pointless discussion," said Losef, turning to Inez. "Are there any other technological elements that bear examination at this time?"

"I think we've covered most everything."

The ICN Director flicked a stray strand of hair from her forehead, laid it on her fingertip, studied it as if it possessed great importance. "The Paratwa envoy, Meridian, will be arriving in Irrya in three days. This attack could be construed as a deliberate preamble to his arrival. Perhaps the blatant display of high-tech weapons was meant to serve as a warning to the Colonies."

"Soften us up a little," said Van Ostrand, snorting. "Scare us into accepting whatever terms this Meridian is prepared to offer."

"That scenario seems probable," said Losef.

The lion felt a chill go through him. *The Paratwa have made the Council's greatest fears come true. They have confronted us with unknown technology.*

Inez faced Huromonus, but her questions were really meant for Losef. "What about Venus Cluster? This corporation has already been linked to the Paratwa. Have your investigators learned anything new?"

"No," said Huromonus. "To date, Venus Cluster has proved to be a dead end. So far, all we've been able to learn is that a tway of this assassin had been placed in the position of a VP within the company. Naturally, he disappeared following the encounter with Gillian, Buff, and Martha." Huromonus paused. "It might prove extremely helpful if the ICN could provide some leadership in this area."

On the FTL screens, Jon Van Ostrand bobbed his head in agreement.

Losef gazed at each of them in turn. Then: "I have again presented these wishes to the ICN board. Here is their formal response." She read from her monitor. "The ICN Director's Board deeply appreciates the concerns raised by the Council of Irrya with regard to the issue of the ownership of the corporation Venus Cluster. It is with deep regret that we cannot satisfy your data request.

"You must understand that the continued stability of the ICN policy that regulates corporate ownership is an issue of extreme sensitivity to the Director's Board and, ultimately, of vital concern to the Colonies. Within the infrastructure of today's marketplace, more than eighty percent of corporate investments are totally shielded. We all know the reasons for this strategy, which was initiated fifty-six years ago by the Council of Irrya. At that time, a tremendous amount of seed money was sought for weapons and defense development, in order that the Paratwa threat of today might be effectively neutralized. All of us are fully aware of the frightening cost of maintaining two million Guardians along a state-of-the-art defense perimeter.

"Over the past fifty-six years, much of that seed money was acquired by promising full anonymity to the investors. To create even one exception to this policy—to reveal just one set of corporate investors—could theoretically lead to a massive—and quite instantaneous—monetary crash, brought on by the withdrawal of investments. For better or worse, the sanctity and security of our investment process has served as a primary attraction for investors. For better or worse, the Colonies of Irrya exist within an almost fully deregulated venture capital marketplace. It would be nothing less than criminal of the ICN to threaten this stability.

"The ICN fully recognizes the gravity of the Venus Cluster situation. But even under the circumstances outlined by the Council, we cannot risk—especially at this time, with the grave threat of the Paratwa hanging over us—the revelations that you crave."

Losef calmly scanned their faces. "Any questions?"

Inez released a weary sigh.

The lion knew that the banking consortium's real objections had not been stated. What the ICN truly feared were the Sirak-Brath–based black marketeers, with their massive investments.

It was the black marketeers who would, at the first sign of collusion between the ICN and the Council, take their money and run. It was the black marketeers who realized that public exposure of their investments could very well be the first step in tracing such funds to illegal sources. And it was the black marketeers, acting in tandem, who had the power to bring on an economic depression. Grudgingly, the lion accepted the ICN's reluctance to tamper with a system flawed by such an inherent instability.

But still . . . there had to be some way of penetrating Venus Cluster's secrets.

Huromonus smiled. "Perhaps someone could leak the information to us?"

Losef shook her head. "Leaking the information could produce the same net results. The clandestine discharging of data also is not a viable option." And then, suddenly, she said: "Recorders off."

They all turned to her, surprised. The lion could not recall Losef ever overriding the electronic transcribers once a Council meeting had begun.

"We're all ears," offered Inez.

"We are not blind to our duties here," said Losef. "The ICN has proposed a compromise. Acting solely through me, and within the sanctity of this Council, the ICN will confirm ownership of Venus Cluster. You will have to provide the initial data, but if your data is on the mark, we will validate. Confirmation—that's the best we can do."

"Better than nothing," mused Van Ostrand.

"It's a start," Inez agreed.

The lion was about to quiz Losef on just what exactly the ICN would consider as proper initial data when Huromonus held up his hand.

"A message from an E-Tech Security contingent stationed in Pocono Colony," he announced, reading from his terminal. "Doyle Blumhaven's body has just been found. It was discovered at the bottom of an unauthorized ski slope, in a small ravine."

Huromonus silently proceeded to scan the screen. Lines across his forehead fissured; his whole face cracked into a deep frown. When he continued, an undercurrent of grim anger flowed beneath his words.

"A group of snow hikers came across the body. Upon first examination, they thought that it might have been an accidental death—a fall. But examination revealed that Blumhaven's head had been severed from his torso and then apparently crudely sewn back on. The initial autopsy reveals evidence of cauterization along the neck. The decapitation was caused by a Cohe wand."

"The monster struck again," whispered Inez.

The lion again recalled the short message that the tway had displayed for him at the end of the massacre. Sixteen sparkling green words. Sappho's warning: YOU CAN LIVE UNDER OUR DOMAIN OR YOU CAN DIE UNDER IT. THE CHOICE IS YOURS.

The lion shuddered.

Gillian stood poised in the airlock, waiting for the craft's external sensors to announce equal pressurization. He wore a full-G spacesuit, the strongest and most heavily armored one aboard the shuttle, and he had mounted a thruster rifle to the arm pad of the bulky silver gray garment, the barrel of the rifle aimed at the lock's still closed outer airseal. His Cohe wand remained inside the suit; the subtle hand pressures required to use that weapon were effectively neutralized by the stout arm gauntlets.

Hull microcams should have provided a view of what was outside the airlock, but, like the shuttle's windows, they seemed to have been ... blackened? No matter. He was ready for whatever was on the other side of that door.

The problem was, he should not have been ready for anything.

Shuttles were not designed to be submerged in eleven thousand feet of ocean. When those huge teeth had closed around him, when the bizarre organism/contraption began to swallow the craft and draw it down beneath the surface of the Atlantic, Gillian had quickly triggered the emergency high pressurization system. ET3, the shuttle's standard nitrogen/oxygen air mix, had been gradually altered to ET11, a 22 psi low-oxygen synthesis of helium and argon.

But according to the medcom, even ET11 should have become unbreathable at somewhere around seventy-five hundred feet. Not to mention that the pressure certainly should have crushed the relatively thin hull well before *this* incredible depth was attained.

I'm over two miles below the Atlantic Ocean. And I should be at least two ways dead.

Obviously, there were scientific operations here that he did not understand.

Jalka/Aristotle, whispered his monarch, echoing Gillian's logical assumption. But still . . . how could Jalka/Aristotle have developed such incredible technologies?

Empedocles did not answer.

"PRESSURE EQUALIZED," announced the airlock.

Gillian drew a deep breath and opened the seal.

The lock had been butted against a roughly tubular tunnel. The tunnel was about eight feet in diameter and curved away to the left, dimly lit by what appeared to be erratically spaced patches of luminescent blue . . . ceiling?

No, not ceiling. More as if the walls had simply merged together in spots: in some places, in a very smooth linear fashion, at other locations, more randomly, forming a composite of organic strands, like woven muscle.

He crossed the threshold and made his way around the bend in the tunnel. Helmet sensors, constantly analyzing external conditions, printed their findings on the main status panel above his inner visor. The air mix was a bit high in oxygen but well within breathability parameters; the average outside temperature was sixty-eight degrees. It seemed to be a thoroughly hospitable environment.

No matter. Gillian was not about to sacrifice the security of his spacesuit. Despite the apparent cordiality of this place, deviance abounded.

He walked around the bend, came to place where the tunnel merged into a much wider area. It was a brightly illuminated room with a glowing ceiling, roughly rectangular in shape, but with its uneven walls in constant motion, like starched sailcloth endlessly wafted by stiff breezes.

He took one step into the new area and froze. The right side wall began to glow with a fierce orange light, so intense that his faceplate automatically polarized as internal sensors adjusted to the onslaught of high-intensity illumination. And then, just as abruptly, the wall returned to its previous nonluminescent state. His visor followed suit.

The wall stopped moving, assumed a brittle translucent quality, becoming a vast curving sheet of frosted glass. Soft reddish afterglows appeared in a few areas, like warm spots within the boundaries of a recently quelled campfire, fading embers fighting darkness.

The warm uneven patches went through yet another metamorphosis, becoming fully transparent. On the other side—or within the wall itself—a series of odd formations were revealed. Gillian was not even certain that what he was seeing was physically real. Could the entire partition be merely the projection of some incredibly complex holo?

He approached carefully, extended his hand, pushed his gloved fingertip into something that felt like hardened jelly. The wall shuddered. Instinctively, he jerked his hand away.

Definitely not a holo. The partition had reacted as if it were alive.

On the other side of the transparent wall, within a small round chamber, a quintet of large murky gray stalagmites appeared to be growing from the faintly misted floor. If his eyes could still be trusted to gauge size and perspective accurately, the wobbly formations varied in height from eight to fifteen feet, with base diameters anywhere from thirty to sixty inches.

Even as he watched, the five stalagmites started to . . . crystallize? Hollow cavities were revealed within.

Each stalagmite contained a lifeform. Gillian stared intently, caught up in the sheer strangeness of the uncloaked organisms. And from the nether regions of consciousness, perhaps given greater impetus by the singularity of his concentration, came the voice of Empedocles.

Each stalagmite is a mere cylinder, housing that which is ultimately important. You do understand: outside is merely the shell. Inside those sculptured forms exists authenticity: that which is truly vital.

"Go away," he ordered.

His monarch laughed—a sensation transfigured immediately into a quivering rush of feeling ascending their common spine.

Three of the stalagmites contained densely coiled snakes, or creatures that resembled snakes. The heads were the wrong size and shape: too boxlike and easily twice the girth of the snakes' bodies. Scaled skins varied in hue over the twenty-foot length of each creature: muted sea greens melted discordantly into stunning streaks of deep violet, outlined in amber. Most disturbing of all were the eyes—frozen in wide open gazes that looked more human than reptilian.

Massive DNA restructuring, proclaimed Empedocles.

The fourth stalagmite encapsulated an eight-foot-high rat-like creature, suspended upright, with elongated forepaws dangling in front of the creature's face, giving the overall effect of a canine begging for food. The entity also possessed a weird pair of ragged protuberances emerging from the smooth dark fur of its underbelly. From each of the two lumps, a set of small leathery hands hung limply from short folds of pale skin. Each hand boasted four long digits.

Notice the fingers, remarked Empedocles. *They are configured in opposing sets of two. Designed for gripping.*

Gillian turned to the final stalagmite, largest of the quintet. Inside, standing at least eight feet high, poised on squat hind legs, was the weirdest creature of all: a black-fleshed monstrosity—definitely humanoid—sprouting two heads from the stem of one impossibly long neck. The twin faces, clearly Negroid, stared blindly at Gillian. Both sets of eyes were pinched tightly shut in a way that reminded Gillian of a frightened child trying to make the world go away.

He shuddered. Even that stream of thoughts which was Empedocles momentarily grew silent and introspective, attempting to interpret precisely what it was they were observing.

"Failed genetic experiments?" Gillian wondered aloud. "A museum of entombed blunders?"

These could be the successes, countered his monarch.

"I don't think so."

Again, note the ratlike creature with the double set of hands attached to its belly. Phylogenetically, an almost impossible natural mutation and far too complex for an accidental experiment gone awry. No—we are looking upon deliberate specialized adaptations.

"Specialized for what purpose?"

Empedocles, having no answer—or not willing to reveal one—again withdrew.

Gillian moved farther along the wall, stopping at the next transparent section. Within, three more stalagmites angled from the floor. This set had also "crystallized," revealing their interiors.

Here, there was no confusion of form and function. Each of the stalagmites contained a naked human being—two males and a female—their common phylogeny clearly discernible. Each had long dark brown hair, high-set cheekbones, and sharply angled chins. Their eyes were wide open but lifeless, trapped in either slumber or death.

Gillian felt his heart beginning to race as he gazed at the three figures. There was something strangely familiar about those three ashen faces. . . .

A flood of what seemed to be memory/images was instantly transferred into his body as strokes of pure feeling, cascading along his arms and legs, through his shoulders, up across his chest, and out along the muscles of his neck. He sensed that Empedocles was being overwhelmed by the same interplay of energies.

So intense was the bombardment of feeling that Gillian believed he might be under attack, possibly from a needbreeder. Instantly, he closed his eyes, trying to prevent what could be an optic assault from reaching the deeper crevices of consciousness. Fingers flashed across the tiny control board on his belt, manually polarizing his visor to full opacity. But the prickling deluge of energies continued to course through him.

Not an attack, concluded his monarch. *We have been spared by a natural process. A massive flow of nondifferentiated feeling, induced by the sudden opening of long-dormant mnemonic channels.*

"Repressed memories," whispered Gillian, knowing it was true. He opened his eyes and restored his suit to primary status.

Acceptance of what was happening to him parted the floodgates. Long-repressed vistas became visible; consciousness returned to a density of emotion/physicality that had defined the parameters of Gillian's early childhood.

"The faces," he heard himself say, knowing that they were what had triggered his reaction. Faces from his own early years; images from an arena of consciousness shuddering with primordial richness.

The faces ... the same faces.

Gillian knew who they were.

The two men were of the so-called Ash Ock scientists. Their names were Yoskol and Eucris.

They may not be Yoskol and Eucris, cautioned Empedocles. *They may be clones. Even holos.*

It did not matter whether they were real persons, genetic copies, or mere apparitions. They were indisputably mirrors into Gillian's past.

Yoskol and Eucris had been among the few humans responsible for attending to the basic needs of the young Empedocles. Deep in the Amazon basin, more than one hundred miles east of Capoeiras Falls, in the Brazilian rain forest facility known as Thi Maloca, lay the closest thing to a home that Gillian had ever known. Thi Maloca—all seven hundred and fifty square acres of it—ostensibly existed as a pharmaceutical implant research and manufacturing center, a near-perfect operational cover for its deeper function as the breeding and training labs for the Ash Ock.

Gillian and Catharine had spent most of their early years within the boundaries of Thi Maloca. Yoskol and Eucris, as well as serving as their teachers and guardians, had also been the ones who had first brought the puerile Empedocles into the presence of the facility's true overseer, Aristotle. And Gillian now recalled that it had been Yoskol who, on many occasions, had escorted him and Catharine to their combat training sessions with Meridian.

Yoskol and Eucris had disappeared from Thi Maloca when Gillian and Catharine were very young. Those two men had been the last of the human scientists—the genetic engineers who were supposedly the creators of the Ash Ock breed—to depart. Afterward, Gillian and Catharine had come under the day-to-day guardianship of Brazilian locals, loyal to Meridian, who lived in the *favelas* surrounding the pharmaceutical company.

And by the late years of the twenty-first century, when Gillian and Catharine had reached adult status, they too had come to accept the widespread belief that their elder brethren—Codrus, Aristotle, Sappho, and Theophrastus—had murdered the Ash Ock scientists.

They disappeared from our lives, mused Empedocles, with uncharacteristic flatness.

And from our memories as well, added Gillian.

He stared at the woman in the third stalagmite and immediately found himself buffeted by a wave of even deeper precognizant impressions. Ripples of heat coursed up and down his chest; he acknowledged a throbbing hunger, a need, a purely nonsexual lust. With a flash of insight, he recognized that this feeling corresponded with other recent sensations: Full-body flush. Full-body hard-on.

But this time, Gillian did not feel the urge to engage in combat. It was almost as if he had descended some linear chain of emotions, dropping to a deeper level, a place where fighting was no longer his only option. Here he could simply feel the feeling; he did not have to utilize the catharsis of violence to redirect the emotional onslaught. He did not have to lash out in order to maintain equilibrium.

"Who is she?" he heard himself whisper. Despite the perplexing physical effects, Gillian could not recall ever having met the woman.

His monarch explained. *Her name is Sasalla. When we were in our infancy, she was there with us in Thi Maloca. I remember the shape of her nipples and the smell of her bosom and the roving stroke of her palm. She is Sasalla. She was our wet nurse.*

"How can you be sure?"

You can recall her only through vague physical memories. But I remember much more. While the infants Gillian and Catharine were helpless bundles of nonlinear awareness, I was, at a very basic level, intellectually alert. As a monarch, I began to conceptualize even before birth.

Gillian frowned. "Pre-natal intellectualization is not possible."

Yes, it is. Iconic awareness: as valid and as powerful as the later symbolic representations of words and images. I was intellectually conscious within the wombs. I knew that I was to be born. All of the Ash Ock were prenatally sentient. It was part of our heritage.

Gillian stared at Sasalla's face. Abruptly, his eyes started to mist over, and he realized that he was momentarily in touch with very early rhythms of pure emotion. He whispered, "She was the closest thing we had to a mother."

Empedocles pulled Gillian back from an abyss of deep feeling. *She was not our mother. We had no mother. She was a wet nurse, nothing more: a female chosen to provide base gratification and bonding. Such things were necessary to ensure later developmental coherence.*

Gillian suddenly understood something else. "You guided me away from my emotions. You created a tension between us."

Yes.

"Flexing," he whispered, awed by his discovery, knowing that he was seeing the outlines of a prototypical pattern that would later become that very syndrome which, to varying degrees, forced all Paratwa to lose control periodically.

Empedocles explained. *You now see the origins of the flex, as they are specific to the Ash Ock. The lesser breeds come upon the process in a slightly different way. But for we of the royal Caste, the roots of our flexing urges emanate from the sheer dissimilitude between the level of consciousness inherent in the monarch compared to the level inherent in the tways.* His monarch hesitated. *I'm not sure that the other Ash Ock ever understood this.*

Gillian was glad that Empedocles had prevented his surrender to ancient feelings. There was too much danger here; it was obvious that they were being shown these particular images from their past for a reason.

His monarch agreed. *We are, in a very real sense, being bombarded by graphic icons nearly as powerful as mnemonic cursors. We are being emotionally manipulated. I am now certain that it is Jalka/Aristotle.*

Gillian, with an effort of will, forced himself to turn away from Sasalla and the others. There was one more clear patch at the end of the wall. He moved toward it.

Behind this third transparent section stood a solitary stalagmite, ten feet high, with a slightly thicker base than the others. But for whatever reason, the "crystallization" process had not occurred here. There was definitely *something* within the murky translucence of this stalagmite, but it remained a dark blur, barely fathomable.

Gillian could feel Empedocles studying it, probing for interpretation. *It looks too big to be another human—*

A noise—like a bucket of water splashing across pavement. Gillian whirled, fingers ready on the trigger of the rifle.

An opening was taking shape in the wall behind him; the partition began to cross-split, as if invisible perpendicular lasers were slicing through the gently swaying material. Four skin-like flaps peeled back to reveal another large chamber.

We are being asked to continue our explorations, explained Empedocles.

"I would never have guessed."

His monarch chuckled; Gillian felt the sensation as wet leaves being rubbed across the inside of his skin. *Have you noticed that you have been speaking aloud to me of late? Can I take this as a public acknowledgment of my existence? Are you one step closer to accepting the inevitability of what we must become?*

Gillian proceeded quickly through the opening.

The new room was even more massive than the previous chamber—at least a hundred feet long and seventy wide at this end, narrowing into what appeared to be another tunnel, similar in nature to the tube that had butted against the shuttle's airlock. Here, more than a hundred stalagmites erupted from the floor, but these were skinnier and more colorful than the ones serving as stasis capsules or tombs. Each spindly base seemed to be composed of interwoven strands, deep sky blues laced with semitransparent bands of emerald. Some of the stalagmites widened into irregularly shaped tabletops; some reached all the way to the ceiling to connect with kindred stalactites. Still others terminated in bizarre melanges of electronic equipment, as if pieces of high-tech gear were growing directly out of their upthrust surfaces.

But the weirdest sight rested atop a stalagmite located near the center of the room. A small naked girl lay on her back. She had no arms or legs. Her eyes were closed; the cherubic face seemed at peace despite the fact that a set of thin cables emerged from her vagina. The cables led to an adjacent stalagmite, where they attached to the back of what appeared to be a standard computer terminal.

"Now what the hell is that?" muttered Gillian.

Empedocles did not answer.

The armless, legless child looked to be about five years old. Gillian was reminded of another mutant child—the one from fifty-six years ago, the one molested by Reemul. He had the uneasy feeling that there was a relationship between the two.

Empedocles prodded. *This whole chamber . . . you've seen something like it once before. I can sense the periphery of a pattern within your mind . . . a recent experience, the vague boundaries of a mnemonic connection.*

Gillian frowned, knowing that his monarch was correct but unable to make the link. "I don't know—"

It came to him in a flash.

"The FTL! The guts of the transmitter that we discovered in Codrus's secret communications facility beneath the Shan Plateau." It was obvious. All the patterns were there, waiting to be properly configured. "This chamber—in fact, everything we've seen so far—comes from the same line of development as the FTL transmitter."

Gillian could feel Empedocles agreeing with his conceptualization. But his monarch expressed other doubts: *The assumption that Therophrastus was the creator of the FTL must now be reexamined. Unless he designed this chamber before the starships left the solar system.*

"Maybe Theophrastus is here right now?" proposed Gillian. "We could have been led into a trap. Maybe there is no Jalka/Aristotle. Maybe we've entered Sappho's secret domain."

"An interesting supposition," replied a male voice.

Gillian pirouetted—a 360-degree spin-crouch, finger snug against the trigger of the rifle. He saw no one. The chamber remained lifeless.

The voice continued. "I used to talk to my master too, back in the days when I was alive."

"Good for you," said Gillian. The voice seemed to be directionless; reverberating tones emerged from the floor, from the ceiling, from the very walls. "Who are you? Where are you?"

"I am called Timmy. I'm right here."

A stalagmite directly in front of Gillian—one that ended in a smooth tabletop—ruptured. From the narrow slit, a holo took shape, emerging from the cracked surface like a flow of construction lava shooting from a freefaller's welding pak. The bubbling light rapidly melded into the contours of a full-sized man.

He was big, over six feet tall, with immense shoulders and a huge frame cloaked in a simple gray robe. Layers of fat encroached on the puffy round face. The eyes were unbalanced; the right one seemed to be more wide open, more alert than its counterpart.

Be extremely careful if we ever meet this creature in the flesh, warned Empedocles. *That right eye appears to be an organic microprocessor.*

Gillian acknowledged his monarch's perception. Such wetware, from the high-tech glory years of the twenty-first century, could disguise a hundred perils, from simple antiscan devices to fire control units, able to target and launch an intermixed concoction of body-mounted weaponry in the blink of an eye. And such wetware could cloak even more subtle dangers: neuronic "smackers"—optic pulses capable of distorting an opponent's natural balance; the deadly projected energies of the hypnotic needbreeder; the subliminal cadences able to trigger an opponent's implanted mnemonic cursor.

"Welcome to my home," said the holo, smiling. "I'm glad that Lester Mon Dama's message reached you."

Gillian studied the projected figure, compared it to his own memories of what Aristotle's tway had looked like. There were definite similarities; this *could* be Jalka, with about a hundred extra pounds added to his frame. "What do you want?"

"Ah, Gillian—you always were the impetuous one. Now, Catharine—she was a bit less rash. Maybe that is why the two of you made such good lovers."

Gillian swallowed. Thinking of Catharine in that way cut to the core of ancient pains.

Timmy continued. "When death took your tway and lover,

when you were forced to lead a life of singularity, when you denied your own reality to escape the madness of being torn in half—it was then that your mutation truly began."

"Mutation?" Gillian challenged. "I don't know what you mean."

"Yes you do. You can't lie to me, Gillian. I know what Empedocles wants. I know that he is pressuring you toward acceptance of the permanent whelm, tway and monarch fused forever. No more Gillian, no more Empedocles. Your monarch is driven by an unquenchable urge to gain complete physical control of the unbalanced creature you have become."

Utterly true, whispered Empedocles.

"Incest," continued Timmy. "Do you know what it means?"

"Of course," he snapped.

"Back in the days when you were whole, did you, Gillian, ever feel that you were engaging in an incestuous relationship with Catharine?"

He gave an honest shake of his head. "No. We were tways of a Paratwa, not brother and sister. As fetuses, we did not come from the same family group. The human-inspired taboos against incest, which are based primarily upon real genetic concerns against the dangers of inbreeding, did not apply to us."

"When you made love to Catharine, was Empedocles always there?"

Gillian acknowledged an extreme feeling of discomfort, an almost brutal twisting of the guts. He did not like where this Timmy's questions were leading. "What do you want?" he demanded. Why have you brought me here? And just what is this place?"

Timmy chuckled. "I promise to answer all of your questions. In time. But for now, I expect you to respond to *my* questions. As children, you and Catharine were always excellent students, unafraid to venture into new, unexplored territory. I want you to be brave once again.

"I *can* help you in overcoming the turmoil of being two discrete consciousnesses perennially at war for control of the same body. But there is a price for my assistance. I demand your complete obedience." Timmy's face assumed an asymmetrical pose; the wetware orb opened wide while his real eye narrowed to a fine slit. "You—and Empedocles—will become students once again, as you were for Aristotle, back in the days when he still lived."

Gillian frowned. "Your monarch . . . he's dead?"

"Yes, my monarch is dead. My tways are dead. I am a new consciousness, one that came into existence only when my last tway—Jalka—surrendered to the urges of his monarch, Aristotle. At the moment of their final merging, both of them ceased to exist. A fresh consciousness, possessing all of the memories of tway and monarch, was born.

"And I know, Empedocles, that this is what you want. But be forewarned—while it will grant you a coherence of the body by day, the emotions of memory will haunt your nights. There will be a price to pay that neither of you can remotely fathom. Timmy is a concoction from such a netherworld. He is a product of surrender, of defeat and, as such, can never truly savor the rewards of victory."

"And you offer an alternative?"

"I do. I can make you whole once again."

"How?" Gillian demanded.

"Answer my earlier question. When you and Catharine made love, was Empedocles always there?"

Gillian forced himself to recall an intimate occasion with Catharine. Pain-encrusted memories stroked awareness like sandpaper rubbing bare flesh.

He blurted out the answer, then quickly closed down what he knew to be a channel cutting into the deepest agonies of his life. "Yes, Empedocles was always there. You know that. The interlace binding Ash Ock tways never completely dissolves. It's merely weakened to the point where the two halves can operate independently. Most memories—but not all—are fully shared."

"Precisely," said Timmy. "So even when you and Catharine made love—even when you entered that state of unrestrained passion which took you the farthest away from the

primarily intellectualized consciousness of your monarch—
even then, he was there."

I was there, admitted Empedocles.

Gillian nodded.

"So—no matter how repressed—your monarch has always
existed within you. You, the tway Gillian, still exist. And the
memory of your other tway, Catharine—even it survives."

"Yes."

The holo disappeared. Gillian heard a noise behind him.
He spun around. The real Timmy stood ten feet away. Gillian made eye contact before he could think not to.

"Kascht moniken keenish," uttered Timmy. *"Kascht mulaf-was—
belj moniken shle-os."*

Mnemonic cursors, warned Empedocles, but it was too late.
The strange sounds poured through Gillian, instantly burrow-
ing beneath the field of his awareness. He tried to raise the
thruster rifle, but his arms refused to obey.

Timmy approached, chuckling. Gillian tried to turn away,
and when that failed, tried to at least break eye contact. It
was no use. Muscles refused to carry out his conscious commands. He may as well have been frozen in a block of stasis
ice.

Timmy closed to within two feet. Gillian stared helplessly
into the unblinking artificial eye, recalling that only weeks ago
he had heard some of those same bizarre word/sounds. *Kascht
moniken keenish*—that phrase had been spoken by Slasher, tway
of the tripartite assassin.

Slasher must have known only the preamble, deduced Empedocles. *Kascht moniken keenish probably opens a channel into our deepest
chasms of body-thought. But this Timmy—he must know the entire root
language. The Ash Ock scientists must have implanted control cursors
when you and Catharine were children.*

Gillian tried to nod his head, but even that simple action
was impossible. He could feel his heart still beating; blood was
pumping and his breathing seemed unimpaired, but all other
locomotive abilities had been short-circuited.

*The mnemonic cursors obviously contain built-in safeguards against
causing a complete shutdown, which would be fatal.*

Gillian sensed that his monarch was fascinated by the entire process.

First, the wetware eye was utilized to arm the cursors. Then Timmy used the words themselves to take command of our musculature.

Is there anything we can do? asked Gillian.

Not at the present time. But if and when we escape, we must find a way to neutralize such a weapon.

Timmy grinned, as if he was fully aware of the internal dialogue taking place between Gillian and his monarch.

"Pretty good trick, huh? I'll bet that the two of you would like to take a shot at me right now. Maybe if you could move, you'd tear this little optic microprocessor right out of my eyeball. Maybe you'd tear my tongue out as well. No more nasty sounds from Timmy to make you into a vegetable whenever it suits him."

The smile vanished. "But Timmy knows of a better way. Timmy knows that even the deepest implanted mnemonic cursor can be overridden by a fully functioning monarchial consciousness. Timmy knows that when Empedocles is once again restored to his rightful place as a complete Ash Ock Paratwa, he will possess the power to neutralize any such attack.

"Do both of you have the courage to take the hard road? Do you truly possess the strength of will necessary to become a complete entity once again? Can you accept Catharine's replacement—the new tway that I have chosen for you?"

A ravenous fever soared through Gillian's body; anticipation infused with delicate tremors of fear, the wondrous dread of rediscovering that an ancient fantasy might yet be made real. *Can it really be?* he wondered. *Can this Timmy truly provide another tway for us?*

"You will make love again," whispered Timmy. "It will be like it once was with Catharine. You will again experience that density of feeling that nothing human can hope to rival. You will be whole. You will be Paratwa."

I will be whole, thought Gillian, caught up in the thrill of the dream even while a more cynical part of him insisted that such a thing could never be.

Perhaps it is possible, suggested Empedocles, and Gillian knew that his monarch also had been enraptured.

Timmy stepped back. *"Kascht moniken keenish. Kascht kataz fal ruosh."*

Gillian's muscles unlocked. He took a deep breath, closed his eyes, and lunged forward. The robed figure did not even try to escape. One of Gillian's heavy suit gloves fastened on Timmy's neck while the other slammed across the wetware orb, blocking any further optic contact.

Gillian opened his own eyes, observed his prisoners' thick jowls part into a leering smile.

"Go ahead," said Timmy. "Kill me. My death should be easy, especially for a tway of Empedocles. A snap of your wrist should accomplish the task, breaking the spine and pinching the aortic trunk—"

"Shut up."

Timmy laughed. "Are you afraid?"

He may truly wish to die, said Empedocles.

Gillian shook his head. "I don't think so." He released Timmy.

The creature that had once been Jalka/Aristotle looked disappointed. "Since you have chosen to spare my life, I suppose that I'm bound to help you spare yours. Are you prepared to become a Paratwa once again?"

"Yes I am."

"No," whispered Susan, roaring to her feet, pushing off against the monitor bench as if it were a live enemy, deserving of anger. "You're crazy! You're completely out of your mind!"

She had observed Timmy's encounter with Gillian, as her proctor had requested. She had sat in the weird little com chamber, becoming totally intrigued by their strange visitor—an event Timmy had intimated might occur. In fact, the entire experience had been oddly pleasurable up until the moment Susan realized that Timmy somehow intended using her as a replacement for Gillian's lost tway.

"You're mad!" she hissed, whipping the flash daggers from the flakjak's pockets, slashing the multihued beams down across the face of the monitor. The screen imploded; gray-green sparks, traveling in clusters, etched tiny trails across the bench top.

I'm to become the twoy of a Paratwa! The idea was so utterly preposterous that, in another time and place, it would have been barely worth consideration. But here, on the floor of the Atlantic Ocean, inside this massive *thing* Timmy cryptically referred to as a "cell of the Os/Ka/Loq," Susan knew that all occurrences were to be taken seriously.

The twoy of a Paratwa! That's why I possess a fetally modified neuromuscular system—why I'm a genejob! That's why you brought me here! That's why you've been manipulating my entire life!

Susan and Gillian. Two halves of a restored Paratwa.

Madness!

She shook her head. *No. I won't permit it to happen.* She felt a sense of control returning to her. Deactivating the flash daggers, she nested them back in their pockets.

"I won't allow it," she announced, knowing that he could somehow hear her words. "You brought me back to life, Timmy. I thank you for that. But now that you have done so, I won't permit you to rob me of my true consciousness."

She wondered if she had any choice in the matter.

"The massive jaws of cold steel fear! The heart-wrenching throbs of torsos crushed in the grip of relentless terror!"

FL-Sixteen freelancer Karl Zork delivered his lines with the impassioned grimace of a man accustomed to shouting for attention. Ghandi leaned back in his chair and lowered the volume. He was alone in the windowless CPG boardroom—a long narrow rectangle coated in soft blue velvet, its crystal chandeliers bursting from the ceiling like a sextet of engorged penises.

"Black Wednesday is almost upon us!" yelled Zork, his ruddy face filling the wafer screen. The monitor hung suspended above the center of the imitation mahogany table by a pair of energized threads attached to opposite walls.

"The steam heaters are cranked to max—the boiler is ready to explode—"

"—And we all face death by scalding," interjected Zork's telecast partner. Theandra Morgan, a tall stunning blond, appeared in close-up. Today, her long tresses had been shaped into delicately waffled tails.

The shot cut back to Zork, who was bobbing his head and scrunching his zigzag red beard beneath an apelike fist. "Hell to pay in a day! Yessiree, tomorrow's the big one. Tway Meridian, servant of our Enemy, arrives in the Colonies. Tway Meridian, assassin of the Jeek Elementals, comes waltzing into the chamber of the Council of Irrya. Naturally, our *brave* little Councillors will roll out the red carpet, set up the champagne glasses—"

"Kiss ass," added Theandra. 'That's what they used to call it back in Century Twenty."

"A long political tradition." Zork hunched forward across his desk, gazed passionately into the camera. "Don't like such shenanigans, good people of the Colonies? Piss you off when your so-called leaders get ready to sell your feet out from under you?" He wagged an angry finger. "I'm so mad I could belch fire!"

"Light one for me, Karl," added Theandra. "But the truth is, we don't know exactly how the Council is going to react to Meridian's arrival. However, certain elements of intercolonial society are letting their views be known."

She glanced down at her desk, pretended she was reading from a file. It was an affected mannerism, designed to match the style of the old-time freelancers who shunned all unnecessary technology, including prompters. Public opinion polls widely hailed Theandra Morgan for her close attention to historic detail.

"This morning, Karl, in the area surrounding the Irryan Capitol building, an estimated eighty thousand citizens gathered to protest the arrival of the Paratwa envoy. This huge demonstration, organized by the Order of the Birch, was intended to voice the feelings of what many experts now believe is a majority of intercolonial citizenry."

"Damn straight," muttered Zork, appearing beside her in a two-shot.

Theandra continued. "The murderous spree of this Paratwa assassin has produced a confluence of opinion. The latest outrages—the brutal massacre at the lion of Alexander's retreat and the killing of Doyle Blumhaven—have certainly added fuel to the fire."

"Hell to pay!" promised Zork.

"Although the Irryan Council is not in session until tomorrow, these eighty thousand demonstrators left no doubt as to what they expect of our leaders."

The Zork/Morgan two-shot dissolved into an image of the main street in front of the Capitol building. The camera angle, high above, probably taken from one of the adjacent stilted skyscrapers, revealed a swollen mass of people. Fists were raised, berating the sky. Even before the audio cut in, the palpable fury of the crowd was obvious.

"Never Forget What They Did to Our Earth! Never Forget That They're Forever Cursed!"

"No Deals Today! No Deals Tomorrow!"

"Long Live the Order of the Birch!"

Ghandi watched closely, fascinated by the shouting crowd, by the visceral images of collective rage. He imagined himself standing before them, announcing that he was the human responsible for paving the way for the return of the Paratwa.

Insane thoughts.

The screen returned to a tight shot of Zork, his head wagging in sympathetic fury. "No more Mister Nice Guy, Theandra! It's time to stop kissing ass and time to start *kicking* it! You know I'm not one for patriotic bullshit, but just the idea of these Paratwa scumheads being allowed back into the Colonies almost makes me want to resign from FL-Sixteen and join the Guardians!"

Ghandi had been watching the Zork/Morgan report for a number of years now—a faithful addict. He recalled several other occasions when Karl Zork had allowed his zeal to threaten resignation. Naturally, he had never carried out any of his caveats.

"Go for it, Karl."

"I damn well might!"

Once, Ghandi had viewed his obsession with the FL-Sixteen freelancers as simply a guilty pleasure. These days, however, he knew the compulsion bore deeper roots. His own inner fury—the waltz of the microbes—achieved a kind of temporary satiation under the nightly spells of the raging Zork. Whatever Karl Zork proclaimed, whether his reports carried fragments of truth or remained complete prevarications, was not important to Ghandi. The freelancer's manifested rage was the primary attraction. That rage provided Ghandi, and probably many other Zork/Morgan fans, with a cathartic outlet for his own emotional ferocities.

"There's more hot news," stated Theandra. "FL-Sixteen has just uncovered new information relevant to the mystery surrounding the disappearance of Susan Quint, grandniece to Councillor Inez Hernandez."

Ghandi came upright from his slouch and leaned across the table.

"As you might remember, Karl, Susan Quint had been missing since the time of the Honshu massacre, over six weeks ago. In fact, Inez Hernandez just conducted a private funeral service for her grandniece—sans body, of course."

Zork scowled. "Theandra, I just hope that when it's *my* time, they'll have the decency to make sure there's a corpse before they start in on the eulogies."

"I'm sure they'll be decent about you, Karl. At any rate, knowledgeable sources now say that Susan Quint was in the Honshu terminal, that she witnessed the massacre there, and that she possibly recognized one of the assassins—one of the tways. She escaped but was later believed to have been hunted down and murdered by the creature."

Ghandi frowned. Except for the fact that Calvin had never found Susan Quint, that she had *truly* disappeared, the freelancers were reporting nothing that wasn't already known.

Zork echoed Ghandi's thoughts. "So tell me something new, Theandra."

She produced a warm smile. "Karl, recall our story from a few days ago, when we reported that the man Gillian, the extway who hunted down and destroyed the liege-killer fifty-six years ago, had been illegally reawakened from stasis? Gillian was the one involved in that deadly skirmish last month at Venus Cluster."

"Bravo!" chortled Karl, clapping three times. "Anyone with the balls to hunt Paratwa is my kind of hombre!"

"A chip off the old block," agreed Theandra. "At any rate, we also reported that Gillian disappeared several days ago, after being contacted by that priest from the Church of the Trust."

"Lester Mon Dama."

Theandra's smile brightened. "Well, Karl, it turns out that Susan Quint also knows this priest. When she was still a little sliver—when her zoned-out parents killed themselves—Lester Mon Dama was there to comfort her."

Zork did not look impressed. "Ancient history, Theandra. It's probably just a coincidence that Susan Quint and Gillian both know the priest."

"Here's some more ancient history for you. Twenty-four years ago, three Church of the Trust practicing obstetricians died in a car crash. Their vehicle went out of control on a transverse boulevard right here in Irrya. Somehow, it went straight through the guard rail—a two-hundred-foot drop right onto the cosmishield strip. Naturally, their car never touched the sun sector. Burn screens cut the vehicle to pieces before it could do any damage to the glass."

"Hell of a way to go," offered Zork.

"After an investigation, the crash was officially ruled an accident, although the owner of the vehicle was briefly investigated for manslaughter. It seems that the car's navcom survived partially intact and showed possible signs of tampering. No one ever proved the owner deliberately sabotaged his car, but a few of the E-Tech Security investigators on the case apparently suspected as much." Theandra paused. "And guess who the owner of this car was?"

"Lester Mon Dama?"

"Score one for you, Karl. It turns out that Lester Mon

Dama was buddy-buddy with all three of these doctors. And one of these dead obstetricians actually cared for Susan Quint's mother during her pregnancy."

"Coincidences are mounting," Zork admitted.

"They certainly are. And here's another one for you. These three doctors took care of a lot of pregnant women, all of whom were devoted members of the Church of the Trust. And ninety-four percent of the babies delivered by these obstetricians were female."

Karl frowned. "A Church mandate, perhaps? The women were ordered to bear female children?"

"There's no evidence of such a mandate. But there is evidence that at least some of these young women—if not all of them—have flowered into extraordinary adulthood. The ones that we've been able to locate—all of whom are now in their twenties—are, by the standards of our era, stunningly beautiful. At least five of them are super athletes. Three play on championship gee-well teams. One is currently ranked third fastest on the Pocono speed slopes. Another goes by the moniker of Slim-Trim Three. She is a famed competitor in Sirak-Brath's brutal Fin Whirl."

Zork narrowed his eyes and rubbed his zigzag beard, as if he were lost deep in thought. "Theandra, I'm going to take a wild guess and say that these women you're describing are genejobs."

"Put money on it, Karl. It's more than a fair hunch to say that these three obstetricians were responsible for fetal modifications—highly *illegal* modifications, I might add. And circumstantial evidence would indicate that Susan Quint was also a genejob."

"But where's all this leading us, Theandra?"

Ghandi asked himself the same question.

"Frankly, Karl, we don't know. One thing's for certain. Lester Mon Dama has some explaining to do. But guess what?"

"Lester Mon Dama has also disappeared?"

"Jackpot, Karl. The priest has been missing since the day he contacted Gillian."

"Mighty strange happenings."

Ghandi agreed. Often, Zork/Morgan blew stories way out of proportion to the facts, reaching conclusions that stretched the parameters of imagination. But in this instance the freelancers were not even attempting to speculate about what it all meant. In Ghandi's mind, that fact alone blessed their data with the ring of truth.

And Susan Quint as a genejob made sense. Calvin, after failing to kill her in the Honshu massacre, had suspected as much. But what could be the purpose behind such genetic modifications? Surely not just to create a batch of super-athletic females. Was Susan Quint, and these other young women, part of some crazy Church of the Trust scheme? Had the missing Lester Mon Dama arranged for the fetal modifications?

Before Ghandi could consider the puzzle any further, the boardroom door fragmented into a checkerboard array of miniature rectangles, which quickly dissolved into pink vapors. The vent system was still sweeping the remnants of the high-tech door up into the ventilation system when Colette charged across the threshold. Ghandi rose from his chair, surprised by his wife's appearance. "I thought you were going to—"

"You saw the report?" snapped Colette. Behind her, the door began recoagulating.

"Yes, I was watching—"

"You have conclusions, Corelli-Paul?"

Her hands were shaking. Forehead creases, normally faint and delicate, rippled with open fury. He studied her face, looking for signs of Sappho, signs that she had melded with her distant tway, merged into the Ash Ock monarchy. The voice seemed to belong to Colette, but it was difficult to tell for certain with so much anger blemishing her features. Colette rarely displayed such fury. But Sappho? Who really knew the extent of *that* one's emotions?"

"I'm not sure what to think. Zork/Morgan didn't summarize—"

"Zork/Morgan doesn't possess the collective intellect for such a task! You do. Analyze. Coordinate data."

"I'm not sure what it means—"

"Guess!"

He gazed at her helplessly.

"Fool Ghandi!" Skirt flaring, she leaped up onto the board table, stomped her low heels sharply into the grained plastic, and then began a turbulent waltz—pure three-quarter time—from one end of the table to the other. Her shoes smacked against the imitation mahogany, producing a sharp interplay of clicking sounds that reminded Ghandi of tap dancing, but distorted somehow, weirdly nonsynchronous, almost vulgar and malevolent. He stepped back from the table, too astonished for words. In their twenty-five years together, he had never seen her do something so extraordinarily bizarre.

She continued dancing back and forth on the plastic surface, heels crackling furiously, arms flapping at her sides as if they were useless appendages, unrelated to the flow of her silent romp. Words poured from her mouth, slurred and syrupy.

"Incomp'tence modified . . . by the inherent weaknesses of this dist'rted *kascht*. It reeks of the lacking!"

She froze in midstride, unnaturally, as if she had run into an invisible barrier. "Reeks of the lacking!" she repeated, whirling to face him. Her head snapped back, as if it had been taken over by some invisible force. Her mouth opened wide.

A braying sound—an animal cry bubbling with undercurrents of what Ghandi sensed to be desperate rage—shook her torso. Never before had he heard such a harsh utterance. It was so far beyond the range of human sounds that for a moment Ghandi felt disoriented, uncertain of his surroundings. He fell back against the wall, into the blue velvet, grateful for the pressure of something that could be touched.

She leaped from the table, landing a pace in front of him. Her arms came forward; fingers trickled across his shoulders, began massaging flesh through the thin fabric of his gossamer shirt. Hungry digits, armored for lust. He stared fearfully into her eyes.

She gripped his upper arms and shoved him hard against the wall.

"Reeks of the lacking!" she hissed, pinning him against the

velvet. "Don't you know what this means, Corelli-Paul? For once, can't you *see* the obvious!"

He swallowed nervously, tried to concentrate his thoughts, looking for a way to escape. Whatever stood before him was certainly not Colette, at least not the Colette that he knew.

"You're Sappho," he murmured.

She released him, stepped back a pace. Distance seemed to produce cogency. Some of the madness departed from her face.

"I am Sappho. You have witnessed the whelm of an Ash Ock, the dialectic pressure of tways uncontrollably inversed against their monarchy, the equation of perfect balance, which forces the arising of the Paratwa."

He swallowed. "I've heard of it."

A cackling laugh escaped from her. "You've heard of it! *Bravo!*—as the freelancers would say. But you still don't know what I'm talking about, do you?"

"I don't know what you're talking about," he admitted.

A fresh spasm of fury overwhelmed her. "It was Reemul! Fool Reemul! He failed to carry out orders! Reemul didn't kill *him!*"

"Kill . . . who? Gillian?"

"Gillian! Hah! A mere afterthought. Disposal of tainted material—elimination of *his* handiwork. No, not Gillian. He did not matter. But the one who trained Gillian *did* matter! The one whose twisted vanity turned him against us—that one is still *alive!* Reemul did not accomplish his assignment . . . at least not his full assignment. One tway must have *survived!*"

"Who . . . are you talking about?" Intense curiosity began to override Ghandi's fear.

"Genejobs! Female fetuses, altered by *him!* Hundreds, probably, all created for the sole purpose of finding the right one, the one who can be fitted to Gillian's intact interlace, the one who can be used to restore Empedocles!"

Ghandi knew enough of Paratwa history to take an educated guess. "You're talking about . . . Aristotle? He survived the Apocalypse?"

"Aristotle," she whispered, as if the word were a curse. "Yes, he still lives—at least some incarnation of him, some aspect of what he once was. No other creature in the Colonies could possibly hope to reverse the ravages of Empedocles's affliction. No other possesses the skill to counter arrhythmia of the whelm." Her face suddenly paled. "The cell of the Os/Ka/Loq ... he may have been the one responsible ..."

"What?"

Sappho shook her head. "Nothing."

Ghandi's eyes widened. "Did Aristotle create the program in the archives, the one your sunsetter has been trying to destroy?"

"Yes, Aristotle created Freebird." She reached her hands out toward him, but this time gently, in the manner of Colette. Palms caressed his cheeks; fingernails played at the corners of his mouth. Ghandi had the distinct feeling that she desired, almost desperately, his full comprehension, desired that he understand the sum totality of Ash Ock intrigues.

Her mouth came forward; her lips touched his chin. She kissed him gingerly on the lower lip. Heat flooded Ghandi's face, but it was an unfamiliar warmth, a passion born of strangeness.

"We thought that only the program remained. We thought that only the E-Tech computers still housed our enemy. But it's now obvious that we were wrong. Aristotle himself—or a part of him—still lives."

She pulled back. A strange expression fell across her face. *What is she feeling?* Ghandi wondered. Sorrow, perhaps, but something else, residing beneath the sadness, buoying it, providing a watery veneer to hide deeper underswells, vaster disturbances. *Loneliness?* That seemed to offer a closer approximation, a more vigorous delineation of the brooding murmurs that distended her surface. But even loneliness could not fully explain the depth of her affectation. There was something else, something that Ghandi suspected he would never be able fully to understand.

For the first time in twenty-five years he felt pity for her.

Reaching out, he grasped her pale elfin face in his hands, held it inches from his lips, suspending her yearning, forcing them to meet as equals.

An incredible sensation passed through him. He felt a renewed sense of control, willpower returning, his true self emerging from the shadows of strictured wisdom, vaulting microbes reduced to proper insignificance.

A tremor of fear passed through her. She snuggled against him. "Aristotle . . . knows things that threaten us."

Ghandi caressed the back of her neck. "And that information is contained in Freebird?"

"Yes. But now we have to contend with the creator as well as his program."

Ghandi's heart raced, pulsing with new virility. He bathed in it, allowed it to bubble up inside him, swelling awareness with liberties sacrificed half a lifetime ago for the advancement of Ash Ock schemes. He allowed her to press against him, but he kept her face delicately suspended inches from his own, maintaining a gulf through which intentions could still be ascertained.

"I have questions."

"Yes."

"When you were on the table . . . in the whelm. You uttered a word that I never heard before. *Kascht.*"

"*Kascht* is a part of . . . space." She hesitated, as if groping for a more precise definition. "*Kascht* is a place . . . a time. It is an area of sorts . . . an area that either does or does not permit the resolution which enables . . . full communication."

Ghandi did not understand, but he had the impression that she was being truthful. He suspected it was a problem of semantics. He pressed on. "And that other phrase. You uttered it several times. Reeks of the lacking?"

"This *kascht* within which you exist, where the Earth exists, where the Colonies exist . . . this *kascht* reeks of the lacking. It does not permit the normal resolution. It does not allow full communication. It is an aberration."

With that last word, her face broke into a pained grimace. For a moment, he thought she was going to cry.

"An aberration? What sort of aberration?"

A specter seemed to cross her face; aquamarine eyes flared wide open, and Ghandi had the curious sensation that he was being observed by more than one person. And then the moment passed and Sappho was gone and it was just Colette again. He understood. He had just witnessed the transition, the return passage, monarch into tway.

His wife pulled away from him.

He asked, "Sappho . . . she was speaking of . . . an aberration—"

"Please, Corelli-Paul . . . enough has been said. No more. Please."

"All right." He turned to the hanging monitor, still tuned to FL-Sixteen. A commercial was just beginning: a well-dressed young couple, holding hands, walked down a crowded and noisy Irryan boulevard. Tension was apparent on their faces, tension obviously accentuated by the disruptive amalgam of too many people occupying too small an area.

Colette said, "I'm going to have Calvin investigate the background of this priest. Perhaps there are trails leading to Aristotle."

"Didn't Calvin already look into that when the freelancers reported that Gillian had been contacted by Lester Mon Dama?"

"Yes, Calvin made a few discreet inquiries. But it was not a priority. Now it is. Aristotle must be found. He must be destroyed."

Ghandi nodded. "This information possessed by Aristotle? What is it? How does it threaten you? Does it have something to do with restoring Gillian's tway, bringing Empedocles back to life?"

Colette hesitated, as if debating whether or not to respond. Then abruptly, she spun and headed for the door. The portal disintegrated, reformed behind her. Ghandi was alone again.

And he knew that bringing Empedocles back to life—somehow making Susan Quint into Gillian's new tway—was not Colette/Sappho's primary concern. An *afterthought*, she had said, in reference to Gillian.

It was Aristotle who poised the true threat. Aristotle and his secret computer program, Freebird.

But what was the information that poised such a threat to Ash Ock plans? Had Aristotle developed some sort of ultra-weapon, something that the Colonies could use to repel the returning Paratwa?

He shook his head. No, not a weapon—at least not a weapon as traditionally defined. But something that Aristotle knew jeopardized the royal Caste. Like Gillian/Empedocles, Aristotle was of their breed. Did the Ash Ock possess some secret Achilles' heel? Had Aristotle learned of it? Was that why, as Sappho had just intimated, Reemul the liege-killer had been sent out to kill Aristotle?

Ghandi sighed. There were too many questions and not enough data. He could dance in circles all day and get no closer to answers.

On the monitor, the commercial was ending. Now the young couple who had been walking down the crowded Irryan boulevard were reclining side by side in a tilted airbed, in a spacious sleep chamber colored in soothing earth tones, mostly pale ambers and dark shades of brown. The lovers were still holding hands, but their faces were now hidden by metallic shrouds. Her leg moved softly across his; his hand squeezed hers. The gentle movements, the inclination of their bodies, all suggested a gestalt of peace, serenity.

The scene dissolved to a wide-shot. A lush field of green grass stretched to the horizon where a range of distant mountains rose from acres of dark pines. Three distinct peaks stood in bas-relief against a piercing blue sky, their nipples coated in golden-white ice drippings. The sponsor's name faded in across the bottom of the screen.

PABLAZI EXPERIENTIALS . . .

. . . OUR LINE OF HOLO REE-FEES WILL MAKE YOU FEEL AS IF YOU'RE ACTUALLY THERE.

Pablazi Experientials was not a CPG company, but Ghandi recognized this advertisement for programmable holo shrouds as the handiwork of CPG's gut-ad department. The message behind this commercial was clearly the work of his wife.

The secret dream of humanity: the return to the Earth. These days, at Colette/Sappho's urging, that theme was being utilized to sell everything from ree-fee shrouds to profarming harvester/planters.

From the edge of awareness came the glimmering of an idea, a blending of disparate elements, which seemed to suggest that Sappho's "return to our roots" motif and Aristotle's secret knowledge were part of the same mystery. But he could make nothing more of it.

Perhaps Colette/Sappho would suffer another bout of strange behavior. Perhaps, next time, she would reveal all.

Jon Van Ostrand bore the appearance of a man who, if granted a choice, would rather have been far away from the stunned silence of the Council of Irrya. Although physically he remained beyond Jupiter's orbit, nestled in the relative security of his heavily fortified op-base satellite, the grim visage appearing on their FTL screens gave every indication that the Supreme Commander of the Intercolonial Guardians had dreaded today's meeting.

"How big?" whispered Inez Hernadez, reflecting the disbelief of all.

Van Ostrand broke eye contact with the Council, swept his gaze downward to read from the status terminal embedded in his desk. The lion could hear the strain in his voice, Van Ostrand's own echoes of incredulity at the magnitude of the discovery.

"The intruding starship is approximately two thousand one hundred and fifty miles in length, ovoid in shape, with a middle diameter approaching nine hundred miles."

Inez shook her head. "You're talking about a vessel that is thirty times the size of our largest Colony."

"Thirty times the *length* of Irrya," clarified Van Ostrand. "In terms of mass, this vessel could easily contain all two hundred seventeen of our cylinders."

"And when did this ship first appear?" Asked Maria Losef. Her tone, as usual, remained free of any discernible emotional shadings. Losef may as well have been asking a question about the weather.

"This single vessel entered out outermost detection grid less than an hour ago. I headed back to the FTL the moment I received the report.

"Interesting coincidence," said Edward Huromonus dryly. "We have Meridian outside of chambers, preparing to address Council, and suddenly this ship appears."

The lion experienced yet another uncomfortable physical sensation; a prodding pain, deep in his guts. For the past few days, he had been suffering from what his Costeau doctors had diagnosed, early this morning, as stomach cramps brought on by extreme stress. They had recommended a lengthy vacation.

Their suggestion had caused the lion to laugh aloud—a cathartic release of tension, to be sure, but still his first such display since the attack on the retreat, four days ago. For the doctors' benefit, he had mimicked the obedient patient, solemnly promising to follow their advice.

He knew that the stomach pains represented a bodily manifestation of his terrible shame, his cowardice at the retreat massacre. He had betrayed a lifetime of values in the stroke of a moment, and he was honest enough with his own feelings to realize that it would take time to truly *feel* the depth of that betrayal. Even his earlier rage had been squelched by the exigencies of having to continue to function as the lion of Alexander, Councillor of Irrya. Responsibilities demanded such self-repression. Responsibilities dictated that righteous rage be transformed into stomach cramps.

From the center of the round table, from the pentagon of FTL screens, Van Ostrand continued with his report. "The vessel is decelerating toward the Colonies at a current rate of just under point-two-percent lightspeed. Velocity and direction almost precisely match those of Meridian's shuttle, which we first detected forty days ago."

"How long until first intercept?" asked Huromonus.

"Two days, providing the vessel maintains current intrusion course parameters. In two days, fifteen of our advance targeteers—all nuclear-armed—will enter the strike zone. And in four days, our first wave of primary attack forces—

two hundred and ninety-six ships, including sixteen Ribonix-class destroyers—will come within offensive range."

Van Ostrand raised his chin and cleared his throat, proceeded with newfound enthusiasm. Like most militarists, the recital of impressive statistics enhanced his resolve.

"Advance penetration gear has been activated. Not surprisingly, we have as yet been unable to pierce their outer shell. The vessel is projecting a massive electromagnetic field, possibly for the specific purpose of fouling external data intrusion. At closer range, however, some of our more esoteric equipment may be able to get a peek inside. For now, all we know for certain is that the outer skin of the vessel displays a multiplicity of irregularities. The shell does not appear to have been mechformed, in the manner of one of our own ships or colonies."

Inez frowned. "You mean this thing could be a hollowed-out planetoid? Something along those lines?"

Van Ostrand hesitated for just a fraction of a second. "No, that does not appear to be the case."

When the Guardian Commander did not expound on his answer, Huromonus raised his eyebrows and asked: "Just what *is* the case?"

"As I've said, we are at a very early stage of data interpretation. But our initial analysis indicates an outer shell that appears to be composited of erratically interwoven segments. Again, at this point, our own phasing mistakes may be yielding a great deal of misinformation. In fact, it's entirely possible that our entire data index is in error; long-range scanning gear may be effectively distorting due to this vessel's tremendous electromagnetic field."

Inez cast a wry glance at the lion. Van Ostrand was trying hard to avoid a direct answer.

Losef was not about to let it pass. "What are you reluctant to tell us, Jon?"

The Guardian Commander gave up. "All right. Providing we're getting correct data, it looks like we're dealing with a two-thousand-one-hundred-and-fifty-mile-long organic starship. The damned thing doesn't look like it was manufactured. It looks like it was grown."

For a moment, no one responded.

"Grown?" Inez finally muttered, her word filling the vacuum of silence.

Van Ostrand shrugged.

A fresh wave of pain tore through the lion's midsection. He reached his hand beneath the table and gingerly pressed a needle pad against his shirt, barely noticing the prick of the medicinal dart. An instant muscle relaxant—the only medication he had been willing to accept from his doctors.

A *starship over two thousand miles long*. Where could such a thing have originated from? Had Theophrastus, Ash Ock scientific genius, created it? Sprouted it in his garden, nurtured it to full size? *What in the hell are we dealing with?*

Losef, as usual, urged restraint. "It's possible that this vessel is camouflaging its true structure—a deliberate attempt to provoke astonishment and awe, amplify the obvious psychological effects induced by its sheer magnitude."

Van Ostrand nodded vigorously, liking the idea. "Yes, that could be the case. We don't know for certain just what we're faced with here. We're still not close enough."

Huromonus turned to Inez. "Didn't the pre-Apocalyptics dabble in mechgrowth?"

"Yes, but according to surviving records, they were never able to advance such discoveries beyond the nanotech level. They certainly never developed such techniques to the point where they could consider growing two-thousand-mile-long starships."

"We could be dealing with an organic shell of some sort," suggested Huromonus, "and *not* the vessel itself."

"That's possible," said Van Ostrand.

Losef held up her hand. "A specific discussion along these lines is precursive. I suggest we confine our debates to a more factual arena."

"Good idea," said Inez, scanning her monitor. "Jon, I'm curious about something. I've run some quick calculations here. A vessel of this incredible size, decelerating at point two PSOL, should have been detected by our outermost warning grid weeks ago. Yet it was not spotted until now. I can conceive only two possible explanations. One, the vessel was traveling at a very high PSOL, and then slowed to point two percent light in an incredibly short time. Or two, it boasts an antiscan technology far beyond the level of our own."

"My people are leaning toward the antiscan theory," said Van Ostrand. "As Edward suggested, it is probably not coincidental that this intruder was discovered just as the Council is preparing to receive Meridian's tway."

The lion nodded in agreement. Meridian's other half, aboard the vessel, could have ordered such antiscan devices shut down just as this tway was about to enter Council chambers. The lion recalled Nick's repeated warnings about this Jeek Elemental, the Paratwa believed to be chief lieutenant of the Ash Ock.

He is one of the deadliest assassins ever bred. This is the Paratwa who was primarily responsible for developing Gillian's great combat skills. This is the Paratwa who mastered the even finer art of political intrigue under the tutelage of both Sappho and Aristotle. Be incredibly wary of him.

Inez turned to Van Ostrand. "You've also not mentioned the direction of this intruder's approach. I take it that this vessel is coming at us from the same coordinates as Meridian's shuttle?"

"Precisely the same coordinates."

Yet another mystery, mused the lion. Nearly six weeks ago, when Meridian's tiny shuttle had been detected, its direction of approach to the solar system had been seventy-five/thirty-five degrees polar from the axis of departure utilized by the Star-Edge fleet over two-and-a-half centuries ago.

Assuming that 12 PSOL—a velocity within the known limits of Star-Edge technology—had remained the highest rate achieved, the Paratwa fleet theoretically could have reached one of the targeted star systems—Epsilon Eridani, perhaps— established a planetary base—assuming hospitable planets were found—and managed this return to the Colonies, all within the accumulated time frame.

But neither Meridian's shuttle nor this massive vessel had come from the direction of Epsilon Eridani, or from any of the other targeted star systems. They had, in fact, arrived along a rectilinear path that, if projected toward a source, led to star systems over half a million lightyears away.

Several theories existed to explain the directional mystery, and over the past month, the Council had discussed them in great detail. The most unsettling concept credited the Paratwa with achieving relativistic velocities, perhaps even surpassing the near-mythical speed of light—a not impossible limit according to FTL theorists. At FTL velocities, such directional changes might be rendered inconsequential.

Like his fellow Councillors, the lion wanted desperately to believe that the Paratwa had *not* attained relativistic speeds. And, fortunately, there did seem to be some evidence negating the FTL theory. For one thing, when the Colonies had first learned that their great enemy had survived the Apocalypse by retreating into deep space, the Paratwa had still been fifty-six years away. Obviously, the tripartite assassin, and perhaps Sappho as well, had arrived in the cylinders ahead of this huge vessel, but their accelerated arrival could be explained in terms of normal velocities. The simple fact that it had taken this massive vessel fifty-six years to reach the cylinders seemed to indicate that the Paratwa still operated within sublight limitations.

"Perhaps," suggested Huromonus, "it is time to invite this Meridian to provide some explanations."

Van Ostrand grimaced. "Maybe he'll even be willing to tell us why his masters had your predecessor murdered."

"The mysteries surrounding Doyle Blumhaven's death will be uncovered," promised Huromonus. "As will the disappearances of Lester Mon Dama, Susan Quint, and Gillian."

Inez looked away. Before the meeting, she and the lion had discussed yesterday's freelancer stories. But Inez had not been impressed by the latest revelations. She still insisted that her grandniece must have been slain by the assassin.

We all try to corral our pain, thought the lion.

Inez said, "I'm still not sure that a face-to-face meeting with Meridian is a good idea. We could just as easily conference via terminal."

Losef said, "There would be no logical reason for this Paratwa emissary to kill us."

Inez glared at her.

"Since his arrival," offered Huromonus, "Meridian and his animals have been examined and reexamined. Multiple teams have scanned the Jeek and these two dogs. If Meridian or his pets bear concealed weapons, biological plagues, or even mild cases of the common cold, we would have found them. But they're clean . . . at least, as clean as our technology is able to ascertain."

The lion kept his thoughts to himself. There was no reason to rehash the possibility of advanced Paratwa technology; all of the Council realized that the idea was now a silent codicil to every facet of their debates.

Inez glanced at the lion for support. He forced a smile.

"Inez, if this tway so desires, he could probably kill us all with his bare hands in less time than it would take to get a security squad in here. But we have to face him." The lion hesitated. "We'd appear as complete cowards if we failed to meet Meridian in the flesh."

"I know you're right," said Inez. "What really bothers me is Meridian's insistence that these dogs must accompany him everywhere, even into chambers. I just can't understand why."

A faint smile touched Huromonus's cheeks. "This morning, I asked Meridian that very question. He replied, and I quote: 'I would be very lonely without my darling little friends.' "

Van Ostrand rolled his eyes. Losef toggled her keyboard to the intercom channel and requested that Meridian be sent into chambers.

The lion had seen Meridian's image already; shortly after the Jeek assassin had rendezvoused with one of Van Ostrand's attack fleets, pictures had been transmitted back to the Colonies. He now realized that the pictures failed to convey the essence of this Paratwa.

When the black door opened, when Meridian came strutting across the threshold like a piece of stiffened sailcoth borne on the crest of an invisible wind, the lion was instantly reminded of ancient videos he had once seen depicting the Zoe Coxcombs—one of the more infamous of the late twenty-first-century vivisection clubs. The Zoe Coxcombs, composed of fastidiously dressed male homosexuals, had specialized in penile amputation/reattachment techniques in their ever more bizarre quest to achieve the perfect orgasm.

Meridian wore a charcoal gray three-piece suit. The buttonless Eton-style jacket barely came to his waist; the vest was fastened with hook-and-eye loops, each hook a large jewel of a different color: emeralds, rubies, and sapphires, no two alike. Thin blond hair, edged with gray, drooped into an even set of bangs that fell primly across his forehead. A bloat—an organic earring—hung from his left ear, its tiny set of conducer strands emerging from the puffy white surface and vanishing into the tway's ear canal. The bloat pulsed serenely, like a beating heart, aligned with some unknown rhythm in Meridian's body.

He was six feet tall and pencil-thin, with a pale gaunt face that almost suggested emaciation. He looked to be in his early sixties, but the lion reminded himself not to make any assumptions about the tway's age; there remained too many uncertainties in that regard. Meridian had lived across a span of almost three centuries: it remained unknown whether the Ash Ock had held him in stasis for long periods, whether they had somehow extended his natural lifespan, or whether his age was the result of relativistic velocities.

"Welcome to the Council," began Losef. "Introductions, I assume, are unnecessary."

The tway's alert green eyes scanned each of their faces; he nodded to them in turn. His eyes seemed to dwell on the FTL pentagon—on Jon Van Ostrand. Meridian smiled at the Guardian Commander. Van Ostrand glared back.

His dogs entered the chambers. The borzoi—the Russian wolfhound—did the walking, its brown silky hair the obvious result of careful grooming. The hound was tall, at least thirty inches at the shoulders. Its head was upthrust, the face almost haughty. The second animal, the miniature poodle, rode on the Borzoi's back. It stood backward, facing the wolfhound's tail, like a sentry watching its rear. The poodle's frizzy hair was white and clipped fairly short. A small tan beret, carefully angled, lay perched atop its head.

The black door closed.

"My delight is inexpressible," said the tway of Meridian, speaking in a rich low baritone. "This moment should be captured; posterity demands a record." He glanced around the twenty-sided chamber, at the leather-veneered walls, at the rare wood-framed paintings revealed through the security of their humidity partitions, at the huge chandelier suspended from the darkness of the high arched ceiling. "I hope you are recording these moments with hidden cameras?"

Losef smiled politely and motioned Meridian to a seat across the table from the lion. "Do your pets require any arrangements?"

The tway sat down and ran his palms across the polished round table. Thin lips widened into a smile. "Delightful environment. Furnishings reminiscent of old Earth." He turned to the dogs. "Beside the doorway, please. Statue alignment. Refrain from barking."

The borzoi trotted quickly back to the portal and sat on its haunches at the left side of the entrance. The poodle leaped from its back and assumed an identical pose at the other side of the black door.

"Is it a binary?" asked Inez, unable to mask the uncertainty in her tone. She kept staring at the dogs.

"Two distinct animals," replied Meridian, with obvious amusement.

The lion recalled hearing tales from the archives about pre-Apocalyptic binary experiments performed on all manner of living creatures. Most such experiments ultimately had ended in failure. In particular, some of the interlinks made with dog fetuses had produced puppies who, after a few weeks or months of so-called normal binary behavior, had gone insane and ripped one another to pieces. According to the few remaining records from some of the genetic labs, no dog tways had ever survived to adulthood.

It remained to be seen whether Meridian was telling the truth about this pair.

"They appear well trained," said Huromonus.

"They do as they are told."

Inez scowled.

Losef continued. "This Council appreciates the opportunity to meet with you."

"It is my duty and pleasure."

"For the record, your other tway remains aboard the vessel that recently intruded into our solar system?"

Meridian laced his fingers together and laid his palms on the table. "The word 'intruded' connotes a specific bias."

"Allow me to rephrase. Your other tway is aboard the vessel that recently entered our defensive grid?"

"Yes. I am here and there."

"And you address this Council as the official emissary of the Paratwa aboard this vessel?"

"Yes."

"And Sappho is the leader of those Paratwa?"

"Our vessel is called the Biodyysey. Sappho has a great deal of input relative to the Biodyysey's course and actions, if that is what you mean by 'leader.' "

"Do you have any introductory remarks?"

"Such remarks were contained in my initial communication."

"Do you have any suggestions about where we can begin these talks?"

"Indeed I do."

And then he was on his feet, his arm hurtling downward, something small and bright emerging from his fist, a burst of white luminescence erupting from the edge of the table where the object impacted.

The lion flashed back to the events surrounding the massacre, to that first terrible instant when his mind rendered chaotic atrocities into patterns of danger. He flew from his chair, prepared to meet whatever threat Meridian had introduced.

Inez cried out, spun to face the dogs. Huromonus and the lion pivoted to follow her gaze. But the animals had not moved. They remained poised in their flanking positions at the doorway.

Losef arched her eyebrows.

A pillar of white luminescence was slowly rising from the tabletop, a column of pulsating energy soaring up past the chandelier, reaching for the ceiling.

"No cause for alarm," Meridian assured them, smiling while his fingers played with one of the jeweled hooks on his vest.

The white column halted its vertical growth some eight feet above their heads. It disintegrated. Sparkling dust fell softly toward the table; swabs of color began to take shape within the gentle rain of mist, tiny collusions of form and hue. The swabs coalesced rapidly, each one mutating into a floating miniature of one of the Irryan Colonies. The largest, obviously Irrya, was nearly two inches long; the others varied respectively in size. Detailing was incredibly precise and appeared to be the result of photographic data as opposed to purely artistic interpretation. He knew without counting that all two hundred seventeen Colonies were represented.

It was the most stunning display of holo technology the lion had ever seen.

Even the geometric spatial relationships between the various tiny Colonies looked correct; Irrya hung at the proper minute angle to its most adjacent cylinder. Saskatchewan Omni. He spotted his small home colony of Den, out near the edge of the display. Only the actual distances between the colonies were exaggerated. Severe selective compression had been necessary to contain the entire manifestation within the limited space of the Council chamber.

"Saints of the Trust," murmured Inez, gingerly moving her face closer to one of the cylinders. She squinted down at the tiny model. "This looks like Northern California. I can even see green forests through one of the cosmishield strips. The animal Preserve." She jerked her head away. "Things appear to be moving inside . . . clouds . . ."

Meridian beamed, obviously enjoying their amazement. "This is not merely a static display. It is a real-time fully animated representation of the Irryan Colonies."

"Most impressive," offered Losef, without conviction. "Does this holo have a specific purpose?"

"For the moment, consider it as a memento of what is."

A faint chill ran through the lion as he resumed his seat. From his position behind the holo, Meridian went on.

"The Paratwa wish their return to be a peaceful one. We do not look forward to the deplorable tragedy of conflict."

From the lion's position, one of the tiny Colonies appeared to hang directly in front of the tway's mouth. As Meridian continued to speak, it appeared as if he were trying to eat the cylinder.

"Our vessel, the Biodyssey, represents a level of technological achievement well beyond your capacity. We have detected the approach of your first wave of assault ships—fifteen vessels, all told." He turned to the FTL screens. "Councillor Van Ostrand, I have been instructed to inform you that should these vessels attempt to inhibit our passage, or should they attempt offensive action against us, they will be immediately annihilated. We provide this warning to you in the sincere hope that a state of outright war between our peoples can be avoided."

Van Ostrand, looking angry, was about to respond when Losef held up her hand. "You are invading our sovereign space," she said calmly.

"We are returning to the place of our beginnings," countered Meridian. "The roots of our existence beckon."

To the lion, such words sounded strangely like the metaphysical platitudes of the Church of the Trust.

Huromonus achieved the same interpretation. "The Ash Ock are generally credited with the invention of one of our religions. Are you, sir, a devoted follower of the Church of the Trust?"

Meridian smiled. "I am, sir, devoted only to logic. The Biodyssey has traveled a long way. Ancient longings have hardened into a resolve that becomes more like a structural configuration with each passing day. No energizing mythos of religion compels us. The Paratwa are driven only by the inexorable strategy of reason.

"The Solar system was once our home. It will once again be our home. We will not be swayed from the achievement of that dream."

"According to the Irryan charter," stated Losef, "neither the Earth nor the Colonies are yours for the taking."

The tway shrugged. "A charter; a rationalization for maintaining the status quo. Meaningless in real terms."

"You intend to ignore our sovereign rights?" asked Inez.

"We intend to achieve our dream."

The lion scowled. "Much as you sought to achieve your dream in the late twenty-first century, by attempting to wipe out humanity."

Meridian stared at him coldly. "Back then, the Paratwa were given no choice. War was declared upon us. Many so-called charters were composed that negated the right of binaries even to *exist*. We were pronounced a human mistake. We were scheduled to be exterminated. Our so-called attempts to wipe out humanity were actually the desperate actions of a race of conscious entities to survive."

Huromonus said, "I believe our data archives provide a very different interpretation of the pre-Apocalypse."

"Indeed? Why am I not surprised that the E-Tech archives would be filled with massive distortions of the truth?"

Huromonus, in what the lion recognized as one of his trademark legalistic mannerisms, stroked his speckled goatee. "You suggest that the Paratwa did *not* murder one hundred and fifty million human beings?"

"The human race suffered severe casualties throughout that era. Were the Paratwa directly responsible for all of those deaths?" Meridian shook his head firmly. "Distortions. Factual errors compounded by unbridled hatred."

The lion felt his fury mounting. He stood up and pointed a finger at the tway. "Was it a *distortion* that attacked my home four days ago, murdering my friends?! Was it a *distortion* that has been on the rampage in our Colonies for months, killing innocent citizens?! And fifty-six years ago—Reemul! Was he also merely a misinterpretation of the facts?!"

Meridian hesitated; his eyes grew distant. The lion got the impression that the Jeek's other tway was conferring with someone. Sappho and Theophrastus, probably. Finally:

"Humans and Paratwa have been at war for centuries. No one denies this. And when Paratwa make war, they do so with two basic criteria—winning and achieving the victory with as little loss of life as possible—on *both* sides.

"Reemul is ancient history. Both he and Codrus, who awakened him, are long dead. Reemul was of my breed, but unfortunately, by almost anyone's standard, he was clearly insane. His excesses never carried the full sanction of the Ash Ock. To use him as an example is patently unfair. Have there not also been crazed humans over the years, operating totally beyond the boundaries of law and order?

"As to the attack on your retreat, need I remind you that you have been willfully harboring—and for a time without knowledge of this very Council—several sworn enemies of the Paratwa, including that vicious little man Nick, who is known to us as the Czar? Can you truly fault my leaders for sending a warrior to deal with ancient and brutal foes?"

The lion gritted his teeth. "Yes, I fault you. I accuse you and your kind of murder, plain and simple. Nick was right about you, Meridian. You're nothing but a well-trained liar."

The tway rose slowly from his seat. His arm flashed downward. The holo disappeared, the miniature Colonies of Irrya vanishing in a swirl of colored dust. He turned calmly to Losef.

"I request an adjournment. I see now that the emotions of the moment will not allow a reasonable discussion of our peace initiatives. Perhaps a few days to cool off. I still maintain high hopes for reconciling our differences."

Losef glanced around the able. "You've just arrived, Meridian. We have many questions for you—"

"I'm afraid I must insist."

The lion felt his fury continuing to grow. He wanted physically to lash out at the tway, to cause him pain.

Meridian approached the lion, halted two paces away. "I understand your rage, and despite what you may think, I even sympathize with it. But may I remind you, and with no threat intended, that in the attack on your retreat, the Ash Nar deliberately spared your life. You, the lion of Alexander, the man whose lifelong opposition to us has been nurtured by an unfortunate childhood encounter with Reemul."

"Ash Nar," whispered the lion, not trusting himself to raise his voice. "So that is what you call your tripartite murderer."

Meridian turned to the others. "For the record, the various

attacks by the Ash Nar were based on military decisions beyond the scope of my authority. But I assure you that if this Council and the Paratwa can reach a common basis of understanding, all such offensive military actions will end.

"And now, with your permission, I would like to have a few days to enjoy the boundless attractions and pleasures of Irrya"

Inez looked astonished. "You want to go *sightseeing*?"

"Yes."

Even Losef appeared to be at a loss for words.

Huromonus cleared his throat. "We would like your assurances that this Biodyysey will initiate no offensive actions against our approaching ships."

"You have my word. The Biodyysey will initiate no conflict, provided, of course, that your own fleet maintains a non-threatening posture.

"We will talk again in a few days." Meridian turned to his dogs. "Standard ambulation alignment. Follow me."

The poodle hopped back up on the borzoi's back, again facing its rear. The wolfhound rose, waited for Meridian to pass, and then trotted obediently out the door, three paces behind its master.

After the door closed, Losef turned to the lion. "Your fury does not contribute to effective discussions. No matter what your feelings, I must formally request that you exercise a greater degree of control during our official dealings with Meridian."

The lion scowled, but he knew that Losef was right. "I apologize to Council. I will maintain a calm demeanor in the future."

"Good." She turned to the others. "Comments?"

Van Ostrand shook his head. "Where did that holo come from? How could we have missed something like that?"

Inez looked glum. "It appears that we can't even *detect* aspects of their technology."

Huromonus gave a philosophical shrug.

Losef said, "I'm afraid we must face some unpleasant realities here. It would appear that our worst fears are coming true: we are being confronted by multiple aspects of a superior science." She paused. "We must at least consider the possibility that the Paratwa are undefeatable in a direct confrontation."

"That's nonsense," muttered Van Ostrand. "We've been shown just enough of their so-called superior technology to scare us into accepting whatever terms this Meridian deems to offer us. I wish to state for the record that we cannot simply assume their invincibility without a fight."

"Are you suggesting we attack this Biodyysey?" asked Losef.

"The Paratwa shall be defeated."

The lion frowned. Van Ostrand, even at his most militaristic, usually did not sound quite so imperious.

He suddenly wanted the meeting to be over. Until they knew more, further discussions would be a waste of time. Right now, he wanted desperately to talk with Nick.

The midget possessed an understanding of Paratwa psychology that easily surpassed that of anyone on Council—and probably anyone within the colonies, for that matter. In fact, Nick's presence today might have proved invaluable. But Nick had considered it vital that, at least for the time being, the lion continue with the charade that he was in a coma. And the midget had other priorities.

Freebird—that's where Nick says our real hope lies. The program could well contain secrets that would enable them to defeat the Paratwa. The invaders were not all-powerful. Despite apparent technological superiority, they could be defeated.

The lion sighed, not believing it for a moment. His willingness to grasp at such a fantasy meant only that reality no longer offered reasonable options.

Gillian found himself trying to remember a place he did not know.

Crisp distorted sensations—images—flashed through awareness, like rapidly changing pictures of a distant waterfall, photographed scenes shown one after another, an endless cascade of forward motion. Liquid eruptions from his own past, literally moving too fast to be comprehended.

Empedocles clarified: *The problem is that you are moving too slowly. The images are discrete; this you perceive. But you must look at them more closely. You must look at them from the deepest valley of your own consciousness, from that place where even I cannot go. You must drop down into your own temporal depths, to the landscape where only the creature* Gillian *exists.*

"How?" he wondered, hearing his solitary word multiply itself, echoing and reechoing along a fading tier of amplification, a stone skipped across water until it becomes nothing.

Become nothing, urged his monarch.

Gillian did not know where he was. He could not remember where he had last been. A chain had been broken, continuity destroyed.

It is not important, said his monarch, using a tone that Gillian knew was intended to soothe him, to prevent Gillian's fear from overwhelming awareness, to prevent terror from superseding the lost knowledge of where he existed.

Am I dreaming or am I awake?

Empedocles did not answer. Gillian quickly realized that the question was meaningless. *I am inside myself. That is all that matters.*

He sensed pleasure within Empedocles; Gillian's correct assessment of his situation produced satisfaction within his monarch.

You must enter the deepest valley of your own perception. It is a place where I can neither lead nor follow. You must go alone.

Gillian stared into the cascading images, trying to see through them, or beyond them.

Slow yourself. Perceive the spaces, the separations.

He glazed at them more closely, but they seemed only to move faster, become more incomprehensible. So he tried the opposite tack, deliberately focusing his attention away from them, allowing the streaming pictures to be glimpsed only through peripheral awareness.

It worked. The simulacra slowed. He still could not make out what each individual image represented, but he began to perceive the spaces separating them. Each distinct image possessed a shadow; each casting of light carried with it an equivalent slab of darkness.

Light . . . shadow . . . light. . . . Ad infinitum.

And the shadows seemed to be pointing away from the illuminated images. That was important. Darkness lay at right angles to the light.

For a moment, he considered that he was going mad, that he had become lost in some sort of obverse consciousness, a conceptual rhythm completely at odds with his established intellectual norm. Nothing made sense. Nothing could be understood.

Yes, urged his monarch, willing him to follow that line of reasoning. *Nothing can be understood.*

Insight blundered into truth; in a flash, he knew what the images and the shadows represented; he knew precisely why he could not comprehend their nature. Empedocles's assessment was correct. The images came from Gillian's own prenatal awareness, from a time before intellectual conceptualization was possible: icons of pure perception, predating the ascension of his logical mind. Back then, his only referential context was the pictorial stream itself, the endless flow of images, the slip of light and shadow across a mental pathway too primitive to grasp anything beyond the simple rhythm of the flow itself: shadow . . . light . . . shadow . . .

But now he understood. *I am seeing my own earliest representation of what it means to be a Paratwa.*

Here was the binary coagulation, the endless dervish of forward movement that linked him and Catharine. Here was his own primordial vision of the interlace—the two-way waltz—the alternation of light and shadow that, when properly aligned, made possible the existence of their monarch Empedocles.

I am the light. Catharine is the shadow. Two entities, telepathically interlaced, spatially phased ninety degrees apart, like twin compass needles forever spinning, forever perpendicular, always together and always apart.

And from Catharine's perspective, *she* would be the light, and Gillian the shadow. From Catharine's perspective, *he* existed ninety degrees off center.

But Catharine was dead. She had no perspective.

The pain began as a dull ache in the pit of his stomach, grew quickly into a mass of unpleasant ripples somewhere beneath the level of existence that he defined as flesh. An inner world of electric currents aligned themselves, creating subliminal havoc, forcing his body to react.

A full-body spasm bolted him upright.

Catharine is dead.

He corralled the pain, controlled it, repressed it, made it return to the shadows from which it had arisen.

He was seated on a small cot in a tiny hexagonal room with warm golden walls and no windows. Recognition came. It was the meditation chamber located in Thi Maloca, the Brazilian Ash Ock base where he and Catharine—and the others of their breed—had been created. The meditation chamber was the place where he and Catharine usually retreated when they needed to close themselves off from the demands of their highly structured world. It was a place reserved for them alone. It was the place where they usually made love.

The light and the shadow, whispered Empedocles. *Focus on those aspects. Consider the fact that both still exist. Consider the fact that the shape and essence of the interlace has not changed. It remains intact.*

Anger came over Gillian. Of course the interlace was intact. If it had not been intact, his monarch would no longer be here to torment him.

Remember the nature of what has been lost, urged Empedocles. *Remember what it means to be truly a part of the whole. Remember a time of no anger, no guilt—when you were of the Ash Ock.*

Gillian tried. But he could only recall the bitterness and longing, the smashed fulcrum, the crescendo of loss.

Empedocles went on. *I am alive. You are alive. Catharine is gone, but the capacity of the triumvirate can be restored. I never realized that such a thing was possible, but now I know the truth. This tway of Aristotle—this pale remnant of departed majesty—can actually help us reverse the terminal disease of our arrhythmia. This Timmy can bring us back.*

Gillian thought about it for a while, concluded that it remained a fantasy, a dream born of desperation. *If restoration is really possible, why hadn't Aristotle's tway restored himself?*

Maybe he could not. Maybe it was too late for him. But such questions are not important. We will learn the truth of him eventually. For now, all that is of consequence is that Timmy can bring us back. We can be whole.

How do you know? How do you know he is not lying to us?

Empedocles writhed with excitement. Gillian sensed the emotion as a deep tickling; feathery strokes on the inside of his skin.

Can't you feel it? cried his monarch. *This place! It is like nowhere we have ever been!*

Gillian frowned. He got up from the cot and gazed serenely at the soft golden walls, at the security of this hexagonal chamber. *This is our meditation chamber. We've been here many times. . . .* He stopped, suddenly aware that something was terribly wrong.

I can't be in the meditation chamber. It's gone, destroyed centuries ago. Following the raid that had killed Catharine, E-Tech had subjected Thi Maloca to nuclear annihilation.

"Where am I?" he demanded, no longer trusting in his private dialogue with Empedocles to provide truthful answers. He moved to the nearest section of wall, reached out to touch it. His hand passed right through the golden partition as if nothing was there.

"It must be another holo," he whispered, feeling cheated.

"Awake," uttered a voice.

Gillian awoke. He was still lying on his back, but within some weird darkened place—a wide curving tube with light glimmering at both ends. Timmy stood quietly beside his bed.

Gillian tried to sit up, discovered that he could not. His muscles were so weak that he could not even raise his arms.

"Is this real?" he asked.

"Another form of reality," Timmy explained, the fat face leering over him, full of amusement, full of itself. "But to answer your question with the digital precision you demand:

Yes, this is real. This is reality as you have been accustomed to defining it."

"Why can't I move?"

Timmy stared. "You don't remember?"

Gillian shook his head. Even that slight motion took an extraordinary effort. "Yes. Now I remember . . . you asked me to take off my suit . . . to follow you through . . . a wall. . . . We came to this place."

Recollection bred recollection. It had been Empedocles who had urged Gillian to obey Timmy's instructions. "You gave me something . . . an injection. . . ."

"An infusion," clarified Timmy. "It was a decelerative drug, containing a soporific. It was spread on a neuropad, which I laid across your brow. A direct injection of this particular enhancer would have been instantly fatal."

"Yes! A drug that enhanced my abilities to perceive the interlace!" Gillian shook his head again; this time the movement came easier. He was beginning to feel stronger, in control again . . . at least in control of his memories.

Timmy asked, "You saw the interlace?"

"Yes. And I dreamed . . . about Thi Maloca. . . . I was in the meditation chamber."

"A not surprising side effect of the drug. It is understandable that as your consciousness focused upon the interlace, your subconscious invoked visions of a place that had been pleasant for you and Catharine."

"We were there when E-Tech raided the facility," Gillian murmured. "That chamber was the last place where Catharine and I saw each other as individual tways."

"I did not know that," said Timmy, looking sad.

Gillian forced himself up on his elbows. "Empedocles . . . I can barely feel him now. But his presence was very strong while I was asleep."

"He will be strong again," promised Timmy.

"My monarch said something . . . about *this* place. He said: 'Can't you feel it?' He was very excited. What did he mean?"

Timmy turned away. When he finally spoke, his voice carried a solemnity worthy of any Church of the Trust recruiter.

"All of the Earth and all of the Colonies—this entire sector of space, this *kascht*—it reeks of the lacking. But here within this cell of the Os/Ka/Loq . . . here, there is no such defect. Here, the purities are maintained.

"Your monarch boasts a sensory capacity beyond your own. Empedocles feels the restorative potency of this cell."

Gillian did not understand. But before he could question Timmy further, a hint of movement focused attention. From one end of the weird tubular room, shadows danced across the pale bluish light. Someone was coming.

Susan rounded the bend and saw him for the first time, stripped of his protective suit, naked and alert, a raw slab of a man. In the dim light, sweat shimmered across his flesh. He did not look young and he did not look old; instinctively, she knew that those keen gray eyes had seen places and times far beyond the experiences of her own twenty-six years. She felt her palms tightening on the handles of the flash daggers. But she did not unpocket them.

Timmy stood beside the man, a smile filling his jowled face. "Welcome, Susan. Allow me the pleasure of formal introductions. Gillian, meet Susan Quint. Susan, meet Gillian."

She halted ten feet from the bed.

"Susan Quint?" whispered Gillian, shocked. "You're Inez Hernandez's missing grandniece! You vanished after the Honshu massacre!"

Susan grimaced before she could think to restrain herself. Although she occasionally thought about Aunt Inez, it had seemed like years since anyone had actually spoken to her about her former life.

She found her voice. "Are they still looking for me?"

Gillian nodded, awed into silence. She was more beautiful than Inez's holos had portrayed. Tall. Long-legged. Molded from some patrician form that perhaps once had garnished the walls of an earthly estate. She looked too extraordinary to be a real person. She did not look at all like Catharine, and she looked exactly like Catharine.

Susan felt her fingers tightening on the flash daggers.

"Susan still resists her fate," explained Timmy. "She continues to entertain notions of something she refers to as 'freedom.' She refuses to acknowledge that ultimate freedom is nothing more than the acceptance of our true natures."

Susan knew she could kill both of them, here and now. She could whip out the daggers and strike. Timmy would go down quickly. Gillian was still weakened from the drug infusion. In that state, he would be no match for her speed.

Gillian perceived her intentions and her doubts. "If you're going to attack, then attack." He hesitated. "I know what it means to contain yourself, hold in all that raw energy. But that's a mistake. Choose a path. Follow it."

She had vowed to resist Timmy's mad plans for her. Becoming a tway of a Paratwa ... the very *notion* of it was ludicrous. How could he truly expect her to do such a thing?

But Gillian's words meant something. They were real. He was real. She released her grip on the flash daggers and moved closer to him. Timmy stepped back from the bed, allowed her the intimacy.

This is insane. She reached down and touched his bare arm. His flesh radiated warmth. Her own arm, from fingertips to shoulder, tingled. A scampering parade of delicate images seemed to crest at the corners of his lips.

Gillian felt it too: a heat between them, more intense than the passions of sex, more inclusive, closer in nature to the ancient longings of infancy. It was a base need, flesh touching flesh. He thought of Sasalla, his wet nurse, her sleeping body now contained within the stalagmite prison. He thought of his cribmate, Catharine, the cherubic smile on her tiny elfin face, her hands patting and touching him.

Catharine.

Full-body flush.

Gillian reached out. He drew Susan down onto him, pulled her mouth close to his. She began to cry. Warm tears spilled onto his hands.

"Cry," he whispered. "Cry for what was lost."

Susan tried one last time to turn away, succeeded in pivoting her head just far enough to see that Timmy was gone. She was alone with Gillian. She was together with him.

From the depths of Gillian's consciousness, Empedocles

projected his blessing; soothing thoughts poured across a waterfall of endless desire.

It is the algorithm of rediscovery, the process of rebirth. Today, in the sanctity of this cell of the Os/Ka/Loq, we begin our return.

Irrya fell rapidly into the darkness, the Colony shrinking in perspective, homeland warmth dissipating, the village consumed until it became a mere shell, sharply etched against the cloak of night. The lion, observing the transformation from the flight deck window, found himself wondering how something that had recently felt so real and solid could be abruptly rendered insignificant.

It was bewildering.

The rapid loss of gravity as the shuttle dropped away from the Capitol also contributed to his growing sense of unease. Yet he could only indirectly fathom why today's deorbital was affecting him so. He had shuttled out from Colonies countless times in the past half century. It was a simple routine, one that begged to go unnoticed.

I'm tired. That explains it. Today's Council meeting, following Meridian's departure, had been long and tedious. But his own retort sounded whimsical, unconvincing. He continued to observe the scene through the forward portal, hoping for comprehension.

The growth of a spacescape: from the human scale of the docking terminal to the widening arc of a land sector seen from the outside—a sliver of dirty white metal pinched between encroaching ribbons of glimmering cosmishield glass. And then the Capitol was stretching itself out, yawning into a seventy-mile-long cylinder, becoming a thing beyond even the mere technological—a fallopian tube with one end aimed at the Earth and the other at the stars, transferring its seeds from past to future.

Seeds from past to future. That was important. Perhaps someday those seeds would be returned to the planet, to the lands and oceans from which they had first arisen. But even as he acknowledged such a hope, he feared it could never happen. The Earth was gone. Forever.

He now recognized that this visual metamorphosis, this falling away from home, offered yet another effigy to his altar of foreboding. *How can we repel an invading force that most certainly possesses technology centuries ahead of our own? How can the Colonies hope to fight an enemy who has returned in a single starship larger than all of the cylinders combined?*

His guts began to ache again. He forced himself to ignore the pain, determined to avoid the use of yet another needle pad.

I'm at war with myself.

The thought brought to mind an event from ages ago, when he had first arrived in the Costeau Colony of Den, in the company of his mother. It had been shortly after she had told him the true story of his dead father; the man whom the twelve-year-old Jerem Marth had never known. In the heat of an argument, she had related what his real father had been like: an opium-addicted smuggler, a pirate thief, a Costeau rejected even by his own clan.

He had not been able to accept his mother's portrait. In a fit, he had lashed out at her. She had lashed back, her own pain triggered by his bitterness. Out of control, full parental fury unleashed, she had hit him.

That event had caused him to run away.

It's the same feelings I suffer from today, the same overwhelming discord of repressed emotions that temporarily drove me away from my mother fifty-six years ago.

In both instances, he had been faced with circumstances beyond his abilities to control. In both cases, he had sought to escape from his feelings. As the child Jerem Marth, that escape had been, of necessity, literal—a wild flight to Sirak-Brath. But as the lion of Alexander, evasion now assumed the more subtle cloak of adult denial.

His shuttle companion spared him from further introspection. "I need that course data now."

The lion withdrew his attention from the receding cylinder and turned to Vilakoz, who sat in the adjacent pilot's seat. The lion handed his security chief a tiny data brick. Vilakoz snapped it into a receptacle, frowned as the monitor translated.

"This heading and coordinates take us into an empty sector. Is this a rendezvous?"

"Yes," said the lion. "A rendezvous."

Vilakoz stared at him for a moment, waiting for more information. When the lion remained silent, the towering pilot turned back to his controls.

A good man, thought the lion. Vilakoz had not inquired about why they were only ones aboard the craft; normally, the Alexanders utilized five-person crews. The security chief knew when to keep his mouth shut, when to accept unspecified parameters.

Vilakoz was a lucky man, too, according to his doctors. He still carried a set of thick diagonal scars across the bridge of his nose where the medics had performed restructuring. Vilakoz's facial encounter with the tripartite assassin's energized attack gauntlet had come perilously close to being fatal: another inch or so upward and the force of the blow might have caused brain damage.

The lion, however, knew that luck had not been a factor. The tripartite assassin did not rely on chance. It had needed Vilakoz alive to effect its escape from the Alexanders' retreat. The security chief's survival had simply been another aspect of the plan.

The lion did not want to dwell further on such matters. "Have you picked up any signs that we're being followed? Anomalies that might indicate long-range tracking?"

"We're alone. No other vessels in the neighborhood and no shadows."

The lion nodded. "I'm going to take a nap." He manually adjusted his acceleration couch into its hard-G contour, more suitable for sleeping. "Wake me up as soon as we arrive at the coordinates."

"Dream the dreams of Ari," murmured Vilakoz.

Become whole, the lion instantly translated. It was an ancient Costeau expression, a cross-cultural idiom used by many of the major clans. Ari Alexander, the first lion, had been one of the founding fathers of the Costeau movement.

He fell back into the softness of the couch, but he did not dream the dreams of Ari. Instead, he drifted immediately into a weird realm of consciousness barely distinguishable from that state he considered definitive of the waking world. Within this phantasma, hundreds of the Irryan Colonies began to slowly emerge from his abdomen in a grotesque mimicry of birth, a labor of terrifying proportions.

The illusion thankfully departed when the lion slipped into a deeper place, where pleasure and pain merged, where all images and thoughts condensed into one vast extrusion of ancient stone, poised on the periphery of a great abyss.

He awoke to someone squeezing his arm, shaking him gently, and for a few precious moments he thought it was his wife, Mela, priming him for a new day. The fantasy dissolved, palpable sensations driving it back to a netherworld of desire. Vilakoz appeared in its place.

"We're here," announced the pilot.

Mela remained at their true home, in the Costeau Colony of Den. Until recently, the lion had shuttled there regularly—at least twice a week. But the turmoil of the past few months had put an end to his frequent homecomings. Although they communicated every day, the lion badly missed the primacy of her touch. It had been nearly three weeks since they had last been together. Mela gladly would have made the journey to Irrya. But the lion insisted she remain within the sanctity of their ancestral home.

She would be safer there.

Vilakoz extended a weightless arm in front of his face, aimed a finger at the window. "Up there, about sixty degrees. That bright reddish light is a repo freighter with Sirak-Brath registry. ID blip says they're on a four-colony hop, picking up industrial wastes for recycling back at 'Brath." The security chief paused. "Is that our rendezvous?"

The lion wiped the last trace of slumber from his eyes and nodded. "Blip them our code and prepare to dock."

Five minutes later, Vilakoz had matched velocities with the massive freighter. When they had closed to within a thousand feet, a group of eight frau clams—miniature robotic tugs—shot from the midsection of the transport, their orange and lemon trajectory lights blinking madly, like a swarm of angry fireflies. The tugs dove beneath the shuttle to plant friction hooks along its underbelly. Vilakoz easily could have docked without the frau clams, but most of the big corporate freighters refused to risk even the slightest possibility for error that an unknown, and possibly inexperienced, shuttle pilot might bring to a berthing.

The freighter transmitted a command, and Vilakoz obliged by shutting down the shuttle's primary engines. The frau clam octet guided them toward a circular opening at the freighter's rear. A moment later, the transport swallowed them whole.

The lion unstrapped his weightless body from the couch and pushed off toward the gripboard leading to the main rear airlock. Vilakoz prepared to follow.

"No," said the lion, shaking his head. "I need you to remain on board. I'm to go alone."

Edward Huromonus was the one responsible for this rendezvous, and the E-Tech Director's security precautions bordered on the paranoid. The lion had been asked to depart from Irrya using an undisclosed flight plan and with an absolutely minimal crew. Upon docking, only the lion would be permitted to leave his shuttle and enter the transport. Huromonus had been unwilling to offer even a token explanation for the secrecy, revealing only that a matter vital to the security of the Colonies was at stake.

The lion waited impatiently in the air lock for several minutes while a generated voice informed him that slight pressure differentials were being equalized. But he knew that such a simple task should not be taking so long. There must be another reason for the inordinate delay.

Finally, the lock went green and the seal slid open, revealing a grimy but spacious and well-lit corridor. One small man stood across the threshold. He wore a white bio suit. The helmet was flipped back, revealing a pale but cheery face.

"Howdy," said Nick.

The lion's shock was genuine. "What are you doing here?"

"That's a hell of a greeting. I thought you'd be happy to see me."

"Did Huromonus call you too?" asked the lion, realizing as he asked the question that such a possibility made no sense. Only the lion and a handful of trusted clan members knew that the midget was not in a coma. "You were supposed to remain in Den. What the hell is going on?"

"More big trouble, I'm afraid. Come on. Our host is waiting to explain everything." Nick pointed to a storage locker. "You gotta wear one of these zoot suits. Biohazards are a *very* big concern around here."

The lion entered the freighter, being careful to maintain alternating heel contact with the friction deck. He managed to contain his abundance of questions while he squirmed into the garment.

With helmets sealed, they proceeded to the end of the short corridor. There was another lengthy wait while a shiny air sampler mounted above the closed portal scanned for contamination. The lion glanced back at the lock leading to his shuttle. A second air sampler had been mounted there, which explained why it had taken so long for his own airlock to open.

"Retrofitted through this whole freighter," Nick explained.

A plague ship? wondered the lion.

They passed through two more secured portals before arriving in a small compartment jammed with assorted monitoring equipment, most of which also looked new. Edward Huromonus stood poised at a console. Beside him was a slim white-haired woman in a knee-length medical smock.

"You can remove your zoots," said Huromonus. "It's safe in here."

As they peeled away their bio suits, Huromonus introduced the woman. "This is Doctor Joan Opal. She is a molecular pathogeneticist, employed by E-Tech. Joan?"

The doctor pointed to a large monitor showing a slightly

elevated fisheye view into a room severely damaged by an explosion. Three bodies could be seen protruding from the tangled wreckage.

In a calm professional tone, she began. "You're looking at this freighter's primary hazcon—hazardous contamination chamber—located three decks below us. It is used by the repo crew to check out any category Three biohazards that might be picked up at one of their stops."

The lion nodded. E-Tech laws required any material so classified to undergo testing and examination before a freighter would be permitted to dock at another Colony. Such regulations were still vigorously enforced, even now, hundreds of years after the Apocalypse, when they had first come into being.

Doctor Opal continued. "A small suitcase, approximately eighteen inches by twelve inches, with a burnished bronze surface, was one of a number of items that the hazcon team brought here for examination. A standard external check provided no clue about its contents. Ultra/x-ray/tilsus readers were employed next. According to the report, those methods also were unable to penetrate the suitcase."

The lion frowned. "Is that possible?" Certainly the penetrative rays of a tilsus reader should have been able to peer through the thin walls of a suitcase.

"The hazcon team also was perturbed by their lack of results," said Doctor Opal. A scowl crossed her face. "But at that point, instead of following procedure and calling E-Tech, they attempted to open the suitcase themselves."

"A fatal mistake," added Huromonus. "Those are their remains you are seeing."

Doctor Opal went on. "They apparently had some trouble opening it. It took the three of them almost an hour. We don't know precisely what happened at this stage of events. By now, since they were guilty of a technical violation of E-Tech regulations, they understandably did not want themselves recorded. They tanned the strip—reported a 'glitch' in the surveillance system. A/V recording was lost, with the exception of a few audio conversations with the freighter's captain."

The lion nodded. He could not actually fault the hazcon team. The vast E-Tech bureaucracy generated incredibly complex rules and regulations. Captains and pilots across the commercial spectrum frequently bypassed what they perceived as inordinate amounts of red tape.

Nick added, "When they did manage to get the suitcase open, it blew up."

"They were killed instantly," said Huromonus. "We suspect the charge was of a type similar to that used in geo cannons."

Doctor Opal concurred. "They did follow *some* aspects of standard procedure. All three of them activated crescent webs. Had the explosion come from a normal charge, the cushioning effects of the webs may have spared their lives . . . at least momentarily."

The lion thought back to the massacre at the retreat, where a geo cannon was assumed to have been used by the tripartite.

"The intensity of the explosion ruptured the security of the hazcon. A deadly aerobic virus was apparently contained within the suitcase. It got into the main air system before the captain was able to initiate proper emergency measures." Doctor Opal scowled again, obviously distressed by what she perceived as flagrant incompetence on the part of this captain and undisciplined crew. "The freighter had twenty-six men and women aboard. There were two survivors, who were lucky enough to be out on the hull doing routine maintenance. When they reentered the vessel, they found a dead crew. Fortunately, the pair were smart enough to remain in their spacesuits. The blipped an SOS straight to E-Tech."

"This all happened about seven hours ago," said Huromonus. "Joan and her people got here quickly. They set up their detection gear and managed to detoxify several compartments. The freighter has been classified Biohazard Five—our worst-case designation."

The lion turned to Nick. "And how did you get here?"

The midget shrugged. "You know me well enough by now. I couldn't just sit passively in Den, waiting for the Ash Ock to decide my fate. I called Eddie here and spilled my guts. The whole shebang—everything we know so far. I told him what I felt needed to be done. He sent a shuttle to pick me up. Coincidentally, this mess occurred right after I left your home Colony. Eddie passed along info about the accident and it sounded important. I asked to be brought here." Nick paused. "I requested that he bring you here also, as quickly and as secretly as possible."

The lion sighed. Nick should have obeyed orders.

The midget attempted a half-hearted grin. "Hey, ya can't keep an old manipulator like me out of the mainstream! I like to go with the flow, see where it's going."

Huromonus, studying the lion's face, said: "Blame me for these events."

The lion blamed himself. "So this exploding suitcase contained a plague virus. And I assume that there's a connection with the Paratwa."

Doctor Opal's eyes widened. She had not been briefed on that aspect.

"Joan, welcome to the big-time," chortled Nick. "Now why don't you tell the lion just how our exploding suitcase was found."

"Of course." She cleared her throat. "This freighter visited the Colony of Toulouse. That's one of the cylinders that still utilizes old-fashioned recycling towers for waste disposal. They believe in promoting active citizen involvement in the recycling process. It's a good practice, one that I wish more Colonies would follow. E-Tech would have a lot less trouble enforcing the sanitation laws—"

"The suitcase, doctor," Huromonus gently chided.

"Yes, I'm sorry. Now the E-Tech sanitation laws require that these recycling towers be cleaned out every five years, recoated with chemobiotics, the irradiators scrubbed, et cetera, et cetera. This suitcase was found in a category Three biohazard chute in the Au Fait Recycling Towers—in a six-week turnover shaft. The location of the suitcase within the chute indicated that it had probably been there for over five weeks. Another few days and it would have reached the incinerators and probably been rendered harmless."

"Or," interjected Nick, "it would have been remotely triggered to explode *before* it reached the incinerators, thereby rupturing the security of the recycling tower and spreading this killer virus into the Colony's atmosphere."

Doctor Opal nodded. "Gauging by the force of the explosion that occurred here, that scenario was a distinct possibility. Unfortunately, our society does not consider category Three biohazards dangerous enough to warrant serious containment." She scowled again, displeased at such laxity.

"At any rate, the cleanup crew, as per their contract, removed all waste matter from inside the Au Fait Towers and transported it to this freighter."

"Tell us about the virus," urged Huromonus.

"It's an aerobic mutagen, absolutely the deadliest one I've ever seen. At close range, one whiff of air tainted with this virus would kill any mammal within a matter of minutes. Even diluted to nearly undetectable levels, the virus would prove fatal to every human who breathed it. They would die within days." She paused. "Had the contents of this suitcase been released from the Au Fait Recycling Towers in Toulouse, it would be a safe bet to say that the cylinder's normal ground-level sweep currents, coupled with spin-rate Coriolis deflection, would have spread the virus through the Colony in a matter of hours. Unalerted to its presence, the projected fatality rate could have been upward of ninety-five percent. A few survivors in the bowels of the docking terminals perhaps, and at the ends of the Colony, where people might have received enough warning to don protective suits."

The lion stared at the monitor, at the three corpses in the hazcon chamber. "We were very fortunate it happened here, out in space."

"Yeah, a lucky break," said Nick, grimacing.

Doctor Opal continued. "The virus, once inhaled, initially induces an acute multiplicative infection of the upper respiratory tract. Delirium, headaches, and muscle pain are the other early symptoms. But the fever is the real killer, Core body temperature is quickly elevated to the range of forty-six to forty-nine degrees centigrade. The victim literally burns up. Comatosity ensues at this stage. Death occurs a short time later. And even after death, the virus keeps ravaging the body. Metastasis, primarily by way of the lymphatic system and the bloodstream, continues almost relentlessly." She shook her head. "This virus possesses a pathogenicity that is stunning in its ruthlessness. In fact, I cannot conceive of such a mutagen arising from natural genetic processes. I have no doubt whatsoever that we're dealing with a designed microorganism."

Nick jumped in. "But wait till you hear the worst part of all this. It turns out that over five weeks ago, at the time this suitcase was believed to have been placed in the recycling chute, a man committed suicide by jumping off the top of the tower. His name was Philippe Boisset, and until the moment he killed himself, he was considered to be a stable, functional individual. I'll give you one guess about where Mister Boisset had been just about twelve hours before he killed himself."

"In Irrya," whispered the lion. "At Venus Cluster."

"Bingo."

The lion sat down on the edge of the console, almost overwhelmed by the sudden rush of comprehension. Venus Cluster—the secretly owned corporation that had served as the front for one of the tways of the tripartite assassin, until Gillian, Martha, and Buff had stumbled into the deadly mess. Here was the missing connection. Here was the reason behind the so-called Order of the Birch massacres, going on for these many months.

"Couriers," said Nick. "That's who the intended victims of these massacres must have been. They were couriers, manipulated into carrying these infected suitcases back to their home colonies, hiding them in who knows how many secret locations. And then each courier was killed, either tricked into showing up at the site of a massacre, murdered individually, or forced to commit suicide."

Doctor Opal looked shocked. "The Paratwa are responsible for spreading this virus? To every Colony?"

"We believe so," answered Nick. "This looks like their handiwork."

Huromonus nodded. "Joan, I know that you are already quite aware of the security elements involved in this situation, but I now feel obligated to reiterate that what we are discussing here is to go no farther than this room."

She nodded vigorously. "Of course."

"It's gotta be a needbreeder," said Nick. "That's what this tway—Slasher at Venus Cluster—must have been using to trick all of these couriers into following his commands. Probably hundreds of innocent men and women, carefully selected by the Paratwa ultimately to spread this threat throughout the cylinders. Men and women chosen on the basis of their impressionability to the effects of the needbreeder, brought to Venus Cluster, hypnotized, given a viral-infected suitcase, sent back to their home Colonies to hide the suitcases, and then on to their respective rendezvous with the assassin. A few individuals who were especially susceptible to the effects of the needbreeder, like this Philippe Boisset must have been, could be disposed of in a simpler manner. The ultimate manipulation—persuaded into taking your own life."

Huromonus spoke calmly. "We must assume that this virus has been hidden in almost every Colony, if not all two hundred and seventeen of them."

"Bet on it," said Nick. "And I suspect that nothing less than pure dumb luck led to the events aboard this freighter, although I'm not sure that such luck is actually going to do *us* much good. But it seems obvious to me that since this suitcase was deliberately hidden in a six-week disposal chute, at the end of that six-week period the incineration of the suitcase would have served to destroy the virus before it could spread throughout Toulouse. Therefore, it's very possible that this suitcase was going to be remotely triggered *before* it reached the incinerators. We may have only a few days left to us before all hell is scheduled to break loose."

The lion turned to Doctor Opal. "Any possible antidotes within that time?"

"Not a chance. This sort of virus is extremely difficult, if not impossible, to counter. It's a true ecomutater—able to constantly adapt its viral coat in order to bind to a wide range of receptor molecules on the surface of the cells. Such an ability necessitates a multifaceted approach in developing a cure." She sighed. "My E-Tech lab is one of the finest in the Colonies, but I'd need six months just to map out the variations. Even then, I couldn't promise anything. I'm not even certain that the heights of pre-Apocalyptic science could have coped with such a malignant invader."

"Many of the victims of the massacres had minor viral infections," said the lion. "Was that the same virus we're dealing with now?"

"I believe so," said Doctor Opal. "Nick and Director Huromonus have provided me with some of your earlier data concerning these infected victims, although until now I was not aware of just how these victims had perished. Be that as it may, my best guess is that our virus possesses multiple developmental stages. In its earliest variations, it would seem to resemble a variant of Type C influenza. Only in its later stages, within a living human body, would it mutate into the deadlier permutation."

The lion was puzzled. "How would the intended victims of the massacres—these couriers—have contracted this virus? It sounds like they must have opened the suitcases."

"That would be my best guess," said Doctor Opal. "They opened the suitcases and were thus exposed."

Nick agreed. "We think that there was some sort of testing procedure that each courier had to perform to make certain these viral bombs were properly activated. In fact, that could explain why the Paratwa utilized such a complex plan for contaminating the Colonies in the first place. Our nasty Ash Nar assassin could not simply hide the suitcases himself; he could not expose himself to viral contamination during the testing procedure. Therefore, there had to be multiple victims, each one tricked—needbreeder hypnotized—into planting a suitcase in a secret location and then conveniently committing suicide . . . or arranging to rendezvous with the tripartite just in time for a massacre."

Doctor Opal nodded. "If these couriers, each of whom were likely contaminated during the testing procedure, had *not* died within a few days of initial exposure, the viruses in their bodies would have begun to mutate into lethal configurations. Only the couriers' deaths prevented this from occurring. The viruses remained in their milder forms and did not develop into their pandemic mode."

"A typical Ash Ock plan," said Nick, "accomplishing multiple objectives. These couriers are killed not only to prevent them from spreading the virus but to prevent anyone from learning where the various suitcases were hidden."

"Once a colony was exposed," asked the lion, "would there be any hope for a rapid decontamination?"

Doctor Opal's attention drifted back to the large monitor, to the fisheye view of hazcon destruction. For the first time, she seemed truly struck by the magnitude of what they were facing. "I'm not even certain a Colony *could* be fully decontaminated," she said quietly, "at least not one hundred percent. For starters, a cylinder's entire atmosphere would have to be flushed. Then we'd have to send teams in to search for hot spots—areas where the aerobic mutagen managed to find other suitable host cultures. At best, it would be a long and tedious process."

They were silent for a moment. To the lion, the ramifications of the virus seemed to slam shut a final door. *It's hopeless. We've lost. The Ash Ock defeated us a long time ago, but we just didn't know it until now.* Despite his feelings, he forced himself to continue. "Any chance of locating these suitcases within the next few days?"

Nick shook his head wearily. "We can try. We might find some of them by tracing the steps of the massacre victims known to have had mild infections. But statistically, I doubt whether we'd be able to locate more than a handful of the suitcases. These viral bombs were hidden by hundreds of different people, all of whom are dead. And even if we somehow captured the tripartite assassin, I doubt we could persuade him to talk."

"And you see no possibility with Meridian," concluded Huromonus, in a tone that suggested he and Nick had already discussed that scenario.

The midget shrugged. "I'd torture the bastard myself if I thought it would help. But the Ash Ock probably would not have given Meridian's tways such specific information."

The lion asked, "Have any other Council members been made aware of this situation?"

For a moment, Huromonus was silent. Then he turned to Doctor Opal. "Joan, would you mind leaving us?"

"Of course," she said, unable to hide her disappointment at being precluded at this stage of their discussion. She hoisted a large ingress from the console, strapped it over her shoulder, and departed from the compartment. Huromonus waited until the door had resealed before continuing.

"Nick and I wanted you brought here to learn of this situation because we fear that if any word leaks out, the degree of intercolonial panic could be immeasurable. So far, no one who is aware of the virus has been permitted to leave this freighter."

"That sounds merely like a postponement of the inevitable," said the lion. "If the Paratwa intend to release this plague within a few days . . ." He trailed off with a shrug.

"Your point it well taken. But we believe that the Paratwa do not actually want to trigger these viral bombs. We think that Meridian, at our next Council meeting in two days, will use the threat of releasing the virus as a bargaining point."

The lion released a bitter laugh. "That's one hell of a bargaining point. More like, 'Do as we say or you're dead!'"

Huromonus and Nick exchanged frowns. The lion understood the meaning of their expressions.

Nick stared at him. "You think we've already lost, huh? The Paratwa can't be beaten."

"Not in the long run."

Huromonus, in an utterly placid voice, asked, "What do you propose that we do?"

The lion sighed. "I don't know. It's their move, I suppose. We'll have to wait and see."

"Fuck that," growled Nick. "I'm not waiting, and I sure as hell don't intend to give up. Remember what we talked about a couple of weeks ago? I told you that I could never live under their domain, and you said you felt the same way."

"We may have no choice."

A flush of anger colored the midget's face.

Huromonus held up his hand. "There's an additional complication to all of this. Doyle Blumhaven, my late predecessor, had a way of making crucial information disappear. Since Doyle first put me in charge of the action/probe, one of my personal goals has been the reassimilation of such misplaced data.

"As you know, the Irryan Council has traditionally charged E-Tech with the task of running detailed security checks on all individuals who were being considered for appointment to the Council."

The lion recalled his own security check, some two-and-a-half years ago. Doyle's people had searched vigorously—some of his fellow Costeaus had claimed *too* vigorously—for any undisclosed data in the lion's past that might have cast disparagement on his goals of becoming the first clan representative to Council.

Huromonus went on. "About eight years ago, Jon Van Ostrand underwent such a security check. But it turns out that the report on our Guardian Commander suffered certain deletions before it was turned over to the Council for consideration."

"Deletions?"

"In the official version, Jon Van Ostrand freely admitted to having several friends and associates who were members of the Order of the Birch. This was not exactly an unexpected revelation. A group that espouses war as the only practical solution to dealing with the returning Paratwa naturally would be expected to have at least some support within the military. Van Ostrand, a career officer, probably could not help but know some Birch idealists.

"But the portions of the security report that were *not* handed over to Council—the portions Doyle Blumhaven chose to delete—cast a very different light on Jon Van Ostrand's connections with the Order of the Birch.

"According to these undisclosed portions of the report, which I recently uncovered, Jon Van Ostrand possessed more than just a passing relationship with the Order of the Birch. He was, in fact, an active member within one of the Birch's more secretive factions . . . a faction known to be dedicated to the complete destruction of the Paratwa."

The lion frowned. "Are you sure?" It was difficult to accept that Van Ostrand could have kept such unwholesome connections hidden from the Council.

"I am certain. Jon Van Ostrand, Supreme Commander of the Intercolonial Guardians, the man in charge of our entire defense network, is a Birch hard-liner."

The lion shook his head, troubled by the very idea. "Are you sure your information is up-to-date? After eight years of serving as a Councillor, Jon's belief may have mellowed."

Nick's cheeks sagged, pulled downward by a deep frown.

Huromonus shrugged. "Possible, of course. But my legal experience in dealing with fanatics has led me to conclude that the genuine variety—dedicated zealots of Van Ostrand's ilk—are rarely tempered by age. Over time, such people merely develop greater abilities to hide their ... enthusiasms."

"Why would Blumhaven want someone like Van Ostrand to be the Guardian Commander?" wondered the lion.

"Why, indeed?" replied Huromonus. "For it's now very clear that Blumhaven had been under Paratwa dominion for a long time. My predecessor was almost certainly responsible for the inputting of the sunsetter twenty-two years ago. And more recently, as well as ordering the raid on your retreat, Doyle made the arrangements for the raiders to rendezvous with the so-called ICN observers—which turned out to be the assassin."

"This makes no sense at all," said Nick, still scowling. "I mean, we've already got a shitload of circumstantial evidence linking Doyle Blumhaven to the Paratwa. Assuming that Blumhaven was an Ash Ock errand boy, why would our enemies want him to arrange for an authentic gung-ho "kill-all-the-Paratwa" freak to be put in charge of the whole damn defense net?"

"Maybe in this instance," suggested the lion, "Doyle was acting from his own conscience. Maybe the Paratwa didn't know anything about the Van Ostrand appointment."

Nick gave a grim chuckle. "No way. The Ash Ock would never have missed something that critical. They certainly would have had more than a passing interest in any individual being considered to oversee the entire Colonial war machine."

"Agreed," said Huromonus.

"So where does that leave us?" asked the lion.

"I don't know," muttered Nick.

"Let's examine this entire situation from the beginning," proposed Huromonus. "Eight years ago, Doyle Blumhaven discovers the true nature of Van Ostrand's radical connections. And he provides this information to his Paratwa masters. But the Paratwa, instead of letting Blumhaven simply hand in the report to the Irryan Council, which from their perspective would appear to be the sensible thing to do, order Doyle to remove just enough data to allow Van Ostrand to achieve passing grades."

"With you so far," said the midget. The lion nodded.

Huromonus continued. "So Van Ostrand becomes an Irryan Councillor. And for eight years he functions in this capacity."

"More like seven and a half years," corrected the lion. "Frankly, since Jon left Irrya six months ago to be with his troops, he seems to have severely blunted his effectiveness as a Councillor—"

"Hold it," said Nick. "Van Ostrand's been gone for six months?"

"Yes."

"Son of a bitch," said the midget. "And when was the first Order of the Birch massacre?"

"About five months ago."

It was Huromonus's turn to frown. "What are you implying?"

Nick spun to face the lion. "You say that Van Ostrand's not been as effective a Councillor in recent months?"

"That's right. Jon's not always within reach of the FTL. Often he misses meetings, or portions of meetings." The lion shrugged. "His priorities are different from those of the rest of us. Obviously, with two million troops and a massive armada to command, he is kept very busy—"

"He left Irrya six months ago," said Nick, "in order to establish his operational base out beyond Jupiter. And he left just about one month *before* the first of the so-called Order of the Birch massacres occurred."

The lion hesitated. "What's the connection?"

"Follow me here for a moment. Let's assume we're on the right track. Let's assume that, for reasons unknown, the Paratwa want someone like Van Ostrand in charge of the defense net. This is a very important facet of their plans. They want someone in command who will need very little provocation to attack them.

"But there are five members of the Irryan Council. Van Ostrand, in order to attack, would, at least legally, require the support of two other Councillors. But what if Van Ostrand is allowed to command his mighty navy not from the distant Council chambers but from an op-base satellite closer to the battlefield? What if he's permitted to function in the manner of a field commander? Given our Guardian Commander's Birch background, would it not seem more likely that in a situation where all hope would appear to be lost, Van Ostrand's impulse would be to attack that monster spaceship with everything he's got? And to hell with civilian control—to hell with whatever the faraway Council of Irrya decided?"

The lion nodded slowly. "I suppose that makes sense."

"Okay. So the next step in our convoluted Ash Ock plan is to get Van Ostrand out there. He must be convinced to leave Council chambers, make the journey out past Jupiter, and once there, plan on *staying*. Concurrently, the Ash Ock are preparing secretly to hide these viral suitcases throughout the cylinders and murder most of the couriers within the context of these massacres.

"So two plans are tied together, in typical Ash Ock fashion. Maybe a month or so *before* the Paratwa assassin is scheduled to start its string of massacres, Doyle Blumhaven is ordered to have a nice private talk with Van Ostrand. We'll never know exactly what was said, but I can guess the gist of it.

" 'Jon,' says Blumhaven, 'I've known for a long time about your true affiliations with the Order of the Birch. It was I who excised those facts from your security check, over seven years ago. I want you to know that you have my full support, Jon, for I too am secretly dedicated to the ideals of your Order. But, Jon, we have a problem. If the rest of the Council becomes aware of your Birch connections, they will certainly see to it that you are removed as Guardian Commander. You will be replaced with someone weaker, a moderate. We must not allow that to happen.'

" 'Jon, you should leave Irrya at once. E-Tech has received information that other highly radical factions within the Order of the Birch are preparing to take violent actions in a misguided attempt to ensure that the Paratwa do not return. If such violence erupts in the Colonies, your Order will come under intense scrutiny. No matter what my own personal feelings are in this situation, I may be forced into providing the Council with information that could expose your true affiliations.

" 'I suggest, Jon, that you take command of the defense net at its source. Put your best people in charge . . . fellow idealists like yourself. If and when the time comes, the loyalty of your commanders must be unquestioned. Nothing less than the security of the Colonies is at stake.' "

Huromonus cut in. "We have data to support this last part. Van Ostrand definitely has been juggling command assignments over the past six months. His admiralty is now composed of men and women who, if they are not Birch hard-liners like himself, certainly lean in that direction. Same goes for the commanders of his primary attack fleet, including most of the captains of those big Ribonix Destroyers."

The lion shook his head wordlessly. Each Ribonix-class Destroyer carried enough nuclear payload to decimate half a planet.

Nick slithered onto the edge of the console. "So Van Ostrand heads for outer space. And by the time he arrives at his new op base, we have a pair of crazed killers on the loose back here in the Colonies, proclaiming themselves members of the Order of the Birch. Van Ostrand gives a silent prayer of relief, genuflects toward Doyle Blumhaven's worthy spirit, and hopes that his true affiliations will remain hidden—at least until he's in position to strike down the devil Paratwa.

"The bottom line is this: I predict that in two days at our next Council meeting with Meridian, the Paratwa are going to threaten to release the viruses unless we immediately agree to whatever terms they present. And when Van Ostrand hears Meridian's threats, he's going to come to the conclusion that the Colonies have lost, that the Ash Ock are heading toward their ultimate victory.

"And Jon Van Ostrand, Supreme Commander of the Intercolonial Guardians, is going to say, 'What the hell—we may as well make a war out of it.'"

Huromonus nodded solemnly. "The Guardians could launch an all-out offensive against the Biodyysey."

"And they could be wiped out," whispered the lion.

"That's a good bet," said Nick. "So far, all of the evidence suggests that Paratwa technology is so far ahead of ours that in a direct confrontation, we wouldn't stand much of a chance. I think we have to assume that the Paratwa possess enough high-tech firepower to destroy the entire defense net. If that's the case, their task might be made easier if they're facing a Commander who will throw everything but the kitchen sink at them. Maybe the Paratwa hope to annihilate whole portions of the fleet in one bold move."

"Then it's over," said the lion.

A wolfish glare swelled Nick's cheeks. "It ain't over till it's over. Besides—sometime stinks here. I know this is going to sound crazy to you, but I get the weirdest feeling about this whole mess. I think that the Ash Ock are *desperate*."

"*They're* desperate?" the lion muttered.

"Yes, damn it. I know how those bastards think! I know the Ash Ock style, and I'm telling you, this ain't it. The Paratwa have been planning for centuries. Suddenly, everything's moving at fever pitch. They're coming at us like gangbusters, as if there ain't no tomorrow. They mix us up and they shake us up and whammo! Instant Victory. Our entire fleet gets vaporized—any Colony that refuses to surrender gets the virus." The midget wagged his finger at the lion. "No, this ain't like them. Something's all wrong here."

"Fine," said the lion. "So what exactly do we *do* about it?"

"Freebird! That program has to hold the key to this whole mess. We gotta bust Freebird wide open, and we gotta do it quickly—in the next two days—before Meridian starts throwing ultimatums at Council."

The lion sighed. Nick would never give up hope; when it came to a Paratwa victory, he remained beyond the call of reason. "These gut instincts of yours about Freebird. I believe it when you tell me that this program must be somehow important." He shook his head. "But important enough to deny the Paratwa their victory?"

"Yes! Freebird was so important that the Ash Ock had Codrus secretly manipulating intercolonial society for over two centuries, helping to keep E-Tech strong so that the archives would remain essentially secure, so that no one would accidentally stumble onto this program. Freebird was so important that after Codrus died—after the Colonies began gearing up for the Paratwa return—the Ash Ock sent their advance team back to the cylinders just so they could sic their sunsetter on it! Freebird was so important that the Paratwa killed Adam Lu Sang as soon as they learned about his knowledge of Freebird and the sunsetter. The massacre at your retreat probably occurred for a multiplicity of reasons, but don't kid yourself—Adam was their main target. I've been a thorn in the Ash Ocks' guts for a couple of centuries now, but even I wasn't that critical. The assassin didn't even bother to make sure I was dead. It was Adam they wanted, and now I know why. Adam was far more dangerous to them because he had *inside* access to the E-Tech data vaults. Adam had a guaranteed means of getting to Freebird!"

The lion frowned, "I don't understand."

"I didn't either, not until I thought about it after the massacre. Then I remembered a conversation that Adam and I had, back when we were first looking for ways of penetrating Freebird's secrets. Adam joked that there was one sure way of doing it—a method that was technically possible but ultimately ludicrous from every other standpoint." Nick paused. "But now, with the absolute threat of a Paratwa victory hanging over us . . . now, maybe it's not so ludicrous after all."

Huromonus faced the lion. "Nick has requested full access to the E-Tech archives."

"I helped design those archives," said the midget. "I know how the data is contained. If I can physically get inside the data vaults, I can do what Adam only joked about.

"We're in desperate straits here. If we don't take desperate action ourselves, then we're going to perish. There's a way to drive Freebird out of there, a way to ream Freebird of its data. And we've got less than two days to do it." Nick turned slowly to Huromonus. "Edward here is understandably reticent in accepting my suggestion. That's another reason why I asked him to have you brought here. I thought you might help me to convince him."

"Convince him of what?"

"Nick wants to do something that I am sworn to prevent," said Huromonus quietly. "Quite simply, he wants to initiate a sequence of actions that will probably result in the destruction of most of the E-Tech data archives."

The lion felt a frigid smile warping his face. Deep down, at that same level where his stomach pains had gripped him only a short time ago, he now sensed the beginnings of an acid laughter, a harsh blend of astonishment and disbelief.

"Destroy the E-Tech archives?! That's insane!"

"Maybe it is," agreed Nick. "Maybe it is."

"Do you know what this place is?" asked Gillian.

Susan ran one palm across his bare chest while the other nestled against his cheek, a playful finger reaching out to tickle his ear. "Timmy calls it a cell of the Os/Ka/Loq."

"I know. But what exactly is that?"

Grinning, she rolled on top of him again, moved her hands to his shoulders. "What is what?"

"Os/Ka/Loq? Do you know what it means?"

She furrowed her brow, pretending to give serious consideration to his question. "I think I've figured it out. I think it means 'the place where passion never ends.'"

He swung his arms across her back, palmed a buttock in each fist, gently pinched. "I'm being serious."

She laughed. "Why?"

"Everything comes to an end."

"You have my end," she pointed out.

He laughed too. "What's going to happen to us after we get tired of making love? We can't stay in this bed forever."

"Why can't we?"

"You're not being rational."

"I don't have to be. You said I'm your shadow, right?"

"If I'm the light, you're the shadow. If you're the light, then I'm the shadow."

"That means we're inseparable opposites, forever attracted to each other."

He paused. "Yes. But you're forgetting about Timmy."

"No, I'll never forget about Timmy."

"He won't allow us to make love forever."

She whispered, "Maybe we can persuade him to change his mind."

Gillian sighed. "You don't understand about Timmy."

"Yes I do." She slid a finger across the bridge of his nose. "Timmy needs us more than we need him. He needs to ... restore your Paratwa. I believe he's dedicated his life to that purpose."

He stared up at the beautiful face, saw Catharine there. "You should be afraid."

"I am. Do you want to make love again?"

"You're insatiable."

This time, her frown was real. "No, not insatiable. I used to be that way. Sometimes, I used to make love to a dozen different men every week. Now I realize that what I was really doing was searching for you."

He kissed her lightly on the chin. "Timmy designed you to be my partner. You can't help feeling the way you do."

"I know. But we're halves of a whole. The same desires apply to you."

They were silent for a while. Eventually, she asked him about Empedocles.

"Is he here now?"

"He's always inside of me. But right now, his presence is very weak. I can barely feel him. I believe that my monarch—"

"—our monarch," she corrected.

"I believe that *our* monarch is deliberately keeping himself in the background. He's permitting us to get to know each other."

"He's permitting us to heal."

"I suppose."

"Am I like Catharine?"

Gillian smiled. "Sometimes you're exactly like her. Other times you're not."

"How about when we make love? Am I like her then?"

"No. Then you're like you."

Susan felt pleased. "Is Catharine still . . . inside of you? Is a part of her still alive?"

"No, not alive. But the interlace is still intact. What Catharine was . . . her potential . . . it still exists. And of course there are my memories of her." He paused. "They used to flow over me sometimes until I felt as if I were going to drown."

"And now?"

And now, for the first time in ages, I can remember her without being overwhelmed by pain. He kissed Susan lightly on the chin. "I want us to be together always." A rush of feeling ascended his spine—the distant Empedocles expressing his pleasure.

Susan nodded. "It's crazy, but I want it too. I keep trying to tell myself that this whole concept of becoming a tway . . ." She squeezed his shoulders. "It's insane! It makes no sense whatsoever! It's the most obscenely ridiculous idea I could ever imagine!"

"And you want it," said Gillian.

"I want it more than anything else I've ever wanted in my life. My *body* wants it."

"No choice."

"I know. My body demands fulfillment."

"Timmy designed you that way."

"I know that too." She hesitated. "I always wanted to have a choice. By the time my parents died . . . by the time they committed suicide . . . I had no choices left to me. Everything was decided for me." New insight flowed through her. "That's the real reason I tried to have sex with so many different men. I could choose. I could keep on choosing. I never had to stop. I could always have the freedom to make a new decision about a new lover."

"That's not freedom."

"I know. I know that now."

"Those men . . . were they pain relievers as well?"

She stroked his arms. "Yes. That too. They made life bearable."

Gillian came to a realization, sharing it with her even as he formulated its parameters. "The Ash Ock . . . that's one of their great powers."

"What is?"

"They not only possess the ability to be conscious of all these inner drives that tways—or humans—are usually unaware of, but they truly understand the inherent multiplicity of behaviors which, taken together, define intelligent creatures." He struggled to make himself clear. "You were having sex with all those men for different reasons. On one level—a physical plane—you were using them, at least to some extent, as pain relievers. Simultaneously, on an emotional level, you were doing it so that you could always, ostensibly, have the power to choose."

"All part of the same thing," she suggested. "Just different aspects of my pre-Timmy neurotic behavior."

"But the Ash Ock . . . they're *always* aware of the interrelationship of those levels. They're always conscious of what we—tways or humans—are usually forgetting. That's why they can generate such complex plans. That's why they're always doing things for more than one particular reason. They see it all. They don't have a subconsciousness—at least, not as we understand it. We have levels of consciousness. They don't. For them, it's one great arena, viewed from end to end within the same sweep of vision." He paused. "I don't believe my monarch ever dreams."

Susan studied a dimple on his neck. "Perhaps when your monarch is fully awake, his tways are his dreams."

"Yes. That's possible." He stared up at her, suddenly seeing her face as a golden mask, covering his own. It was a vision—an iconic image of the way things once were . . . and

the way they would be once again. Two tways, able to see
themselves from the inside and from the outside at the same
time, able to mirror each other. Ash Ock consciousness. Ash
Ock Paratwa.

The vision departed, leaving in its wake a fresh storm of
speculations. His thoughts turned to the assassin—the tripartite.

"The Honshu massacre . . . where you ran into the killer.
I think I understand something. You always thought it was a
coincidence that you were there, right?"

"Yes. Are you suggesting that it wasn't?"

"I believe that the tripartite wanted you there. It was supposed to kill you. An Ash Ock—Sappho, perhaps—ordered
your death. But things went wrong. You were too fast. You
got away."

She frowned. "The whole thing was just a terrible coincidence. I must have met one of its tways somewhere. It made
inadvertent eye contact with me—"

"No!" said Gillian, bursting with revelations. "No, the eye
contact was deliberate! We always thought that you must
have somehow seen more than you realized in that terminal.
Because of that, the assassin wanted you dead—at any cost.

"But that wasn't it at all! You were supposed to die in that
terminal because you were the grandniece of an Irryan Councillor—to be precise, because you were Inez Hernandez's only
living relative!"

"But why?"

"I don't know," he admitted. "Not exactly. But I think I
have a general idea. The Paratwa have been manipulating
the Irryan Council, trying to alter their attitudes, trying to
make sure that they're in the right frame of mind . . . for
something." His palms tightened on her buttocks, squeezing
her in the desperate hope that flesh would provide the final
answer. It was all there, just at the edge of consciousness, the
full intricacy of an Ash Ock scheme waiting to be plucked.

"The assassin tried to kill me in order to somehow manip-
ulate Aunt Inez? That doesn't make much sense."

"Considered by itself, maybe not. But considered as one

small aspect of their plan, it might make a great deal of sense."

"Then why would the assassin have made eye contact with me? I mean, if it was expecting me to be there, it should not have acted surprised . . ." She hesitated, filled with new doubts.

"Yes!" urged Gillian. "Think it through!"

"All right, I must have met one of the tways before Honshu. But that part I already knew." She frowned. "I don't understand . . ."

Gillian sensed the sudden intuition vaulting through her, perceiving it as a clenching of her buttocks. He grinned wildly. "We had it ass backwards, so to speak."

She whispered, "Honshu wasn't the first time the assassin tried to kill me. It tried once before that. But something went wrong. It never got its chance."

"Right!"

"So it arranged for the Honshu massacre. . . . It learned that I would be passing through the terminal—it scheduled my death along with the other ones!"

"That's right—a Paratwa assassin, acting under the multiple-objective commands of its Ash Ock master!"

"It made eye contact with me—"

"—because it wanted you to *know*! It wanted the satisfaction of your *fear*! It wanted you to realize that this was not some complete stranger about to end your life. This was someone you were acquainted with—"

"—someone whom I must have offended! He was angry with me! There was the satisfaction of vengeance in those eyes!"

"Which you never saw at the time, never realized—"

"—until now! He was . . . my lover. No! Not my lover. He was—"

"—a would-be suitor. He had intended to be just another one of Susan Quint's countless seductions—"

"That's how he was planning to kill me the first time! A rape-murder!"

"And when he failed to seduce you that first time, was denied his opportunity to kill you—and then failed again in the terminal—he sent those two corrupt E-Tech Security officers to your apartment to finish the job—"

"They were going to rape me! One of them told the other to drag me into my bedroom so that they could 'do it on the bed!' The sick bastard! He wanted those officers to finish me the same way he had originally intended!"

An undercurrent of emotion, gilded with anger, swept through Susan, and then suddenly she was lost in a maelstrom of light and shadow. She saw *herself*, saw her own face, observed that face staring up at herself. Her conceptual framework—her own secret sense of *being*—threatened to disintegrate, blasted by the consequences of this impossible vision. Deep within, she longed for that collapse even as another part of her retreated in terror.

Fear triumphed. With a violence rooted in desperation, she pushed off Gillian, lunged from the bed. Her left foot caught his right one. Off balance, she stumbled into an aqua-green stalagmite serving as a bedside table, grabbing at its uneven edge in a frantic attempt to regain equilibrium. The stalagmite did not cooperate; it bent in the middle like a rubber hose, sending its twin beakers of ice water splashing across the floor. She landed on the fresh puddle, butt first.

The commotion of her ungainly movement. The noise of it. The feel of her bare ass resting in a lake of frigid water. Gillian laughing, amused by her clumsiness. Those things should have annoyed her, embarrassed her. But she welcomed them. They were of the senses. They were real.

Gillian continued to chuckle. "That was a cute display. Any particular reason for it?"

She stood up, drew a deep breath.

"I was inside you," she blurted out.

His smile faded. "Are you sure?"

"Of course I'm sure!"

He tried to sympathize. "The first time . . . it must be a terrifying experience. Becoming a tway . . ."

She stood there in front of him, naked, arms folded across her breasts, trying to shield herself.

"As time goes by, it will become easier," he offered, feeling oddly saddened, knowing that he was mourning the loss of her innocence. The process of cojoining had begun. From now on, they would begin to count time together. From now on, their intimacy would lead inexorably toward the coalescence of a Paratwa. Those precious moments of being able to come together—as discrete entities—were gone forever. The purity of separateness was no more.

"What now?" she asked, recovering some of her composure but still feeling helpless, like a little girl lost.

"The second time will be easier," said Gillian.

His voice soothed her. His words did not.

He said, "It's this place that brings us together. This cell of the Os/Ka/Loq. Inside this vessel, thousands of feet beneath the Atlantic Ocean, the purities have been maintained." He did not fully understand the meaning of what he was saying, but he knew he was speaking truth.

"The purities," Susan whispered. She turned slowly, gazed at the strange wavering walls, at the profusion of stalagmites, some with obvious functions, others melding into electronic arrays whose purposes could only be guessed at.

He held out his arms. "Come to me again."

She took a hesitant step toward him. "I have no choice."

"No choice."

The prime data-retrieval section, located deep in the first-floor vaults of E-Tech's Irryan headquarters, was a small circular room jammed from floor to ceiling with computer equipment. On several occasions over the years, the lion had been given tours of the more publicly accessible areas of the massive vaults. But until now, he had never been inside this section. Nick referred to it as the "heart and soul of the archives."

The midget sat before him at one of the consoles. A trio of

E-Tech programmers were in the room as well, two males and a female, all incredibly youthful, all three faces displaying that same passionate dedication that had underscored Adam Lu Sang's spirit. Cheerleaders, Nick called these three. They buzzed through the cramped chamber, checking readouts, accessing information, painting multicolor data portraits across monitor screens with a nimbleness that the lion found oddly disturbing.

He suspected that what annoyed him was their intense perfectionism, their focusing of raw energies into microlaser precision, their concentration on the immediacy of the moment to such a degree that they were sure to miss the overall picture, the larger perspective. But he reminded himself that these three had been Adam Lu Sang's friends, as well as early supporters of the slain programmer's theory that a sunsetter was responsible for the data destruction within the archives. And now, the youthful trio remained the only high-level programmers whom Edward Huromonus had been willing to trust for the upcoming task. The remainder of the vault personnel, including many of Doyle Blumhaven's appointees, had been denied access. Trusted security guards, with orders to use deadly force, had been posted outside this prime data-retrieval section to ensure that Huromonus's dictates were obeyed.

"All set!" hollered one of the programmers.

"Fault lines correlated," added another.

"Archives—get ready for your first trembler!" chortled the third.

The lion sighed. The trio also reminded him of pampered colonials—rich juvenilia, mainly—who hired Costeaus to take them into the outer reaches of colonial space to "experience" adventure. Earlier, he had mentioned his comparison to Nick.

"Nah," the midget had replied. "They're more like cheerleaders."

The name had stuck.

"Eddie's here," announced Nick, glancing at a security monitor.

The door opened, admitting Edward Huromonus. The

E-Tech Director looked inordinately cheery. "I've got good news."

Nick raised his eyebrows. The cheerleaders froze en masse, then, in tandem, turned to Huromonus. The lion was reminded of a cluster of ancient radar dishes, all swiveling to track the same source. Three sets of ears locked in on their target, preparing to receive virgin data.

"I correlated your latest sunsetter data," began Huromonus, "with information that my people managed to wring from one of Doyle's former compatriots in E-Tech Security. This Blumhaven crony is currently facing a host of serious criminal charges. He has been persuaded that cooperation is the most proper course of action."

"Change of heart, huh?" quipped Nick.

"Indeed. And from what he has told us, it appears that those weird trails left by the sunsetter at multiple nexus points throughout the archives were created for the purpose of covering its tracks."

"I told you," said one of the cheerleaders, wagging his finger at the others. "The sunsetter scampered outside the archives!"

"Yes," confirmed Huromonus. "For a brief period, following the Honshu massacre, the sunsetter must have utilized one of these nexus points to exit the archives and enter the transit computer net. After accomplishing its task there—and before returning to the archives—it deliberately made contact with a slew of other nexus junctions."

"To disguise its true purposes," surmised the lion.

"That's right," said Nick. "Paratwa psychology, pure and simple—a perfect example of their style, just like the massacres. If you have to kill one person, kill thirty others at the same time to camouflage your intentions. If you have to hide your presence in a computer net, make a lotta false tracks."

Huromonus went on. "Our informant claims that Doyle Blumhaven ordered him not only to ignore a certain discrepancy between two different sets of transit computer records but to replace the first set with the second set. The first set was retrieved from the transit system by E-Tech Security immediately following the massacre. The second set—data presumably altered by the sunsetter—was substituted some sixteen hours later."

A wild grin appeared on the midget's face. "Go ahead— make my day. Tell me that there's a name on that first set that's missing from the second one."

Edward Huromonus's smile grew.

"Bingo!"

"You whacked it, Nick!" yelled one of the cheerleaders.

"Yeah, but I couldn't have done it without you folks. Hell, you know these archives like the backs of your hands."

The lion noted how the trio swelled with pride. To the cheerleaders, Nick was not a mere computer programmer; he was a living legend—one of the pre-Apocalyptic geniuses, restored to life. At the very least, the midget must be considered an angelic presence here, if not an outright god. A compliment from Nick was probably considered a gift from heaven.

"We not only have a *name*," said Huromonus, "we have the *corporation* that this individual is employed by."

"Thank you, Susan Quint," murmured Nick. "Wherever you are."

The lion mouthed silent agreement. If the assassin had killed Susan Quint in the Honshu terminal as it had intended, the Paratwa would not have been forced into the ultimately more dangerous action of altering the transit records.

"Our missing name belongs to one Calvin KyJy," continued Huromonus. "He is the special aide to Corelli-Paul Ghandi, founder and executive officer of CPG Corporation, the fifth largest company in the Colonies. There is, however, some contradictory evidence that seems to indicate that this Calvin KyJy was in the Colony of Michigan Deuce at the time of the Honshu massacre."

"Just another smokescreen," said Nick.

"We suspect as much."

"I know this Ghandi," said the lion. "At least I've met him a few times over the years."

Huromonus nodded. "I know of him, but our paths have never crossed. Until now. I just finished some basic background checking. Corelli-Paul Ghandi founded CPG corporation twenty-five years ago."

"That time frame clicks," said Nick. "We know the sunsetter's been in the archives about twenty-two years."

"And Ghandi founded CPG Corporation in a rather spectacular manner. One day, he was merely a common crewmate on a Costeau shuttle. Almost overnight, it seems, he managed to arrange enough serious financing to cover the start-up costs for a new high-tech company. A most difficult task, to say the least."

"Where'd his funding come from?" asked Nick.

"Some money came from legitimate enterprises. But a great deal of the financing is believed to have emanated from black market sources."

"That good old anonymous investment process," grumbled Nick, "legal and fully supported by the ICN." The midget shook his head. "Jesus, your society brings new meaning to the concept of money laundering."

The lion remembered something. "At the time, the story was that Ghandi, on an illegal prospecting foray to the surface, discovered some sort of high-tech cache. And he returned from the last expedition alone. I recall there was a real furor over that. There were even some accusations that he murdered his crewmates down on the planet."

"Correct," said Huromonus, "although there was never enough solid evidence to implicate him formally. Ghandi's story was impossible to dispute. He claimed that his crewmates were lost on the surface when a violent tsunami hit the Chinese mainland. He claimed to have survived only because the shuttle captain had left him aboard ship and he managed to lift off before the sea wall hit. An E-Tech base in China did register a tsunami on the day in question.

"Ghandi was charged and convicted of illegal surface prospecting—a fairly minor violation. He had to pay a stiff fine, but that was the extent of his legal problems."

"Let's assume," said Nick, "that our boy Ghandi actually came across the Paratwa down there. And he stuck some sort of deal with them."

"How would they have gotten to Earth?" the lion asked.

"Probably a small shuttle," replied Huromonus. "After all, Meridian entered our defense net by shuttle. And the Council has already discussed the likelihood that the Paratwa possess very sophisticated antiscan technology. If that's true, then twenty-five years ago—a time when the majority of the defense net was not even in place yet—one small ship easily could have gotten through."

"It's perfect," said Nick, shaking his head. "Son-of-a-bitch! I should have thought of this before. I always assumed that the tripartite assassin, and whatever other Paratwa came with him, somehow figured out a clandestine way of entering the cylinders. I could never work out the details, though. It always seemed so incredibly complicated . . . so risky.

"But they didn't come to the Colonies! Instead, they must have used this antiscan gear to penetrate E-Tech's planetary tracking. They landed on Earth. I should have seen it!"

The lion noted that the cheerleaders were frowning. Nick had overlooked something. Their computer god possessed imperfections.

"I'll be damned," muttered the midget, still stunned by his oversight. "The Paratwa landed on Earth, suckered this Ghandi's shuttle down, killed his crew, probably destroyed their own shuttle, and then had Ghandi transport them up to one of the cylinders. He probably docked first in one of the real out-of-the-way pirate Colonies—a place where few questions would be asked. He dropped his new friends there, then flew the shuttle back to his original departure terminal where he gave everyone the bullshit story about his crewmates being lost in this tsunami."

"It adds up," said Huromonus.

"Damn right! And this Calvin KyJy—Ghandi's so-called aide. He must be the third tway. The backup. The one that Susan could have identified."

"Then this Ghandi must be functioning in the manner of Doyle Blumhaven," mused the lion. "He's just another front man for the Paratwa. Do you think the tripartite could be running their operation?"

"I doubt it," said Nick. "No, there must be someone else. Maybe an Ash Ock lieutenant—someone of Meridian's rank . . . or maybe even the actual tway of an Ash Ock."

The lion recalled the Ash Nar assassin's ominous warning

at the retreat—the words that supposedly came from Sappho herself. *You can live under our domain or you can die under it. The choice is yours.*

He allowed himself a deep sigh, hoping to prevent his guts from clamping into new torment, hoping to prevent physical reacknowledgment of his cowardice, of the utter hopelessness of defeating the Paratwa. But surprisingly, the stomach cramps did not come. For the first time since the retreat massacre, he felt a sense of hope. Huromonus's revelations offered fresh possibilities. *Even my body recognizes that there may be cause for optimism.* The thought almost made him chuckle.

"I've ordered a full data probe of CPG Corporation," said Huromonus. "In a short time, we'll have a complete profile of the company and its chief officers."

"Excellent," said Nick.

The lion asked, "Anything new on these freelancer stories regarding Gillian's and Susan Quint's connection with Lester Mon Dama, the Church of the Trust, and these female gene-jobs?"

Huromonus shook his head. "Zork/Morgan, the FL-Sixteen freelancers who broke the story, have not been very cooperative. We're still trying to track down their sources, as well as investigate some of these women who Zork/Morgan claim have been genetically modified. But as yet, we've generated no hard data. And Lester Mon Dama is still missing."

The lion nodded. "Could there be a connection between this priest and CPG Corporation?"

"An interesting possibility."

Nick shrugged. "We can dance in circles all day trying to make sense out of that mess. But right now, I say we get back to the task at hand. It's time to shake up the archives. It's time to catch ourselves a Freebird."

"It's time to crack the surface!" hollered a cheerleader.

"The big quake's a'coming!" hollered another.

A pale blue background speckled with soft cotton puffs dissolved across the main screen; a representation of Earth skies that once were as common to the planet as human beings. The lion stared, briefly entranced by the pure imagery:

dreams of a place he had never known vacillated with a deeper feeling that their upcoming actions would somehow forever deny them access to it.

But the archives had to be sacrificed. Freebird had to be driven from the self-imposed depths of its data fortress. And according to those who knew better, destruction was the only way.

Nick aimed a finger at the screen. "Again, this is the representational aspect of Freebird, sort of its 'public image'—its front. But the real guts of this program must reside in a floating core drive that—at any particular moment—is probably scattered in hundreds of discrete locations throughout the archives. That's why it's so difficult to track. The core drive is never in one place long enough to get a handle on it. That's why we haven't been able to ream it of its data, and that's also why the sunsetter has been unsuccessful—at least, so far. This floating core drive is what enabled Freebird to make it up to the Colonies in the first place, two-and-a-half centuries ago. It was fast enough and smart enough to have escaped detection and detoxing when the archives were originally transferred from the planet. But all that's about to change." The midget grinned at Huromonus. "Gee, I sure hope this works."

The E-Tech Director sighed. "I would, Nick, prefer a more positive attitude. Future generations will doubtlessly remember me as the man who ordered the decimation of the archives, the man who wiped out much of the collected knowledge of humanity's past."

"Yeah, this could be the greatest loss since the library at Alexandria got trashed."

"Indeed. And I would prefer, at least, that future history texts provide a codicil to my actions. Something on the order of: 'He did it for a good reason.'"

"Hey," offered Nick, "not to worry. No matter what happens, they'll always remember you as 'Crazy Eddie.'"

Nervous laughter sounded from the cheerleaders. Even the trio's good-natured bantering had dried up as the moment of reckoning approached.

"I think we're ready," said Nick.

"Do it," ordered Huromonus.

Nick turned to the cheerleaders. One of them typed a set of commands and muttered, "Here we go."

Another said, "This is for Adam." The other two nodded in silent accord.

Earlier, Huromonus had outlined the combination of factors necessary to accomplish archival decimation: "Full-scale destruction can be initiated only from within this prime data-retrieval section. It remains the only location where all of the major nexus points can be simultaneously accessed. And as the acting E-Tech Director, I am probably the only one who can guarantee our security while this catastrophe is being engineered." A rueful smile had crossed his face. "We are going to send a cry out to every E-Tech programmer within hailing distance. Some of them will use any means possible to stop us."

The lion had agreed with Huromonus's assessment.

For several moments nothing happened. Ivory flurries continued their endless parade across the sharp blue skies.

And then sirens began to scream.

Activity erupted across every monitor within sight. A chill raced through the lion. The prime data-retrieval section was coming to life in a way that its creators had never intended. Coming to life to prevent its own death.

"First shock wave's spreading!" yelled a cheerleader. "Multiple tangents hitting the primaries—all back-up systems are producing security algorithms!"

"Back-ups are beginning to initiate cut-off procedures! In twenty-five seconds, they'll terminate the com links!"

"Get ready for shock two," Nick calmly ordered.

The big one, thought the lion. The first barrage of Nick's multiple-stage electrospasm—an overload blast of high-voltage current simultaneously introduced into every major nexus point—was intended primarily to *alert* the multiple back-up systems scattered across duplicate archival facilities in a dozen Colonies. Shock wave one, although literally incinerating circuits while it spread rapidly from system to system, was deliberately designed *not* to leap across the nexus points linking primary and back-up facilities.

Nick had explained the strategy in his inimitable way, using analogies that both the lion and Huromonus could easily understand.

"To force Freebird out in the open, we not only have to destroy the archives here in Irrya, we have to wipe out the duplicate systems as well. Shock wave one forces the back-up security algorithms to pop out of their safe little foxholes. They stand up, as it were, take a look around, and try to discover the reason for the calamity within the primary system. But they don't perceive any direct threat—the first shock wave has not touched their systems—so they don't go into their instant defensive modes and disengage RF/Laser com matrices. At this point, they will still be perceiving the problem as being limited to the Irryan system, although they will begin a standard countdown leading to emergency cutoff.

"And that's when we hit 'em with everything we've got—shock wave two. We mow down the security algorithms, preventing com disengagement. And then we blow the back-ups to hell!"

A cheerleader shouted, "All security algorithms up and out of their foxholes! Fifteen seconds to cut-off!"

That was Nick's signal. "Shock wave two. . . . Now!"

Fresh sirens howled, contributing to the din. A cheerleader grabbed Huromonus by the elbow.

"Sir, the guards outside the vaults are signaling! Two senior programmers have arrived! They're demanding entry! They're threatening the guards with extreme sanctions if they're not allowed to pass!"

Huromonus gently lifted the cheerleader's hand from his elbow. "Are the programmers armed?"

"No, sir!"

"Are the guards armed?"

"Yes sir! I catch your meaning, sir!" The cheerleader spun back to one of his consoles.

Another cheerleader shouted, "All security algorithms are down! Cutoff procedures terminated!"

"Hit 'em with the aftershocks," commanded Nick.

Another series of electrospasms spread through the system. More sirens wailed. Monitors displayed dizzying explosions of color and data—nonsensical arrays of light and motion—the outlines of desperation, of a network fighting to maintain sanity in the face of massive traumatic shocks to its deepest circuitry.

"I've got a tracer on what looks like a core drive? It could be Freebird!"

Nick leaped from his chair. "Location?"

"I'll have a rough physiograph in ten seconds!"

"Make it five!"

"Got it! It's right here in Irrya! The core drive is scampering all over the place, trying to avoid getting fried in any terminated circuits!" The cheerleader hopped from foot to foot, as excited as a three-year old. "Look at that sucker move!"

"Go to mommy!" urged Nick. "Show us the way!"

Another cheerleader yelled. "We've got calls coming into E-Tech from all over the Colonies! The back-up facilities are screaming for explanations!"

"Let 'em scream," Nick hollered. "Just stay glued to that core drive!"

"It's heading for a nexus!"

"Bingo! We must have fried a good portion of its floating memories. It's running home to mommy—or at least to where it thinks mommy is."

"I've got a precise nexus location," announced a cheerleader. "It's a standard subsystem terminal at the following coordinates. Southern Irrya, Epsilon sector, one point two-three-six-six miles north of the polar plate, two-five-nine degrees!"

"Close that nexus!" ordered the midget.

"Doors are shut and latched! That core drive is going nowhere!"

"Got you, you son-of-a-bitch!" howled the midget. "We've trapped it!"

The lion risked an interruption of their delirious agitation. "Any trace of the sunsetter?"

"Negative?" shouted a cheerleader.

"We didn't expect much success there," said Nick, his voice instantly calmer. "A sunsetter is way too compact. And it's designed to hide itself in a network, and stay hidden no matter what's occurring." He risked a quick glance away from his terminal, caught the lion's eye. "Besides, like I told you . . . it's not the sunsetter we're after."

The lion nodded. The coordinated destruction of the archives was far too complex to offer them a realistic shot at both of the warring programs. They could effectively track one or the other and Nick's priorities had been clear. He wanted Freebird.

"I've got data on Freebird's check-in terminal," said a cheerleader, sounding much calmer, as if he was taking his cues from Nick.

"The subsystem terminal is located in a private dwelling . . . a house owned by the Church of the Trust."

"Well, now," muttered Nick. "Our old friends. Why doesn't that surprise me?" He turned to Huromonus. "We've got to raid this house—right now. Our zap of the archives no doubt revealed to the sunsetter the same information it revealed to us. The Ash Ock might already be zeroing in on this location."

"They might send their assassin," said the lion, trying to keep a disturbing amalgam of emotions out of his voice.

Nick's response was suitably grim. "We'd better bring a lot of firepower."

Ghandi had never before seen Ky and Jy completely naked. Even at the chalet, in those cold-blooded moments surrounding Doyle Blumhaven's murder, the tways had worn translucent gowns, the sheer fabric providing just enough of a buffer to hide the flesh beneath Ky's left armpit and Jy's right one— the only portions of its collective body which Calvin found embarrassing.

It was difficult accounting for such reticence. The Ash Nar

could kill with impunity, publicly ejaculate on a dead man, and probably do things to helpless animals that would discomfit lifelong sadists. But for as long as Ghandi had known him, the identical twins—Ky and Jy—remained inordinately modest about exposing their strange scars.

Colette had warned Ghandi never to speak of the tways' blemishes in Calvin's presence.

When Ghandi stepped through the CPG shuttle's midcompartment airseal into the tiny exercise chamber, the twins were floating, naked and wet, beneath the open hatch of a steamjet cubicle. Obviously, they had just come out of the shower following a workout. The last person they were expecting to see was Ghandi. He rarely came to this section of a shuttle. When the Ash Nar was aboard the same CPG fleet vessel, Ghandi usually preferred to remain sequestered with the crew on the upper decks.

Today, he was not quite sure why he was making an exception.

Instantly, the tways pinned their arms against their bodies: fast enough to prevent him from seeing their scars, fast enough to call attention to their movements.

Ghandi planted his friction boots on the edge of a whip cycle, pulled himself forward into a "seated" position in the weightless compartment, and favored the tways with a grin.

"Afraid to let me see you?" he challenged, knowing well the dangers inherent in such provocation.

It was not as if he was throwing caution to the wind. Ghandi liked to think that he remained at least somewhat concerned about his own future. But since that weird performance by Sappho in the CPG boardroom several days ago, since experiencing those incredible sensations of once again having some semblance of control over his life, it seemed more natural for him to take risks, to challenge the status quo maintained by the force of Colette/Sappho's will.

And who was more representative of that status quo than Calvin, as rigidly obedient and territorially protective as a litter of well-trained dogs.

Ky and Jy were pitched about ninety degrees from Ghandi's perspective. Two sets of eyes glared at him; four angry dots propped one above the other, in a line so straight that it begged for a vector to connect them. As usual, the tways wore just enough facial makeup to hide their identical genetic features. Today, Ky's cheeks appeared more swollen than his brother's, and his closely cut auburn hair provided a distinct contrast with Jy's wavy blond tresses.

Ghandi allowed his smile to widen. He approached his target from a new angle, his mouth wielding fresh taunts.

"I didn't mean to pop in on you like this. I didn't intend to make you feel so ashamed. I know how embarrassed you are about your scars."

Hatred. Murderous rage.

Following Sappho's boardroom behavior, Ghandi's newfound strength had, within a matter of hours, disappeared. He had been left only with a vague memory trace, the echoes of departed feeling, conceptions of what the emotion had been like. Agitated microbes had returned to dance through his body, mocking his subservience, his weakness. He had tasted virility—virility in the fullest sense of the word—and now he longed for repeated doses. He could not imagine a more potent drug, a more desperate addiction.

If he made Calvin too angry, the tways might risk Colette/ Sappho's wrath. Calvin could kill him, here and now. But for Ghandi, the rewards were worth the risk. Truly, his addiction was that powerful.

"It must be difficult for you," he pressed. "Here you are—by your own admission, the deadliest Paratwa assassin ever bred—yet you're scared to show old Ghandi a little set of blemishes."

Floating in the weightless chamber, the tways somehow fell into positions resembling full-G crouches. Their bodies compressed, coiled. Tiny aquatic particles detached from their flesh, drifted away; other beads from the steamjet shower remained affixed to their skin, held there by forces that Ghandi, at a fundamental level, did not understand.

"You'd rather kill me then expose yourself. I can see the shame in your eyes."

They pushed off each other, came toward him. In zero-G, the movement appeared unnatural—a violation of the laws of inertia. One of them should have been shoved in the opposite direction. Ghandi was not ignorant of *all* natural forces.

They halted their momentum by grabbing converse edges of the whip cycle, positioning themselves in line with Ghandi's axis, flanking him at a range of less than a yard. The smell of mild cocoa cologne, applied during final steamjetting, emanated from their bodies. It would not have been Ghandi's first choice.

Unpleasant sounds came from Jy's mouth. Snarls and a deep-throated hiss, like a cat might make when cornered by a larger beast.

The other tway—the one who had acquired the public moniker of "Slasher," the one whose musculature had been trained to use the deadly flash daggers—spoke. Ky's voice sounded as calm as the surface of a gee-well.

"You are saying things that are not yours to say. Colette is not here to protect you. You are putting your life in danger."

Ghandi forced a dry laugh. "Frankly, Calvin, I expected a better attitude from you. We're not talking about my death here. We're discussing your cowardice."

A streak of motion. Ky's fingers snagged Ghandi's neck. Now both tways were glaring and hissing at him.

The pressure of Ky's viselike clamp was painful, yet bearable. Ghandi refused to be intimidated. He glared back at the tways, knowing that he was pushing this thing far beyond rationality, knowing that he was truly risking an explosion of Ash Nar rage.

But the microbes remained at rest; his body had achieved an inner tranquility that he had not known in ages. It was the repose of authentic fearlessness. He recalled what it had been like to be a Costeau, to be unafraid of one's action, to live fully, forever skimming across a wave of consequences. It was a freedom of the spirit he had sacrificed long ago.

Ky's grip was not yet tight enough to dam another stream of words. Ghandi whispered:

"The clans used to have a saying: 'The heart of a coward bequeaths the mind of a fool.'"

The tway's fingers crushed inward. But only for an instant. Then Ky released his grip and somersaulted violently across the chamber. He hit the opposite wall, compressed his legs, and sprang back toward Ghandi.

Jy reached out, grabbed his twin's arm, retarded his velocity. Ky came to a halt beside his brother. The rage had departed from his face. In fact, both tways now regarded Ghandi with a curious dispassion.

"Show yourself," urged Ghandi, knowing that he had pushed Calvin to the point where only two absolute choices remained. *He must either grant my request or kill me.*

Ky raised his left arm above his head; Jy raised his right one.

The banana-shaped scars, mirror images of one another, began just beneath their armpits and extended downward almost to their hips. Ghandi was a bit disappointed. His curiosity, cock-driven and fueled by inner turmoil, had now achieved its maximum state of fulfillment. Seeing Calvin's surgical disfigurements had instantly reduced their importance, making Ghandi aware—at least momentarily—of what little separation truly existed between the mythic and the mundane.

Nevertheless, it had felt good to outdistance the tways.

"When were you disconnected?" he asked, now genuinely curious and, to his own surprise, strangely affected by Calvin's willing exposure—no matter what forces had impelled the Ash Nar.

Ky and Jy responded in full stereo. "I was four years old when Sappho's doctors performed the operation."

Ghandi tried to imagine what it must have been like for the tways prior to separation: Siamese baby boys, learning to crawl, walk, and function as a whole.

"You were a difficult creation . . . for Sappho?"

Ky answered, "The interlace, in its most natural state, remains dualistic."

Jy continued, "A tripartite consciousness required special provisions. In our wombs, I was two tways—Calvin and KyJy. Then Ky and Jy were split. But not split entirely . . . until the operation."

Ghandi shook his head. "This was done on the Biodyssey. . . ." He hesitated, trying to formulate his thoughts into a precise question. "You were separated within a *kascht* that did *not* reek of the lacking?"

Again, they answered in unison. "Yes. Probabilities dictated that I could not have been created here. The difficulties would have been magnified a thousandfold."

Ghandi had the feeling that he was on the verge of comprehending something . . . some important facet of Paratwa reality. But suddenly the tways' eyes widened.

"I am being summoned," said Ky.

"Your presence is also requested," added Jy. The tway grabbed Ghandi's arm. "You will travel with me. I will show you the flight of an Ash Nar."

Quickly, they took hold of him and propelled him through the open seal, into the midcompartment. Walls and tables, terminals and lockers; everything sailed past Ghandi's eyes as he tumbled and twisted through the larger space. It was as if he had become a child's suspy ball—a sphere filled with just enough helium to maintain itself at a specific distance above the ground, forced into spontaneous lateral movement by the omnipresent spin-rate accelerations found in every Colony.

Calvin's four hands mimicked that Coriolis force, pushing and shoving Ghandi, the tways' bare feet repeatedly kicking off the walls, expertly maintaining a desired conjunction of velocity and direction.

Through the midcompartment, Ghandi's head barely missing the edge of an airseal, now tumbling out-of-control like a spacecraft in zero-G with one retro jammed wide open . . . yet he had never felt safer in his life. He had driven Calvin to a place where only those of iron will could hope to survive; he had shown the Ash Nar that he was willing to die rather than surrender. And now Calvin was driving *him*.

Ghandi laughed wildly, exhilarated by the sheer tumultuous sensations of manic flight, knowing that he had no control, knowing that Calvin would not permit any harm to befall him.

For the moment, he sees me as one who has matched his own courage. For the moment, he respects me as an equal.

And then Ghandi was somehow *twisted*—a course change of ninety degrees—and he was slowing down, velocity and spin rate rapidly retarded by a quartet of softly slapping palms. One final somersault and he vaulted through the open portal into the study/dinette.

The tways killed his momentum, flipped him upright; his friction boots reglued themselves to the grated deck.

Colette stood a dozen feet away, glaring at him. Ghandi grinned and swayed like a drunk, his equilibrium still disturbed from the mad ride. But emotions bubbled. He felt invigorated.

Next to Colette stood Calvin's third part, the namesake tway who remained physically distinct, the one whose body assumed the role of the seducer, the one who always provided the Ash Nar with its deepest glories of sexual conquest and ultimate gratification. In stark contrast to tway Calvin's sexual hunger, Ky and Jy remained virginal: the privilege of immaculate masturbation was their only means of relief.

The twins never needed to touch themselves. They could masturbate on command, just by thinking about it. An entire process and mythos reduced to the simplicity of urination. Even Colette admitted that the ultimate psychological processes underlying the tripartite's sexual functioning remained a thing not fully comprehended.

But Ghandi felt that he understood this facet of the tripartite's makeup.

Calvin endured an almost quaint sensitivity in regard to his twins, perceiving them as an impairment of his Ash Nar perfection, their physical and emotional blemishes inducing weakness, creating a constant source of vulnerability. And Calvin did what most humans did when confronted by the perceptions of internal frailty. He overcompensated. He attempted to depersonalize his shortcomings.

"That's a stupid smirk," snapped Colette. "Remove it."

Ghandi continued grinning at her. "Why are you angry?"

"Don't contradict me," she warned.

He remained silent, aware that there must have been fresh setbacks for Paratwa schemes. Nothing else could make her this furious. Maybe the whelm would come once again, illuminate monarch Sappho even as it carried his wife away.

"Lester Mon Dama is nowhere to be found!" she continued. "Likewise for Gilllian and Susan Quint! Therefore, Aristotle remains an enemy cloaked in shadow!"

Ky and Jy attempted a stereo rebuttal. "The search continues—"

"Silence! Do not speak of that which you do not understand! Ramifications of your failure—" She paused, then began to speak very fast. "But *all* has not been a failure, has it? As planned, the Toulouse skygene suitcase has been found. The profarming plans have been proceeding as expected. Intercolonial acceptance ratios now indicate a cross-cultural willingness to return to the planet."

The tempo of her words increased, seemed to pour from her mouth like water from an open spigot. "Our gut-ads have been successful. Within six months of our victory, two hundred and fifty profarming communities *will* be in place, scattered across the surface of the Earth. The Biodyysey's crops will be deposited in fertile ground. Reseeding will take place according to plan. This *kascht* which reeks of the lacking will indeed bear fruit. A first harvest will indeed occur on schedule."

She stopped, as abruptly as she had begun. Then: "Is that not true?"

"Yes," admitted Ghandi, feeling uneasy. Once again, Colette was betraying a novel pattern of behavior. He wanted to ask her what was wrong but realized that such a tactic would be a mistake.

A bitter grimace tightened her lips. "But at this point, the reseeding is of secondary importance, is it not? More important is the fact that only moments ago, the E-Tech archives suffered an assault on an order of magnitude unrivaled in its history!

"The archives have been deliberately blasted with electroshocks! Massive irreversible devastation has taken place! Our sunsetter has failed us!" A spasm seemed to pass through her. Her shoulders scrunched together and misery ravaged her face. She turned to tway Calvin.

"The Czar is still alive! This is his doing! You did not kill him at the retreat!"

Calvin extended his fingers. YOU SAID THAT THE

CZAR'S DEATH WAS NOT A PRIORITY. YOU SAID THAT THE PRIMARY REASON FOR THE ATTACK WAS TO KILL ADAM LU SANG AND DISPLAY OUR TECHNOLOGICAL SUPERIORITY—

"Fool!" she screamed, arms batting the air in front of her face, as if something terrible was approaching. "Must I spell out *everything* for you?"

Calvin responded with uncharacteristic rectitude; Ky and Jy bowed their heads, spoke in stereo.

"I made a mistake. I should have made certain the Czar was dead. It was entirely my error."

"And who will suffer the consequences!" cried Colette, her arms now flapping wildly, trying to ward off the invisible demons. "Freebird has been caught! Trapped in Irrya! The Czar will already be on his way to the check-in terminal. He will flay the skin from Aristotle's cursed abomination! He will learn Freebird's secrets!"

Ky/Jy offered: "We'll be docking in Irrya very shortly—"

Colette screamed in agony, grabbed her right shoulder with her left hand, squeezed as if there were a fire beneath the thin fabric of her blouse.

Ghandi moved toward her. "What is it?"

She thrust herself backward, into a console. "Get away from me! Don't touch me!"

Ghandi, mystified, turned to the tways. But if Calvin understood what was happening to her, he was keeping the knowledge to himself.

Another scream escaped from Colette, a wail of agony even more penetrating than her initial outburst. Still clawing at her shoulder, she fell to her knees. Tears began streaming down her cheeks.

A chill went through Ghandi. *Something horrible is happening to her other tway.* He moved forward, wanting to help or at least comfort her.

But Ky and Jy grabbed Ghandi from behind. Calvin's fingers splattered fresh letters.

DO NOT REACT. THERE IS NOTHING THAT YOU CAN DO FOR HER.

Another bitter shriek—a high-decibel wail of outright

pain—filled the study/dinette. Ghandi could not help himself. He lunged forward, desperate to break the Ash Nar's grip.

It was no use. One of the tways yanked him backward while the other swept his feet out from under him. Ghandi slammed hard onto the grated deck.

DO NOTHING. INTERFERENCE WITH THE DISINCORPORATION COULD BE CONSIDERED A REASON TO INCREASE ITS DURATION OR INTENSITY.

Ghandi shook his head, bewildered.

IT WILL NOT BE FATAL TO HER. SHE IS BEING MADE TO SUFFER ONLY A LIMITED DISINCORPORATION. OUR TASK IS TO BEAR WITNESS. THAT IS THE OBVIOUS REASON WHY YOU AND I WERE SUMMONED HERE. SHE WAS ORDERED TO PROVIDE OBSERVERS. IT IS AN INTEGRAL PART OF THE PUNISHMENT.

"Punishment?"

FOR HER FAILURES.

Desperate sobs shook Colette's frame. Heart-wrenching wails. *Her other tway is being tortured!*

Ghandi could not stand it. Seeing his wife undergoing such turmoil was worse than that sheer internal helplessness associated with the mad dance of his microbes.

"No!" he hollered, roaring to his feet.

This time, the tways were less forgiving. Ky's bare leg nailed the back of his knees like a steel rod. Pain shot through him as he again collapsed to the deck.

THIS IS THE WAY THAT IT IS DONE. IT MUST BE.

"Why?" he moaned.

A WARNING. SHE HAS LED US TO A PLACE WHERE SUCCESS AND FAILURE ARE HINGED ON THE SAME AXIS. THIS IS A CONFIGURATION THEY DO NOT TOLERATE. IT IS . . . AN ORGANIZATIONAL ERROR.

A shudder passed through Ghandi. "Who? . . . Who is doing this to her? The other Paratwa?"

YES. THE OTHER PARATWA.

A final scream. Colette's eyelids fluttered. She slithered to the deck, face forward. Unconscious.

Ghandi crawled across the deck toward her. Calvin did not stop him.

"My love," he whispered, cradling her head in his arms, stroking her hair. "It will be all right," he murmured. "I promise."

Colette awoke, opened her eyes, attempted a fragile smile. "Pain incorporates," she whispered. "It teaches the individual the importance of the society."

"Be still," he hushed.

"Corelli-Paul . . . we once told you that you might have to make a great sacrifice. Someday, you would have to become the public scapegoat."

"Whatever you wish," he vowed.

She shook her head. "No, I—Colette—do not want it to happen. I want you to be unshackled. I want you to be liberated. If there is a sacrifice to be made, then I will make it."

He gazed at her silently, seeing for the first time a creature strictly guided, a creature as bound to a specific direction as he had been for these past twenty-five years. Colette/Sappho was powerless to alter the rigorous limitations of her existence. Like Ghandi, she could not truly escape.

She gripped his arm. "I need to recover my strength. I must sleep now, Corelli-Paul. For a short time only. Just until we dock."

Calvin moved out of the way as Ghandi scooped his wife into his arms, carried her to their cabin, laid her on the bed, covered her with a single sheet.

"My love?" she asked, as he turned to go.

"Yes?"

"I never dream."

Ghandi frowned. It was something he had wondered about for many years. "You're not missing much," he offered, trying to keep his tone casual, trying not to choke on a sudden terrible pain that rose from his guts.

"Corelli-Paul?"

He turned away so that she would not see his agony. "Yes?"

"I wish that it did not have to be this way."

He left the bedroom quickly, too upset to reply. He knew

what she was trying to say. He could not bear to hear her succeed in expressing it.

He was never going to see her again. When she awoke, she would be gone. When she awoke, she would be Sappho.

Gillian led their exploration, but it was not by choice that he performed in the role of guide. Susan insisted upon walking a full pace behind him, at the outer limit of his peripheral vision, like a cognizant shadow, cloaked in its own trepidation, waiting and watching, unwilling to lead and too terrified to follow.

He understood and sympathized, knowing how hard this must be for her. But he moved on.

They had last seen Timmy ... how long ago? Hours? Days? He had truly lost track of time. Gillian's possessions consisted of shirt, pants, boots, and his Cohe; the spacesuit and its accoutrements had disappeared, along with the thruster rifle. Susan, likewise, had only the clothing on her back and the matched set of flash daggers rigged in flakjak pockets.

They had been exploring the vessel's seemingly endless compartments and chambers, ostensibly searching for a way back to Gillian's shuttle. There was no reason to assume that they would find their way out without Timmy's help. And although they had come to the conclusion that their "host" must be monitoring their progress, there remained no reason to expect his assistance.

A section of wall obediently cross-split as they approached, flaps peeling back to create a new portal. Gillian admired the efficiency of this place—this thing called the cell of the Os/Ka/Loq. The vessel contained nothing so specific as a permanent entryway. Doors existed where and when you wanted them.

He crossed a threshold into yet another new chamber, more virgin territory, hearing Susan's footsteps behind him, hearing a soft mushy sound as the flaps automatically re-sealed, and he knew without looking that within seconds, all signs of the doorway would vanish.

It was a process that brooked admiration.

This new area was the largest one they had yet entered: a cavernous chamber some fifty feet in width and height and, like other areas of the vessel, illuminated by erratic patches of luminescent blue ceiling. The length of the chamber was impossible to gauge. Stalagmites sprouted from the floor, but here there existed a literal forest of them, hundreds perhaps, of all shapes and sizes, in a plethora of colors distinctly dominated by shades of blue and green. A few of the upthrust masses extended all the way to the ceiling.

Some of the stalagmites had simply grown into the domed covering, forming nonsymmetrical columns; others, having aspired to such heights, apparently lacked the chemistries to attain full melding. Like rootstock unable to penetrate inhospitable ground, those stalagmites had split at their ends, forming tendrils cascading in all directions—their denial transferred into lesser achievements.

He recalled seeing something similar, centuries ago, on Earth: ancient campus buildings splotched and streaked with dark green organic masses. Ivy, it had been called. But here, even the sections of ceiling not covered by groping tendrils appeared somehow alive, like vibrant tapestries, gently dancing under the tutelage of invisible winds.

Susan muttered, "I was in a profarming Colony once, on an assignment from La Gloria de la Ciencia. They were experimenting with new strains of wheat, and there were some sort of genetic malformations inside a certain test rotator. The inside of the rotator was filled with stalks, bending and twisting in every possible direction. The stuff was so dense that it was strangling itself. But it just couldn't stop growing."

"Like here," murmured Gillian, sensing his monarch again stirring, pushing and pulling against the boundaries of consciousness, seeking full freedom of movement, a permanent way out of his prison of dual singularity.

Fulfill me, urged Empedocles. *At this very moment, you are trapped within a process that you cannot even dimly comprehend. You are a victim of forces beyond your understanding. Fulfill me. Make me whole, and I will dream a better dream. My consciousness will take us beyond this place.*

Gillian shook his head. *I'm not ready yet.*

"There was nothing they could do," droned Susan. "The genetic malformations inside the rotator were impossible to restructure. They had to dump the entire mass. I was working as a Progress Inspector. It was my duty to complete a full report and dispatch my findings immediately to my division head. Within La Gloria de la Ciencia, obverse funneling was the name o' the game—the preferred method for the dissemination of data. But there were always complications—"

"Stop," ordered Gillian, stepping quickly to the left, moving around the massive trunk of a deep blue stalagmite streaked with ribbons of flaming yellow.

Susan ignored him. "La Gloria de La Ciencia's methodology for establishing informational parameters was also very sophisticated. There were no bureaucratic roadblocks built into the structure of the organization that might damn the data flow—hinder the stream of information—"

"Stop it," Gillian growled, louder this time. He circumnavigated the massive trunk of the stalagmite, came full circle to face her. She froze, glared at him in anger.

"The data flow must never be dammed, not within a network idealistically dedicated to assimilation of lost technological knowledge—"

Gillian lunged forward, grabbed her shoulders, shook her. "Stop it! You're speaking gibberish!"

"I can't help it!" she cried, wrenching herself from his grip. "Don't you understand? I'm scared, Gillian. I'm scared about what's going to happen!"

"I know. But you have to get it under control."

For Susan, it was worse than the terror Timmy had subjected her to out on the Ontario beach, worse than knowing that his bab knife had pierced the flesh over her stomach and that he might release the tiny blade to cut through her body. No, this terror flowed from deeper roots, gaining its strength from a place beyond the mortal fears of suffering pain, of risking death. Since that first moment with Gillian, when she had been swept outside herself to witness Susan Quint from the perspective of another, her conceptual framework devastated by the intellectually transcendent force of the vision . . .

Their words and thoughts flowing back and forth with incredible speed and clarity, a rush of excitement, a coalescence—like intelligent monosynchronous transceivers barring all extraneous frequencies, achieving total wavelock, delimiting communication until only the mocking perfection of a single overlapping sine wave remained. . . .

The sensory turmoil of becoming, for that impossible instant, another creature. Twenty-six years of self-conceptualization—however repressed and emotionally twisted—swept away in a moment. Twenty-six years of learning who she was relegated to the recycling core. . . .

And afterward, knowing that she had been a victim of her own expanding tempest of feelings and thoughts, churning with Gillian's feelings and thoughts. . . .

It was too much. She did not think she could again step out onto that unrailed balcony, lean over the edge, fall into that chasm that would remake her life into something greater and lesser than what she was. She did not think she could become a Paratwa.

Gillian again tried to explain, tried to provide a cloak of rationality to offset her terror. "There are great disturbances associated with the whelm. The forced interlace—the dialectic of tways into monarch, monarch into tways—is a simultaneity of expansion/compression that is so inherently powerful that it generates the most primal fears. But you must try to contain those fears, or adjust to them somehow. You must come to terms with your future."

"I can't. There must be another way."

His words grew bitter. "The whelm is the only way that the interlace can still be manifested."

Susan heard the sadness in his voice, the echoes of feeling that suggested: *once there had been another way.*

And she knew that if she were to prevent the whelm from reoccurring, she would have to make sure that their thoughts and emotions never again flowed together.

But that regimen did not take into account her desperate desire to become entwined with Gillian—a physiological and psychological need to be with him forever.

A scream of pure frustration escaped her. "I don't know what to do!"

Gillian understood. "I know that you're concentrating on aspects of your old life—your former job as a La Gloria de la Ciencia Progress Inspector—in the hopes that keeping your memories alive will prevent a repeat of the coalescence. But if you keep yourself occupied by thoughts and feelings that have never really been of much importance to you. . . ." He trailed off with a shrug. "You might indeed prevent the whelm, but you'll also make yourself even crazier."

She knew he spoke the truth.

He reached out, pulled her toward him, cradled her head against his chest, ran his fingers through her silken hair.

Even the simple pressure of his touch triggered spasms that shook her to the core, threatening to induce that contradiction called the whelm. But at a certain level, she did not care. It felt good to be soothed.

Beware! warned Empedocles. *Things are not as they appear. Both of you are caught within a vortex—transformational energies that could easily swirl you to oblivion. Remember always—I am the way out. Remember!*

Gillian ignored his monarch, continued stroking her. "I know what it's like to be this afraid, to not know what to do. I know that you want to remain intact." He hesitated. "But I honestly don't think that it's possible. You can't avoid this thing. You have to let it happen."

She hugged him desperately. And suddenly he was pulling away from her, violently.

"What's wrong—?"

Black light streamed from his hand, whipped above Susan's shoulder. Behind her, something hissed in agony.

She whirled, flash daggers gliding from her pockets in one fluid motion, cartoon images thrusting forward, into the blocky reptilian face that bore down upon them from above.

Shafts of blood spurted from the snake's gargantuan mouth, spraying her from head to toe. She leaped sideways, out of the path of the descending head. It crashed to the ground at her feet.

High overhead, still slithering down the trunk of the stalagmite, was the rest of the creature's body—a twenty-foot length of brilliantly colored lizard, its stump oozing viscera, yet still vibrantly alive, twisting to and fro, perhaps seeking reunification with its departed head, which had been cleanly severed by the slashing black light of Gillian's Cohe.

"Behind you!" she yelled.

The second snake launched itself from the heights of a soaring gray stalagmite. Gillian's position was too awkward for an effective counterattack. He had no choice but to dive from the path of the flying reptile.

Susan leaped in the opposite direction. The snake abandoned Gillian as a target, whipped toward her. It froze, drew back its head, hissed.

A third snake, on the ground, came slithering out of the stalagmite forest. It too suddenly stopped and raised its head to focus lifeless eyes upon Susan. A chill went through her.

"What now?" she whispered, keeping the flash daggers pointed at the coiled snakes. The blocky heads were poised less than ten feet in front of her, easily within striking distance.

"Don't move," ordered Gillian, getting to his feet again, carefully moving to the snakes' left flanks.

The creatures lunged at Susan. Gillian's wand thrashed the air. With one downward slice, the curving whip of black energy decapitated both of them.

The two heads crashed to the deck at Susan's feet. Like the first slain creature, the bodies of the pair kept whipping back and forth, refusing to surrender unto death. She deftly sidestepped the churning necks until finally their movement slowed, and they assumed postures of acceptance. There was a moment of calm. . . .

And then more noise emanated from the forest. Susan turned, saw a ratlike creature the size of a small horse scampering out from behind a stalagmite. On the rat's back rode a tall, naked black man with two heads sprouting from one long neck. All four of the twinhead's eyes were pinched tightly shut.

Gillian again moved close to Susan. "I know these creatures," he murmured. "The snakes, the two coming toward us now—they were all being kept in some sort of stasis aboard this vessel."

"For what purpose?" she whispered.

Deep within, Gillian sensed joyous feelings passing through his monarch, great satisfaction and relief, as if long-raging fires finally had been quenched.

Now I understand, murmured Empedocles. *This nonexperimental amalgam is providing what was lost. I do not need to dream. But you must. It is the only way to restore the deepest connections.*

"Connections?" wondered Gillian.

"Con-nec-tions," mimicked the left mouth of twinhead, as if pronouncing an English word for the first time.

Twinhead smacked his rat mount atop its head. The creature scrambled forward. Susan gasped. The stirrups holding the bizarre creature to his ride were actually a double set of four-fingered hands, emerging from the rat's belly to clench twinhead's bare ankles.

Twinhead's eyes remained closed. The ratlike creature halted less than two yards away from them.

The right mouth of twinhead asked: "Who is you? Is you one or is you two?"

Gillian just stared, not knowing how to answer.

The mouth asked, "Why you kill the snakes?"

"They attacked us," Gillian replied slowly. "What . . . are you?"

"What you think I is?"

"I . . . don't know."

"How about I is an unconscious creation from the depths of your own mind? How about I is not really here?"

Susan drew a deep breath. "This is just too bizarre. This is not happening."

"Not ha-pen-ning," mimicked twinhead's left mouth.

Gillian shook his head, confused. "What *is* happening?"

Empedocles's thoughts streamed across awareness. *Feel your body! Feel it!*

Gillian tried. He could not. There was nothing there to feel.

He remembered. Fifty-six years ago. Facing Reemul. That sensation of total disunity, a complete loss of body-image, all physical sensation vanishing, his entire being reduced to a mental construct, cut off from all sensory experience.

The same thing's happening to me now!

"Not to you alone!" cried Susan, with sudden comprehension. "It's happening to both of us!"

Twinhead's eyelids popped open. Susan screamed.

Four empty sockets, devoid of all mass. Eyes that did not really exist. . . .

Twinhead, his rat-beast mount, and the dead snakes disappeared. The stalagmite forest melted into the contours of the small chamber where Gillian and Susan had made love.

Final alignments occurred. Dual awareness soared together into the thundering epiphany of the whelm. Empedocles awoke, leaped from both sides of the bed, two sets of feet landing on the floor at the same instant.

We were dreaming, thought Gillian.

So real, countered Susan. *As if we were awake. But we never left this chamber.*

We dreamed together. That's what was needed for him to finally awaken. That was the missing element.

Awe touched Susan. *As we slept, our imaginations interlaced. And he emerged from our dreams. And now we've become dreams of his.*

No. The Ash Ock do not dream. They do not possess a true subconscious. What we have become is amalgams incorporated into the entirety of his being. Most often, he will not even notice that we exist. Generally, we are as invisible to his perception as a blood corpuscle might be to the mind of a human. Even though the corpuscle might float freely throughout the body, the holism of consciousness would rarely take notice of it as a distinct entity.

Gaia of the body, thought Susan.

A sense of deja vu struck Gillian as he considered the entire process from his internalized vantage point. *I remember, now: this is what it feels like to be the tway of an Ash Ock when the monarch is whole.* He felt oddly amused by the forgotten familiarity of the experience.

Susan sensed his amusement as a warm tingling at the back of her neck ... or as what she conceived of as being the back of her neck. In truth, she realized, she possessed no such thing as a neck. Her body was no longer hers. It belonged to the monarch. She was only an amalgam with memories of the body.

Gillian went on, intrigued by his own percipience. *These feelings—they are forgotten by the tways each and every time the monarch arises. The individualized tway does not remember what it feels like to be reduced to this state. Each coming together is a rediscovery of what was forgotten from the last time. If one could remember, then the tway might very well resist any future monarchial attempts to become whole.*

Wonderful, replied Susan. *What you're saying is that we're currently trapped within a pretty miserable state of existence, one that's not worth repeating.*

Gillian felt her sarcasm come at him like a dark storm cloud bristling with nodes of fury.

How long do you think we'll be confined? she asked. *How long until we're reawakened ... as individual tways?*

He had no answer.

"It's happened!" cried Timmy, his bloated body filling the doorway, his shapeless gray robes quivering with excitement.

Empedocles studied the outburst, calmly observed the emotions spilling from Timmy's mouth, like the side sprays of water from an undisciplined spigot.

"You've returned! Arrhythmia of the whelm has been reversed!"

"I have come back," announced Empedocles, speaking through his Gillian-tway. He stretched his arms out, relished his restored freedom of movement. Strange new muscle groups—characteristics of the Susan-tway—demanded acclimation. He took in great gulps of air, utilizing the Paratwa method of slightly out-of-sync dual breathing to pump oxygen through his two halves.

Timmy licked his lips. "It feels good, yes?"

"It feels."

"Kascht moniken keenish," uttered Timmy. *"Kascht mulaf-was—belj moniken—"*

"Save your words," said Empedocles. "They cannot control *me.*"

Timmy smiled. "You are truly whole."

"I am whole."

Timmy blinked erratically. "My wetware eye ... it's been giving me circuit problems for a long time now. Sporadic malfunctions. Very annoying. I'd be better off without the silly thing."

Empedocles ignored the display of self-condescension. He shifted his speech to the Susan-tway, feeling more comfortable in his new half with each passing moment.

"Does anything of Jalka—or Aristotle—remain within you?"

"I am Timmy," reaffirmed the bloated creature. "What I once was is no more. Of course, there are usable memories. Data from the past. But the true consciousness of both tway and monarch are gone. They died making me into Timmy. The pain of having lost my tway—"

"I am not interested in your pain," interrupted Empedocles. "Why did you bring me back? What was so important about my restoration? Decades of effort to achieve this moment? Why?"

A tear formed on the lip of Timmy's remaining eye. "You truly don't know?"

"If I knew, I would not ask."

"You are Ash Ock" whispered Timmy. "You are my last brethren."

Empedocles considered the words. Then: "I am not the last of the royal Caste. There is Theophrastus. And Sappho."

"They betrayed me."

Empedocles detected a faint trace of stiffness in Timmy's tone. "Perhaps you seek to settle an old score? Did you bring me back so that I could become your avenging angel?"

Timmy shook his head. "No, that's not it at all."

"I am puzzled. Enlighten me." Empedocles spread his four

arms, palms upward, in a gesture of friendship. "This vessel—
this cell of the Os/Ka/Loq, resting on the bottom of the
Atlantic Ocean . . . you must have great knowledge of its purposes."

"I do. I know why it is here."

Empedocles permitted a warm smile to play across his
faces. He was beginning to understand the drives of this obese
remnant of the royal Caste. Such knowledge could prove useful.

"Timmy, I wish to become your student. I wish to learn all
that you know. Will you be my teacher?" He paused for effect. "Will you instruct me as I was once instructed by your
. . . predecessors?"

Timmy looked ready to burst into tears. "Yes, Empedocles!
Yes, I will be your teacher!"

Empedocles continued to present a friendly and eager facade. *A fat fool, a prancing shadow—all that remains of the majesty
that once was Aristotle. Theophrastus and Sappho betrayed you, so you
say, but perhaps it was you who betrayed them. Either way, I will learn
the truth of it. I will allow you to educate me, and then I will decide
whether you are worth keeping alive.*

Timmy stepped out into the corridor. "Come with me," he
implored. "We will go to my private chambers for discourse.
And then I will show you things that you have never imagined!"

"I am yours to lead."

Susan felt coldness arising from where she imagined her
shoulders to be.

He's a monster! she cried out. *Timmy made him whole, and now
he considers murder as repayment!*

Gillian was not shocked. Now, he remembered how it was
when his own consciousness was reduced to an amalgam,
when Empedocles controlled his body. *He is an Ash Ock
Paratwa. There is a certain . . . arrogance.*

Susan steeled her emotions. *All right—he's an arrogant bastard.
So what can we do about it? How do we become twoys again?*

We must wait for the proper conflux of circumstances to dissolve the interlace. We must stay alert, ready to take advantage of the onset of such circumstances.

Susan hesitated. *He's not going to want to permit that, is he?*

Not willingly. Empedocles will strive to maintain his monarchial wholeness for as long as possible.

Not acceptable! snapped Susan. Gillian felt the heat of her anger blast across the face of his awareness.

Be careful, he warned. *I said before that we are like mere corpuscles in his body, but there are situations where he can indeed perceive us. Strong emotions call out to him. He cannot read our thoughts per se, but he can analyze violent outbursts of emotion. And through our displays of feeling, he may be able to comprehend our intentions.*

Susan forced calm. *Yes. I see that he is very good at understanding the emotions of others.*

Gillian continued. *If we maintain a purposeful tranquility, the depths of our tway-thoughts will remain hidden from his perusal. We can freely communicate without his knowledge. The tways always have their little secrets.*

For a time they were silent, entering an even deeper state—a wellspring far below the level of dreams.

Susan was the first to return to the realm of thought. She projected herself carefully, allowing no sadness to color her words. *I didn't think becoming a tway would feel so . . . empty.*

You did not know how it would feel, answered Gillian. *And I did not remember.*

The lion had never been this far south in the Capitol cylinder. He stood with Nick at the corner of two gloomy and deserted streets, behind a smashed cement wall with plastic reinforcing strips splaying from its shattered top. Beyond the wall, row upon row of small grimy houses, mostly deserted, fell away into the dense fog. Southern Irrya remained one of the most blighted areas in the Colonies, rivaling even the slums of Sirak-Brath.

The target house, a two-story structure with a glimmering green terrapane facade, squatted in the middle of the block. According to records, the house was one of the few in this sector still boasting valid occupational permits.

The lion shivered in the chill breeze that swept down from the polar plate—the massive wall capping this end of the cylinder. Irrya's southern terminus was a mile and a quarter away, rising majestically from the swirling ground fog, like a dark sentinel smudged with patches of light. The smaller areas of illumination marked the location of industries on its vertical surface; the larger splotches defined the perpendicular cities.

In most of the Colonies, polar-plate real estate remained relatively cheap. Although most citizens were not eager for vertical housing under variable gravitational conditions, many deemed it superior to living below the fogline, preferring the odd geometries of the perp cities to the dankness of circumpolar streets.

"Some things never change," muttered Nick. "*Poor* on top of the mountain is better than *poor* down in the valley."

"I suppose," said the lion, pulling the flaps of his thin jacket up around his neck—a futile attempt to keep the penetrating dampness away from his body.

Nick shivered. "Christ, it's nasty down here. Reminds me of old London on a bad day."

"I should have known to dress warmer," said the lion. "Southern Irrya . . . it still suffers from an old-style climate. This area has not yet benefited from nom-normalization upgrading."

"Say what?"

He explained. "Originally, it was always wet near Colonial polar plates . . . something to do with the air current flows and natural condensation processes within cylinders. But in the past thirty years or so, they've developed techniques for combatting the problem. They call it nom-normalization."

"Ah, I get it," said Nick. "In other words, up near the northern plate, where your retreat is, funding was found for this 'nom-normalization.' Whereas, down here, it's ghetto life as usual."

"Something like that," admitted the lion.

The midget gave a philosophical shrug. "Still, I guess that says something about Costeau social integration. At least your people are no longer at the bottom of the economic heap."

"A few of us have escaped." The lion pointed a finger at the fog-shrouded plate. "But more than sixty percent of the people living up there in those prep towns come from the clans."

Nick wiped his brow with the back of his sleeve. "Are you trying to do anything about that?"

The lion glared at him. "I did not choose to become a Councillor of Irrya for the *prestige*."

Nick grinned and tightened his collar. "Ya know, you're starting to sound like your old self again. Pissed off and almost as righteous as a Church of the Trust recruiter."

My old self, mused the lion. Nick was right about that, at least up to a point. He was feeling much better: his stomach pains had retreated, and he could not deny a newfound optimism, a sense that the Paratwa might actually be defeatable. But on a deeper level, internal conflicts remained. The lion knew that he had yet to come to terms with the primal source of his turmoil.

In the face of death, I was a coward.

At least now he was able to confront the feeling a bit more directly, admit its veracity without hiding behind other emotional reactions: shame, anger, and the defamation of surrendering to a supposed fate. But whether he could ever truly overcome that deep feeling of cowardice remained to be seen.

"Ya know," said the midget, "we're not too far from a historic site. Over fifty years ago, a few blocks from here, Gillian and your father first tangled with Reemul."

The lion nodded. "I know." Aaron, his adoptive parent and the only father he had ever known, had been gravely injured in that battle against the liege-killer; Aaron's sister and another Costeau had perished.

Memories of his father cut to the heart of the lion's distress. *What would Aaron have thought of my cowardice? Would he have been disgusted by my actions? Would he have been ashamed to call me his son?*

A sudden warmth suffused the lion, driving away the emptiness of the past days. Aaron had been too much the realist to have condemned an only son to eternal damnation for one cowardly act. The lion smiled, imagining what Aaron's exact words would have been.

You messed up but good, boy. You shafted yourself. Don't do it again. Next time, get it right!

He promised that he would.

From a dilapidated and deserted building at the end of the next block, Edward Huromonus and an eight-person squad of helmeted E-Tech Security personnel jogged out into the street. The assault group wore gray field uniforms, transceiver helmets, and active crescent webs. Each carried a heavy-duty thruster rifle. They ran in pairs, following Huromonus's quick pace.

The E-Tech Director halted his squad in front of them. Huromonus instantly leaned over to clench his knees and suck down great gobs of air.

Nick chuckled. "Eddie, you're getting too old for this shit."

Huromonus straightened. "You and the lion are not exactly models of youthfulness."

"Yeah, but we can still kick ass." Nick grinned fiercely at the lion.

The leader of the squad, a tall olive-skinned woman, stepped forward. "Sir, we have confirmation. The final units are in position."

Huromonus nodded. "There are now approximately seven hundred and seventy-five Security troops within an eighteen-block radius of us, plus two dozen airborne assault craft with enough scanning gear to track a stray microbe. If the tripartite does show up, we should at least have a fair chance of stopping it."

Nick's abrupt frown indicated what he thought about their chances.

They all understood. It was not so much a matter of numeric odds as it was the sheer speed of the tripartite assassin, its ability to be in three places simultaneously, and its use of unknown weaponry far beyond Colonial state-of-the-art.

The midget shrugged, then gave a nasty smile. "Oh, hell—if our Ash Nar friend does show up, we'll make it one bitch of a fight." He turned to face the squad leader. "Isn't that right, Sergeant?"

The woman twisted her rifle's sprocket lock to the FIRE position and stared gravely at Nick. "I lost a friend at the Alexander's retreat."

Huromonus picks his people well, thought the lion.

"All right, Sergeant," said Huromonus. "Give your signals. And remember—we're looking for information. If there's anyone in there, make every effort to take prisoners."

The Sergeant nodded.

"But," added Nick, "if something aims a weapon at you, blast the shit out of it!"

The Sergeant lowered her visor and leaped out from behind the wall. Her squad followed.

They covered thirty-five yards in five seconds. When they were less than twenty feet from the house, a high-circling jet assault craft, hidden in the fog, launched a slo-mo missile. The rocket drifted lazily from the mists, targeted the doorway, then lunged forward at attack velocity.

The doorway and its surrounding superstructure exploded inward. The Sergeant and her unit charged through the opening.

Huromonus, monitoring via transceiver, provided rapid updates.

"They're in the entry hall . . . sweeping the downstairs area . . . scanners reading negative . . . no targets. . . ."

A second explosion sounded from the back of the house.

"Squad two just hit the rear door," intoned Huromonus. "Still no targets . . . no discernible equipment masses . . ."

Nick shook his head grimly. "There's got to be a terminal in there."

"Nothing on scanners. . . . Wait! They've located a target . . . upstairs. . . ." Huromonus tensed. "Target is armed!"

The lion held his breath.

"Got him!" shouted Huromonus. "They've neutralized the target. . . . He's alive. . . ."

Nick charged out from behind the wall. The lion and Huromonus jogged after him. By the time the three of them had reached the destroyed entrance, the whole street had erupted into a wild melee of noise, light, and motion. E-Tech Security troops poured from surrounding houses; others charged from bleak alleyways or came streaking from the mists on skysticks. Assault crafts hovered above the street, their optic scanners gouging reverse shadows in the dense fog as they sought enemy targets.

Nick raced into the house and up the stairs. The lion and Huromonus stayed right on his heels. They turned a corner, passed through an empty bedroom, and entered a windowless chamber with white fabric walls.

The Sergeant and three of her troops were there, surrounding a chair occupied by a bearded man in plaid shirt and pants. Nearby was a desk with a built-in terminal. The screen was still active, displaying a set of jagged patterns. The lion recognized the pastiche as a distinct aftereffect of archival decimation. It barely hinted at the enormous loss of stored data.

On the far side of the room, the wall bore several dozen erratically spaced shelves, which appeared to have been quickly snapped onto the white fabric with little concern for neatness. Each shelf was crammed full of ancient telephone directories in protective wrappers. A few separate covers, also sealed in translucent preservation envelopes, had been framed and mounted in a tight cluster beside the shelves.

"Pacific Northwest Bell," Nick read. "Bell of Pennsylvania. Wisconsin Bell. Bell Atlantic." He faced the seated prisoner. "Thinking of calling someone?"

The man gave a weary smile. "I've a weakness for twentieth-century telephonic materials. I've been collecting this sort of thing since I was a boy."

"His name's Lester Mon Dama," provided the Sergeant. "He's the only one here. He was working at the terminal when we came in."

"Booby traps?" asked Nick.

"Nothing our scanners can pick up. The terminal's clean . . . at least in terms of specific detonatable devices. Whether he's planted programming traps—"

"We'll handle those," promised Nick.

Lester Mon Dama spoke. "You're the Czar. I should be honored." He pointed to the distorted monitor. "This massive archival destruction. It was your doing, wasn't it. Very ingenious. An act of such temperament—such utter desperation— simply was not considered a viable possibility. My master made no preparations to guard against such madness."

"Who is your master?" asked Huromonus.

"He calls himself Jalka."

"Who is Jalka?"

"He is my master."

Nick scowled. "You've got a firestorm of trouble coming your way, priest. I strongly suggest cooperation."

"I would have it no other way."

"Good. How about some real simple stuff. Where's Gillian?"

"And Susan Quint?" added the lion. "Is she still alive?"

"I do not know."

"Where is this Jalka?" asked Nick.

"I cannot say."

"Perhaps," offered Huromonus, "we should define cooperation." He stepped to the back of the chair, out of the priest's field of vision. "I wish for you to understand that there are no criminal charges against you at this time. The authorization for this raid falls under the provisions of the E-Tech Security D&D3 Act—"

Lester Mon Dama held up his hand. "I waive all rights. Further discussion of legalities will not be necessary."

"And you understand that you may be charged with future violations arising from our search efforts?"

"I understand."

Two of the archival cheerleaders burst through the doorway—a male and a female, with portable terminals attached to their chests. They looked incredibly agitated, their eyes flicking back and forth, their heads darting madly across the breadth of the chamber. One of them locked his gaze on the side of the Sergeant's helmet, moved in closer to study some particular detail. The lion had the impression that the pair did not get out of the vaults very often.

"Over here," instructed Nick. "Don't waste any time."

The cheerleaders scampered to the desk. The female began attaching color-coded bungee feeders from her portable terminal to the back of Lester Mon Dama's computer. The male zeroed in on the keyboard. Fingers smacked noisily.

Huromonus came back around to the front of the chair. He knelt in front of the priest, so that they were eye to eye.

"There is a story," began the E-Tech Director, "being told by the freelancers. It regards the mysterious deaths of three friends of yours, some twenty-four years ago. They were obstetricians. One of these doctors not only cared for Susan Quint's mother during her pregnancy, he actually delivered Susan. She was altered in the womb, turned into a genejob."

The priest stared at the floor.

"In fact, a slew of female babies were fetally modified by your three obstetrician-friends." Huromonus paused. "Was that the reason Jalka ordered you to kill these doctors? So that no one would ever find out that they were responsible for creating hundreds of illegal genejobs?"

A tic seemed to come alive in Lester Mon Dama's neck. He twitched violently. "I do not recall these events."

"Is there anything you do recall?"

"Very little."

"We're off to a piss-poor start," warned the midget.

"It's here!" shouted the cheerleader at the keyboard.

"Freebird!" added the other.

Lester Mon Dama lifted a shaking hand toward his face. The Sergeant instantly grabbed his wrist. A second guard pointed the tip of a small scanner at the priest's speckled beard.

"Nothing," said the guard. "Still squeaky clean."

Huromonus raised an eyebrow. "You *did* do a full scan?"

The Sergeant nodded. "Right before you got here. But sometimes it pays to doublecheck."

Huromonus nodded with approval.

"Care to talk about Freebird?" asked Nick.

The priest was silent for a moment. When he spoke, his words seemed distant, obscured by some invisible curtain. "Although you may disbelieve me, I truly know nothing about this program, other than the mere fact of its existence."

"How long have you been in this house?" asked Nick.

"Many days. Jalka instructed me to hide here after I made contact with Gillian."

"When we drove Freebird out of the archives, why did it come to this specific terminal?"

"Through this terminal—through me—Jalka monitors Freebird. I suppose that this was the natural place for the program to hide."

"What do you know about the sunsetter?"

"Only that it has been attempting to destroy Freebird."

Huromonus frowned. "Does Jalka contact you through this terminal?"

"Yes. Or through other terminals."

The E-Tech Director assumed his best prosecutor's tone. "Am I to understand that you know where Jalka is right now, but that you are unwilling to provide this information?"

"That is correct."

"At this time, is there any information about Jalka that you wish to volunteer?"

Lester Mon Dama's shoulders jerked violently, and then a look of deep sorrow appeared on his face. He glanced at the busy cheerleaders, then turned to the wall of telephone directories. Sadness colored his words. "All of us maintain certain loyalties. I am sure that a person of your position can well appreciate this facet of existence."

"Of course," soothed Huromonus.

"I can tell you nothing of Jalka. But I can offer my cooperation in other areas." He faced the Sergeant. "Please remove the protective wrap from the directory labeled Bell Atlantic."

Huromonus nodded to the Sergeant. The guard with the scanner carefully unsealed the ancient book from its preservation envelope and flashed his probe across it.

"A sad day," moaned the priest. He stared up at them. "I am sorry . . . truly sorry. I know that you do not understand, but these books are pre-Apocalyptic. They are representations of a time before time. They are very precious to me."

The lion glanced at Nick. A deep frown had settled on the midget's face.

"Book's clean," announced the guard.

"Would you hand it to me?"

Huromonus nodded and the guard carefully deposited the artifact in Lester Mon Dama's open palms. Gingerly, the priest peeled back the covers.

"Bell Atlantic," he murmured. "My entire collection consists of system-wide yellow-page directories, all produced in the early years of the twenty-first century. They contain no individual phone listings, only corporate display ads. By that era, few items such as these were actually being produced on paper. The demand for all printed directories had almost disappeared—especially for ones such as these. They are incredibly rare."

"Fascinating," said Huromonus, maintaining his accommodating tone.

Nick, looking more agitated by the moment, turned to the cheerleaders. "How long yet?"

"Real soon," said the female at the back of the terminal. "Simple stuff—we're past the outer checkpoints already. No serious roadblocks."

"We'll have Freebird up on the screen and ready to ream in five minutes flat!" added her male counterpart.

Lester Mon Dama apparently found the page he was looking for. He squinted, then shook his head. "I'm sorry. My eyesight . . . the tension. I have somewhat of a headache. You'll have to read it for me. Page three-thirty-eight. The display ad in the upper right-hand corner."

The Sergeant waited for Huromonus's signal, then gently picked up the book and began reading.

"Kawaniam Aquatics . . . Designers and Builders of Custom Concrete Pools . . . Construction, Renovations, Maintenance . . ."

A spasm passed through Lester Mon Dama. The priest bolted upright in his chair.

Nick's agitation peaked. His eyes widened with sudden comprehension. "No!" he cried out. "Stop reading!"

"Kascht moniken keenish," uttered Lester Mon Dama, in a voice that sounded as if it came from far away.

"Get a medic!" yelled Nick.

The priest arched backward, then collapsed forward. The Sergeant and a guard grabbed him, prevented his body from tumbling to the floor.

Nick gripped Lester Mon Dama's wrist, checked for a pulse. He laid his other hand across the priest's forehead. "Son-of-a-bitch!"

"What happened?" demanded Huromonus.

"God damn it!"

"Sergeant," ordered the E-Tech Director, "get a med team in here at once. And have them prepare a revival unit at the nearest location—"

"Don't bother," muttered Nick, his fury abating. "There's nothing to be done for him. He's dead and he's going to stay dead."

The lion ventured a guess. "Mnemonic cursors?"

"You got it," said the midget, shaking his head. "I should have suspected. The phone books, the way he kept referring to this Jalka as his master. Shit! I should've read the clues."

The lion tried to console him. "You couldn't possibly have known."

"Yeah, maybe."

"I'm not sure that I fully understand," said Huromonus.

"It's simple. Lester Mon Dama was being controlled by implanted mnemonic cursors. I mean *really* controlled. When you do an autopsy, I'm willing to bet you're going to find enough remnants of mnemonic cursors to stock a warehouse.

"This poor bastard was being governed from the word go. These phone books all must contain numerous sets of code sequences, disguised as simple display ads and such. When Lester was confronted by certain situations, the mnemonic cursors directed him to open particular books and read specific selections. Those selections, in turn, triggered other sets of mnemonic cursors, which then forced him into new patterns of behavior."

The lion shuddered, recalling pre-Apocalyptic tales of such things.

"A retroslave!" chortled the female cheerleader.

"Yeah," muttered Nick. "That's what they used to call them . . . back in the good old days."

"Simple data processing and storage technology!" proclaimed the male cheerleader, grinning weirdly. "The phone books provided an almost infinitely large memory—gigabytes of usable data, with the mnemonic cursors themselves serving as the core drives, able to access the massive memory network upon proper command sequencing."

"More like old-style CPUs than core drives," corrected the other cheerleader.

"I don't think so. Historically, central processing units predate the introduction of true core drives—"

"Enough!" commanded Huromonus.

The cheerleaders shrugged and resumed their work at the terminal.

The E-Tech Director faced Nick. "Why can't we attempt revival?"

"Look at his forehead."

"Bright red," replied Huromonus, feeling the priest's brow. "He's burning up."

"It's a particular type of mnemonic cursor known as a consummator. Anyone implanted with one possesses a code—a phrase which can be used to arm the actual cursor. In this case, a particular advertisement for swimming pools. Upon reading that phrase—or hearing it read—Lester Mon Dama was then obliged to utter the final sequence that triggered the consummator.

"When activated, a consummator causes massive neurotransmitter activity throughout the brain. Widespread synaptic ravagement is the result—a fever of brain cells, quickly destroying most memories. Even if you managed to revive him just to the point of being able to do an RNA scan, there wouldn't be any useful information left to access. You might be able to revive his body, but you'd have nothing less than a total vegetable on your hands."

"He knew," whispered the lion. "He couldn't bring himself

to read the words of the ad. Deep inside, some part of him must have recognized that he was bringing about his own death. He complained of a headache, of not being able to read."

"That's right," said Nick. "In the end, that was all the freedom he had left to him, the only way of resisting his own suicidal actions. Being captured by us must have triggered the actual self-termination sequence. His body tried to fight it, but he was in a no-win situation. Poor son-of-a-bitch."

"An entire life of manipulation," murmured the lion. By comparison, the lion's own recent troubles—his cowardice—seemed terribly irrelevant.

"This Jalka must have been responsible for the implants," said Huromonus.

"Bet on it." Nick cast a steely gaze at the slumped-over priest. "Jalka—whoever you are, you've just made my shit list."

"Freebird!" cried the male cheerleader. The terminal screen dissolved into a sharp blue sky dabbed with puffy white clouds.

Huromonus turned to the Sergeant. "Remove the corpse. Then wait for us outside."

The Sergeant and the guards picked up the priest's body and bore it from the room.

"Program's open!" yelled the female. "Ready for serious reaming!"

"Good work," said Huromonus.

"Nothing to it," she replied. "These rescue programs are holy terrors inside large networks, but once you trap them in a small system, they're bird shit on a pogo stick!"

Nick stepped up to the terminal, began pecking at all the keys.

Freebird's signature blue skies vanished. A menu appeared.

"Cute," said Nick. "Freebird is offering multiple output modes for its data. Looks like we have a choice of about sixty major languages, plus seven mathematical formats and something referred to as 'Os/Ka/Loq base iconic.'"

"How about standard English?" suggested the lion.

"Sounds good to me." The midget typed the command.

Words appeared. A long document. They began reading.

It was a tale from the pre-Apocalypse, written by the Ash Ock Paratwa Aristotle. It was a revelation of life amid the royal Caste, telling of manipulation and deceit on a scale heretofore unimagined.

It told of Sappho and her tways; one, a beautiful and seductive woman; the other, a tiny deformed girl, born without appendages. And it told of another breed of Paratwa, called the Os/Ka/Loq.

"By the memory of Ari," whispered the lion, as the significance of what they were learning penetrated consciousness.

Huromonus's voice quivered. "This is . . . unbelievable."

They read in silence for a long time. When they reached the end, Nick was the first to speak.

"I think I know what they fear," he said solemnly. "We may have found a way to defeat them.

At what price? wondered the lion.

The oval chamber, barely large enough to contain teacher and student, brewed a malignant odor from its quivering soffloor, from the inverted valley of its illuminated dome, from its walls draped in late-California nouveau plastique embroideries. Empedocles, upon entering the cramped space, realized that this was where his obese instructor must sleep. Timmy would have grown accustomed to the smells; intrinsic aromas would have steadily retreated from his field of awareness, entering a vast and expanding zone of disused social graces, a place of decaying dreams.

The smells of death.

Timmy assumed the lotus position, leaned against the wall at one end of the oval, spread his gray robes across his lap. Empedocles sat down on both sides of his old proctor, forming an obtuse triangle with Timmy at the vertex. The monarch's quartet of ears discerned the faint slithering of the entry flap resealing itself, coalescing back into a seamless whole.

His instructor began. "I am going to tell you a story that you have never before heard. It concerns the long-hidden truths of the Paratwa. This is a tale known in its entirety only to Sappho, Theophrastus, and Meridian. And to the Os/Ka/Loq."

Empedocles, believing that a few bytes of personalized rhetoric would help Timmy render his tale with even greater lucidity, made an offering through his Gillian/tway. "I am glad to be with you again," he lied. "I recall with fondness our walks through the forests . . . our long discussions while hiking the trails of Thi Maloca."

Timmy's natural eye compressed; a pained grimace appeared on that side of his face. "Yes, I recollect some of those walks, even though it was Aristotle whose company you actually kept. My monarch has been dead for a great many years."

"So you have stated."

"Obviously, I still have access to his memories." Timmy squinted. "Yes, I remember . . . the Amazon basin. Aristotle must have found it most enchanting. The sunsets through the forest trees, the waterfalls." He gave a vigorous nod. "Yes, it must have been very beautiful."

"Yes," said Empedocles.

Timmy closed his natural eye. His artificial one responded by opening wider, as if some complex internal equilibrium needed to be maintained. "It was the last decade of the twenty-first century, in those final years before the decimation known as the Apocalypse.

"You were still at Thi Maloca. Your training had almost come to an end. In a short while, you were to have been brought into the larger world, gathered into the Ash Ock fold. But like Aristotle and Codrus, you too would have been denied access to the true plans and objectives of the royal Caste." Bitterness darkened Timmy's words. "For the actual determiner of Ash Ock destiny was Sappho, and only

Theophrastus and a handful of the Paratwa lieutenants were entrusted with the secret knowledge.

"Eventually, however, Aristotle learned the truth. But by then it was too late. My monarch did not perceive the nature of the trap until the snare was about to descend."

Timmy bowed his head, fell into silence. Empedocles waited impatiently, eager for continuation but aware that it would be a mistake to wring history from this obese artifact.

At last, Timmy looked up. Both eyes opened wide. "And so the trap closed on my monarch. And he was destroyed."

Empedocles interjected via the Susan/tway. "Then your other half was indeed lost back in the days of the pre-Apocalypse?"

"Yes."

"And Jalka, the surviving tway, later fused with Aristotle."

"I became Timmy," he replied, in a voice brimming with great sorrow.

It's so sad, thought Susan, sensing echoes of grief in the hush of Timmy's solitude. *It must have been terrible for him.*

Gillian projected agreement, then repeated his earlier warning. *Beware of exposing your emotions too openly. If Empedocles senses our feelings, he will use such knowledge to maintain the monarchy.*

Susan imagined herself nodding her head, knowing that Gillian could clearly understand such mnemonic gesticulation. *You're right,* she added. *I'll have to keep my feelings gagged . . . no matter how much I hate such self-repression. It reminds me of my pre-Timmy life—*

—You're doing it again, chided Gillian.

Sorry.

Timmy's like a fractured amalgam, instructed Gillian. *He's a recluse destined to scavenge amid junkyards of former glory, forever searching for tarnished parts, knowing all the while that there is no hope for authentic reconstruction.* Gillian paused. *There—did you perceive how I did that? I subsumed the emotional content of my thoughts within a strict informational mode.*

Yes . . . I think I understand. She gave it a shot. *I, Susan, am like a tree whose roots have been torn from the soil, whose physical adoration for her newfound love, Gillian, has been abruptly—and despicably—rendered Platonic.*

Gillian cast a wry smile toward her, keeping it faint enough to avoid Empedocles's attention. *That was pretty good. Just be careful with the more potent feeling-oriented words, like* despicably. *Words like that can easily convey emotional charges if you're not careful.*

What about love? she asked with care.

That word also requires prudent handling.

She vowed, *I will make greater efforts toward perfection in this area.*

A weirdly cheerful grin blossomed on Timmy's face. He gazed back and forth between Empedocles. "It is still hard for me to believe that you have returned. All these years . . . all these efforts. . . . But success has come at last. You are whole once again. Your glory has been restored. It is good to have you back."

Empedocles rested a hand from each tway on Timmy's shoulders. "It is good to be back," he uttered in stereo, thinking: *This fool requires the humors of sentimentality and nostalgia to maintain clarity of thought. He is like a child who needs constant encouragement.*

Timmy cleared his throat, forced composure. Empedocles withdrew his hands, dialectically painted Gillian/Susan with expressions of sadness/expectant delight. "Please go on," he urged.

"Yes," said Timmy. "I must go on . . . to a time before Aristotle's demise. I must begin the story there, in the year 2095.

"The Earth is almost finished. Techno-madness is engulfing the planet, mindless mini wars are being fought everywhere, and even the most optimistic human senses that the end is drawing near. The world is being ravaged by the twin cancers of unrestrained progress and unlimited profit. The individual reigns supreme even as the fabric of society disintegrates. Balance has been lost. Chaos awaits.

"And Sappho . . . she secretly *welcomes* these things; she revels in the very idea of total nuclear/biological decimation, the termination of all life on the planet.

"She was the true overseer of the royal Caste, although her

leadership was carefully filtered through a decision-making process involving all four of us. She was most subtle in this. Even Aristotle, in the beginning, did not comprehend that most of our actions ultimately coincided with Sappho's desires.

"Codrus, alas, never grew conscious of her hidden domination. In fact, Codrus even failed to comprehend that Sappho actually welcomed the Apocalypse." Timmy scowled. "As a specialist, Codrus was brilliant, but he carried unto death a naïveté that was, in many ways, truly astonishing.

"And then there was Theophrastus. Generally, our scientific maestro applied his formidable logic to support Sappho's ideas, although he was most careful to maintain an air of political neutrality. In fact, he often publicly disputed her suggestions. But, actually, Theophrastus was unswervingly loyal to her.

"There was the Star-Edge effort. One of Theophrastus's tways, using the name Teddy Carrera, had successfully infiltrated and took control of that grand project. Ostensibly, the plan was to gather as many Paratwa as possible and retreat into space—to escape the Apocalypse by colonizing another world."

A brittle laugh filled the tiny chamber. "Colonizing another world! Ahh, what secret delight Sappho must have taken in that, knowing that Aristotle, Codrus, and perhaps a thousand other Paratwa had been inspired to believe in this great ideal! We would escape the Earth's decimation. We would create a culture, a civilization, based on Paratwa rule. The binaries would, at long last, be free of humanity's persecution."

Timmy shook his head. "It was a fantasy, of course, but a potent one; a fantasy that Sappho was able to use to rally the breeds, and eventually bind many of them into the service of the royal Caste. Sappho understood the nature of such a deep desire, a secret dream shared by many of the Paratwa. She understood how to cultivate that dream, how to build it into a thing capable of generating fanatic loyalty."

Empedocles permitted genuine curiosity to emerge from both faces. "The Star-Edge project was a sham?"

"From the very beginning. There was never any intention

of colonizing other planets." Timmy grinned and patted the Susan/tway's arm. "But I race ahead of myself here. This is not proper conduct for a teacher."

"Not proper," Empedocles murmured, thoroughly intrigued by the disclosure.

"As I stated, it was Sappho's secret lust for the coming Apocalypse that initially aroused the suspicions of Aristotle. He could make no sense out of this. Why did she want the world destroyed, humanity annihilated? The Ash Ock collectively recognized that, in most situations, it was preferable to conquer rather than destroy. Yet Sappho's hidden agenda ran counter to this inherent goal. While her public persona sought ways to prevent the Apocalypse, she secretly plotted to guarantee its occurrence.

"Aristotle's growing suspicions in this area lead him to examine other assumptions. One of these involved the birth order of the Ask Ock.

"As you know, the Sphere of the royal Caste indicates that Codrus was the firstborn, followed by Aristotle, Sappho, Theophrastus, and, much later, yourself. The accepted truth was that we four seniors—" he smiled "—were born nearly simultaneously, with less that a week separating us in age. As children, we all remembered one another quite clearly. Our tways played and romped together within the confines of Thi Maloca. But whenever Aristotle utilized his iconic memory to recall his earliest days, he had the feeling that Sappho was present before any of the others.

"One day, Aristotle casually mentioned this novelty to Codrus. And somewhat to Aristotle's surprise, Codrus too reflected that his own oldest and deepest iconic memories involved Sappho.

"Aristotle came to the conclusion that the birth order was false. A lie had been told and retold until even our basic iconic awarenesses accepted its verity. In truth, Sappho must have been the firstborn. She had disguised this fact for the same reason that she had disguised her true role within the Ash Ock."

Timmy paused, raised his eyebrows. Empedocles knew that the old remnant was waiting for his "student" to provide a conclusion. Empedocles responded through his Gillian/tway, "It would seem as if Sappho sought always to camouflage herself under cover of the group mind. She practiced invisible politics—inducing actions that could not be traced back to her doorstep."

"Very good. Yes, Sappho indeed thrived on such subterfuge. In the beginning, Aristotle assumed that her 'invisible politics' was merely an elegant means of controlling the royal Caste. But later he came to understand that her deceptive ways were also an integral part of a most peculiar psychological makeup.

"At any rate, now more curious than ever to uncover Sappho's secrets, Aristotle began to study her every action, follow her every move. She possessed numerous odd behavior patterns, and one of the most curious of these involved her frequent treks to Brazilian coastal cities. During most of her travels, the plenary tway traveled alone, but when a journey was to be made to one of these Brazilian seaports, the partial always accompanied her."

"Plenary tway?" asked Empedocles. "Partial?"

"Ahh, yes. Sappho's configuration. Again, I race ahead of myself. Please forgive me.

"There had been a serious genetic mishap during Sappho's lab gestation—at least, that was the accepted story, which by this time, Aristotle regarded with a great deal of skepticism. Be that as it may, one of Sappho's tways possessed severe physiological defects.

"Her halves could not have been more different. The tway known as the plenary was a beautiful and seductive woman, a spellbinding creature, a witch able to attract men the way parched soil sucks in rainwater. In start contrast, her other tway, referred to as the partial, never grew beyond the size of a small child. The partial was born without arms and legs. She was cursed with neurosynaptic malformations that, when she was awake, caused almost constant facial neuralgia. The severity of these malformations made it impossible to attach even the most basic prosthetic devices."

Empedocles recalled the armless, legless child he had come across during early explorations of the underwater vessel.

"In our younger years," continued Timmy, "in Thi Maloca, the plenary used to transport the partial around in a simple electric carriage. Later, the partial was placed in a semipermanent gyropros. This fully robotic container, as well as automatically handling the partial's bodily functions, permitted a limited means of self-transport. The partial eventually learned to control basic gyropros movements via simple auditory commands."

"The partial was . . . intelligent?" asked Empedocles, realizing that his questions was imprecise even as he uttered it. But Timmy did not challenge his vagueness.

"Oh, yes, the partial was intelligent . . . or, at least, she appeared to be. Even with her crippling affliction, she was able to develop a small vocabulary of word-sounds to direct gyropros movements—no small achievement, considering the severity of her handicaps.

"Now, you must understand that by this time, Aristotle was challenging *all* of his previous beliefs. He was restructuring his entire conceptualization of Sappho, and doing so in a manner based strictly upon observation. He no longer accepted the accuracy of even his own memory. All data were recorded and cross-checked, then either verified or eliminated. Aristotle was convinced that such a conservative method was the only way he could learn the hidden truths of the Ask Ock.

"But this method, although accurate, was not providing him with a great deal of information. And although he had developed a theory about Sappho's crippled partial, there seemed no safe way of testing his hypothesis. His frustrations mounted. Finally, he concluded that he had to begin taking serious risks if he was to expand his data base. He concocted a plan.

"One day, when Sappho's plenary tway had departed— leaving the partial behind—Aristotle paid a visit to Sappho's current residence. The tways were both living in a private European scraper along the old border of Yugo/Hungary. Sappho occupied a ninety-first floor suite. The scraper was one of those ultraexpensive, ultrasecret hotels, where the entire staff, even the lowliest of servants, were prevented from transferring data to the outside world. At the end of each shift, the workers were thoroughly searched, scanned, and administered cribloc injections to erase all short-term memories. Each day, the entire operating staff had to be given a refresher course, relearn such forgotten details as the layout of the hotel and the names of the guests.

"The royal Caste had access to one another, of course, so Aristotle knew Sappho's home arrangements. He arrived at the hotel with the knowledge that only the partial would be there. Utilizing a needbreeder, his own cribloc injections, and some careful bribes, Aristotle managed to have the partial's breakfast tainted with an untraceable soporific. And so Jalka, tway of Aristotle, in servant's regalia, penetrated hotel security and entered Sappho's suite.

"The partial, having been fed her drugged breakfast by the gyropros, was unconscious." Timmy again closed his natural eye. "I remember it clearly. Feeding tubes were still attached to the partial's tiny mouth. Spittle dripped from her chin. And the gyropros' eclectics had become trapped in a logic loop, repeating the same progress, over and over. The machine's arms would withdraw the tubes from her mouth, wash her face, reinsert the tubes, determine that she was not swallowing, then again withdraw the tubes. Obviously, there had been a severe failure in the eclectics' programming—"

"What did Aristotle learn?" prodded Empedocles.

"Learn ... oh, yes. First, Aristotle disabled the eclectics and locked down its sensors. Then he integrated his own scan template—complete with a false set of customized spatiotemp memories—into the suite's internal security net. He had thought of all possible ways that his clandestine activities might be detected, and he had taken appropriate precautions. He could conceive of only one possible means for Sappho to find out about his secret visit."

"Through the tway herself," concluded Empedocles.

"Precisely. The plenary, who was currently thousands of miles away, should have been wondering why her handicapped partial had fallen asleep in the middle of breakfast—an odd occurrence, at best. But if Aristotle's theory regarding the partial was correct, then even that possibility would pose no threat to his safety.

"And so the examination of Sappho's partial took place. In less than twenty minutes, Aristotle had learned that his theory was even more correct than he could have imagined. The partial—this armless and legless thing that lived the majority of its existence strapped into the gyropros—was not really alive, at least, not in the fullest Ash Ock sense of the word.

"The partial's true internal makeup was disguised by a self-generated skin screen. But beneath the protective field, the partial was fabricated out of biochips—sophisticated nano-cellular components—and of a type totally unfamiliar to Aristotle. These biochip components mimicked standard human organ configurations, with one notable exception. Inside the partial's vaginal canal was an interface organ with nodal connectors."

Empedocles nodded both heads, remembering that the tiny child he had come across had been vaginally attached to a computer terminal.

"Aristotle concluded that the partial was certainly no tway. He realized that she was, in fact, nothing more than a complex android, designed to react appropriately to the plenary's body patterns, to provide the illusion that she was one half of a Paratwa, even down to the detail of appearing to be able to split from the plenary, to function—in her limited manner—as an independent tway.

"Aristotle had the foresight to bring with him a variety of surveillance devices, and upon learning that the partial was an android, he decided to take the added risk of implanting holotronic recorders beneath its flesh. These recorders were the least detectable type of scanner available, passive in the extreme. Unfortunately, this fact also dictated their primary limitation, namely that accessing their accumulated information would necessitate their removal from the partial at a later date. Still, Aristotle deemed the recorders the only reasonably safe means of secretly monitoring the partial's immediate aural/visual arena. Perhaps at some later time, he could extricate the recorders and gain a wealth of new information."

Timmy shook his head. "Aristotle safely exited the suite before the soporific wore off, but as you might well imagine, he was now more mystified than ever. Answering one question had created numerous new ones. Why had Sappho created a "fake" half? If this partial was not Sappho's real tway, then who was? Was the plenary even a Paratwa? Could Sappho be merely human? Who had designed and created the partial? Where had such sophisticated and unknown nanocellular components come from? What was the purpose of that interface organ in her vaginal canal?

"The more he learned, the more utterly bizarre the reality of the royal Caste began to appear. Neither Aristotle nor his tways were capable of suffering true paranoia, but after the visit to the partial, his suspicions had certainly reached an apex.

"Concurrently, Aristotle also had begun to investigate the backgrounds of Thi Maloca's Ash Ock scientists—the so-called creators of the royal Caste. This quickly bloomed into yet another great mystery. Aristotle's secret inquiries and data traces revealed that all of Thi Maloca's scientific contingent had fake histories. The 'creators' had been recruited from all over the globe, yet data roadblocks existed wherever Aristotle attempted to research their immediate genealogies. Ultimately frustrated, he was forced to the conclusion that the Ash Ock scientists had come out of nowhere. They had no pasts.

"It was at this point in time when Aristotle decided he needed to safeguard his growing tapestry of strange facts. He had penetrated the fledgling E-Tech archival network, which was being prepared by agglomerating masses of data from the world's computer systems. Within the archives, Aristotle discovered a very powerful rescue program, called Freebird. Using it as a prototype, he fashioned his own particular model. *His* Freebird, secretly hidden within the archives, would become a repository for all the data he was compiling on Sappho and the royal Caste. If something should happen to Aristotle . . ." Timmy hesitated, stared solemnly at the floor.

"Go on," urged Empedocles, hoping to refocus him before another bout of melancholia produced silence.

Timmy looked up, startled. "Where was I?"

Empedocles forced patience. "You were discussing Freebird."

"Ahh, yes. Aristotle transferred every new scrap of information he discovered into Freebird's memory. Should Sappho discover his secret investigations and attempt to take ultimate sanctions against him, Aristotle could threaten to open Freebird and turn its information over to E-Tech. Freebird was intended to be his 'ace in the hole.' In the event that things went wrong, the program might serve to rescue Aristotle from disaster.

"His obvious next step was to investigate Sappho's plenary tway. She had to hold the keys to this entire enigma. Aristotle concluded that he had to learn more about her clandestine trips to these various Brazilian coastal cities.

"And so Aristotle waited until the next occasion when both tways journeyed together to South America. After Sappho's tways returned and the plenary had once again departed on other business—leaving the partial alone at the European hotel—Aristotle sprang into action.

"Another complex sequence of events . . . another soporific injected into the partial's food . . . and tway Jalka again entered Sappho's suite. The recorders, implanted months earlier, were successfully removed from the unconscious android.

"Aristotle journeyed back to his own current operational base in Cape Town, South Africa. And it was there, in the sheltered privacy of his villa, where he accessed the implants' aural/visual data and uncovered the truth of the Paratwa."

Through the ears of Empedocles, Gillian listened, at first fascinated by this story that transcended all that he had heretofore known or suspected. But as Aristotle's tale continued, he found himself wishing for a sort of oblivion, a deevolution of data, a way to reduce this expanding sphere of cognition. He wanted to be able to somehow revert, fall backward in time, be carried on a temporal stream toward a simplicity of form and function. He wanted to blot all new knowledge from consciousness.

Had he been in control of his body, he suspected that he would have gone looking for another fight. Full-body flush; a cathartic release of psychic turmoil. But being an amalgam offered no such opportunity. There was no escape.

Susan perceived Gillian's torment though she could not understand the reason for it. To her, Timmy's story was utterly intriguing. *What's wrong?*

I'm afraid, he responded calmly, maintaining a degree of composure to prevent Empedocles from sensing his discomfort.

Afraid of what?
I don't know.

Timmy slipped into his best instructor's pose: backbone straight, chin tilted back, eyes pinched slightly closed as if trying to gaze upon vistas far beyond the cramped odorous walls of the chamber. Empedocles recalled that such a posture had usually preceded Aristotle's drier lectures.

"There are five basic forces of nature," Timmy began. "Gravitation, electromagnetism, the strong nuclear, the weak nuclear, and the T-psionic.

"It is the fifth force, the T-psionic, which accounts for the phenomenon of the binary interlink, the ability of a Paratwa's tways to remain telepathically linked no matter what distance might separate them. The T-psionic is the newest of the five, not having been discovered until the middle of the twenty-first century, when the McQuade Unity was developed, permitting Paratwa to be bred. But even at the height of Earth science, in those years before the Apocalypse, there was never a clear and full understanding of the properties and parameters of the T-psionic force. However, it was suspected that within the complexity of life on Earth, the vast carpet of organic activity that was once the sine qua non of the planet—*gaia,* as it were—it was suspected that within this familiar sphere, the T-psionic remained an essentially weak force, reaching its full resonance only among the mind-linked Paratwa.

"In fact, many twenty-first century scientists believed that the T-psionic force actually occurred at varying intensities throughout the universe, just as gravitation, for example, varied according to the amount of mass present within a particular area of space. One theory suggested that the closer one came to the center of a galaxy, the greater the intensity of the

T-psionic force. It was also believed—quite rightly, as it turned out—that the degree of T-psionic force existing within our own spatial arena, out here near the edge of the galaxy, remained at a particularly low level.

"Now let us imagine another place—another world, far closer to the galactic core—where the force of the T-psionic was not weak but immensely strong, where the attributes of this T-psionic force directly influenced the primordial biosphere of an emergent planet. Imagine a world where the impetus of evolution, consistently patterned by the ability of *all* organisms to generate telepathic linkages, eventually led to the development of intelligence.

"Imagine this strange world where everything communicated, where the distinctions between plant and animal, between herbivore and carnivore, between male and female even, remained of minor import, at least in comparison to our own planet—where inter- and intraspecies domination developed as the primary motif. Imagine the ultimate rise of a particular combination of cooperating organisms upon this world—an intelligence composed of a multiplicity of interacting lifeforms, telepathically cojoined to achieve common ends. At its highest level, an intelligence consisting of pairs— tways—each telepathically linked half composed of a vast conglomerate of lesser cooperatively existing organisms. Such tways themselves would be untroubled by the necessities of procreation; their individual components would take care of such specific needs, at various paces, in varying styles.

"Let us give a name to this alien master race, these sets of tways made up of mutual conglomerates of cooperating organisms. Let us call them the Os/Ka/Loq.

"We do not know when the Os/Ka/Loq first grew their great organic interstellar vessels. Five thousand years ago? A hundred thousand? A million? Suffice it to say that they became a spacefaring species a very long time ago. They sent out many of these massive vessels, filled not only with their own tways but with representative organisms from the entire sweep of cooperative life existing on their homeworld. Each great vessel, as it were, was a miniature gaia.

"These immense starships scoured the galaxy, navigating

not according to any spatial or temporal relationships—as human beings might—but choosing their directions primarily on the strength of T-psionic impulses. The stronger the force of the T-psionic in a particular sector of space, the more intensely the Os/Ka/Loq vessel was attracted in that direction. And where an Os/Ka/Loq starship came upon another planet bearing life, whether intelligent or not, they sought to reseed it with their own syntheses of life.

"The Os/Ka/Loq, quite naturally, never developed what we might refer to as a sanctifying respect for intelligent species. That concept simply did not occur to the occupants of world where the T-psionic force was so inordinately potent. Lifeforms on planets where the T-psionic force remained weak were perceived as perversions of what was natural. They were reseeded with what *was* natural—organisms from the Os/Ka/Loq's home planet. Native populations were either vigorously eliminated or, where possible, coupled. The presence of an intelligent species on a world was never a factor in Os/Ka/Loq plans. Intelligence itself, although admired as a sophisticated evolutionary adaptation, was not the Os/Ka/Loq's guiding factor in what they considered superior life. Alien organisms were graded in importance according to the strength of their telepathic linkages.

"There was a particular Os/Ka/Loq vessel, known as the Biodyysey, which had drifted into our immediate spatial sector, our *kaşcht*. Since the T-psionic force remained relatively weak within the boundaries of this *kaşcht*—which encompasses our solar system as well as many nearby stars—I can only speculate as to why the Biodyysey came here. Perhaps the Os/Ka/Loq had already reseeded all of the inner galactic worlds. Perhaps they perceived Earth, with its poverty of T-psionic force, as a new challenge. I cannot say precisely. All that is known for certain is that at some time in the early years of the twenty-first century, one of the Biodyysey's probe ships secretly landed on Earth. Or, should I say, landed beneath the ocean, several hundred miles off the coast of South America. You are now, of course, within that probe—this cell of the Os/Ka/Loq.

"There was a solitary Os/Ka/Loq intelligence aboard this

probe—a tway—who naturally maintained T-psionic contact with her other tway aboard the Biodyysey. The methodology of Os/Ka/Loq exploration provided for numerous probes, each containing a tway, to be ejected from the mother ship. Each probe was to seek out hospitable planets and prepare them for reseeding according to Os/Ka/Loq principles.

"The particular tway who landed here on Earth urged her brethren to consider our *kascht* as the place of their next reseeding. Despite the fact that our *kascht* reeked of the lacking—that is, its T-psionic force remained exceptionally weak—this tway was able to convince her fellow Os/Ka/Loq explorers that the Earth was their best choice. Far from the galactic core, with reseedable planets likely becoming harder and harder to locate, the Os/Ka/Loq aboard the Biodyysey came to an agreement that the Earth would be their next target.

"And so the Biodyysey steered a course toward the solar system. And here on Earth, far beneath the waters of the Atlantic Ocean, the tway aboard this probe set about making the necessary preparations for the mother ship's arrival.

"Her Os/Ka/Loq name is unpronounceable—just as the word Os/Ka/Loq itself was coined for the benefit of humans. But by now, you must certainly know who I'm talking about."

"Sappho," murmured Empedocles.

"Yes . . . Sappho.

"She set about studying the lifeforms on our planet. Rather quickly, I presume, she came to the realization that our world offered some unique hindrances to the reseeding. That low-level T-psionic force that dominated our spatial neighborhood had led to the development of life on Earth where the concepts of domination/submission had been carried to extremes. From the Os/Ka/Loq point of view, the Earth must have looked like one crazy place, with nearly every species on the planet fighting for survival. Instead of the basic Os/Ka/Loq notion, which might be aptly expressed as *cooperation of the fittest*, our world boasted something quite different."

"*Survival* of the fittest," offered Empedocles.

"Indeed. Survival of the fittest. Our planet lacked what the Os/Ka/Loq perceived as even the basic stabilizing influence of a moderate T-psionic force. On Earth, millions of years of intense rivalries among countless species had produced a wild continuum of plants and animals, all at odds with one another, all fighting for a piece of the pie. Individuality carried to extremes."

Empedocles adopted twin frowns. "These Os/Ka/Loq must have had some notion of individuality? If this tway of Sappho was here on Earth alone, she must have been making at least some of her own decisions."

"That is correct. The Os/Ka/Loq, although maintaining telepathic alignments with all lifeforms that developed upon their world, still existed as individual conglomerates of entities. It is the degree of the T-psionic force that distinguishes us from them. The T-psionic force is extremely weak here on our planet, but it does exist. On the Os/Ka/Loq homeworld, it is far stronger, but even there it has limitations. Individuality exists in both places. Like most facets of the universe, the process ultimately comes down to a matter of relativity.

"I once came across a monograph Theophrastus did on the subject of T-psionic field strengths. He postulated that there might be an ultimate place of T-psionic interaction, where the force would be so strong that *no* possible individual distinctions could ever come into being. Only one lifeform would ever exist there; one entity composed of everything, a cell unto itself.

"At any rate, here on Earth, this tway of Sappho began the secret exploration of our world. She sent out small robotic probe ships, which gathered numerous lifeforms to return to this cell for analysis, for genetic experimentation."

"The things in the cages," said Empedocles, through the mouth of Susan.

"Yes. Early experiments, for the most part. Later, of course, as Sappho became more skilled working with our genetic material, her results improved remarkably. But in the beginning, there were numerous bizarre mutations. Some of the more unusual ones were preserved."

"A museum for their aberrations," said Empedocles.

"Yes, a museum of sorts. But Aristotle always assumed that from the point of view of telepathic entities like the Os/Ka/

Loq—themselves composed of a multiplicity of awareness-linked organisms—the idea of aberration would not have been a well-developed concept. No matter how bizarre the mutation, the Os/Ka/Loq would remain telepathically linked with it. Therefore, it would be part of their consensual consciousness, no more alien to them than your arm or leg might be to you. But here on our planet, within a *kascht* that reeked of the lacking to such a high degree, such mutations could have proved inordinately fascinating. Twinhead, for example. An utterly unique individual for *two* reasons. First, twinhead possessed little or no telepathic consciousness. And second, his actual appearance placed him a great distance from the genetic prototype. He was a true one-of-a-kind. A true museum piece.

"Anyway, the tway of Sappho made good progress with her experiments. Within a few years, she was successfully recreating 'normal' human beings, at least normal in appearance. Many of these humans were later used in Thi Maloca, enslaved to Sappho's will via mnemonic cursors."

"The so-called Ash Ock scientists," mused Empedocles. "That's why you couldn't locate histories for them. The scientists all were born and raised here, within this cell."

"Precisely. But the scientists themselves represented only the beginning of Sappho's plan. What she ultimately sought was a foothold on our world, a way to transplant stronger aspects of the T-psionic force into earthly form. By the mid-twenty-first century, she had succeeded. It was Sappho who actually was responsible for the astonishing breakthrough known across the globe as the McQuade Unity. The famed Scottish lab credited with discovering these primitive telepathic masses merely had served as a front for her efforts.

"It was Sappho who made possible a limited form of direct T-psionic prowess for the human race, for the artificially grown McQuade Unity, when injected into a pair of dissimilar fetuses, caused those fetuses to grow and develop as one.

"It was Sappho who designed and introduced the binary variation of telepathic wholeness that became known as the Paratwa."

Empedocles had always considered himself immune to astonishment, seeing it as an emotionally based reaction to a rapid overload of fresh information, something that could be overcome through concentration and analysis. But when both of his mouths dropped open—when he experienced genuine surprise—he realized that, under the right conditions, any parameter could be exceeded.

Timmy continued. "And it was Sappho who first transferred her own genetic material, her own *consciousness*, into a female fetus, thus, in a way, serving as her own creator, making herself into the first and only Paratwa of mixed species. One tway human, one tway Os/Ka/Loq. Firstborn of the royal Caste. The human portion—the plenary—endowed with a T-psionic field capable of extending her lifespan far beyond the limited boundaries of human beings."

"Six hundred years," whispered Empedocles.

"Yes. Well in excess of what pre-Apocalyptic science was capable of granting, despite transplants and regenerative techniques. Aristotle always suspected that six hundred years was only a fraction of an average Os/Ka/Loq lifespan. But six hundred years was a most impressive achievement, nonetheless, considering that the genetic material used to create Sappho's plenary was strictly Earth-based.

"When she was still a small child, the plenary tway, who was fully iconically conscious, arranged for the Ash Ock scientists to produce three more Paratwa. Those three were to be trained as specialists in disparate fields.

"Codrus would be the financial expert, Aristotle the political master, and Theophrastus, the research scientist. A bit later, it was decided that a fifth Ash Ock would be necessary. But I'll explain the reasons for your creation in a moment.

"Sappho also fabricated her partial 'tway,' building the android from nanocellular components readily available within this cell. In fact, the form of biochip technology found in the partial, which had earlier mystified Aristotle, forms the basis for almost their entire scientific attainment. The Os/Ka/Loq grow most of their tools—the massive seedships, these smaller probes, many of their weapons."

"FTL transmitters?" asked Empedocles.

"No. The FTL *was* a true invention of Theophrastus. And

although he based it on Os/Ka/Loq technology, I believe he specifically designed it so that it could be manufactured instead of grown . . . which explains how and why the FTL was able to be replicated by Colonial scientists.

"The basic genetic structures of all Paratwa utilized earthly DNA. But for the Ash Ock fetuses—including Sappho's plenary—the particular McQuade Unity injected to produce the telepathic interlace differed substantially from the type used in the creation of the other breeds. This McQuade Unity had been endowed with an invisible aspect of sorts . . . an undetectable distillation of what the Os/Ka/Loq possessed naturally, yet a variation specific to our *kascht*."

Timmy released a sigh. "I confess my scientific inadequacies here. My explanation does not do justice to the phenomenon of the Ash Ock. But I'm afraid that only Theophrastus—or the Os/Ka/Loq—could define the depth of our existence more clearly. Suffice it to say that we of the royal Caste have nothing in our genes that makes us the way we are. This should clarify something that you certainly must have been curious about over the years."

Empedocles gave a double nod. "No medical exam ever detected evidence indicating that my tways had greatly extended lifespans."

"Precisely. Just as your very existence as a tway of a Paratwa remained unfathomable, so too did your extraordinary life expectancy, for both concepts have nothing to do with DNA and everything to do with the T-psionic. And this fifth force of nature still remains basically immeasurable by the methodologies of earth science.

"However, there was an unexpected side effect involving the creation of the Ash Ock. The tway-sets were endowed with a certain . . . weakness. The Os/Ka/Loq creature known as Sappho, with one tway on the Biodyysey and one tway on Earth, had been a solitary consciousness—up until that moment when the tway here on Earth transferred her consciousness into human form. From that instant, Sappho was able to exist as a pair of distinct halves. The side effect gave rise to the most unique aspect of the royal Caste: the ability of the Ash Ock Paratwa to live in both worlds, to be either one or two, to be able to split into separately conscious tways or unite into monarchy."

Empedocles shrugged his Gillian/tway. "I always suspected that having conscious halves was a flaw. The natural perfection of monarchy was forever being interrupted by these lesser awarenesses, these side effects." He stopped abruptly. Fresh comprehension filled him with excitement. He smiled, allowing both faces to express his triumph.

"Ahh, my good student," said Timmy, grinning also. "I see now that you finally understand. Be of good cheer, Empedocles. From now on, your problems in this area will be notably diminished."

Gillian steeled his emotions, using every bit of willpower at his command to prevent an undercurrent of devastating terror from bursting out of him and entering their monarch's field of vision. *I know why I'm afraid,* he projected.

Susan waited.

Gillian drew what he imagined to be a deep breath; he tried to induce those mnemonic aspects that had once been his lips to propel the terror out of him. But the words refused to come.

What is it? asked Susan, perceiving his reluctance, his growing fear. *Whatever it is, Gillian, you have to say it. Even if he hears you. Just say it.*

Gillian imagined himself nodding his head. The words came. *I can't go back again.* He imagined his breath coming in short palsied spurts. He imagined himself hyperventilating.

Susan projected bewilderment. *What do you mean?*

I can't go back again, he repeated. *I can't return to my body. I'm trapped here.*

I . . . don't understand. You said that we just had to wait for the proper conflux of circumstances. You said that under the proper conditions, we could dissolve the interlace. . . .

I was wrong. He sensed bitter laughter rising from his guts. *I was so afraid of the alternative—becoming like Timmy, Gillian and Empedocles melding together into a new consciousness—that I lost sight of the truth.*

What truth? demanded Susan, not worrying whether or not

Empedocles sensed her emotions—frustration mixed with a growing fear.

Gillian forced himself to continue. *Here, within this cell of the Os/Ka/Loq, where the purities of the T-psionic force have been maintained, Timmy was able to correct arrhythmia of the whelm. But that was not all he was able to do. Besides incorporating you, Susan Quint, into the wholeness of Empedocles, thus bringing back a fully dualistic Paratwa, Timmy also arranged it so that I could never escape this amalgamated state of consciousness.*

Susan found herself refusing to accept his conclusions. *How do you know?*

The mnemonic cursors! They've put some kind of a hold on me. I can feel it! Within my body—within the consciousness of Gillian—these control cursors have been configured to prevent me from ever attempting to dissolve the interlace. Timmy must have issued specific commands to the cursors while I was in one of my dream states. He arranged for me to be subsumed forever to the will of the monarch. I can't break free!

Susan forced resolve into her words. *If Timmy issued those commands to your mnemonic cursors, then he must also know the counter phrases that would reverse their effects. We just have to figure out a way to persuade him. Or else, we have to gain access to that control language.*

How? We're trapped in here as amalgams! And we need more than just access to that control language. Remember, my particular mnemonic cursors must first be armed by Timmy's wetware eye. Gillian felt a wave of defeat pour from consciousness. *It's no use. Timmy is the only one who can bring me back. And he won't do it willingly!*

Susan understood. A chill escaped her. *And now Empedocles knows all of this. Our monarch now realizes how important Timmy is to you.*

Empedocles's triumphant feeling produced a new sense of resolve. "Why was I created?" he demanded. "Why did Sappho need a fifth Ash Ock?"

Timmy smiled. "For the Apocalypse, of course. I do not know for certain whether or not the nuclear/biological decimation of 2099 would have occurred without Os/Ka/Loq assistance. The human race was becoming more and more self-destructive in its own right. In fact, it's even possible that humanity's pre-Apocalyptic excesses were the prime factor attracting the Biodyssey to this world in the first place. It was—as those contemporary semiotic-driven freelancers might phrase it—'ripe for the picking.'

"But whatever the case, the Os/Ka/Loq planned for the Apocalypse to occur. We, the Ash Ock, along with Paratwa from dozens of other breeding labs, were destined to be the agents of planetary decimation. Sappho created the royal Caste specifically to unite the thousands of Paratwa so that humanity's destructive tendencies could be accelerated and brought into line with the Os/Ka/Loq timetable. But apparently, the drive toward global havoc fell behind schedule."

Empedocles murmured. "That's why I was created. To ensure that the Apocalypse occurred on time."

"Yes, that was the primary reason. Also, Sappho was beginning to fear the sheer savagery of some of the binaries. Many Paratwa refused to grant allegiance to the Ash Ock because the royal Caste were not warriors. The Ash Ock did not live by the binding creeds of the assassin. Because of that perceived shortcoming, many Paratwa still refused to trust the Ash Ock.

"In addition, there were a handful of Paratwa in outright revolt against the royal Caste, a handful shrewd enough to perceive that the Ash Ock were actually attempting to achieve the Apocalypse. These few Paratwa actively opposed Sappho and her minions and worked to defend the Earth against the royal Caste.

"And as a final problem, there were a handful of erratic Paratwa—the walking time bombs like Reemul—whose frequently unpredictable actions also threatened the sanctity of the Os/Ka/Loq timetable.

"In short, too wide a conceptual gap existed between the ordinary breeds and the Ash Ock. Many of the assassins were beginning to buy the Ash Ock 'dream' of a united race of Paratwa, but many others remained unable, or unwilling, to grant their full allegiance.

"And so, you were created. Empedocles—the Ash Ock warrior, whose mastery in combat would help doubters become Ash Ock sympathizers." Timmy grinned. "You were to bring new stability to the concept of a united Paratwa, so that the Os/Ka/Loq vision of Earth destruction could occur as planned. In fact, even though the E-Tech raid on Thi Maloca and the death of Catharine cut short your 'career,' the very fact of your existence proved beneficial. Meridian's allegiance to the royal Caste was further sealed by a challenge to train you and make you the best of the assassins. And Meridian's early reports on your abilities, coupled with my own high recommendations, did serve to bring some wavering Paratwa into the fold.

"Of course, Sappho and Theophrastus were aware that you yourself could, theoretically, also become an eventual threat to their plans."

Empedocles nodded twice. "That's why they implanted my tways with mnemonic cursors and arranged a specific technique for arming those cursors."

"Exactly. It was to be a means of control, albeit a limited one, for only your tways could fall under the manipulation of that protolingual tongue—which, incidentally, came from a deep-brain language developed by the Os/Ka/Loq. But your monarchial consciousness remained capable of overriding any mnemonic cursor." Timmy paused. "They did not want to provide *that* severe an inhibition upon your natural abilities.

"And so, to a small degree, your influence did help maintain the Os/Ka/Loq timetable. The Apocalypse occurred on schedule. Gaia—the totality of Earth's organic concoction—was essentially erased from the planet. This tapestry of life, which reeked of the lacking, which was perceived as totally unnatural by Os/Ka/Loq standards, was wiped out to prepare the Earth for reseeding.

"You see, the great strength of Os/Ka/Loq lifeforms—their ability to develop in telepathic harmony with one another—also remains their greatest weakness. Without extreme efforts on their behalf, the tapestry of Os/Ka/Loq life could not hope to compete with organisms from environments where T-psionic energies remained spartan. In particular, within the *kascht* of ultracompetitive Earth organisms, where the concept of survival of the fittest reigned supreme, the Os/Ka/Loq lifeforms would have stood little chance of survival. The delicacy of their interdependence requires a less threatening, more gentle ecosphere.

"Although Earth remained weak in the T-psionic force, it did possess the proper attributes for sustaining organic life. Despite the vast differences between Os/Ka/Loq and Earth organisms, the planets themselves shared what was indeed a rarity throughout the Os/Ka/Loq-explored galaxy. Both worlds existed within that proper window of biological opportunity, which permitted carbon-based lifeforms to thrive near maximum levels."

Empedocles produced two mild frowns. "The Os/Ka/Loq obviously possess tools far superior to Earth-based technology. Why such a convoluted plan for destroying Earth's organic tapestry? Why not simply come here in their starship—this Biodyysey—and wipe out the planetary gaia? Then simply terraform the world to their own specifications?"

"Excellent questions," complimented Timmy. "And you are correct in your assessment of their technological superiority. But still, they do have limits. For one thing, they do not possess FTL travel. Einstein's paradigm continues to thwart them. Consequently, they move very slowly throughout the galaxy.

"But what you perceive as a convoluted plan is not really that way at all. In actuality, the Os/Ka/Loq, after countless millennia of experience, have adopted a most expedient method for 'terraforming' alien worlds for reseeding. Remember, this cell that we are in—this seed ship—was just one of many sent out ahead of the Biodyysey, in all directions. And each of these cells, containing an Os/Ka/Loq tway, explores within a specific temporal range of the mother ship. As far as I understand, that range has never been greatly altered throughout their spacefaring history.

"When this cell—when Sappho—first reported of conditions here on Earth, the Biodyysey remained approximately three Earth centuries away from our planet. As I said, these individual cells *always* explore within a specific temporal range of their main vessels. The Os/Ka/Loq are a very calculating, very deliberate species. Long ago, they must have developed this modus operandi for reseeding hostile planets." Timmy paused. "Can you grasp the significance of that temporal framework?"

"I believe so," Empedocles replied slowly. "My Gillian-tway gained certain knowledge from the Czar, regarding the natural renewal of the Earth's gaia. The planet is returning to life, coming back form its nuclear/biological devastation. The ecosphere is currently ready to accept a concentrated effort leading toward complete restoration."

"Precisely," said Timmy. "The Earth is indeed coming back to life. The Os/Ka/Loq, ages ago, established what they obviously consider the best method for reseeding. First, nuclear/biological devastation. And then, after the majority of evolutionary strains are wiped out and the prime carpet of life destroyed, a wait of 250 to 300 Earth years, until such time as the natural process of planetary regenesis begins anew. At the point where true ecospheric turnaround starts to occur—when a planet begins to cleanse itself of its poisons—the Os/Ka/Loq introduce custom-tailored organisms to facilitate the process.

"From reseeding countless worlds, the Os/Ka/Loq have learned to predict accurately the effects of nuclear/biological decimation upon specific ecospheres. They have learned to control the parameters of destruction in order the ensure that their seedships arrive at the most opportune times.

"But on Earth, what Sappho and the Os/Ka/Loq did *not* foresee—at least, not until it was too late—was the tenacious insight of numerous individual human beings, many of whom perceived the coming of the Apocalypse with the same clarity as Sappho. And these individuals made their own plans to save the race by bringing E-Tech into existence, by coopting the space cylinders, which were already in the advance stages of construction, and using them as a preserve for the human race.

"And when the Apocalypse finally came in 2099, when the Ash Ock and many of the Paratwa escaped in the Star-Edge fleet, they left behind a real threat to their ultimate goals. Namely, the Colonies of Irrya."

Empedocles arrived at another conclusion. "The Star-Edge

fleet headed into deep space not to colonize other worlds but to rendezvous with the Biodyssey."

Timmy nodded. "Of course. And Codrus was left behind in the Colonies, along with a few other assassins being held in stasis. Codrus was, as I have indicated, never the intellectual equal of the rest of our breed. He would have been of no great use to the Os/Ka/Loq, unlike Theophrastus, whose inherent genius was immediately recognized.

"But Codrus could still contribute to the Os/Ka/Loq goals. First, he would inhibit the Colonies' technological advancement. Although the Os/Ka/Loq were—and still are— far beyond humans in terms of scientific application, they did have some real concerns about the incredible growth rate of human technology over the past few centuries. They acknowledged the possibility, however slight, that the Irryan Colonies, if scientifically unshackled, might indeed reach a level of technological sophistication that could pose a threat to their returning Biodyysey.

"But Codrus succeeded in keeping E-Tech strong. Technological advancement was effectively controlled and stifled, at least until fifty-six years ago. But by then it was too late for humanity ever to catch up.

"Codrus also hindered any concerted Colonial efforts at artificially revitalizing the Earth. The Os/Ka/Loq, having timed the arrival of the Biodyysey to coincide with the precalculated natural restorative cycle of the planet, wanted no alteration of that time frame. And so Codrus, secretly working through the auspices of the ICN, effectively prevented any large-scale Ecospheric Turnaround projects from taking place." Timmy smiled. "Everything was going along quite nicely for the Os/Ka/Loq until fifty-six years ago, when Codrus's control slipped, leading to a complex sequence of events that ultimately brought *us* together, here and now."

There has to be a way to stop him, projected Susan. *After all, these control cursors are located within your physical body, not mine. Maybe I can dissolve the interlace?*

Gillian acknowledged the truth of her statement. *But how? It takes both tways, acting in tandem, to reverse the whelm. . . .* He hesitated, recalling the events of fifty-six years past, when he had faced Reemul. Back then, Empedocles had also returned, only to be dissolved a short time later by the fury of the liege-killer's attack. But Gillian knew that those events had occurred under an entirely different set of conditions. That whelm had been very fragile, with only one tway—Gillian—available to give rise to the monarchy. Today's circumstances were different.

Susan read his thoughts. *There has to be a way!* she insisted. *Timmy may very well be our only hope.*

Susan imagined herself swallowing her fear, forcing herself to repress a growing sense of terror. *If that's true, we have to act quickly.*

You're right! If Timmy's the only one who can bring us back, we don't have much time.

"Council of Irrya, September eighteenth, 2363," began Maria Losef. "Confidential database, standard access."

"Confidential database?" wondered Jon Van Ostrand, his amplified voice tinged with sarcasm, his rugged face contorting into multiple sneers on the pentagonal FTL screens. "These days, that seems to be a real misnomer. We may as well hold these meetings in a freelancer studio!"

"The disclosures that you refer to have caused minimal damage," Losef said soothingly.

"Minimal?" Exasperated, Van Ostrand shook his head. "How many protesters did you say have gathered outside Council chambers?"

Edward Huromonus, with typical poise, read the latest figures from his monitor. "Estimates are upward of four hundred and fifty thousand in the surrounding streets. Plus at least another three hundred thousand scattered in smaller groups throughout Irrya. Many other Colonies are also experiencing vigorous assemblages within their governmental sectors."

"Millions of protesters," complained Van Ostrand. "And all of them knowing not only that this Paratwa vessel has entered our defensive net but also that fifteen of the Guardians' advance targeteers have assumed attack positions. Worse yet, the protesters have learned the strength and makeup of our primary force. They even know when our first wave will come within offensive range!"

The lion could not fault the Guardian Commander for his acrimony. Certainly, it was not misplaced. But Van Ostrand could not be told the truth, at least not yet. It would certainly not do for him to learn that the lion, Huromonus, and Inez Hernandez had been responsible for leaking the details of these Guardian attack plans to the freelancers.

Huromonus cleared his throat. "About ninety-five percent of these protesters favor an immediate attack upon the invading starship."

"I wasn't aware that the details of defensive strategies were open to public debate," snapped the Guardian Commander.

"The voices of democracy have spoken," Inez Hernandez added, without so much as a trace of irony.

"Spare me!"

The lion was not really surprised by Van Ostrand's anger. Nick had foreseen this reaction. Birch hard-liner or not, Van Ostrand possessed enough egotism to want to arrive at his own decisions. Never mind that Irryan citizenry was firmly in his court; if the Guardians were ordered to attack the Biodyysey, Van Ostrand wanted it to be his own decree, not something influenced by the vagaries of public opinion. He remained, in the most traditional sense, a military man. The lion just hoped that this aspect of Van Ostrand's personality did not jeopardize Nick's ultimate plan.

Losef continued to assuage. "It's quite possible that your anger is misdirected. I doubt whether anyone on this Council would have had reason to leak these details."

Wrong, thought the lion. *We had very good reason*.

"Meridian may have been responsible," suggested Losef.

The Guardian Commander glared. "Probably so. Which is why this Council should have held Meridian incommunicado between Council sessions, instead of letting him roam freely throughout Irrya."

"I understand," said Inez, staring up at the chandelier, "that Meridian has been on an extended shopping spree in several of our major retail districts."

Van Ostrand grimaced.

Losef held up her hand. "Jon, where the leaks originated is of no consequence at this point. You know as well as we do that holding Meridian incommunicado would have been a futile effort. As a tway, he remains in contact with their vessel. Other Paratwa are already here in the Colonies. It's obvious that we're dealing with an information loop beyond our ability to neutralize."

For a moment, Van Ostrand looked ready to offer fresh complaints. Instead, he nodded grudgingly. "All right, I suppose you're correct. And if my anger has been misdirected, I apologize to the Council."

"Thank you," said Losef. "Now perhaps we can move on to the task at hand. Meridian is waiting outside chambers—"

"Let him wait a while longer," said Huromonus. "There are some things that the Council must discuss in private."

And these things, mused the lion, *may well determine whether the Colonies survive the coming storm.*

It had been Nick's idea to leak the details of the Guardians' offensive posture. The midget's plan, based on the incredible knowledge that they had accessed from Freebird, seemed, on the surface, desperately ludicrous. Yet the lion and Huromonus—along with Inez Hernandez, who had been updated on all that they had learned so far—agreed that it was the Colonies' only hope.

The lion thought back to their own *private* pre-Council meeting, held only hours ago. Nick had been there, along with Inez and Huromonus. The E-Tech Director had begun the session by reporting what they had learned about CPG Corporation.

Inez had asked: "Has Losef confirmed CPG Corporation as the secret owner of Venus Cluster?"

"We've not yet made the request," said Huromonus. "Nick believes—and I concur—that we can't risk alerting them."

The midget explained. "Losef and the ICN cannot be relied on to do what's best for the ultimate security of the Colonies. Fifty-six years ago, I didn't trust this banking/finance consortium, and recent events have not changed my feelings. I mean, think about it. The Colonies are risking annihilation at the hands of the Paratwa, and the goddamned ICN won't reveal who owns Venus Cluster!"

"Do you think they're involved somehow?" asked Inez.

"No. But I think their mindset is unalterable. They're like the global megacorps of the twenty-first century, whose loyalty to the financial currents transcended all other concerns. The ICN will deal with anyone, even the Paratwa, as long as the money flow is not disturbed. They'll sell out the human race, if that's where the maximum profit can be had."

Huromonus shrugged. "Frankly, I no longer believe that we need ICN confirmation. This Security report on CPG Corporation is most illuminating. There is a woman. She has been the wife of Corelli-Paul Ghandi for almost twenty-five years. Her name is Colette."

They had been intrigued by Huromonus's information. The lion recalled having met Colette at various social functions over the years. "Colette Ghandi possessed a genuine inner poise," the lion related. "I recall her as being very attractive, in an outright sensual way. And she seemed extremely supportive of her husband. She was even using his last name."

"A real old-fashioned wife," grumbled Nick.

Huromonus continued. "Records indicate that Colette Ghandi is forty-eight years old. She was born to an unmated Costeau, on a shuttle voyage between the colonies of Teheran and Washington Montana."

"Cute," said Nick. "No official colonization records, right?"

"That is correct. And her mother supposedly died shortly after giving birth. The father remained unknown. She was raised by Costeaus, but not within any particular clan." Huromonus paused. "Data indicate a most interesting history, but one that is nearly untraceable. Supposedly, she first met Ghandi approximately six months after he returned from his final, ill-fated jaunt to the surface."

"She's gotta be the one," said Nick, his face beginning to flush with excitement. "The timing fits. Maybe Ghandi and his crew actually ran into this Colette down on the surface. Maybe she and Ghandi killed his other clan mates, then transferred up to the cylinders in Ghandi's shuttle, along with our nasty tripartite."

Inez nodded. "And they brought the sunsetter with them, ready to be introduced into the archives to seek out and destroy Freebird."

"You got it," said the midget.

"Could she actually be a tway of Sappho?" the lion wondered aloud, disturbed by the possibility that he may have actually met their most formidable Ash Ock adversary.

"It's possible," said Nick, staring off into the distance. "Jesus Christ . . . Sappho herself. After three centuries, we just may have found the invisible bitch."

"Of course, her role in the Paratwa manipulations has been greatly redefined," pointed out Huromonus. "The information from Freebird makes it clear that Sappho is just one of a great number of these Os/Ka/Loq."

They had fallen silent for a time, again struck by the monumental and far-reaching aspects of what had been learned from Freebird. That wealth of information compiled by Aristotle still seemed too enormous to accept.

Huge Os/Ka/Loq space vessels scouring the galaxy, seeking habitable planets to reseed. A tway of Sappho transferring herself into human form, becoming the creator of all Paratwa. The occurrence of the Apocalypse as a deliberate aspect of far-reaching Os/Ka/Loq plans. The Star-Edge fleet retreating from the devastated Earth, not to colonize other worlds but to rendezvous with Sappho's seedship, the Biodyysey. A probe vessel from the Biodyysey resting at some unknown location on the ocean floor. Alien manipulation on an incredible scale.

The lion shook his head, abruptly returned his attention to

the Irryan chambers. Huromonus was beginning to address Council, as planned.

"I belive we must take *immediate* offensive actions," urged the E-Tech Director. "By 'immediate,' I mean, right now—before we resume discussions with Meridian. The Paratwa must be shown that we are committed to fighting their invasion."

"What do you propose?" asked Losef.

Huromonus made his pitch. "I would like this Council to authorize those fifteen advance targeteers, which are already in assault position, to launch an all-out attack against the Biodyysey."

Losef glanced at Van Ostrand then back to the E-Tech Director. "I remind you that this Council has a verbal agreement with Meridian not to initiate conflict."

"I am aware of that agreement. But our own interests must take precedence. We must launch an attack so that the Paratwa realize the severity of our commitment."

Van Ostrand frowned.

Losef said, "Whatever your rationale, the Paratwa will quite properly be angered by such a rash and uncalled-for action."

"Let them be angry. I request an immediate vote upon my request."

"As Council President, I object to any vote . . . at least until Meridian has been permitted to address us."

Inez said, "I second Councillor Huromonus's motion for an immediate vote."

The ICN Director stared coldly at Inez. Losef's limited procedural powers had just been overridden. "Very well, we shall vote. The ICN votes no. Let the record also show that we find this sudden call for a vote on such a serious issue to be ill-advised, ill-defined, and perhaps ultimately devastating to the safety of the Colonies."

"I vote yes," said Huromonus.

Inez nodded. "Yes. Attack the Biodyysey immediately."

The lion clinched it. "I also vote yes."

Had the occasion been less serious, the lion actually might

have enjoyed Losef's reaction. It was rare to see the ice dyke misplace her iron control.

"This is absurd," said Losef, turning to the FTL screens. "Jon—do you wish to register a vote?"

Van Ostrand did not try to hide his bewilderment. "I'm not sure that an *immediate* attack is warranted—"

"Decidedly not," snapped Losef. "And in this situation, you are not only a Councillor of Irrya, you are the highest ranking field commander. On a tactical level, you are far better able to assess the pros and cons of such an attack ... an attack whose inspiration would appear to be politically motivated."

Good, thought the lion. *In the heat of the moment, Losef believes that the rationale behind our actions is a direct result of the massive protests occurring throughout the Colonies. She assumes vox populi underlies our decision.*

The Irryan citizenry had been driven into an anti-Paratwa frenzy by a truly odd combination of factors. The Order of the Birch, who opposed any peaceful settlement with the returning binaries, had certainly contributed to the political climate, as had the powerful freelancers, most of whom sympathized with Birch ideals. The Paratwa themselves, through the rampages of the tripartite, had also advanced the cause. The Ash Nar assassin had carried out its mass killings while boasting of loyalty to the Order of the Birch. Not until Freebird was cracked had Nick finally and truly grasped the myriad significance of that association.

And finally, the conspirators themselves—Nick, Huromonus, Inez, and the lion—had leaked information that advance targeteers of the Guardian fleet had come within striking distance of the massive Paratwa "warship." That news had exploded across the freelancer channels, providing even more fuel for the massive protests.

It had been Nick's idea to call the Biodyssey a warship.

Social manipulation on a grand scale, the lion mused. *The ancients used to call it "playing god."* But he quickly reminded himself that their efforts remained distinctly amateur when compared to the century-spanning variety of manipulation practiced by the Os/Ka/Loq.

Huromonus went on. "Our decision is not politically motivated. We believe that the Paratwa must be shown that we are deadly serious."

"Ridiculous!" charged Losef.

The lion agreed. But, he hoped, both Losef and Van Ostrand would conclude that a decision to attack the Biodyysey *was* politically motivated. Van Ostrand, especially, had to be convinced that Huromonus, Inez, and the lion had an ulterior motive. If Van Ostrand learned the entire truth—the truth contained in Aristotle's Freebird—the Guardian Commander could very well act in a predictable military manner, thus dooming their only chance for victory.

Losef regained her steel composure. "Jon, on a tactical level, you must follow your own experience regarding this proposed assault. If, in your mind, you perceive that such an attack would be, at this time, militarily detrimental to our cause, then you must refuse the order of this Council."

The lion, Huromonus, and Inez remained silent. They had discussed this very possibility: that Losef might encourage an outright refusal of a Council edict. They had decided that a vocal reaction, however appropriate under the circumstances, could very well do more harm than good. Van Ostrand had to be very delicately nudged into doing the right thing.

The Guardian Commander was obviously displeased by the entire chain of events. He turned sideways, began a private consultation with someone off-camera—probably Admiral Kilofski, his Chief of Staff. Static poured from the FTL speakers as a wordwand came to life, blocking the audio transmission and visually distorting Van Ostrand's mouth to nullify lipreading.

The lion stared at the screen, grimly aware of just how much hung in the balance. Two men, in an op-base satellite out past the orbit of Jupiter, were very probably making a decision that would determine whether or not the human race had a future.

Finally, Van Ostrand deenergized the wordwand and returned his attention to chambers. "For the record, you may register my vote as an abstention. But it *is* my duty to carry out the dictates of this Council. I will order the advance targeteers to open fire immediately upon the Biodyysey."

The lion released his breath. Huromonus and Inez appeared to share his relief. Losef ignored them all, concentrated on her terminal. The ICN Director's Board was likely making note of its collective displeasure.

Inez faced the FTL. "Jon, how many Guardians are aboard those fifteen targeteers?"

"There are about three hundred crewmembers altogether," replied Van Ostrand.

"Wish them our best," said Inez, in a voice so utterly calm that someone who did not know her well might have perceived her response as callous.

But the lion *did* know her well. He heard the harsh emotional control.

Their collective decision to sentence the men and women of the targeteers to death had not been an easy one. Inez, Huromonus, and the lion *knew* what the others could only guess at: the Biodyysey would annihilate those fifteen ships with no more effort than it might take a human to dispose of a swarm of trapped flies.

It has to be.

The lion typed into his own terminal, informed Nick that events were moving according to plan.

Empedocles slept for a time, relishing the pure sensations of physicality, feeling his chests softly rising and falling as lungs processed oxygen with the unique synchronicity inherent to Paratwa. He slept primarily to refresh his bodies. His mind required no such repose; he remained alert throughout his rest period, analyzing information, formulating previously vague ideas and concepts into precise plans of action. He slept the dreamless slumber of the Ash Ock, thinking effortlessly about what needed to be done.

When he awoke, Timmy was there, standing at the edge of the sleep chamber, the bloated face filled with anxiety. Empedocles was not certain whether Timmy was merely eager to continue with the enlightenment process or if the fat creature actually realized that today was to be his last day of life. Either way, it did not really matter.

Timmy led his tways to the large chamber where the Gillian/half had first discovered the bizarre plethora of stasis-frozen lifeforms. The three large and erratically configured windows along the wall remained transparent.

Inside the first circular tomb rested the grouped stalagmites containing Sappho's earliest genetic experiments; chamber two held the Ash Ock scientists: Yoskol, Eucris, and his wet nurse, Sasalla. Timmy ignored both arenas and walked directly to the third section of visible wall, the one occupied by the solitary ten-foot-high stalagmite.

His proctor rubbed a fat palm against the opaque section immediately above the jagged window. Inside, within what Empedocles now knew to be the standard Os/Ka/Loq version of a stasis egg, the long stalagmite began to 'crystallize,' revealing its contents. Observing from two oblique angles, Empedocles gazed with fascination as the dark blur rapidly achieved clarity.

Timmy did not have to speak; Empedocles knew that they were looking upon the original Os/Ka/Loq form of Sappho's tway, the half who had transferred her consciousness into the human form of the plenary. And although this Os/Ka/Loq was in a condition of stasis, it was not asleep.

The encapsulated alien writhed. Every square inch of its bluish green flesh seemed to be an independent entity, coiling and twisting and bubbling; the entire epidermis squirming as if a million snakes were crawling beneath its surface. A multifunctional conglomerate of semiautonomous organisms, all telepathically linked, all contributing to a commonality of function and purpose. *Cooperation of the fittest.*

Empedocles, with gestalt comprehension, realized that the breadth of Timmy's earlier description did not do justice to such a creature. This pulsating and twisting mass lacked earthly corollaries; its radical dissimilitude served instantly to render all other familiar lifeforms into a distinct subset of their own. He now perceived the greater—and more subtle—meaning of that Os/Ka/Loq word, *kascht,* which served not only to describe place but to indicate a form of biological classification above the taxonomic realm of kingdom: one *kascht* contained all of the organisms known to have originated on planet Earth. And another *kascht* encompassed the naturally telepathic conglomerations that had arisen on the homeworld of the Os/Ka/Loq.

The alien appeared to be nearly nine feet high . . . or perhaps nine feet long, for Empedocles had no way of judging whether it had an innate gyroscopic sense of "up" or "down." The creature had no legs; instead, it rested on a bulkier mass of squirming flesh at its base, which tapered gradually into a somewhat flattened hemisphere at the top. He suspected that its present shape was a mere adaptation to current gravitational conditions. In fact, to such a creature, the concept of *shape* would be simply another useful variable; more than likely, it possessed an elasticity resembling that of chilled mercury. Its telepathic infrastructure would be capable of rearranging the body to suit most any environmental condition.

There was no indication of whether the creature possessed a means of locomotion, but again, Empedocles knew instinctively that it would be able to move in a variety of ways: by crawling, hopping, or rolling; perhaps by generating temporary legs to imitate human ambulation. Probably, it could even readjust its cooperative structure into an aerodynamic configuration, soar through the skies. Or adapt a hydrodynamic profile, swim through waters of any density. The very essence of this Os/Ka/Loq suggested a degree of locomotion unimaginable within the limited constraints of an earthly *kascht*. By comparison, the human form appeared truly lacking.

Timmy shook his head slowly. "An amazing creation. From time to time, I've seen appendages come out of its body. I've seen it extrude sensory organs, of an enormous variety. Over the years, I've seen at least a dozen specialized eyes temporarily emerge from beneath its skin, each unit or set incredibly different in appearance, each eye undoubtedly capable of monitoring a different portion of the electromagnetic spectrum. Other organs have come and gone as well. Each one usually forms for only a short time, before beginning its slow dissolve back into the basic infrastructure.

"I've seen mouths, sometimes two or more distinct ones issuing from its flesh simultaneously. I've monitored sounds emanating from those mouths, heard a variety of outcries, some utterly novel, others strangely familiar. I've listened to things that have sounded like the cackling of crows, and more frequently, the braying of horses. Sometimes three or more mouths have evolved to perform in tandem, creating rich harmonic textures, an Os/Ka/Loq music of sorts, almost beautiful in its strangeness. And there have been other sensory nodes, some so totally unfamiliar that they bordered on the grotesque, so alien that I could not begin to guess at their function."

"The true tway of Sappho," murmured Empedocles. "But why does it exhibit life while it remains within stasis?"

"An apparent contradiction," Timmy agreed, "but the telepathic makeup of an Os/Ka/Loq requires this. Preserving a human being within a stasis capsule involves creating a dormant condition for only one unified complexity of life, and freezing that unit at a molecular level. But an Os/Ka/Loq is composed of perhaps millions of separate entities, in complex telepathic interrelationships with one another. I believe that there is no way for an Os/Ka/Loq to be deeply frozen without doing great harm to its holistic aura. An Os/Ka/Loq stasis capsule, like most aspects of their technology, is radically different—true molecular freezing does not take place. It if did, I suspect that the Os/Ka/Loq would begin to disincorporate."

"What is that?"

"Disincorporation would cause the millions of different organisms that compose the creature to begin separating from one another and seek out new configurations. Eventually, if the disincorporation reached a certain critical threshold—if enough discrete organisms abandoned the main body—the

Os/Ka/Loq would die. The escaping organisms would re-incorporate into other forms.

"The Os/Ka/Loq actually utilize this concept of disincor-poration at a social level. In fact, disincorporation forms a basic political tenet of their civilization. Within their commu-nal structure, minority points of view are tolerated only to a certain point. If a particular group of Os/Ka/Loq, sharing like-minded objectives, begins to lose cooperative support within the larger social framework, those minority Os/Ka/Loq may be made to suffer limited disincorporation, both as a punishment and as a warning that their collective viewpoint has drifted too far from the Os/Ka/Loq center."

Empedocles continued staring at the writhing creature within the chamber. "And this organism possesses no con-sciousness. That aspect of its being has been transferred into the plenary?"

"Correct. You are looking at a mere body of Sappho, not her mind and spirit."

Empedocles pondered for a moment. "If this creature were to be disincorporated right now, would Sappho's plenary also die?"

"No. The plenary has now become the true half of the Os/Ka/Loq Sappho. The monarch is an authentic hybrid. In a certain sense, Sappho's transferral into human form was actu-ally a limited type of disincorporation. What remains within this chamber is merely an empty shell. The plenary can never return to her original body. The earthly half of Sappho will be in human form for the rest of her life."

Empedocles nodded both heads. "Then this place is indeed a museum."

"Yes," said Timmy quietly. "A repository for lost bodies or souls."

Empedocles arched his heads away from the Os/Ka/Loq. "How did you first enter this cell? Does Sappho know that you've come here?"

Timmy chuckled. "If the plenary knew that this cell still ex-isted, she would have emptied the oceans to locate it. No, there is much that Sappho does not know. She may not yet even realize that a tway of Aristotle has survived her betrayal."

"Tell me the story of this betrayal?" urged Empedocles, acknowledging a new sense of urgency. He was whole again, restored to Ash Ock fullness. And Sappho and Theophrastus remained complete entities as well. "Tell me what happened to you."

Timmy looked appropriately sad. "Yes, I suppose it's time." He reached up and popped the microprocessor eye out of its flesh envelope, deposited the glimmering white orb in his waist pocket. Within the eyelid, a slip of transparent flesh descended like a miniature window shade, the membrane blotting the dark well, protecting the exposed depths. The eyelid itself remained open.

Empedocles gazed into the empty socket. The symbolism of Timmy's action was clear. There would be no more tricks, no more manipulations. No more betrayals.

Timmy began. "It happened only a few weeks after Aristotle made that first momentous discovery. This was in 2095, four years before the Apocalypse. Aristotle had returned to his villa in Cape Town, accessed the data from the partial's implanted holotronic recorders, and learned why Sappho had been making those frequent and mysterious visits to Brazilian costal cities.

"She owned half a dozen jet yachts, harbored along a six-hundred-mile stretch of Brazilian coastline, in seaport cities from Rio all the way up north to Caravclas and Alcobaca. On this occasion, with the partial's monitors secretly recording every aspect of the journey, Sappho arrived in Caravelas.

"She boarded her jet yacht alone—just her and the partial, that is—and headed out into the Atlantic. Several hundred miles off the coast, at a point approximately twenty degrees south of the equator, she cut the engines.

"She used a neuropad to render the partial unconscious, took her below deck, and inserted a set of seeker cables into the partial's vaginal canal. The seekers automatically fastened to the nodes of that interface organ, which Aristotle had discovered during his secret examination. Sappho connected the other ends of the cables to a basic terminal.

"That tiny armless and legless android was not simply a camouflage unit to hide the fact that Sappho's real tway was an Os/Ka/Loq. The partial also had other functions. In this case, the android was being utilized to contact and control this cell of the Os/Ka/Loq. Sappho typed the necessary commands into the terminal and the partial's specialized organ transmitted those commands to this probe ship. The cell rose from the ocean floor, creating its own chameleonic effects to prevent detection. The heavy fog bank inhibited visual ID and the superior Os/Ka/Loq antiscan gear thwarted all other electromagnetic technologies, including low-orbit defense satellites. The cell opened its massive jaws, swallowed Sappho's yacht, and then returned to its resting place on the ocean floor, over two miles below."

Timmy paused. "Even now, I cannot say precisely why Sappho returned to the cell that day. An Os/Ka/Loq-version of the FTL transmitter exists aboard this probe, but the plenary did not make use of it. No reason to, of course— Sappho's tways remained in telepathic contact with each other. This cell also boasts a vast technological alchemizer—an automated data-to-hardware system—capable of creating working copies of practically anything in its memory. But during the visit which Aristotle monitored, Sappho ignored that device as well.

"Fortunately, for Aristotle's purposes, the partial, once vaginally disconnected, followed the real tway everywhere, rolling along in the gyropros, still programmed to complementarily pantomime the actions of the plenary. And so Aristotle later bore witness to the inexplicable events which constituted Sappho's entire three-hour visit.

"The plenary came to this chamber. She crystallized the walls and stood like a statue in front of this very stasis vault, gazing in at her former body, silently mesmerized by the writhing conglomerate of this now-mindless Os/Ka/Loq. She remained in that position for over an hour. And then, beginning very slowly—only gradually picking up the tempo—the human tway of Sappho began to dance."

Timmy shook his head. "Perhaps it had something to do with the flexing urges of the Ash Ock. Perhaps it was a dance of mourning, a way to temporarily offset the knowledge that this half of her would never again be able to return to its true form. But whatever the motivation, it was a strange thing to behold. I can only describe her dance as a most bizarre version of an earthly waltz, but even that description does not do justice to what the partial's recorders documented.

"The entire dance continued for almost three hours. When it ended—slowly and gracefully, as it had begun—the plenary tway returned immediately to her jet yacht. Again using the body of the partial as a control unit, Sappho ascended to the surface, and then skimmed directly to Caravelas's harbor."

Empedocles frowned. "That was the only reason she journeyed here?"

"If she had other purposes, Aristotle never learned of them."

Empedocles shrugged both sets of shoulders. "And then?"

"Over the next few weeks, Aristotle collated the vast amount of data gathered by the partial's holotronic recorders. The partial had been operating with the secret recorders for several months and a wealth of information required processing and condensing. But even after studying that mass of data, my monarch remained unaware of the real nature of Os/Ka/Loq schemes. And although Sappho had repeatedly referred to the Biodyssey, Aristotle still knew little about the great seedship.

"He did learn that Theophrastus was fully aware of Sappho's secrets. That fact in and of itself was a severe blow to my monarch. Aristotle felt . . . cheated. He learned that Codrus, too, had been kept in the dark about these matters. Why had Theophrastus been made privy to these great secrets? Why had Aristotle and Codrus been denied?

"Aristotle became very angry. And he decided that it was time to consider Sappho and Theophrastus as actual enemies. He knew that the only way to gain more information—to learn the entire story—would be to get aboard Sappho's underwater vessel. He made his plans.

"A few days later, Sappho's European Hotel was vaporized. All occupants and staff perished under the blistering heat and radiation of a tactical smatter nuke. A Fundamentalist Christian terrorist brigade, the White Lights of Jesus, who were very active throughout Europe at that time, claimed responsibility."

Empedocles permitted a knowing smile to touch the cheeks of the Susan/tway. "These terrorists, I presume, were doing Aristotle's bidding."

"Yes. The White Lights were experiencing some cash flow problems. A series of large credit transferals into their global accounts provided the necessary inspiration for their deed."

"And Aristotle managed to kidnap the partial shortly before the smatter nuke was detonated?"

Timmy nodded. "And Sappho never knew. She assumed that the partial had indeed been destroyed. The plenary owned extra partials, of course—backups stored at various locations around the globe. She merely acquired a new one and bragged to Codrus and Aristotle of her extreme good fortune, telling them that the partial had *not* been inside the European Hotel at the time of the incident." A faint smile wafted across Timmy's swollen cheeks. "Codrus was suitably impressed by Sappho's close brush with mortality.

"At any rate, Aristotle now possessed a key for entering the cell of the Os/Ka/Loq. But even as he made plans to use it, he made his fatal error."

Timmy paused, softly rubbed the back of a sleeve across his real eye. His hands began to shake. "You must excuse me. Aspects of my monarch's demise . . . they still provide difficulties for me. . . ."

"Of course," said Empedocles, allowing impatient frowns to appear on both faces. "Take your time," he urged, meaning just the opposite.

Timmy overcame his turmoil and continued. "The mistake that killed my monarch was a simple one. Aristotle turned to Meridian—the one Paratwa who he thought could be trusted. There was little reason not to trust the Jeek. Meridian, intensely loyal to the Ash Ock, also managed to remain honest and forthright with the other Paratwa who served our cause. And Aristotle considered Meridian something of a friend. While teaching you, the two of them had developed a camaraderie."

Timmy sighed. "And so, Aristotle shared some of his new discoveries with Meridian. My monarch provided just enough information to one of Meridian's tways to whet the Jeek's curiosity. Aristotle concentrated on the facts that had first inspired his own detective work. Aristotle told Meridian nothing about the makeup of the partial. Nor did he reveal the secrets learned from the holotronic recorders." A bitter smile fattened Timmy's cheeks. "My monarch, like all of the Ash Ock, practiced manipulation as a way of life. In Meridian's case, Aristotle had intended to dole out just enough data to inspire the Jeek to undertake his own investigation. Meridian would be supplied the information in stages.

"But stage two never arrived. Less that twenty-four hours after my monarch made his first revelations, both of the Jeek's tways arrived at Aristotle's Cape Town villa. Meridian claimed to be very upset by Aristotle's disclosures. He wished to discuss the various inferences of Aristotle's 'unbelievable' tale."

Timmy stared at the floor. "But Aristotle knew immediately that he had been betrayed. Meridian was a shrewd liar, but Aristotle was shrewder. My monarch listened to what the Jeek was saying and he listened to what the Jeek was *not* saying, and he realized that Meridian was also part of the conspiracy.

"Meridian must have gone directly to Sappho. And she would have ordered the Jeek to return at once to Cape Town, to ferret out the rest of Aristotle's information. And on Meridian's second visit, *both* of the Jeek's tways had arrived at the villa. My monarch was forced to presume that Meridian had been given discretionary orders . . ." He trailed off.

"Aristotle was to be assassinated?"

Timmy squeezed his hands together to prevent them from shaking. "Before the meeting ended, both parties realized where things stood. Although no direct accusations were ever made, Aristotle knew the full extent of the betrayal, and Meridian *knew* that he knew. My monarch, in an effort to buy time, played his final hand: he told Meridian about the secret existence of Freebird within the newly created E-Tech archival computers. Aristotle made it clear to the Jeek that Freebird contained more information than he had revealed.

'Should an untimely accident befall me,' Aristotle warned, 'Freebird's data will fall into the hands of E-Tech.'

"Meridian accepted this threat in his typical fashion—with a sort of cordial aplomb." Timmy hesitated. "You remember that unsettling demeanor of his, don't you?"

Empedocles remembered. Cordial aplomb was indeed an appropriate phrase to describe the Ash Ock lieutenant. Even when the Jeek killed, it was done with a sort of quiescent grace. If Reemul had been considered the mad assassin, Meridian had been the courteous one.

Timmy continued. "At the end of their meeting, Meridian's tways, still as poised as ever, offered Aristotle the two-score."

The two-score, thought Empedocles. *The Paratwa handshake: eight hands clasped together, forty fingers molded in friendship.*

"Aristotle assumed that this was the end. Meridian would kill him in the middle of their farewell gesture. But surprisingly, Meridian shook hands and departed in peace. Only then did my monarch realize that the two-score had been intended as a real gesture of their friendship, that it had been the Jeek's way of saying good-bye.

"Meridian would not be doing the deed. But Aristotle knew that little time remained. Sappho would be dispatching another assassin, one without any qualms.

"Like all of the Ash Ock, my monarch had made numerous contingency plans—fake identities in countries all over the world, caches of hidden supplies, clandestine bank accounts. . . . Immediately, Aristotle dispatched one of his tways to an area north of Cape Town, to his closest storage bunker. Sappho's captured partial was being kept at that location, in a state of induced sleep. Aristotle planned to flee to a town in the Russian Steppes, where he had prepared identities as a geostrand engineer and a NewNam bankrep."

Timmy's whole body began to shake. He leaned against the wall in an effort to control himself.

"But my monarch was too late. The end came quickly. A fire-fall nuke was detonated high above Cape Town. The tway of Aristotle who remained at the villa bore witness to his own incineration."

Timmy clasped his arms tightly across his chest. A final

tremor seemed to pass through him, and then his voice fell to a deep-throated whisper. "Later, when I came to this cell and penetrated the Os/Ka/Loq data net, I learned the identity of the assassin."

"It was Reemul, wasn't it?"

"Yes," murmured Timmy. "The liege-killer nuked the entire city just to destroy my monarch."

Empedocles frowned. "When I've heard the tale of your monarch's death, it was always suggested that Aristotle had been attempting to bribe South Africa's president when the firestorm hit."

Timmy laughed hard, but it was a laugh on the edge of madness. "My monarch did bribe that nation's leader from time to time. But such a story remains just another muddled fable from the final days. Perhaps this particular tale was encouraged by Sappho. She certainly would not have wanted the other Paratwa to learn of dissension within the royal Caste. Better to intimate that Aristotle's demise was related to international politics."

Empedocles nodded slowly, in tandem. "So one of your tways perished. And the other one?"

"Jalka made it to that storage bunker, just beyond the lethal range of detonation. He escaped, but not without injuries. He lost an eye. . . ."

"But worse than that, of course, he suffered the madness. You know what it was like. You too have lived through the horror of being torn in half.

"For many days—weeks perhaps—Jalka wandered aimlessly . . . lost in the pain of what was lost. . . ." Timmy's real eye blinked rapidly, as if it were a malfunctioning circuit. "After a time, Jalka emerged from the bunker. He had survived the devastation. Still, he continued to burn in that womb of pure pain, endlessly reliving the incineration of his other tway.

"But eventually, the spirit of a new being emerged from that womb. Jalka and Aristotle were fused. And from that blasphemy of tway and monarch, I arose. I was born. And I christened myself Timmy.

"I had my appearance physically altered. A black market tech customized a wetware eye for me. I retrieved Sappho's sleeping partial from the bunker. I purchased a jet yacht and skimmed to the Atlantic coordinates where Sappho's cell of the Os/Ka/Loq lay hidden on the ocean floor.

"I attached the partial to a terminal as I had seen Sappho do. It took me a few hours to break the control codes, and in those hours, paranoia washed over me. I kept worrying that Sappho was going to appear. Perhaps she could somehow remotely monitor surface traffic that approached her hidden vessel? But my fears were swept away when the jaws of the great cell broke the surface and enveloped my yacht. As I journeyed into the depths, my confidence returned. Soon, I knew I would possess all of her secrets.

"My confidence was not unfounded. Here within this cell, I first learned of the awesome century-spanning manipulations of this alien race. I mastered their data net and their powerful alchemizer. I assimilated a knowledge of genetic engineering far beyond the dreams of the most rabid earthly researcher. I spent hours on end attached to their feed loops, binging on accelerated memory quantizers.

"And throughout those days and weeks, I waited for Sappho to return to her cell. I made no plans, however, no contingencies in the event that she suddenly 'dropped in.' " Timmy hesitated. "Later, I realized that I had a death wish. I wanted her to come. I wanted the witch to complete her half-finished task.

"But she did not come. I grew aware of my self-destructive tendencies and slowly overcame them. I made a conscious decision to stay alive, though at the time, I did not know why. At any rate, I developed a complex plan.

"I mastered the nav system of this cell, programmed it to function as a submarine. Underwater, I piloted the great probe ship from Sappho's original resting place to a new location, over a thousand miles to the north."

"Where we are right now," mused Empedocles.

"Yes. After moving the cell, I returned to the surface in my yacht, and then headed for the city of Fortaleza, the closest port. I accessed my secret accounts—drained several of them, in fact. I spent a small fortune in order to carry out the rest of my scheme.

"Six days after my return, a jet—believed to be carrying a cargo of refinanced opium—was shot down near the original location of the cell. The Brazilian authorities had received word of the jet's cargo and destination through U.S. Customs. Since the Brazilians were part of an ancient agreement to destroy inbound American drug traffic, and since U.S. Customs was making a fuss about it, the Brazilians were forced to shoot down the jet rather than adopt their standard tactic and demand a percentage cut from the smugglers in exchange for safe passage.

"But this jet was not bearing opium. Its cargo was much deadlier—one hundred and ninety-two tactical nukes, bound for French Canadian Decentralists, in the newly warmed Northwest Territories. And unknown to the smugglers, the nukes had been armed.

"The jet went down, a scant mile and a half from the location where Sappho's cell was supposed to lie. The aircraft sank quickly. One hundred and ninety-two nuclear bombs mysteriously detonated in a thousand feet of water. Media reports later claimed that some of the tidal waves that ravaged the Brazilian coast were over a hundred feet high."

Susan was unable to contain her emotions any longer. *They're both monsters! They talk about death and destruction as if it were something inconsequential.*

They're Paratwa, stated Gillian. *They're Ash Ock—*

I know what they are! But I thought Timmy was different—

—Then you've been fooling yourself. You have to accept the reality of them. Timmy is just as ruthless and manipulative as the others. Paratwa have always looked upon humans the way humans looked upon cattle. And remember what Timmy said about the Os/Ka/Loq. Our intelligence—our consciousness—is not even a factor in the way that they judge other species. Only the degree of T-psionic force of importance—

Go to hell!

Gillian felt her wave of fury wash over him. *You are not angry with me.*

Susan forced control. *You're right, I'm not angry with you. I'm sorry.*

Besides, projected Gillian, *I suspect that we're already in hell.*

Despite their circumstances, she felt soothed by his gentle humor. Her resolve returned. *There has to be a way to break the interlace. If we can't get Timmy to reverse those mnemonic cursors in your mind, then it's up to me—*

—It's not possible, insisted Gillian. *It would require both of us, acting in tandem, and under the proper conflux of conditions, to dissolve the monarchy.* . . . He hesitated.

You have an idea?

Gillian thought about it for a while. *Perhaps there is a way.*

But Susan did not feel cheered by his word, for his thoughts bore an undercurrent of deep and bitter regret.

Empedocles chuckled, using both bodies to spread his laughter through the chamber.

Timmy frowned. "Tidal waves amuse you?"

"Oh, no. Inconsequential amalgams amuse me. The Susan is angry. The Gillian is bitter. They have not yet come to terms with reality. They have not yet accepted that theirs is a bodiless future."

Timmy nodded. "It will take time for them to accept the truth."

"Indeed. Please continue with your story. After that nuclear payload detonated, was Sappho convinced that this cell was destroyed in the explosion?"

"Yes. She did possess a tracking system for the cell—to cover the unlikely eventuality of someone actually boarding the probe and moving it. But I had arranged for the locators inside the cell to be disabled shortly before the immense nuclear blast ruptured the sea floor. Since the immediate area of devastation was too hot for any rescue craft, and since her tracking system indicated complete sensor failure at the other end, Sappho would have been forced to conclude that her cell, if not totally destroyed, at least had been severely damaged."

"But she would have remained suspicious," Empedocles pointed out.

"True enough. The nuclear incident's proximity to the location of her probe ship certainly could not be dismissed as coincidental. But not having the slightest evidence that a tway of Aristotle had survived, Sappho would have had to turn her suspicions elsewhere. Most likely, she arrived at the conclusion that a deep-water explorer—perhaps from one of the more volatile quasi-religious governments, or from one of the hardcore techno-hate groups—had discovered the probe ship and arranged for its destruction." Timmy shrugged. "This was, after all, only four years before the Apocalypse, when global madness had reached its lofty heights. In those days, tactical nuking was considered a normal first-line situational response.

"Indeed, with the Apocalypse fast approaching, I realized that I had to begin making long-range plans for my own survival. I decided to put myself to sleep for a few centuries. But I did not want to enter stasis within this cell of the Os/Ka/Loq. There was always the possibility, however remote, that Sappho and her minions would make an early return from their deep-space rendezvous and that the Biodyysey could somehow locate an individual cell.

"I engineered an underground stasis vault and had it constructed in the Adirondack Mountains, in an area then known as upstate New York. Within a hundred-mile radius of this vault, I arranged to have several small shuttles hidden. And in the early fall of the year 2095, I put myself to sleep. The automatic wake-up system was set to retrieve me from the depths of slumber in exactly two hundred years. If the Os/Ka/Loq maintained their schedule, I would still arise long before they returned.

"And so I awoke, in 2295, twelve years before Codrus set Reemul on his murderous spree throughout the Irryan Colonies, twelve years before your Gillian/tway was first brought from stasis by Rome Franco. To my surprise, the Earth remained virtually uninhabited, except for scattered E-Tech bases and Church of the Trust temples. The atmosphere was still heavily contaminated.

"I had assumed that in two centuries, the Irryan Colonies would have revitalized the planet, at least to a minimal extent. But one of the reasons Codrus had been left behind was to guarantee that the various Ecospheric Turnaround projects did not exceed experimental size. To that end, Codrus was successful. When the Os/Ka/Loq returned, they would find their new planet in a perfect state: fertile, yet virginal.

"I had prepared for the possibility that the atmosphere was still poisoned. Protective garments, weapons, and supplies had been stored in my underground bedroom. I embarked on an eight-mile hike, through bleak windswept hills that had once been covered with forests. But when I arrived at the location of the nearest hidden shuttle, I was distressed to learn that the shuttle had been vaporized, along with the small town where it had been stored. I was forced to head farther north, to the location of the second shuttle. That shuttle had fortuitously survived intact. And nearby was the Ontario Cloister—a facility which at that time was still being used by the Church of the Trust as a surface burial temple.

"I entered my shuttle and flew back down to the South American coast. I reentered this cell.

"For twelve years I stayed here, learning even more about the culture of the Os/Ka/Loq. I monitored intercolonial broadcasts, gained knowledge of the Irryan cylinders. After a time, I even located the trails of political manipulation left by Codrus, and I began to analyze his strategies.

"But then came the clarifying events of 2307. Codrus and Reemul were exposed. Your Gillian/tway and Nick were brought from stasis by E-Tech. I knew at once that Nick had to be the Czar—one of the Ash Ock's most formidable pre-Apocalyptic nemeses. And after your Gillian/tway killed Reemul, I knew who you were. No mere human could have defeated the liege-killer in open combat.

"Excitement flowed through me and I blazed with new purpose. I had mastered enough Os/Ka/Loq secrets to know that a single tway of an Ash Ock could be restored to full glory, that arrhythmia of the whelm could be reversed. It was too late for me, of course—the melding together of tway and monarch had already occurred, and that process remains irreversible. But the reports I was able to gather regarding your Gillian/tway indicated a man disturbed by vast inner turmoil. I was certain that you had not yet melded.

"By accessing Freebird, I discovered that Rome Franco had arranged for your Gillian/tway and the Czar to be put back into stasis for fifty-six years. *Perfect,* I thought, for I knew that decades would be required to implement my plans.

"And for decades, I remained hard at work here within this cell, making my preparations. Then, about thirty years ago, I returned to upstate New York, to the Ontario Cloister. I entered that Church facility, claiming to have come there as a stowaway aboard a Colonial shuttle.

"I made myself useful to the Church elders and they permitted me to remain at the Cloister. I became their chief caretaker. I fixed what was broken, straightened what was twisted.

"But all the while, I was bringing my plans to fruition. I befriended a young priest at the Cloister. His name was Lester Mon Dama. One day, I persuaded Lester to take a long walk with me on the beach. Far from any possible probing eyes, I drugged the priest and took him to my shuttle. Within the deepest recesses of his mind, I implanted a massive array of mnemonic cursors. I made Lester Mon Dama into my retroslave. He was aware, of course, of his indentured status, but he was unable to do anything about it.

"Under my orders, Lester arranged to have three Church of the Trust obstetricians visit the Cloister. All three of these doctors were brought to me. More mnemonic cursors were implanted.

"From my own biological/T-psionic infrastructure, I created a genetic matrix that could be used to overcome the limitations of a normal human neuromuscular system. Over a five-year period, through the efforts of Lester Mon Dama, hundreds of pregnant women were given special injections of this matrix by these obstetricians. Hundreds of female babies were born, all of whom were close to the physical age of Gillian. Following the last of the births, I arranged for Lester to dispose of the three doctors. The obstetricians had served their purpose.

"From one of these hundreds of babies, I was certain that a suitable replacement for Catharine eventually could be found. But I must admit that for a time I was fairly discouraged. None of these young women, whom I monitored from afar—through Lester and through my own access to the

E-Tech archival network, via Freebird—seemed quite right as a replacement for your lost Catharine/tway." Timmy cast a wan smile. "But, eventually, fate called Susan to my attention. And she turned out to possess the requisite qualities for becoming your new half.

"And so, I arranged to have both of you brought to this cell, where restoration could take place. The purities have been maintained here. This cell is a living organism of sorts, ebbing and flowing with energies of the T-psionic force, which even I, at a fundamental level, do not understand. But within this probe, arrhythmia of the whelm could be reversed."

Empedocles alternately nodded his heads. "I am still confused about one thing, Timmy. Why? Why did you bring me back?"

"I told you before. You are Ash Ock. You are my brethren."

"Then your actions were guided purely by emotions?"

"My feelings toward you . . . were all that remained important following the melding of my tway and monarch. It gave me pleasure knowing that I could make you whole again. It gave purpose to my life."

"And that was the only reason?"

Timmy did not answer. Instead, he changed the subject. "I mentioned earlier why Codrus was left behind in the Colonies after the Star-Edge fleet departed to rendezvous with the Biodyysey. But aside from the reasons I've already stated, Codrus was assigned an additional task. He was to keep watch for Aristotle's secret program, whose existence Aristotle had first revealed to Meridian.

"Sappho did not know for certain whether Freebird actually existed. Aristotle could have been bluffing. But even though no E-Tech archivists had located the secret program in over two centuries, Sappho was no longer willing to take any chances. Following Codrus's demise, she sent her plenary tway back to the Colonies with the sunsetter. By setting her data destroyer loose in the archives—by having the sunsetter seek out and destroy *all* old programs—Sappho hoped to eliminate Freebird . . . if it indeed existed.

"But Freebird became aware of the sunsetter first. And last

month, when the Czar began to send his own exploratory programs into the archives, I perceived an opportunity. I arranged for Freebird to show itself at a precise moment, thus tricking the sunsetter into returning to its prime check-in location. I was able to trace the sunsetter back to its source. Thus, I was able to learn Sappho's current identity."

Timmy reached under his robes and withdrew a data brick. "This contains information on Sappho's plenary tway. She now assumes the name of Colette Ghandi. The data in this brick will help you find her."

Empedocles used the hand of his Gillian/tway to take the brick. With his Susan/tway, he stepped behind Timmy. For a few moments, he silently studied his former proctor, front and rear. Then: "You must be aware of another factor that still greatly perplexes me."

"Of course. We both know that you're going to kill me. And you cannot understand why I am not worried."

Empedocles nodded.

An odd smile blossomed on Timmy's face. "Before events proceed to their preordained conclusion, there is one other detail I should mention. It concerns the E-Tech raid on Thi Maloca, the attack which killed your tway Catharine. You know, of course, that this raid occurred only a few weeks after Aristotle's assassination?"

Empedocles acknowledged a tinge of anger. He stared coldly.

"The correlations are obvious," said Timmy. "Empedocles was the student of Aristotle. Sappho could not know for certain whether my monarch had involved you in his traitorous activities, but she could not take any chances. Your training was almost complete. Soon, you would be leaving Thi Maloca to become a full member of the royal Caste.

"But by this time, you were considered expendable—no longer necessary to ensure that the Apocalypse occurred. Sappho had no choice, really. She secretly revealed to E-Tech the location of the Ash Ock labs in Thi Maloca. She arranged for your death as well as mine."

Empedocles felt his anger beginning to swell.

Timmy seemed completely unconcerned. "So now you

know everything. You even possess the appropriate data to realize what it is that Sappho and the Os/Ka/Loq truly fear, although I can see that you have not yet correlated such information into conscious knowledge. Nevertheless, with a little thought, it will come to you.

"At any rate, I now give you my blessings. Empedocles, lastborn of the royal Caste—you are now free to do what it is that you must do."

With his Gillian/tway, Empedocles came forward another step. "Revenge?" he whispered. "Is that what this has all been about? You want me to kill Sappho?"

Timmy sighed. "You still don't understand, do you. All right, *Ash Ock.* I will spell it out for you:

"My monarch, Aristotle, was flawed. That is why Sappho precluded him from her plans, and that is why he ultimately turned against her. I wish to make right the ancient wrong of Aristotle's betrayal.

"I have returned you to full monarchy. I have given you the tools to reestablish yourself among the Paratwa. I have healed you. And now I wish to heal the broken Sphere of the royal Caste.

"I wish for you to be my apology to Sappho."

For a moment, Empedocles was too astonished to respond. He found himself shaking both heads. "You *are* insane."

Timmy shrugged. "Quite possibly. But insane or not, my desires remain clear. I could never have approached Sappho myself. She would never again trust a remnant of Aristotle. But for you . . . the wounds are not so deep. Sappho may accept you, Empedocles. Especially when she realizes that, with all your newfound knowledge, you returned to her instead of to the humans. And you returned with a gift—the head of Aristotle . . . figuratively speaking, I would hope." Another smile fattened Timmy's cheeks.

"You are now a complete Ash Ock Paratwa. Go to Sappho. Allow yourself to share in her coming victory. Assume your rightful place in the new order."

Don't do it! cried Susan, no longer concerned about maintaining even the slightest emotional restraint. She knew what was going to happen. She could feel Empedocles easing up into that moment of ultimate repose—the assassin's crest—when all tension would depart his bodies in a crescendo of violence.

And even though the extent of Timmy's monstrous manipulations and deeds were now clear to her, she could not help but feel sorry for him. *Timmy brought me back from a life of shallowness. He helped restore my essence.*

Gillian lashed out at her with rasping anger. *Don't be a softhearted fool! Timmy brought you back for one reason only—to forever trap your consciousness in here as an amalgam. You were needed only to restore the monarchy!*

I still can't help how I feel.

Gillian projected bitterness. *And now we're going to be trapped in here forever! Timmy's the only one who can neutralize my mnemonic cursors. He's the only one who can return me to my body!*

But you said there might be a way—

It's no use, Gillian yelled. *Once he kills Timmy, he knows that we'll never be able to break the interlace! There's no way out!*

Susan began to understand. She forced herself to respond with complete composure. *You want our monarch to feel the fury of our defeat. You want Empedocles to believe that we've given up hope.*

You are a perceptive person, Gillian replied calmly. *Therefore, feel free to contribute to this common goal.*

Susan screamed.

Empedocles lunged with his Gillian/tway—right arm unfurled, hand fisted, forefinger extended, stiff as a blade. The finger penetrated the fragile translucent membrane protecting Timmy's empty eye socket, plunged straight through into the brain.

Timmy's head jerked back. Empedocles withdrew the finger, used the Susan/tway's arm to snap the presented neck. The massive body spasmed. Empedocles stepped away, watched Timmy slam onto the floor. He stared down at the body, smiling twin smiles.

"Thank you, my proctor. You have been most helpful. And I do believe I will follow your advice."

Projected on the FTL, the Biodyysey appeared neither massive nor threatening. Ovoid in shape, over two thousand one hundred-fifty miles from end to end, the fattest portion of its belly nine hundred miles across, it looked more like an oversized gray egg than an invasion vessel of an alien species. But the lion knew that the seedship of the Os/Ka/Loq bore death within its living shell. He acknowledged a renewed feeling of helplessness while he watched two glittering swarms of red specks approaching the invader from opposite tangents.

"Those are the fifteen advance targeteers," narrated Van Ostrand. "They've been split into two groups for the actual assault."

"How long yet?" asked Inez, her voice still smoothly controlled but her delicate face creased with a frown that even the bacterial skin toners could not mask.

"In one minute they'll reach primary attack coordinates," replied Van Ostrand.

Edward Huromonus raised his eyebrows. "Those targeteers look bigger than I would have expected them to be, in relation to the Biodyysey."

"You're looking at enhancements," said the disembodied voice of the Guardian Commander. "At this scale of magnification, our targeteers would be completely invisible. For video transmission, the images have been colorized and enlarged."

The lion asked, "Now that they're within such close range, have the targeteers been able to make any data penetrations?"

Van Ostrand sounded disappointed. "No, the Biodyysey's electromagnetic field continues to foul even our most esoteric scanning gear."

"A pity," murmured Inez.

Losef, in a voice more icy than usual, announced: "Meridian is demanding to be brought before the Council."

"Why am I not surprised?" wondered Huromonus. "After all, his other tway is out there on that vessel. As the freelancers might put it, Meridian is now staring down the barrel of our gun."

The lion repressed an urge to laugh. The expression could not have been more inappropriate.

"Meridian can wait," suggested Inez.

"Thirty seconds," said Van Ostrand. "Prime attack coordinates—"

A flash of amber light filled the FTL screens, momentarily discoloring the entire vista. Each of the fifteen targeteers briefly expanded to at least three times its imaged size before dissolving back into the darkness. Seconds later, only a hazy pink afterglow remained to mark the location of each Guardian ship.

"They're gone," whispered Inez.

Only the massive Biodyysey remained, dominating the center of the screens. To the lion, the display of firepower seemed to impart the alien vessel with a majesty even further beyond their understanding.

We knew it would happen this way, he quickly told himself, refusing to allow the Os/Ka/Loq's triumph to overwhelm his determination.

The spatial view disappeared; Van Ostrand reappeared. The lion had never seen the Guardian Commander so dazed and unsettled.

Losef broke the silence. "A stupid sacrifice."

"A tragic one," murmured Inez.

Van Ostrand cleared his throat and stared grimly at the Council. "The electromagnetic field . . . it briefly expanded. Final data transmissions from the targeteers indicated some unknown type of energy emission from that field. . . ."

"Anything left of our ships?" asked Huromonus. "Any possibility whatsoever that there were survivors?"

"No. They were vaporized."

The lion thought about the three hundred dead crewmembers, tried to imagine what it was like for them in those final moments. Most would have realized that their chances of surviving an attack against the Biodyysey were nil. The sheer size differential between the minuscule targeteers and the monstrous invader and the fact that the Guardians faced technology of an unknown nature—those factors certainly would have fostered a collective sense that their mission was suicidal.

Inez said, "Their bravery must never be forgotten."

The lion felt her words hit his psyche—rock against pulp—splattering a whole host of what he now knew to be self-delusions.

How dare I even consider my own cowardice of any importance? I faced death and ran from it, then arranged for those three hundred men and women to sacrifice their lives for a greater cause.

He felt his face reddening. He knew he had arrived at the true depths of his cowardice.

I am ashamed of myself. I am ashamed to be the lion of Alexander.

And he knew that he would have to live with that personal disgrace for the remainder of his days. There could be no "forgetting," no resigning guilt to the boundaries of his subconscious, where the displaced power of his shame could launch tenacles of emotional torment into the physical stream of his body. Denial served to split consciousness, divide intellect, emotions, and physical self into discrete entities. To remain whole, he merely had to recall the full impact of his humiliating cowardice. Such self-acknowledgment might serve to lessen his opinion of himself—he would forever remember his numbing fear at the hands of the Ash Nar—but in the long run, such insight would maintain his humanity.

I am the lion of Alexander. And I have been a coward.

So be it.

Newfound determination took root. It was time to implement the rest of their plan. It was time to take the offensive. "I believe we should ask Meridian to enter chambers."

Losef, seeing no objections, keyed her terminal. A moment later, the black door opened. Meridian and his animals—one dog atop the other—entered Council chambers.

The Jeek tway was outfitted in the same clothing that he

had worn during his first visit to Council. The three-piece
charcoal suit, the Eton-style jacket, the vest with its hook-and-
eye loops made of precious jewels, the bloat hanging from his
left arm, its power strands disappearing into the canal; Meridian: archetype of the primeval dandy. Today, however, he
looked less friendly than upon his first visit to chambers.

As he approached, the Ash Ock servant aimed a forefinger
toward the door. His animals read their master's command;
the poodle leaped from the borzoi's back and the dogs quickly
assumed their "statue alignment" on opposite sides of the portal. Meridian moved to the far side of the table and halted beside Losef. "This unprovoked attack was incredibly foolish.
Did you really believe that a mere fifteen tiny ships could
hope to damage the Biodyysey?"

The lion perceived Meridian's words primarily as a challenge aimed at Van Ostrand. He glanced at the Guardian
Commander's multiple visages, saw brooding anger, suspected
that Meridian's tactic was partially successful. Van Ostrand
suddenly looked mad enough to throw his entire fleet against
the Paratwa. *That must not happen.*

The Jeek sighed. "Stupidity is always a waste. But it was
anticipated that, despite warnings, you would attempt to
probe our defenses. Now that you have satisfied yourself as to
our invulnerability, we should be able to proceed with discussions."

The assassin raised his arm and lanced it downward. A tiny
beaming object—a corpuscle of light leaped from his fist,
smacked the edge of the table. A column of white luminescence sprouted into the air, enveloping the chandelier, then
just as quickly decayed into a rain of colored dust. Falling
motes coalesced into bundles, formed hundreds of petite floating cylinders. For the second time, the fully animated, real-
time representation of the Irryan Colonies assumed its shape
before Council.

"Indeed, they are beautiful," murmured the Jeek.

No one responded.

Meridian smiled. "Pick a Colony. Any Colony."

"We prefer to engage in direct deliberations," announced
Losef. "We have no time for games."

"This is not a game," warned Meridian. "Please choose a Colony." He paused. "I might offer a hint. If I were you, I would pick a Colony that you do not like. Select a cylinder that would not prove overly burdensome to lose."

A chill went through the lion. *Here it comes.*

"The Paratwa do not want war. But events have occurred in the past few days that have accelerated us toward the precursive conditions for violent conflict." The Jeek suddenly spun to face Huromonus. "I understand that the Paratwa are being blamed for the decimation of the E-Tech archives?"

Huromonus nodded. "That is correct. You should be proud. Your sunsetter has succeeded in destroying a good part of our human heritage."

Meridian laughed. "An interesting lie. Blaming the sunsetter—which I do admit was ours—for the archival destruction is a most clever tactic. But then, not all of your fellow Councillors were privy to these events."

"I'm afraid we don't know what you're talking about," said Huromonus calmly. "Your words would seem to be aimed at causing divisiveness within this Council."

The lion contained his own smile. *We can twist the truth and spread lies just as well as you can, Meridian.*

"Your cleverness boasts an impressive girth," offered the Jeek. "But let us test the depth of this proficiency. In other words, please pick a Colony. Or would you rather I pick one for you?"

Losef said. "It's your show."

"I sometimes wish that was true," replied Meridian, in a tone that seemed to reflect genuine sadness. He shrugged. "These days, however, I'm afraid that my actions are guided by other hands. One pays a price for one's allegiances."

He extended his palm, closed his fingers around one of the inch-long holographic cylinders. When he opened his hand, the tiny gleaming representation seemed to be stuck to his flesh.

He peered closely at it, shaking his head. "My Colonial geography is rather poor. I do not recognize this particular cylinder." He moved around the table to Inez, displayed his open palm to her. " 'The Glory of Science'—La Gloria de la

Ciencia—those dedicated to the limitless yearnings of logical achievement. As the representative of such a formidably titled organization, would you care to attempt an identification?"

Inez avoided eye contact, gazed coldly into Meridian's extended hand. "It's the Colony of Red Saxony." She turned to the lion. "I recognize it from the distended shape of its southern polar plate."

"Most impressive," said Meridian, closing his fist. When he opened it, the holo was gone.

"In exactly one hour, if the Council has not yet agreed to our peace initiatives, a plague will be released within the Colony of Red Saxony. This virus, an aerobic mutagen that is one hundred percent fatal to humans, will poison the air throughout that cylinder. I give you this advance warning so that you might warn those citizens. Bio- or spacesuits—any sealed garment with its own air supply—should protect people from exposure." A deliberate hesitation seemed to creep into his voice. "Naturally, those citizens should plan on remaining inside their suits for a rather long time. This virus thrives within various cultures, and once it enters Red Saxony's atmosphere, I'm afraid there will be no painless method of decontamination. In fact, it will take years before anyone again breathes freely within that Colony."

The lion scanned the other Councillors, froze his attention on Van Ostrand. Not surprisingly, the Guardian Commander's images bristled with barely controlled fury.

Meridian continued relentlessly. "One hour after Red Saxony gets the virus, we will pick a second Colony for exposure. And one hour after that, a third Colony. At that rate, in about nine days, all two hundred and seventeen cylinders will be contaminated.

"But I suspect the Paratwa will not have to wait that long to achieve a lasting peace with the Colonies of Irrya. I sincerely believe that we can collectively reach an understanding before any cylinder needs to be contaminated."

"Bastard!" snapped Van Ostrand.

Meridian moved directly behind Huromonus and laid his hands on the E-Tech Director's shoulders. Huromonus flinched.

While the Jeek spoke, he softly massaged Huromonus's neck. "Some of you Councillors already know the power of our plague. In fact, at least one Councillor at this table has undertaken investigations into the cellular structure of what we refer to as the skygene virus. That person—especially— knows that we do not bluff.

"A skygene suitcase had been hidden within each cylinder, primed to explode and send its poisons into the atmosphere. The Biodyysey can instantaneously trigger every one of these viral bombs. There is no way to block the triggering signals. . . . Suffice it to say that the communication technology involves FTL-type transmissions."

"Remove your hands from me," ordered Huromonus, with icy control.

Meridian patted his shoulder and pulled away. "As you wish. I certainly did not intend for my physical contact to be offensive." He leaned down across Huromonus's shoulder. "By the way, Edward—may I call you Edward?—we meant for you to find that particular skygene suitcase the repo freighter removed from the Au Fait Recycling Towers in Toulouse. That suitcase was put there in the first place precisely because we knew that the towers were scheduled for cleaning. In other words, the Paratwa *wanted* at least one suitcase to be found and studied. We wanted it to explode aboard that repo freighter. This was not done out of cruelty. The tragedy aboard the repo vessel was a contained event, with minimal loss of life—minimal compared to what may occur one hour from now in the Colony of Red Saxony.

"You were given an opportunity to study the skygene so that your best scientific minds would come to understand the power of our threat. Thus you, Edward Huromonus, know that we are not bluffing."

Losef asked, "Is there truth in Meridian's words?"

Huromonus stared at the FTL. "Yes."

"Why wasn't the rest of Council informed?" demanded Van Ostrand. "Whose side are you on? What the hell kind of manipulative nonsense—"

"Enough!" barked the lion. "The only nonsense at this table is the kind being spread by this assassin."

Huromonus agreed. "Events here are preceding according to Paratwa plans. *That* is what is going on. I had good reasons to keep the discovery of this virus hidden from the rest of Council. And *now* is definitely not the time to discuss those reasons.

"I would simply urge all of you to keep in mind the time-honored political technique known as 'divide and conquer.' Our emissary would appear to be greatly skilled in this tradition."

Meridian laughed. "Guilty as charged. But I hasten to add that, within these chambers, I am not a lone practitioner."

Van Ostrand hunched forward until his face filled the screens. "Be warned, Meridian—we'll never submit to these threats of yours. We'll fight you all the way!"

Exactly what Meridian is trying to encourage, thought the lion, with a touch of despair. The revelation that the repo freighter incident had been merely another aspect of the Paratwa plan was unnerving. *We missed that.*

He hoped they had not missed anything else.

With regal conviction, Meridian continued. "Please understand that the Paratwa are negotiating from a position of absolute military superiority. We are not making idle threats here. If necessary, we will destroy the cylinders. We will decimate you.

"But again, we intend to do everything in our power to avoid the horrors of confrontation. We do not wish to destroy you. We truly desire harmony and a lasting peace with the citizens of Irrya."

He stepped away from Huromonus, began circling the table.

"In the coming days, the Colonists will be asked to make some minor adjustments to their lifestyles. But by and large, the cylinders will continue to thrive and prosper. The majority of your social systems and institutions will be permitted to remain intact, including this Council, the Irryan Senate, and the ICN. We do not wish to destabilize intercolonial commerce. We respect the fact that delicate trade balances must be maintained. Even your freelancers will be permitted to continue their outrageous telecasts." A faint smile touched the Jeek. "Providing, of course, that is what you desire."

Inez muttered, "You're talking about slavery, pure and simple."

"You will most assuredly have new overseers." Meridian pointed to his dogs. "These animals are under my domain. On occasion, when necessary, they must adhere to my commands. But most of the time, they do as they please. They are quite contented.

"I, Meridian, am not a god. The Paratwa are not gods. All living organisms possess overseers, whether consciously perceived or not. I have masters. I follow the dictates of those above me. *Sappho* follows the dictates of those above her. Even the overseers have overseers. It is a way of nature."

"Cooperation of the fittest?" asked the lion.

For one piercing instant, Meridian met his gaze. Then the Jeek turned to Losef.

"I beg of you, let us make the necessary arrangements for a peaceful coexistence. Let us put our hostilities behind us. Our terms are quite simple. You will formally announce to your intercolonial citizenry the nature of this viral threat that can destroy each and every one of them. You will announce that you are transferring control of the Irryan Colonies to a transitional team of Paratwa who shortly will be departing from the Biodyysey. Until that team arrives, I will function as their liaison.

"All of your defense net military units will immediately surrender their vessels to representative forces from the Biodyysey. If we can agree to these basic terms within the next hour, then no skygene virus need ever be released. The brutal tragedy of a conflict you cannot win will be avoided. And a new age of peace—for both human and Paratwa—will begin."

Meridian's arm flashed downward. The holo churned into motes of dust, colors fading, disappearing.

For a time, no one spoke. Finally, the lion turned to Losef. "I contend that Meridian and the Paratwa are unabashed liars. Their falsehoods must be exposed, laid bare. There is a man waiting outside chambers who would like the opportunity to address Council. He is here to tell us the truth. With your permission, I will have him brought in."

Van Ostrand scowled. Losef gave a slow nod.

Huromonus keyed a command and the door reopened. Nick strode purposefully into the chamber. Passing between the dogs, he dropped a small plastique bone in front of each of them. The dogs did not budge.

"You can usually rely on good discipline," said the midget, hopping up to stand on an empty chair beside Inez.

Meridian bowed slightly. "The Czar. We meet at last. I am most honored."

"Howdy, Jeek. From my perspective, I can't actually say its an honor. But I will admit that I'm going to remember the occasion for a long time."

"I share your sentiments."

Nick chuckled. "I doubt it. Still, that sounds like a nice and friendly attitude. I just hope that you can maintain your diplomatic mannerisms over the next few minutes as well. 'Cause what I'm about to say might just get you really pissed off. Please try to maintain your cool."

"I will make every effort."

"Good. Then let's cut to the chase. Several Councillors have been permitting me to listen in on this meeting. . . ."

Losef raised her eyebrows.

"And I've learned a lot. In fact, the last few days have been a real education. But not all of Council are aware of these events. So we'll start with a recap. . . ."

Nick began by outlining the incredible knowledge that they had gained from Freebird. During the presentation, the lion kept his attentions riveted on the Guardian Commander, trying to gauge his temperament as the story unfolded. Soon, Jon Van Ostrand would come to know just how much their collective future was riding upon his actions.

Nick related Aristotle's entire tale. He told them about the Os/Ka/Loq, and how Sappho had arrived on Earth in her probe ship, hundreds of years in advance of the Biodyysey, to ensure that the planet was destroyed in an apocalypse; how she had first created the earthly Paratwa within a *kascht* which possessed only the barest level of T-psionic force, a *kascht* which reeked of the lacking. He told them of Aristotle's betrayal of the Ash Ock. He told them of the century-spanning manipulations of Sappho, the purposes for the Order of the Birch massacres, and the reasons Codrus had been left behind in the Colonies.

And finally, the midget detailed the complex Os/Ka/Loq scheme to replace Earth's native organisms with their own unique tapestry of life. And he described the fatal flaw which would ultimately doom the Paratwa plan.

"The Apocalypse happened pretty much according to Os/Ka/Loq designs. The majority of earthly life was wiped out in preparation for reseeding. But the Os/Ka/Loq—Sappho in particular—screwed up with the Irryan Colonies. We weren't supposed to survive. Millions of human beings weren't supposed to retreat up to the cylinders while the planet was being consumed by nuclear and biological madness. In fact, we can thank the foresight and perseverance of some of our ancestors—those brave humans who worked hard to guarantee that the cylinders escaped destruction and prevented Paratwa infiltration."

Nick shrugged. "Still, all things considered, it wasn't Sappho and the Paratwa who brought the human race to the brink. We were already plunging toward the edge—the Paratwa merely gave us a well-timed push. Even without their help, the continuing dehumanization of our species—the subjugation of human passion to the twin gods of profit and progress—probably would have sent us tumbling into the abyss sooner or later.

"But *sooner or later* wasn't good enough for the Os/Ka/Loq. They had a specific timetable. And here today, we've come to the grand culmination of their ancient project. The Biodyysey has arrived, and it indeed possesses the technological superiority to destroy anything we can throw at it. Their skygene viruses indeed have been secretly hidden within all of our cylinders. The Os/Ka/Loq are ready to infest the Earth. The Colonies have been placed in a position where our demise seems imminent . . . unless we surrender. But even our surrender won't save us. The most that we'll gain is a little time. If we quietly throw down our weapons, the Os/Ka/Loq will simply use us to carry out their reseeding plans, and then send us to hell—as they had originally intended."

Nick paused, turned his gaze upon Meridian. "But we've got an ace in the hole, don't we Jeek?"

Meridian smiled. "What you *have* is less than one hour before the Colony of Red Saxony is poisoned."

Nick arched his eyebrows. "I'm shocked, Meridian. No denials?"

"It would be pointless for me to lie. The bare facts of your story are essentially true. But your interpretation is faulted. The Os/Ka/Loq desire only the planet. Humans will be allowed to remain happy and content within the sanctity of these cylinders."

Van Ostrand looked stunned. "All of this . . . everything . . . the Apocalypse . . . the Paratwa . . . it's all been part of an alien scheme to conquer the Earth?"

"You got it," said Nick. "In a sense, the whole human race has been bent over the table for the past three centuries."

"Quaintly put," said Meridian, allowing his gaze to span the entire Council. "But all that the Czar is relating to you would have been learned by the Colonies in the upcoming weeks. His presentation has merely introduced minor variations to a timetable conceived more than three centuries ago. *Think* about that. Think about a species which deliberately plants seeds not intended to bear fruit for hundreds of years." The Jeek shrugged. "You have merely gained some fragments of knowledge slightly ahead of time. But nothing has essentially changed here. You are still faced with the same choices. If you fail to accept our terms, your Colonies—one by one—will be exposed to the virus."

Nick chuckled. "Don't believe this Jeek for a minute. This is one desperate son-of-a-bitch. He *knows* I've got an ace in the hole. And he *knows* I'm getting ready to play it."

Meridian sighed. "Then please do. It's obvious that the natural course of events cannot precede until you have finished with your . . . games."

"Damn straight," said Nick. "Yesterday, upon accessing Freebird's secrets, the lion of Alexander, with the full cooperation of E-Tech and La Gloria de la Ciencia, implemented our own plan. A massive shuttle armada, with ships from E-Tech and from various Costeau clans, was secretly outfitted with nuclear weapons and biological poisons of every conceivable variety. E-Tech's L5 research cylinders contributed the ecospheric toxins while La Gloria de la Ciencia—prime armaments provider to the defense net—supplied the megatons of nuclear warheads necessary to accomplish our task.

"Less than one hour ago, all planetary bases and facilities on the surface of the Earth received emergency evacuation orders. And in approximately ten minutes, that massive shuttle armada will begin to arrive in low Earth orbit. These ships will arm and launch their deadly payloads toward the planet." Nick paused. "Armageddon has come again. Earth's second Apocalypse is about to consume the place of our birth."

Van Ostrand whispered. "Trust preserve us." Losef leaned back in her chair. She appeared stunned.

Nick continued. "It's a sad day for the human race. Our great collective dream—Ecospheric Turnaround—so close to coming true, will now have to be denied for ages to come. Our world is about to be recontaminated, made unfit for human life ... made unfit for Os/Ka/Loq life."

Nick, with a look of complete disdain, turned to Meridian.

"And Jeek—be advised that we will utilize every effort to *keep the Earth contaminated*. If need be, we will deny it to ourselves forever, in order to keep you and your masters from spreading their perversions upon it."

Meridian stood patiently, as if waiting to make sure that Nick was finished. When the midget remained silent, the Jeek assassin threw back his head and laughed. "Is that it? Is that your so-called ace in the hole?" With a wild grin, he turned to Van Ostrand. "I'm frankly astonished. I was expecting something more in the line of, say ... a new, top-secret military weapon. But ... bombing the *Earth*?" Another harsh laugh echoed through the chamber.

"This is the most extraordinary nonsense I have ever heard. Do you truly believe that recontaminating the planet is going to make the Paratwa disappear? Do you think that this is going to stop us from releasing the skygene virus? Do you think the Biodyysey will simply . . . go away?"

The lion studied Van Ostrand, saw the deep worry in his eyes. Losef was frowning. Even Inez appeared somewhat unnerved by Meridian's confident retort.

"Then do us," said Nick, his voice dropping to a deep whisper, but his words resounding through the chamber with iron clarity. "Do us, Jeek. Do us right now."

"I beg your pardon?"

"Do us. Do all two hundred and seventeen Colonies right now. Release your virus in every cylinder."

The lion pushed back his chair and stood up. "Do us."

Huromonus and Inez followed suit. "There's no reason to wait," said Huromonus.

"No reason at all," added Inez.

For a moment, Meridian hesitated, and the lion sensed that there was turmoil taking place aboard the Biodyysey, where the Jeek's other tway must be standing before Sappho and the Os/Ka/Loq masters.

Nick asked, "Is the translation coming through okay at your other end? Are your lords clearly understanding us?"

Meridian remained silent.

"Well, Jeek, let me phrase things another way. . . . Why don't you and your Os/Ka/Loq disincorporate. Or, in the old earthly vernacular—go fuck yourselves."

The lion added, "No matter what happens to us, the planet's finished. Our shuttle armada can't be recalled. You can wipe out the Colonies, Meridian . . . you can even get rid of this present uncooperative Council if you like, perhaps assemble a more malleable group of individuals, those who might be willing to live under the yoke of the Paratwa. I'm sure you'll have little trouble finding such people. But even so, no matter what you do, the essential facts do not change."

"That's right," said Nick. "The Earth is getting nuked and there's not a damn thing you can do about it."

When Meridian finally spoke, his words were solemn, contemplative. "The Os/Ka/Loq are a most patient species. They have desired the Earth for many centuries. If they must wait a while longer to obtain it, then that is what they will do."

Nick shook his head. "Nah, I don't buy it. A few years, sure. Ten, twenty, fifty, maybe even a century. But how about a *thousand* years, Jeek? How about *five thousand*? Will they wait that long?"

Meridian started to open his mouth to speak, then either thought better of it, or else was ordered to hold his tongue.

"I believe I know what you were going to say," offered Nick. "You were thinking that it was damn unlikely that the Colonies managed to scrape together enough nuclear armaments to truly decimate the Earth for such a lengthy period. And you'd be correct. Even our best calculations limit the extent of surface contamination to under a hundred years.

"But we've taken the trouble to work up a more extensive profile for planetary destruction. We figured out what it would take in terms of megatons to make the Earth unlivable for *millenia*. Our calculations indicate that a dense nuclear saturation of the planet's surface—something which works out to be on the order of thirty-five times the total amount of energy released during the entire Apocalyptic year of 2099—would accomplish this task. That level of nuclear saturation will produce a long-term self-sustaining reaction, ensuring severe ecospheric fallout for at least a thousand years. Global temperature increases will melt the polar ice caps. The ozone layer will be totally depleted."

The lion added, "Such devastation is well within our power. And we know enough about your masters to know that however technologically superior, they are not omnipotent. The Os/Ka/Loq cannot hope to reverse such ravages. We will create conditions which will put the Earth beyond even the most vigorous approaches to terraforming."

Nick faced Van Ostrand. "Actually, all that is required for such destruction are the payloads from about two dozen Ribonix-class destroyers."

On the FTL screens, sudden understanding crossed Van Ostrand's face.

Nick went on. "It's all up to you and the Guardians. And by the way, Councillor, we're now a hundred percent certain that Doyle Blumhaven was functioning as an Ash Ock puppet. And we know that Blumhaven kept your true Order of the Birch affiliations a secret."

Van Ostrand did not look overly surprised by Nick's remarks. The lion assumed that in recent days, the Guardian Commander would have given a great deal of consideration to Doyle Blumhaven's hidden agenda.

"Think about that," suggested Nick. "Consider why the Paratwa wanted someone of your radical nature commanding the defense net."

Van Ostrand murmured, "I would throw everything we had at them."

"Bingo. The only real threat to an Os/Ka/Loq victory is the one that we've just outlined. A mere two dozen of your Ribonix-class destroyers are capable of totally screwing up three centuries of Paratwa plans.

"And the Os/Ka/Loq *know* that. Fifty-six years ago, when Codrus was exposed, their greatest fears arose. The Irryan Colonies began removing many of the scientific/technological limits imposed by E-Tech over the centuries. Most especially, weapons development got full green lights. In short, your defense net was put into place, boasting enough nuclear firepower to bake the planet.

"The Os/Ka/Loq's only advantage was our lack of knowledge. We didn't know the truth about them, and they did everything in their power to keep it that way. They kept the Colonies focused outward—in fact, that's one of the reasons they chose the Order of the Birch as their smokescreen to carry out the skygene courier assassinations. It was another subtle psychological ploy to keep Colonial feelings aligned with the idea of combatting the Paratwa out at the defense net.

"So their biggest concern became keeping us in the dark. And their biggest worry was Freebird. Aristotle's ancient program was like an invisible club hanging over their heads. I suspect that Codrus probably made some serious attempts to root out and destroy Freebird over the years, but obviously he didn't succeed. And when Codrus perished, the human tway of Sappho returned to the cylinders with the sunsetter. And that sunsetter was set loose in the archives for one reason and one reason only: to hunt down and terminate Freebird. In typical Ash Ock fashion, of course, the destruction of the many would camouflage the destruction of the one. Their sunsetter was designed to annihilate *all* old programs to disguise its true purpose." Nick paused. "But we found Freebird in time."

Meridian seemed to be rooted to the floor, his eyes distant, as if gazing upon some faraway vista.

Van Ostrand stared at Nick. "You deliberately arranged for those advance targeteers to attack the Biodyysey, knowing that they were headed toward certain destruction. You wanted me to know what I was up against."

"That's right," said Nick. "The Os/Ka/Loq would like nothing better than to have you throw your entire fleet against the Biodyysey. That's what they were counting on. They figured that once they started releasing their skygene viruses in the Colonies—once things began to look really hopeless—you'd attack furiously, with every ship under your command. They would have the opportunity to decimate your entire fleet, thus ending the one real threat to their final victory.

"Of course, now you know what would happen during such an all-out attack. The Biodyysey's energy field is capable of vaporizing any craft—or missile—which comes within immediate attack range. I suspect that they're quite impervious to harm."

"That is correct," said Meridian, returning his attention to chambers. "And our skygene viruses are still capable of ending Colonial life." He sighed. "Whether or not you destroy your homeworld will ultimately make no difference. I beg of you to realize that your only hope for survival is complete surrender, under our terms. You must understand that no matter what you do, you lose . . ." The Jeek trailed off when he noticed Van Ostrand suddenly walk away from the FTL.

Nick smiled grimly. "Well, Jeek, I can't argue with your logic. But hell—better now than later. I mean, if nothing else, our species will die with a bit of dignity. We know that human beings are nothing more than interesting perversions to the

Os/Ka/Loq. Your masters might keep a few of us alive for a time—as servants or sideshow freaks—but if we surrender, we're finished as a race."

For the first time, a trace of real concern appeared on Meridian's face. He stared at the FTL screens, at Van Ostrand's vacant seat. "This is . . . a very brave decision on the part of Council. But I doubt if your attitude will be much appreciated by the average Irryan citizen. Once the Colonies learn that you've signed their death warrant, the vast majority will revolt. Like most organisms, they will do anything to stay alive."

Nick shrugged. "You're probably right. But either way, your prize is snatched out from under you. The Earth is going to get a nuclear bath—"

"We'll do even worse," promised Van Ostrand, returning suddenly to the screens. He looked as grimly determined as the lion could ever recall.

"I've just given the orders to my fleet commanders. Even as we speak, over nine hundred ships—including forty-eight Ribonix-class destroyers—are setting courses for the Earth. They have been made aware of how vital their mission is. They have been instructed that no matter what happens within the Colonies, they are to unleash their entire payloads upon the planet. Their missiles will broil the planet. The Earth shall be made into an utter wasteland."

Nick aimed a finger at the assassin. "And Meridian—I hasten to point out that once the men and women aboard these Guardian vessels learn that the Colonies have been poisoned, that they have nothing to return to . . . well, I'd be willing to bet that there'd be nothing in the universe capable of deterring them from their mission."

The lion said. "It's your move, Meridian."

The Jeek stood quietly for a moment. Then: "I would like to be alone for a short time."

"Of course," offered Losef, keying open the door. Meridian and his dogs quickly existed.

Inez released a deep breath. "Well, we've done it now, haven't we."

"No turning back," said Huromonus.

Inez looked hesitant. "Have we made the right decision?"

Nick shook his head. "I doubt if there is a *right* decision here. But I'm convinced that we acted properly. This is our only chance for survival."

The lion turned to Huromonus. "What about CPG?"

Nick explained to Losef and Van Ostrand what they had learned about Sappho's identity. Losef, after consulting her terminal, offered confirmation that Venus Cluster was indeed secretly owned by CPG Corporation.

"Your confirmation arrives not a moment too soon," said Huromonus, in a tone leavened with dry wit.

Losef defended her actions. "The ICN has acted properly throughout this affair."

The lion sighed. "Either way, it's no longer of any consequence."

Huromonus read from his monitor. "We have a large E-Tech assault force in place around CPG's Irryan headquarters. Our spotters do not know whether Corelli-Paul Ghandi or the tripartite assassin are there, but Security is positive about Colette Ghandi. She's inside the building."

Inez mused, "At this stage of events, it certainly can't do us any harm to capture the tway of Sappho."

"Decidedly not," agreed Huromonus.

"Go get the bitch," said Nick.

Empedocles was no stranger to vanquishment and the postures required to face defeat. Having been imprisoned within the body of the Gillian/tway for those many years—trapped inside a consciousness rendered incapable of even *perceiving* the existence of the monarchy—Empedocles was accustomed to living as a shadow, a physical pauper, a disembodied icon of Gillian's deepest dreams. It had taken a long time before events finally had triggered Gillian's psyche into rediscovering his true Ash Ock self, a long time before Empedocles could even begin to entertain hopes of escaping a life of cloistered disembodiment. And even after Gillian's primary memories had returned, the monarch consistently had been forced to expend great effort—via his own powers of subliminal persuasion—to focus the tway's drifting consciousness.

But as Gillian's memories returned, Empedocles's frustrations had mounted, for his monarchial future seemed destined to suffer the limitations of time-sharing a single body. Empedocles could not imagine a more perverse bane for an Ash Ock. Still, there had seemed no way to counter such a restriction. Catharine was dead. Only one tway remained.

It was then that the notion of the permanent whelm had begun to sound attractive. The melding of his consciousness with Gillian's certainly did not represent an earnest desire, but it had come to seem the most tolerant of a color-starved palette of options.

And then Timmy had come into their lives. A long-abandoned spectrum was reexamined; strictured vistas again blazed with the hues of former glory. Timmy helped achieve what Empedocles had come to believe was impossible. Through the vehicle of Susan Quint, true monarchial consciousness—thriving contemporaneously within two bodies— was restored. Once again, Empedocles was a complete Ash Ock Paratwa.

Fully reconstituted, he had planned to follow the basic outline of Timmy's wishes. He would seek out the tway of Sappho, bring to her the news that he had slain the last remnant of that ancient traitor Aristotle. Empedocles also would make possible the return of Sappho's stolen Os/Ka/Loq probe ship. Once his actions were verified by the mistress of the Ash Ock, his long-denied rightful place in the Sphere of the royal Caste would be granted.

It did not take long for his optimistic plans to disintegrate.

Boarding the shuttle with the partial "tway" in tow, Empedocles had utilized the tiny android to send the proper command sequences to Sappho's ship. Their ascent from the depths had been fast and uneventful . . . provided one ignored the unknown technology that rendered depressurization effects inconsequential. Nevertheless, the first hint of trouble did not occur until he had reengaged the shuttle's monitoring system.

Harsh urgent warnings blanketed every intercolonial channel that he could tune. Each network was broadcasting a variation of the same basic message: all Earth personnel, whether in E-Tech bases or Church of the Trust cloisters, whether on the surface legally or otherwise, were to evacuate the planet immediately. No explanation was given for such an unprecedented communique.

But Empedocles had a pretty good suspicion of what must have occurred. Freebird had been cracked open, its secrets spilled. The Irryan Colonists had discovered the Archilles' heel of the Paratwa.

Quickly, he had blasted off. Hull microcams revealed the artificial fog bank dissipating, the massive Os/Ka/Loq probe ship automatically sinking back into its watery sanctuary. Empedocles was not certain whether two miles of ocean would be enough to spare the cell from decimation, but there was little enough he could do about it at this point. Without time to familiarize himself with its navigational systems, any attempt to lift off in the probe was sheer folly.

By the time his shuttle had achieved the relative safety of high orbit, hundreds of nuclear-armed missiles already were being fired at the planet. He was thirty-three thousand miles out when he encountered the actual first wave of attackers.

Alarms wailed. Navcom screens erupted. Several of the approaching shuttles blipped E-Tech IDs at him, then proceeded to transmit additional warnings to his craft. He allowed the navcom to phrase his response, providing them with assurances that he was indeed heading back to the Colonies with all due haste. Under normal conditions, the E-Tech vessels probably would have challenged his presence here; he was, after all, flying a smuggler-owned craft. But conditions clearly were not normal.

Onboard sensors provided real-time documentation of the planetary destruction. At his command, the navcom created a spinning holo of the globe, wrapped in geothermal overlays.

A hundred pinpricks of light erupted across the Earth's land masses; within minutes, that number had increased into the thousands. Long-range cameras displayed an even more engaging symmetry as mushroom clouds expanded, overlapped, melded into a vast carpet. For a few extraordinary moments, the land masses of the planet seemed to become solid wavering sheets of golden flame.

And then the firestorm relented and the fierce light faded, and the atmosphere grew dark, almost opaque. Empedocles disengaged all planetary imagery, knowing that there was nothing more of consequence to be seen. He permitted himself twin sighs. Radical alteration of his plans had become necessary.

Originally, he had intended to dock the shuttle in Sirak-Brath—the Gillian/tway's initial point of departure—then take a standard flight back to Irrya. That had seemed the safest way to proceed. But now, there was no time for such caution. He had reset the navcom for an Irryan rendezvous.

Upon docking in the small minor terminal, located nearly twenty-five miles south of the Capitol district, he realized that the remainder of his carefully wrought plans also had been rendered unless.

There was madness on the streets of Irrya.

Side by side, he walked up the terminal's exit ramp and out into a sun-swept boulevard overwhelmed by rioting humans.

There appeared to be thousands of people involved, screaming and ranting and smashing their way through the ground-floor windows of this secondary shopping district. E-Tech Security was out in full force, but obviously they had lost control of the situation. Most of the troopers were huddled tightly along one side of the street, their multiplicity of active crescent webs filling the air with a solid hum that was, somehow, clearly discernible above the shrieks of the rioters. It was impossible to discern motivations for the destructive rampage.

Empedocles turned and dashed back down into the bowels of the docking terminal. He shoved his way through a small group of frightened individuals surrounding an arrival/departure grid. Someone had retuned the monitor to an emergency network and a gray-suited kronkite—a machine-generated newsreader—was reporting on the extent of the intercolonial disorders.

The riots were not isolated events; they were occurring throughout the cylinders. In a serene voice, the kronkite also confirmed what Empedocles already knew: the entire Earth had just been nuked in an attempt to deter the returning Paratwa from their goals. The newsreader offered no commentary on just what those goals might be.

Frustrated, the monarch pushed his Susan/tway through the small crowd, leaped over a high counter, and flipped monitor channels until he located a live freelancer who was reviewing the riots in the context of an entire spectrum of deliriously newsworthy events. Empedocles's rudeness was not appreciated by the assemblage.

"Hey!" yelled a large fingerless man wearing prosthetic gloves. "We're watching for local riot updates! We want to get out of here without being killed! Who the hell do you think you are?"

Empedocles came up behind the man with his Gillian/tway. He raised his leg and slammed his boot heel into the man's kidney. The protester went down. Several humans stared angrily at his Gillian/tway, but a quick stereo glance confirmed that there would be no other challenges.

On screen, the rather elderly male freelancer was recapping the most notable incidents of the past few days. Empedocles listened with growing apprehension.

The reasons behind the riots were varied and complex. Initial protests apparently had come from Order of the Birch sympathizers who objected to the Irryan Council's cowardice in agreeing to meet with Meridian. But the rioting had exploded into uncontrollable proportions over the past few hours, after it was learned that the returning Paratwa vessel—the Biodyysey—had annihilated a small force of Guardian targeteers.

And then new fuel was poured over the growing conflagrations. Unsubstantiated rumors began to spread that the Paratwa had planted deadly viral bombs in all of the cylinders and that the Council of Irrya—by refusing to accede to Ash

Ock demands—was jeopardizing the lives of each and every citizen. There were even reports—as yet uncomfirmed—that one of the Colonies already had been contaminated by the aerobically transmitted disease.

Right now, full-scale riots were occurring in nearly three-quarters of the Colonies. Order of the Birch fanatics, demanding a total attack on the Biodyysey, were clashing with civilians who insisted that the Council of Irrya heed Meridian's threats. None of the rioters seemed to be overly concerned that the Earth had just been nuked; if that issue carried weight, its pull remained an unconscious influence.

Martial law had been declared in most cylinders, but the rioting was so out-of-hand—E-Tech Security forces so severely out-numbered—that the declaration held little meaning. Colonists were either too angry or too terrified to be overly concerned by governmental threats.

The elderly freelancer provided a wealth of other news as well. Empedocles learned about the decimation of the E-Tech archives, an event that was being widely blamed on "Crazy Eddic" Huromonus, whose tenure as E-Tech Director was anticipated to be the shortest in the history of the organization. But Empedocles now understood just how the humans had been able to strip Freebird of its secrets. And he realized that there was a high probability that Huromonus had not been acting alone. The Czar, that ancient and implacable Ash Ock enemy, doubtlessly was involved. Destroying the entire archival network just to ream Aristotle's cursed program smacked of the Czar's boldness.

The freelancer also reviewed last week's massacre at the lion's retreat—a report that held absolutely no interest for Empedocles. He did not care that Adam Lu Sang, Buff Boscondo, and a number of other humans had been slain. But deep inside, he sensed a tinge of emotion emanating from his Gillian amalgam.

The next item riveted Empedocles's four feet to the floor of the terminal.

"There's still no word on the fate of Colette Ghandi, wife of CPG Corporation founder Corelli-Paul Ghandi. For reasons as yet unannounced, E-Tech Security raided CPG's

Irryan headquarters and arrested this woman." An angry scowl spread across the elderly freelancer's face. "No formal charges have yet been filed. E-Tech is refusing to make any comment on what many Irryan judicial experts currently believe may be an illegal detention."

Empedocles released a short bitter laugh. This freelancer was actually upset by an issue that was, under the circumstances, remarkable only for its irrelevance. But his monarchial humor quickly died away.

The tway of Sappho had been taken.

He considered his options, quickly realized that only one course of action remained open to him. It was not going to be easy to get to the Irryan Council chambers. And once there, his chances for survival would be impossible to predict; too many variables now existed.

But lesser destinies simply were not worth consideration. He had come too far to ever again accept vanquishment. There would be no more postures adopted to face the possibility of defeat. From this point on, he would live or die as Ash Ock.

Buff's dead, projected Gillian.

Susan felt his hurt. *She was a good friend.*

Yes. He repressed all echoes of sadness, consigned them to that dark place beyond the horizon of immediate consciousness. Later—if there was a later—his memories of Buff might be recalled. Now was not the time for mourning.

His anger was more difficult to contain.

Susan held her composure. *What do we do now?*

Gillian forced his thoughts back into the flow of an icy stream. *We stick to the plan. When the time comes, when conditions are right, we act—cleanly and without hesitation. Remember, we'll probably get only one chance. Empedocles won't allow himself to be fooled twice by such a tactic.*

Susan allowed an instant's hesitation to mark her uncertainty. *There's no other way?*

No other way, insisted Gillian. *I can feel Timmy's mnemonic cursors. I can perceive the outlines of the mental prison that I'm confined within. I cannot return to my body.*

She argued, *But Timmy also implanted a mnemonic cursor inside me.*

We've been over this before, responded Gillian, suspecting that her contention sprouted not only from a refusal to accept the unpleasant parameters of Timmy's mind trap but from a genuine fear of what needed to be done if they were to dissolve the monarchy. *Your mnemonic cursor is not the same. You told me so yourself. Timmy implanted your control nodule for the distinct purpose of forcing you to seek him out when certain conditions arose. But Catharine and I received the implants for a totally different reason, as a means of controlling Empedocles's tways, in the event that the monarch ever became a threat to the Ash Ock.*

Susan continued to express doubt. *How do you know that Timmy didn't secretly implant other cursors inside my mind?*

He would not have considered it necessary. Gillian paused. *Catharine and I . . . we were different from the other Ash Ock tways. We were the only ones who did not require a mirror for regular interlacing. We were the only ones who could come together merely by thinking about it. And once, when Aristotle was whole, he knew of our special ability.*

You see, Timmy claimed to possess all the memories of his monarch and tways. But I know better. He was lying. I too remember the pains that rise to overwhelm you when you're torn in half, when you lose a tway. Timmy's monarch and surviving tway melded because it was the only way they could truly come to terms with the enormity of that pain.

If you try hard enough, you can blot anything from awareness. And Timmy would not have had to make a great effort to forget memories having to do with individuality, with authentic freedom of choice—those things which he had forever lost.

I don't understand, projected Susan.

It's simple. Timmy forgot about the special gifts of Gillian and Catharine. He forgot the power that we alone possessed: our ability to create or destroy monarchy without the need for any sort of external contrivances. And when he forgot that simple fact, he was led to the assumption that Empedocles's permanent monarchy could be maintained merely by blocking me—Gillian—from returning to my body.

But he forgot about your body. He realized that the amalgam known as Susan Quint, by herself, could do nothing to break the interlace. But he forgot what Catharine and I were capable of doing. Timmy did not remember the extent of my abilities. Therefore, he did not take the added precaution of implanting the more sophisticated varieties of mnemonic cursors inside your mind.

Susan whispered, *Your plan terrifies me.*

I know, he responded gently. *And it's a fear that I cannot help you through. But unless we are to spend the rest of our days as amalgams, we have no choice.*

She did not reply. There was no need.

The private limo had a snow-repellent rainbow roof, a passenger compartment capable of comfortably seating six, that same number of tires—each embedded with rubberized twistik for better traction—and a broad-shouldered woman driver with a minimalist's approach to conversation.

"Where?" she asked, holding the left-side passenger door open for Ghandi and tway Calvin.

"Drive south," ordered the Ash Nar, as he slid into the forward-positioned seat. Ghandi sank into the cushioned elegance of the equally wide couch that faced the rear of the limo, directly across from Calvin.

The chauffeur assumed her place in the separate driver's compartment, started the car, and accelerated out into a snow-free speed lane. Ghandi stared blankly through the window, barely cognizant of the white-caked hills and skier's valleys that defined the very essence of Pocono Colony. He might as well have been riding through the void.

The tway withdrew a tiny device from beneath his jacket, waved it around the compartment, then nodded to Ghandi. "Limo's clean. We can talk."

What's the point? thought Ghandi, feeling another overwhelming surge of bitterness rising from his guts. But he replied anyway, the words flying out of him, sarcastic and uncontrolled. "No holotronic letters today, Calvin? Straight talk, right from the mouth? I'm damn honored."

The tway's eyes seemed to dance from one side of Ghandi's face to the other, with a kind of surgical precision, as if he was examining Corelli-Paul's countenance for possible dissection. "Colette's capture merely serves as a temporary inconvenience."

Ghandi forced a smirk. "She's gone, Calvin. Hasn't that registered yet?"

"It has registered. The ones who have taken her will be made to pay."

"You don't seem too upset, Calvin. I would have expected a bit more rage."

"I am enraged. My twins have already arrived at the chalet. They are in the gym. As we speak, I am pulverizing practice dummies with four fists. Cathartic release is most satisfying, at least on a short-term basis. You should try it."

"Not my style," mumbled Ghandi.

The tway offered a faint smile. "Do you want me to punish you? Do you want me to make you suffer, so that you can more keenly acknowledge your loss?"

Ghandi glared. He was beginning to think that he had made an error in earning the Ash Nar's respect. *I liked him better when he wanted to kill me just for the hell of it.*

"When we get to the chalet, I could administer a mild beating to you. Or a severe one, if that is your pleasure. Perhaps this would help you in overcoming your emotional torment." Calvin grinned.

"I can do without your help."

The tway turned to the window, stared up at a Speed Slope that emerged from the clouds to parallel the road for a short distance. "You never followed your destiny, Corelli-Paul. That is the great tragedy of your life."

"What are you talking about?"

"Yesterday, in the shuttle, when you pushed it to the edge . . . when you challenged me. It made you feel strong, virile. Yes?"

Ghandi did not answer.

"It made you feel . . . *alive.*"

"Do you have a point to make, Calvin, or do you just enjoy babbling?"

The tway returned his attention to the compartment. He locked his eyes on Ghandi.

"Your destiny, Corelli-Paul, was to oppose us. Your destiny was to fight the Paratwa."

Ghandi turned away. "You should have been a psychcounsellor, Calvin. The three of you could have had a hell of a family practice."

The tway shrugged. "You know that I'm speaking the truth. For twenty-five years now, you've followed a dishonest path. You've lived a life held separate from your feelings. You've lived a lie."

The microbes twitched. Ghandi's shoulder jerked violently. "I love her," he heard himself insist. "Colette's real to me. She made it all worthwhile." He met Calvin's steely gaze. His hands began to shake. "It's true. I love her."

"Of course you do. She's your painkiller." The tway paused. "Did you know that Sappho created me."

"What?"

"She created me. The human tway of Sappho required a lifelong companion. So she created me."

"Human tway?" asked Ghandi, bewildered.

Calvin's laughter filled the limo. "You are like most creatures, Corelli-Paul, blinded by the immediacy of your own needs. You spent a quarter of a century with Colette, and still you walk in darkness. You know so little of what the universe holds."

"She wouldn't tell me the truth," he mumbled.

"Of course she wouldn't. There was no need."

Ghandi found that he could barely respond coherently. Words spewed from his mouth in small streams, like bursts of vomit. His whole body began to shake. "I lost her . . . even before E-Tech took her, I lost her . . . disincorporated, you said. . . . She's gone. . . . She's not coming back. . . ."

"Correct," said Calvin. "Colette will never return. Only Sappho remains."

He could hardly hear the Ash Nar's words. Everything was becoming blurred, dreamlike. Calvin took on the appearance of some weird machine, attached to the seat, programmed to eject sentences with icy disdain.

"You used to mock me, Corelli-Paul. You used to compare me to Reemul. But in all candor, I would have to say that Reemul was more like you. That Jeek was also a slave to his emotions.

"Did you know that Sappho once seduced Reemul? When I was still a young boy, she showed me a holo that she had made of their lovemaking session, back on Earth, in the days of the pre-Apocalypse. Sappho wanted me to view his holo so that I would come to understand the nature of manipulation.

"During their one and only sexual encounter, Colette permitted the Jeek the simultaneity of vaginal/anal intercourse. It was clear from the holo that Reemul experienced great enjoyment.

"But after that session, Colette never again allowed the Jeek to touch her. In fact, afterward, Reemul was rarely summoned into her presence. From then on, when the Jeek required personal contact, Colette dispatched the partial tway. . . ."

"Ah, but I forget, Corelli-Paul. You know nothing of the partial." He shrugged. "It is of no consequence. The point of this story is that Reemul was easy to control. He required only a single seduction. From then on, his fantasies sustained Sappho's rule.

"Your seduction was more difficult, of course. With you, a more consistent effort was deemed necessary."

A wave of dizziness came over Ghandi. He fell back into the cushions. "We have to . . . get her back," he whispered. "I . . . love . . . her."

Calvin shook his head. "You are pathetic, Corelli-Paul. Is there anyone or anything that you have *not* betrayed? First, you sold out the human race. Then you served as your own Judas. Where do you go from here? Who remains to suffer your treachery?"

Ghandi stared out the window, numbed into silence by Calvin's diatribe. The landscape, bathed in whiteness, flashed before his eyes—a colorless vista that offered no end.

"Welcome back," Nick said to Meridian, as the Jeek and his dogs reentered Council chambers.

The lion stood at the far side of the room, away from the others, studying Meridian's face, searching for some sign of rationality, some indication that the Paratwa had arrived at the decision that it would be pointless to sentence the entire human race to death. But as before, the tway managed to project an aura of complete indifference.

Nick sat crosslegged on the table, between Inez and Huromonus. Losef, a few chairs away, tensely observed her monitor. On the FTL screens, Van Ostrand munched nonchalantly on a sandwich. Alone among the Councillors, the Guardian Commander appeared relaxed. He had rendered his decision, committed his forces to a specific course of action. Now, whatever anxiety he may have been feeling had been superseded by proper soldierly discipline. From Van Ostrand's point of view, there was nothing left to do but dispassionately await the outcome of the battle.

The lion wished he could at least imitate such tranquility.

Nick said, "We've got the tway of Sappho outside chambers. But then . . . I guess you already know that."

Meridian did not reply. He also did not order his dogs to assume their familiar flanking positions at the doorway. This time, the borzoi stayed at its master's side, obediently keeping pace, while the poodle remained on the wolfhound's back, facing the rear of the larger animal. The poodle briskly wagged its tail.

Nick went on. "By now, I suppose you've gotten a good look at the action on Earth. One hell of a firestorm, wasn't it? For what it's worth, our shuttles also dropped some biotoxins into the atmosphere, although I doubt that they were really necessary. The nukes did a pretty good job. Still, the more the merrier.

"Of course, a month or so from now, when Jon's Guardians get within attack range ..." The midget gave a bored shrug. "Well, I guess we no longer have to spell things out for you."

Coolly, the Jeek scanned the room, briefly locking gazes with each one of them. Finally, he spoke:

"There is massive rioting throughout the Colonies. The populace has learned of your rash decisions. An overwhelming majority of citizens are calling for the removal of the five of you as Irryan Councillors."

Inez smiled wanly. "I've been meaning to take a long vacation."

"Likewise," said Huromonus, nodding to Losef. She keyed her terminal.

The lion circled the table until he was directly across from Meridian. "I believe it's time that we talk to your master."

The door again opened. Two armed Security men escorted Colette Ghandi into chambers.

Her arms were pinned tightly against her sides, wrists shackled to a thin black restrainer belt coiling her waist. Blond curls drooped down across her brow, giving her a slightly dishevelled appearance. Yet despite her current predicament, there was something almost brazen in the way she strode into the room. Colette Ghandi seemed to project herself with such intensity that her mere presence demanded homage.

But it was not just her intensity that riveted the lion's attention.

As he gazed at the woman, he found his thoughts turning to his wife. He recalled that it had been weeks since he and Mela had been together, making love.

"Sappho," murmured Nick.

It was something about her pale skin, the piercing eyes, the way her loose brown skirt swirled at her ankles, the thin cloth wafting between her legs, shaping itself to her crotch as she approached the table. It was something about the space between her breasts, where long fringes of pale orange cloth grew from the white chiffon blouse, crawling through that deep valley, caressing its walls, exploring its secrets.

The lion felt as if the wind had been knocked out of him. He wanted to go to this woman, take her in his arms, make love to her right here and now.

She smiled for him. But abruptly, he found that he could not return that smile. And then the absurdity of what he was experiencing penetrated the fog of his lust. He broke his gaze, turned away from her. But even that action required great effort.

A quick glance around the table confirmed that he was not the only one affected by her presence. Huromonus's eyes had narrowed into slits, and his head seemed to be bobbing up and down, as if he was rapidly scanning her from head to toes. On the FTL, Van Ostrand's hand was frozen inches from his mouth, a string of mayonnaise dribbling from the edge of his sandwich. Losef was running her tongue across the inside of her lips. Inez's forehead rippled into a deep scowl. Even the two guards could not stop staring at their prisoner.

But Nick was grinning from ear to ear. Suddenly, the midget clapped his hands, hopped to his feet atop the table, threw back his head and laughed uproariously. "Wake up, everybody! Get the old hormones under control!"

The spell was broken. Huromonus ruefully shook his head. The others started to relax as well.

Losef dismissed the guards. With obvious reluctance, the two men backed out of the chamber. The black door slid shut.

"Jesus, Sappho!" exclaimed Nick, still grinning. "You're a genuine vamp, aren't you? No wonder most of the Paratwa population followed your orders!"

Her face stopped shining. Coldly calculating eyes fastened on the midget.

"Or maybe," mused Nick, "you're more like a bitch in permanent heat. Maybe you can even turn it on and off at will. But whatever it is, you should have a license for it. 'Cause, uncontrolled, you're a goddamn danger to society."

She finally spoke, her words emerging on the back of a

husky growl. "My name is Colette Ghandi. You have made some sort of bizarre mistake—"

"Don't waste our time," snapped the lion.

"Damn right," said Nick. "We know exactly who and what you are. Colette Ghandi might be your tway, but I know we're not talking to her at the moment. You're Sappho—Ash Ock monarch of the royal Caste."

"Continue such denials," warned Huromonus, "and we'll have you removed."

"Yeah," said Nick. "We can just as effectively deal with Meridian."

The lion saw the barest flash of anger darken her face. But it was almost instantly replaced by an open smile.

"Very well, I am Sappho. But there seems to be a problem of communication here. You do not seem to truly understand that we can destroy you—*utterly*. I would suggest that it is this *Council* which is the true danger to society."

"Yeah, well, that's a matter of perspective, now isn't it." Nick faced the others. "Take a good look at your enemy. Here is the creature responsible for the deaths of millions of human beings. Here before you stands the genesis of Earth's Paratwa. Here stands the seductress of the Ash Ock, who has been manipulating the human race for over three centuries.

"She arranged for Doyle Blumhaven to be murdered after he became a liability to her schemes. She arranged for Jon Van Ostrand to be put in charge of the Guardians." Nick faced Inez. "This is the creature responsible for the attempted murder of your grandniece. By killing Susan Quint during one of the tripartite's intricately scheduled massacres of skygene couriers, the Ash Ock hoped to influence you into accepting the inevitability of their ultimate victory. You would, in essence, become more malleable to their plans. A similar ploy was used to orientate the lion.

"The Ash Ock made you and the lion aware of your own mortality, by stealing something precious from each of you. In your case, Inez, they robbed you of your closest living relative. They believed that when it came time to threaten the destruction of the Colonies, awareness of your loss would make you more willing to do what was necessary to spare the cylinders."

"And from me," the lion conceded, "it was my courage which was stolen." He glared coldly at their prisoner. "Fortunately, that theft was discovered in time. What was taken has now been restored."

Nick tuned to Huromonus. "I'm afraid, Eddie, that you didn't quite fit into their plans so neatly. You turned out to be a bit of a wild card."

"Such is life," said Huromonus. "And what about our Council president?"

Losef gazed vacantly at one of the wall paintings. "I was the easiest one to interpret. No extraordinary manipulation was necessary."

"That's right," said Nick. "The ICN always follows the money flow. It's a sure bet."

"I have always adhered to the path of my duties."

The lion was not certain, but he thought he heard a trace of unfamiliar sarcasm in Losef's words. Perhaps she too had transcended—at least in some small way—the boundaries of her predictability.

Meridian sighed. "The Council continues to waste time. I repeat my earlier assertion: *nothing has changed.* The skygene viruses are still poised for release." The Jeek turned to Van Ostrand. "Unless those last orders to your fleet are countermanded—unless the surface decimation is limited to its current level—the Os/Ka/Loq will cause your cylinders to be made uninhabitable. And if that happens . . ." he paused for effect, "where will you go?"

"To hell, maybe," admitted Nick. "But it's a moot point either way. The Guardian fleet can no longer be recalled. Jon?"

Frowning, Meridian and Sappho turned to the FTL. Van Ostrand finished chewing a final bite of sandwich, then shrugged. "We sent a priority-one blackout directive to our ship commanders. They've been ordered to ignore all future fleet-external communications. Whatever happens in the Colonies will not make the slightest difference to the status of their mission. Even a direct command from the Colonies couldn't stop them at this point. Our ships have been warned that the Paratwa will probably attempt to issue recall orders, using the medium of the Irryan Council. Such orders will also be ignored."

Huromonus said, "Jon, we know that many of your commanders are sympathetic to the ideals of the Order of the Birch."

"That's true," admitted Van Ostrand, his voice growing colder. "Many of my people have a passionate hatred of the Paratwa. And they are now fully aware of the importance of their mission. Nothing will deter them from making the Earth uninhabitable for millennia to come."

From atop the table, Nick wagged his finger at the Ash Ock tway. "Ya know, Sappho, the problem with complex schemes is that when they backfire, they usually do it in a big way."

Something inside Sappho snapped. The lion watched her face begin to change as fury overwhelmed that careful control, that innate sense of haughtiness. Glaring at Nick, she took a menacing step toward the table.

With a sharp movement, Meridian stepped in front of her, blocking her path. He addressed her calmly. "There was a time when the Czar's destruction was within the realm of your options. That time has now passed."

From over the Jeek's shoulder, Sappho continued to glare at Nick.

The lion said, "Meridian, it's our understanding that the Colony of Red Saxony still has not been contaminated, despite rumors to the contrary—rumors undoubtedly spread by the Paratwa."

"To create further discord," added Nick.

"Whatever the reason for the delay," continued the lion, "the fact remains that your deadline has passed. The Colonists within Red Saxony are still breathing air. Your viral bomb has not been triggered."

"This is most puzzling," said Huromonus.

"Yeah," said Nick, displaying a frown. "I mean, you said that you can remotely trigger these skygene suitcases from the Biodyysey. So what's the holdup?"

Sappho tried to shove her way past Meridian, but the Jeek refused to budge. The borzoi and the poodle began to growl.

Nick laughed. "She's a got a real problem, hasn't she Meridian? I mean, three centuries ago, when the original Os/Ka/Loq tway of Sappho arrived here in her probe ship, she managed to convince her fellow brethren aboard the Biodyyssey that the Earth would make for a dandy colony. Our planet had a biosphere similar to their homeworld, the proper temperature range, et cetera. Minimum terraforming would be necessary. Even the most delicate of interrelated Os/Ka/Loq lifeforms could prosper on our world, once the original inhabitants were . . . eliminated.

"So even though an advanced technological species existed on the Earth, Sappho went ahead with her schemes. After all, she reasoned, a good Apocalyptic nuking would wipe out the human race as well as take care of the rest of Earth's rigorous lifeforms.

"But things didn't quite work out the way Sappho planned. Destroying humanity turned out to be a more difficult proposition than first anticipated. We humans proved to be a bit too tenacious. We managed not only to survive the Apocalypse but to thrive and prosper up here in the Colonies. So even though the Earth was appropriately prepped for Os/Ka/Loq reseeding, a great danger remained to foil their plans. The human race now possessed a tactical position whereby we could fairly easily recontaminate the planet. And that wasn't her only problem. There was the traitorous Aristotle and the unknown damage potential contained in his hypothetical Freebird.

"By this time, Sappho, I figure you were already beginning to fall out of favor with your Os/Ka/Loq pals. We now know enough about this telepsionically linked species of yours to understand that they must not have been overly pleased by your growing list of errors. The Os/Ka/Loq run a pretty exclusive club, and any member who starts messing up runs the risk of being—what do you call it—disincorporated?"

A muscle along Sappho's neck twitched.

Nick smiled coldly. "Not a nice word, is it? Disincorporation—to an Os/Ka/Loq, a fate worse than death.

"Still, although your race was unhappy with your failures, you presented them with a modified plan. When the Apocalypse occurred—when you and Theophrastus and the hordes of Paratwa assassins escaped the Earth in the Star-Edge fleet, when you headed out into space to rendezvous with the approaching Biodyysey—you convinced the Os/Ka/Loq that the original timetable for reseeding our world was still valid. Codrus had been left behind in the Colonies to inhibit technological growth and to cripple any large-scale efforts to restore the Earth. And Aristotle's secret archival program, if it even existed, probably would never be found.

"But then Codrus messed up, and the events of fifty-six years ago forced yet another alteration to your schemes. This time, you had to send your human tway back to Earth with the sunsetter, because now that the Colonies were making a concerted effort to play technological catch-up—accessing formerly restricted weaponry and defense data from the archives—there was an even greater chance that someone might stumble upon Aristotle's program.

"So you returned to the Colonies and tried to get things back on track. And as the moment of truth approached—as the Biodyysey entered our solar system—you instituted a headlong rush of events, hoping that rapid-fire happenings would keep us off balance. You assumed that we'd be so overwhelmed and confused by the so-called Order of the Birch massacres, by Doyle Blumhaven's murder, by the attack on the lion's retreat, by the revelation that viral bombs had been planted in all of our Colonies, that we would fail to discover that we actually possessed a fairly simple means of denying your species their ultimate prize.

"From a subtle psychological standpoint, the idea of the virus was particularly clever. Contamination of a cylinder's atmosphere—the loss of breathable air—would serve to inspire survivors into perceiving the Earth with even greater devotion. Air—being stolen from the Colonies—was again becoming abundant on the planet. So, during the early stages of your reseeding, possible threats of terrorist action against the Earth would be lessened. I suspect that CPG Corporation also contributed to spreading the idea that the Earth was a thing of immense value."

Nick paused. "It *is* a thing of great value. But our homeworld was not meant for your species, Sappho. The Earth is ours. And if we have to deny it to ourselves to prevent it from being stolen, so be it."

A weird sound began to emerge from Sappho, like the deep mournful growl of some animal trying to escape its cage. The dogs instantly swiveled their heads, locked onto the source of the disturbance. Meridian took a step away from her.

Nick approached the edge of the table, then aimed an accusing finger down at the tway. "And now, *Ash Ock*, it's judgment day. You stand before humans whom you attempted to perform genocide upon. And you stand before your own Os/Ka/Loq brethren, whom you have failed."

Screeching with rage, trying to wrench her arms free of the restrainer belt, Colette Ghandi, tway of Sappho, lunged toward the table. But she never made it.

Her head jerked sideways, as if it had been struck by an invisible force. A shudder passed through her body. She screamed, stumbled sideways, lost her balance, slammed onto the floor. Her mouth flopped open; guttural inhuman noises emerged to fill the chamber. She brayed. It was a bestial sound, a nightmarish howl.

Shivers raced up the lion's spine. Never in his life had he heard such a hideous lament.

And then she was somehow on her feet again, pirouetting madly across the chamber. The other Councillors leaped from their chairs, scampered from her path.

Out of control, driven by demons the lion knew lay beyond the limits of human imagination, Sappho ran—or was propelled—straight toward the nearest wall. An instant before she hit, her braying seemed to grow louder, taking on an even more excruciating resonance. Paradoxically, in that final moment, her agony sounded almost human.

With a sickening crash, Sappho's head smashed into the clear partition protecting a priceless Van Gogh painting. The force of the collision shattered the pressurized glass; the partition imploded, sending gleaming shards ripping across the golden cornfield.

Sappho whirled. Her face was torn and bloody; tiny shards of glass protruded everywhere. One eye was pierced dead center. Whatever fragment of rationality remained within her now seemed to find its focus upon Meridian.

"Make ... it ... end. ..." It was not a plea. It was a command.

She took a faltering step toward the Jeek. Meridian quickly knelt beside his dogs. "Aggressive alignment," he ordered. "No restrictions."

The Borzoi sprinted across the chamber in two bounds. The poodle leaped from its back, performed a perfect backward somersault, and landed on Sappho's shoulder. It's teeth sank into her neck, piercing the jugular in one mighty bite. The wolfhound knocked her legs out from under her. A shaft of blood splayed a diagonal stripe across the wall.

On the floor, kicking madly, Sappho continued to bray and scream.

"Trust preserve us," whispered Inez.

Meridian, with methodical composure, said, "The process of full disincorporation is somewhat lengthy. It will take several minutes for Sappho's Os/Ka/Loq tway to be completely rendered down into its component organisms. Until that occurs, this tway will continue to exhibit life."

The poodle kept ripping into her neck until finally, with her head half torn from her body, the horrendous cries came to an end. But her body kept arching forward; she was still trying to get to her feet. The wolfhound jumped atop her knees to hold her in place.

Appalled, the lion turned away. He looked at the others. Inez, Huromonus, and Losef were white with shock. On the FTL, Van Ostrand was slowly shaking his head, like a child trying to make something bad disappear. Only Nick appeared as calm as Meridian.

The Jeek said: "The cooperative nature of the Os/Ka/Loq—the essential T-psionic interlinking common to their entire world—precludes many of the attributes referred to as human emotions. To the Os/Ka/Loq, Sappho's disincorporation was a simple necessity, predicated by her final and ultimate failure."

"Cooperation of the fittest," whispered the lion.

"More like cooperate or die," muttered Nick.

Meridian watched his dogs continue their mutilation of Sappho's tway. "Correct. But within the parameters of their ratiocination, they do perceive the essential values of punishment. *Partial* disincorporation often serves their purposes. In fact, a precise measure of pain was recently applied to Sappho in an attempt to make her aware that the complexity of her actions taunted failure.

"But she stayed true to her course, heedless of the changing winds. She promised that within six months of your formal surrender, the first new crop of Os/Ka/Loq organisms would be harvested to walk the Earth's surface."

"Harvested to walk?" asked Inez, her eyes still riveted to Sappho's thrashing body.

Meridian explained. "A new species of specially adapted Os/Ka/Loq mobile plants was created aboard the Biodyysey. The first generation of these plants, sowed in Earth soil, were to grow to maturity within six months. At that time, they would begin to uproot themselves. With assistance, these plants would wander across the face of the Earth, spreading fresh seeds. Within a decade, geometric progression would guarantee that these organisms blanketed the land masses of the planet.

"Thousands of your humans were to have been recruited to assist with the reseeding. Most of these Colonists would have come from your population of skilled profarmers. In the Colonies, CPG Corporation was to serve as administrator of the project, making sure that the necessary hardware—atmospheric revivifiers, harvesters, planters, and the like—was transported to the surface.

"On the Earth, a special breed of Paratwa, created aboard the Biodyysey, were to oversee the actual reseeding. The Ash Joella were to be the new shepherds of your world. Through their efforts, the reseeding would proceed for maximum yield. The Ash Joella would also be responsible for rooting out any ultracompetitive native organisms which might threaten the sanctity of Os/Ka/Loq cooperation.

"Once this new subspecies carpeted the planet, the higher forms of Os/Ka/Loq life would start to migrate down from the Biodyyssey."

"And what about the Colonies?" the lion asked softly.

"You would first be stripped of your ability to do harm to the planet. The skygene virus would be discriminately released within particular cylinders that were thought to pose specific threats to Os/Ka/Loq dominance. Initial plans specified the elimination of approximately twenty percent of your population."

"Initial plans, huh?" muttered Nick. "And what was to happen after *initial plans*?"

Meridian shrugged. "Eventually, of course, the majority of your species was to have been eliminated."

The words should have sent a cold chill through the lion, but they did not. For the time being, his consciousness had passed beyond the stage where such things could affect him. He faced the Jeek. "Then from a species point of view, we did the logical thing. Decimation of the Earth was indeed our only hope."

"Your only hope," affirmed Meridian.

"And what happens now?" asked Huromonus.

Meridian closed his eyes. "The Os/Ka/Loq have temporarily retreated from my presence. They will debate among themselves for a time. Every Os/Ka/Loq on the Biodyysey will assimilate facts relevant to this greatly altered situation. A cooperative reassessment of options will occur. A cooperative decision will be rendered."

Colette Ghandi's remains, with one final burst of energy, managed to sit up. The blood-caked mass of flesh, its nearly severed head hanging limply across the chest, shuddered. The poodle, gnawing at her shoulder, barked madly. The borzoi stood up on its hind legs, lunged forward, and knocked her back down onto the floor.

The tway of Sappho stopped moving.

Meridian opened his eyes. "Disincorporation is complete. The Os/Ka/Loq entity known as Sappho has ceased to exist.

The millions of individual organisms which composed her unique structure will now be spread across the forests of the Biodyysey, where they will be reassimilated with other lifeforms, creating new configurations."

Silence filled the chamber. Meridian's dogs, satisfied that the body was no longer alive, scampered back to their master. The poodle assumed its familiar position on the borzoi's back and began licking its bloody paws.

"They are tways, aren't they?" muttered Inez. "You were lying about your pets."

"Guilty as charged," admitted the Jeek, kneeling to pat the poodle's head. "His name is Lancelot. He's a good dog."

By the time Empedocles arrived in the central capital district, things appeared hopeless; there was no way he was going to get to the sixteenth-floor Council chambers, at least not directly. The rioting humans were so densely packed that he could not even penetrate to within two blocks of the building's main entrances.

He quelled his frustration and once again restructured his plans. The primary entrances might be inaccessible, but there were other, more convoluted ways of at least piercing the lower levels of the massive structure.

Access to the Gillian/tway's memories provided schematic data on the building. Numerous underground driveways existed, most leading to the parking garages. Although Gillian had not been here for fifty-six years, it appeared that the Capitol building and its environs had not undergone any severe structural alterations since that time. And the probability of the mob knowing the locations of all out-of-the-way entrances seemed slim.

Empedocles abandoned his rental car, split up his tways,

and began circling the outer edges of the crowd. The first two garage ramps that the Gillian/tway passed were clogged with rioters, the heavy doors locked to prevent access. But three blocks from the building, on a narrow side street, his Susan/half discovered an unmarked incline squeezed between an ICN bank and a Commerce League exhibition hall. Compared to the swollen crowds just around the corner, this area was practically deserted.

Empedocles waited until his Gillian/tway arrived. Then, mounting twin smiles, he held hands with himself and proceeded side by side down the long ramp.

The garage door was open, but six E-Tech Security guards, armed with thrusters, were posted at the bottom of the incline, where the ramp funneled into the actual garage. Two of the guards moved quickly to block his path.

"Identification," demanded the first sentinel.

Empedocles spoke through his female mouth. "I'm Susan Quint, grandniece of Councillor Hernandez. My friend and I are here to see my Aunt Inez."

The Security man frowned. "Susan Quint? You're supposed to be . . . missing."

"Obviously I've been found."

The second guard, a tall woman, squinted at Empedocles's female half. "You look like her. But we'll still need to see some identification."

Empedocles produced an ID slab from Susan's pocket, handed it to the guard. The pair studied the holo image, then passed it to their leader, a busty hermaphrodite with a cultivated handlebar mustache. The herm ran the slab through a belt-mounted scanner, then nodded.

"Looks like you're who you say you are." The herm squinted suspiciously at Empedocles's Gillian/tway. "And how about you?"

Before the monarch could reply, a fourth guard approached, began muttering urgently into his lip-mounted transceiver.

Empedocles overhead just enough of the man's words to realize that his bluff had failed.

"In Sirak-Brath ... last week ... matches description ... smuggler named Impleton. ..."

Empedocles struck before the other five guards could assimilate the information.

With a flick of Gillian's wrist, the Cohe catapulted from the slip-wrist holster into his palm. The guard who had sounded the warning barely had time to raise his rifle into assault position when the stream of black energy whipped forward, slicing the weapon in half. With a cry, the man leaped backward, dropped the smoking pieces of his thruster to the garage floor.

Using Gillian's arms, Empedocles grabbed Susan from behind. He raised the needle of the Cohe, held it against Susan's neck, forced his female tway in front of himself, pretending to use her as a shield. The monarch compressed Gillian's jaw, felt the dim contours of the powerful crescent web energizing at his front and rear, screening both bodies. He filled Susan's face with a panicked grimace.

"Please!" cried Empedocles, through his female mouth. "Gillian made me bring him here! He'll kill me if you don't do as he says!"

All six guards activated their crescent webs; the silence of the garage was broken by the varying hums of harmonically competing energy fields. The five sentinels who still possessed weapons aimed their thrusters in the Susan/tway's direction. Fierce whispers flooded the air as the sextet chattered madly.

"Quiet!" ordered the herm. The he/she stared coldly at Empedocles. "Release the woman right now. If you do as I say, I promise you won't be harmed—"

"Don't waste my time," warned the monarch, through Gillian. "Do as *I* say, or she dies here and now!"

"Oh, please," he begged through Susan. "Don't let him kill me!"

The herm's handlebar mustache flicked upward as the dual-gendered face assumed a scowl. "What do you want?"

Maintaining a frightened posture with the Susan/tway, the monarch announced his demands through his male half.

"I want the Council of Irrya and I want Meridian. I want them brought *immediately* down to this garage."

The herm hesitated. "Perhaps you'd prefer that we take

you up to the sixteenth floor, where chambers are located. Then you could address Council directly—"

He pressed the tip of the Cohe needle into his female neck until it punctured the skin. A rivulet of blood slithered down Susan's flesh. He allowed a terrified gasp to escape from her mouth.

"Don't patronize me. I know this building—there are too many places to set up an ambush. It would be foolish to tempt your Security forces into any sort of rash action. You're to bring the Council here and you're to do it *now*."

He allowed a soft wail to escape from his victim/tway's throat. "Please help me!"

The herm nodded vigorously, held up his/her hand. "All right, take it easy. We're going to do exactly what the man says. There's no need for anyone to panic." The he/she paused, gazed directly at Gillian. "But you have to understand that the Council may not want to come down here—"

"They'll come. In fact, I think they're going to be rather anxious to see me. And when you get them here, I promise that I'll surrender my weapons and release Susan Quint, unharmed. You have my word on this. I have no wish for violence, but I'm in a no-win situation. My options are limited." And he thought bitterly: *That last part's particularly true. My options are limited.*

Behind him, Empedocles heard the door sealing itself. It did not matter. Either he would leave here freely or he would make his final stand in this garage.

"You're wasting time," he urged. "Summon the Council."

The herm switched frequencies and whispered into the lip mike, then nodded silently while someone issued a response. Finally the he/she spoke for all to hear.

"Your message has been delivered to the Council. They're on their way."

For good measure, Empedocles permitted a swell of relief to escape from Susan. "Oh, thank you! You've saved my life!"

The lion felt a chill go through him when he, Nick, Inez, Huromonus, and Losef stepped out of the spacious convator and into the dimly lit environs of parking garage Eleven-B.

Sixty feet away, half-circled by a coterie of about thirty E-Tech Security and Council guards, stood Gillian. A frightened Susan Quint was pinned in front of him, the needle of the Cohe resting against her neck.

"Well, well," murmured Nick. "What *have* we here?"

Behind them, a sharp hiss sounded as the second convator emerged from its transit tube to dock beside their own CV. The door split open. Meridian, accompanied by a quartet of guards, emerged. The still-bloody Paratwa dog, Lancelot—with the poodle mounted on top, facing the rear—trotted out behind its master.

Nick whispered, "A penny for your thoughts, Meridian. Are they two or is he one?"

The Jeek shrugged.

Beside the lion, Inez Hernandez drew a sharp intake of breath. "Susan! Trust preserve us. It *is* her!"

"Maybe," warned Nick. "And maybe not."

As a group, they moved forward until they were only twenty feet away. The lion wanted to approach even closer, but he yielded to urging from the E-Tech Security contingent, who were understandably nervous about permitting four-fifths of the Council of Irrya to occupy the same space as a madman with a Cohe wand.

An E-Tech Security officer—a major—stepped from the circle of troops. He faced Gillian. "All right, we've done as you have asked. The Council is here. Now put down your weapon, lower your web, and release the woman."

"Not just yet."

Nick took a step forward. "Howdy, Gillian. Been a long time, huh?"

Empedocles nodded his male tways head, recalled when Gillian had last been in the presence of the Czar. The two of them had fought. In fact, Gillian, in a rage, had actually started to strangle the midget. *Too bad you did not finish that particular task.*

The monarch replied, "I trust you have recovered from your injuries. Your neck appears healthy."

Nick produced a skeptical frown. The lion, observing Meridian, saw the Jeek instantly assume an acute posture—

arching forward slightly, rising on the balls of his feet—like a cat suddenly confronted by a dangerous animal. Lancelot—poodle and borzoi—emitted slightly out-of-sync growls.

Inez, blinking back tears, also stepped forward. "Susan. I thought that you were . . . dead. I didn't know. I thought that—"

"I'm all right, Aunt Inez," said Empedocles through his female tway.

"Don't hurt her," Inez pleaded to Gillian.

"I don't want to hurt her," continued the monarch. "But this seemed to be the only way of gaining an audience with the Council on such short notice."

"I don't know who you are," said the lion cautiously, "but at any rate, you have your audience. Now what is that you want?"

Empedocles, hearing the doubt in the lion's words, seeing Meridian's alert stance and the Czar's suspicious glare, came to a sudden decision. There was no point in continuing with his charade of duality. They knew—or at least suspected—the truth.

"I want sanctuary," replied the monarch, slowly withdrawing the Cohe from Susan's neck. "I want sanctuary with Meridian."

Several of the guards began to raise their weapons. "Hold!" ordered Huromonus, turning to the leader. "Major, no one is to take aggressive action here. Is that clear?"

The major spoke into his lip mike. The guards lowered their thrusters.

Empedocles replaced the weapon in Gillian's slip-wrist holster, deactivated the web, and assumed side-by-side positioning.

"Then it's true," murmured the lion.

"You found Jalka," Nick concluded. "And the tway of Aristotle . . . he used Susan to . . . restore your monarchy."

Inez shook her head, unwilling to believe.

Empedocles faced Meridian, spoke in stereo. "Aristotle's dead. I killed his last remnant—the Jalka/tway which called itself Timmy. It was a necessary death. Timmy wanted his own termination to serve as an apology for Aristotle's ancient betrayal of the Ash Ock. It was intended to be his final appeasement to Sappho."

Nick shrugged. "I'm afraid your timing's a bit off."

A faint smile touched Meridian's face. "Sappho's dead. She was disincorporated by the Os/Ka/Loq for her failures." The Jeek paused. "Now, only you and Theophrastus remain. . . . The last of the Ash Ock."

Empedocles felt a torrent of bitterness rising from within—a fierce eruption, born of intense frustration—blossoming outward to reach the flesh as a double cascade of red-faced rage. His quartet of hands tightened into fists. He fought back an urge to lash out with the Cohe.

Since he had left the cell of the Os/Ka/Loq, every one of his carefully conceived plans—with maddening consistency— had collapsed into failure. And now . . . Sappho . . .

Meridian went on. "At this moment, events are in a state of flux. If I were you, I would be most wary of seeking sanctuary with one who served under the Ash Ock." A wide smile filled the Jeek's face. "Even in the best of times, choosing sides can be a dangerous proposition."

The lion glanced sharply at Meridian, then turned back to Empedocles. "May we speak with your tways?"

Inez nodded vigorously.

"My tways are gone," Empedocles replied furiously. "They will not be coming back."

Inez shook her head, unwilling to believe. "You're still Susan. A part of you must remain—"

"She is nothing," snapped the monarch through his female half. "Susan Quint has ceased to exist as a person. She is a mere amalgam, silenced and impotent."

"I don't believe you."

"Your beliefs are of no consequence. I am Empedocles. I am complete, and I will remain complete. So bury your grandniece, Councillor. She is as good as dead."

Inez swallowed hard, then turned away. The lion rested his hand on her shoulder. "Don't despair," he whispered to her. "This is a creature of lies."

Nick spoke softly. "Well, Empedocles, if what you say is true, then things are a bit simpler for us. If our friends, Gillian and Susan, have actually ceased to exist, then we can consider you our enemy without . . . complications."

"True," said the Monarch, allowing all tension to depart from the muscles surrounding the Cohe's slip-wrist holster. He turned his Susan/tway slightly sideways, prepped that body for whipping out the flash daggers from her flakjak pockets.

But he did not fool himself; he realized that he was at a disadvantage for combat. Surrounded by more than thirty armed guards, his tways close together—poor positioning under the circumstances—and lacking even the element of surprise, fighting was obviously not the best option . . . and there was a tway of Meridian to contend with as well.

Still, his speed would allow him to strike first. With one slash of the Cohe, he knew that he could destroy the Council of Irrya. And the Czar.

But Meridian was watching him closely. The Jeek could read his body signs. He understood.

"It would be a shame," said Meridian, turning quickly to the lion and Huromonus, "if all were to end here, in a parking garage. Can the parties involved reach some sort of agreement?"

"Sounds like a damn good idea," offered Nick.

The lion glanced at the other Councillors, then nodded. "I believe that . . . the Council of Irrya would be willing to grant this Ash Ock full asylum."

Loscf and Incz frowned. But no one voiced any objections. The lion continued. "If that is agreeable to you, this Council officially will provide sanctuary—"

"—with one condition," added Nick.

"And what might that be?" demanded Empedocles.

The midget licked his lips. "You see, Mister monarch, I figure that if the Os/Ka/Loq decide to release their viral bombs and terminate the human race . . . well, none of this is going to matter much. But should things go the other way—should the Colonies survive—we're still going to have some big problems to deal with. And one of those problems goes by the name of Calvin."

Meridian began to grin again.

The lion nodded with understanding. "Even as we speak, E-Tech Security is engaged in an intercolonial search for this tripartite assassin. Calvin *will* be located."

"You want me to kill him for you," replied the monarch calmly.

"That'd sure be nice," said Nick.

Empedocles felt his faces grimace. "Perhaps the Colonies might be able to solve two problems simultaneously? Calvin and I could kill each other."

"Gosh!" said Nick, "that thought never even crossed my mind!"

Meridian laughed openly. "Ah, Empedocles—before you accept such an assignment, I would hasten to warn you that there are those who believe that Calvin is the deadliest assassin ever bred. Undefeatable, according to the true believers.

"Yet it is also my understanding that the Ash Nar was most displeased by the humiliation he suffered at the hands of your Gillian/tway in Venus Cluster." The Jeek shrugged. "Quite frankly, I don't believe you have much choice in this matter. If you don't go after Calvin, sooner or later he will come after you."

Empedocles glared at them all, overcome by a diffuse anger aimed at human and Paratwa alike. When he finally responded, he alternated his words between tways.

"It would—"

"—appear—"

"—that my choices—"

"—have been determined."

Meridian, still smiling, said, "You have made a wise decision."

There's a great deal of activity surrounding my twey, Gillian informed Susan. *I'm not exactly sure what's happening, but I believe that my body has entered a near-weightless state.* He strained to comprehend more. *I'm leaning over.... They're attaching something to my feet.... A strange kind of helmet is being put over my head. And there is a certain ... apprehension ... an anticipation within Empedocles. I believe that the crisis point is almost upon us.*

Susan acknowledged his percipience. Tension was undeniably intensifying. Whatever was going to happen was going to happen very soon. She steeled herself. *When the time comes, I'll do my best—*

No! he countered, knowing that the monarch would not be able to read much into that simple emotional response. But even if Empedocles could have deduced the underpinnings of such an outburst, the risk would have been necessary. Susan had to understand. She had to accept clearly that their successful escape from monarchy hinged upon the complete removal of any lingering doubts.

You must believe that we can do it. If you don't, a part of you will fight the process. Anything less than your total faith will serve to defeat us.

And remember—we have to catch him at the proper moment. We're probably only going to get one chance.

I'll be ready, she solemnly promised. *When the time comes, I'll be there for you.*

Gillian knew that she meant it. But whether she truly could endure the coming chaos remained to be seen.

She asked, *Why is it getting harder to ... sense what's happening outside our bodies? It wasn't this way in the garage ... and that was less than eight hours ago. What's happening to us? Does it have some-*

thing to do with the fact that our tways are physically in very different locations?

Gillian sensed a pale trace of fear riding beneath her words, and he longed to provide a soothing answer. But if their one shot at freedom was to have any chance of succeeding, a level of absolute trust had to be maintained between them. He gave her the raw truth.

We're being deliberately quarantined from the real world, but it has little to do with the separation of our tways. The simple fact is, the longer an Ash Ock monarchy remains intact, the weaker the tways become. And in our case, Empedocles is using every means available to repress us even further. Soon, we could become so dissociated that we won't have any chance of overcoming him.

Susan turned her thoughts outward. *It's getting chilly,* she declared. *My tway is in a place where the air is . . . very cold . . . damp . . .*

She could not actually *feel* the change in air temperature, of course. But the idea of coldness was still discernible, entering the amalgam of her consciousness upon swirling vapors, like the memory trace of some vague and distant dream. Automatically, her imagination decrypted those vapors, reconstructing fresh mnemonic referents in their place. Whatever Empedocles's Susan/tway was experiencing now lay beyond her sensory capacity. Nevertheless, information from the real world—albeit heavily filtered—continued to penetrate this prison that confined and encompassed her spirit.

She saw icicles, hanging from the upper lip of a railing. She heard men and women speaking harshly, their words unfathomable, but their tones clearly modulated into rhythms precursive of violence. Another mnemonic referent took shape and she recalled a pleasant taste from childhood: iced vanilla wobblies. Each wobblie—exquisitely crystallized in zero-G—had been mounted on a wafer stick; a baker's dozen were bundled together and set in a tiny edible vase made of reconstituted orange rinds.

For a moment, she imagined herself as a young child again, delighted by that wondrous orange/vanilla taste. And then, abruptly, the recollection disappeared, and she was left with only a fading memory. That joyous intensity—that mimicry of authentic sensation—was gone.

Bitter disappointment nearly overwhelmed her. But when the aching loss of those sensory retrospects hit home, fresh determination spilled into her. *I will have my body again,* she vowed. *When the time comes, I'll be ready.*

Gillian sensed the outlines of her newfound inspiration. *Now I believe that you mean it. Now I believe we're ready to take back what was stolen from us.*

The lion stood huddled with the others, shivering in the cold late-afternoon gusts that swept down from the upper reaches of Pocono's perpetually frigid—and somewhat unpredictable—atmosphere. He pulled the collar of his jacket even tighter up under his chin and leaned over to notch his boot heaters up another five degrees. How anyone could actually live in such a place year-round was beyond his imagination. A thermometer on the oak-paneled wall behind him indicated a Fahrenheit temperature nearly ten degrees below freezing. Two-plus centuries ago, when the new orbiting cylinders were being assigned nomenclatures, it must have been someone's idea of a sick joke to refer to Pocono as a leisure Colony.

"Most unpleasant," affirmed Huromonus, turning his body in a vain attempt to shield himself from another blistering swirl of icy winds.

The lion nodded, regretting that he had not opted for one of the full-body shapers, complete with sealed helmet and filtered breathing mask. But the crack team of first-wave assault troops—two dozen strong—who occupied the spacious front porch of the Ballistic Mystic Hotel along with himself, Huromonus, and the Susan/tway of Empedocles, had all rejected shapers in favor of lightweight ski garb. And there were Costeaus from the lion's own people—the Alexanders—assigned to this E-Tech Security force. Clan pride alone dictated that the lion emulate their toughness.

Nevertheless, he knew he could not stand much more of this intense cold. If Empedocles did not begin the assault soon, the lion was going to retreat to the comfort of the hotel lobby.

The monarch's Susan/tway stood apart from the others, at the tip of the porch, studiously observing the output screen of a small terminal. As the lion watched, Empedocles's female half removed a frozen stick-mounted confection from her flakjak pocket and slid it into her mouth. She bit down hard, lopping off a sizable chunk.

Empedocles, from his peripheral vision, caught the lion staring at him. He smiled and held the remainder of the frozen confection up in front of the Susan/tway's face, contemplating its icy perfection. "They're called orange creamsicles," the monarch offered. "They sell them inside."

The lion shivered. And as if to further taunt him, the hotel's front door slid open. A soothing wave of heat—all too short—caressed his face. Two men emerged from the inner warmth.

Vilakoz, the lion's towering security chief, barely could fit through the door. He looked like some bizarre version of a pre-Apocalyptic speciality android. Like the other troops, he wore skintight ski pants and a white jersey, but mounted on his back was a huge rectangular unit, nearly twice the girth of a zero-G constructor's pak. Gray cables trailed from the device, connecting the unit to a monstrous seven-foot-long rifle cradled in the Costeau's gloved hands. A second set of cables slithered from the rifle's trigger scope, rose upward to attach to Vilakoz's matte black targeting helmet. The Costeau's face was mostly hidden by the helmet. But the bridge of his nose, where the black skin bore the scars of his previous encounter with Calvin, remained visible.

"That looks extremely heavy," said Huromonus, with a nod toward the massive rifle. "I was not aware that the geo cannon came in a portable model."

"It doesn't."

Huromonus arched his eyebrows.

Vilakoz stared grimly across the snow-covered field surrounding the porch. "A clean shot with this," he promised, "and crescent web or not, one of those bastards *will* go down."

"Just remember," uttered the second man, stepping out from behind Vilakoz, "that we're not going after . . . bastards.

The proper word is bastard—singular." Inspector Xornakoff raised a four-fingered hand, called for everyone's attention.

"Don't forget what we're dealing with here," he warned the troops. "This is a creature capable of existing in three separate locations simultaneously. Watch your backs."

Two men at the outer edge of the porch mumbled something. Xornakoff stepped forward. "I didn't quite hear that?"

"Nothing, sir."

Xornakoff smiled and raised his other arm, the one broken in the battle at the lion's retreat. He gently laid the fractured limb—still held rigid in a clear cast—across the man's shoulders. "If you have some doubts, please share them with us."

The Security man glanced at several of his friends, then shrugged. "The strategy here, sir . . . it seems a bit . . . off-base."

"Off-base?"

Another trooper jumped in. "Sir, this chalet that we're going to hit—we know the Paratwa's in there, right?"

"That is correct."

"And we're not looking to take prisoners."

"Paratwa are not partial to surrendering."

"And we're not faced with a hostage situation."

The Inspector lowered his arm from the first man's shoulders. "Get to the point."

The man stared grimly. "Sir, most of us were wondering . . . why not simply take out the whole damn chalet with slo-mo missiles."

A female trooper nodded in agreement. "Yes, sir—that house is so isolated that we could use heavy-duty vapor grenades—blow it right off the side of the hill. There'd be little chance of casualties."

"Military *or* civilian," added another man.

"Those are good questions," admitted Xornakoff, glancing at Huromonus. "But I'm afraid that I'm not the one with the answers. Your orders are clear. The chalet is to be assaulted via conventional means. Explosives will be limited to windows and walls."

Empedocles finished his creamsicle and hurled the stick into the snow. He allowed a sultry passion to underlay the

Susan/tway's words. "If you're afraid of what's going to happen . . . then don't come."

"It's not a matter of being afraid," growled one of the troopers. A chorus of agreement erupted.

"Enough!" commanded Xornakoff. "All of you volunteered for this mission. The parameters of this attack were made clear—"

"—But you do deserve an explanation," said the lion. He started to pace back and forth—another vain attempt to ward off the numbing cold. "By now, all of you know about the Biodyysey and the alien Os/Ka/Loq and their threat to release these deadly viruses. And you know that this tripartite was the one responsible for actually hiding the skygene suitcases throughout the cylinders.

"We can't be certain, of course, but the possibility exists that there will be information hidden within this chalet which might help us deactivate these viral bombs."

Another blast of frigid air swept across the porch; an uncontrollable shiver escaped the lion. He turned away from the troops, put his back to the wind. Huromonus took over the reins in his story.

"We cannot risk indiscriminate destruction. After the assassin is eliminated, the chalet will have to be searched from top to bottom."

"After the bodies are removed," whispered Empedocles, so that only the lion could hear his words. The lion glanced at the Susan/tway's face, saw that it wore a mocking grin.

Huromonus continued. "Remember, the element of surprise remains in our favor. With Gillian—and Susan—leading the assault, you have a good chance. Both of these individuals have gone up against this assassin. They are . . . experienced fighters."

Empedocles restrained an urge to laugh aloud. *Huromonus and the lion are frightened old men! They cannot even admit to their forces that I am Ash Ock, that they are sending Paratwa to fight Paratwa!*

A few skeptical grimaces came from the troops, but the majority of the men and women appeared to accept the lion's story. That made the lion feel bad. He hated lying.

The story was a fabrication. No one entertained any real

hopes of finding something in the chalet that might spare the Colonies from the threat of the viral plague.

It had been Nick who had demanded that Empedocles lead a conventional assault on the chalet. As always, the midget had been most convincing in pleading his case.

"Look—we know that Corelli-Paul Ghandi and the tway identified as Calvin were brought to this chalet some ten hours ago. And we're ninety percent certain that the other two tways, Slasher and Shooter, are inside as well. Yet despite today's events—in particular, the Council's announcement of Sappho's death—Ghandi and the assassin have made no attempts to leave.

"Think about that," urged the midget. "I mean, why the hell are they holed up in there after all this time? They must know about Sappho—every intercolonial channel has been blasting the story of her death. If they had any sense, they'd be looking for a better hiding place, one that can't be traced back to CPG. The bottom line is this: there must be something in that chalet that we don't know about. Which means that we can't just blow the house to smithereens."

The lion was not convinced. He knew Nick all too well. "That's a half-assed rationalization and you know it."

"Fine," said the midget, shrugging. "So I'll give you a better rationalization, the same one that was broached in the parking garage. Send Empedocles in first and maybe these two Paratwa will waste each other. We kill two birds with one stone."

Huromonus shook his head. "I will not order a conventional attack just so that two killers can have at each other."

The midget regarded them wryly.

"Why don't you give us your real reason?" suggested the lion.

"I think you already know my *real* reason."

"I want to hear you say it."

"All right," said Nick grimly. "Gillian was my friend, and he was your friend, and he deserves a goddamn chance. I don't give a shit whether Empedocles lives or dies. But we owe it to Gillian. We owe him a shot at coming back."

"You don't know if he *can* come back," Huromonus argued.

"You're right, I don't know. But I do know that when there is tremendous stress—tremendous tension—the Ash Ock's inner gates are forced open. Combat presents the proper conditions for change to occur, for thresholds to be crossed."

Huromonus said, "Suppose we go along with you? Exactly how do we carry out this assault? Remember, that chalet has a full sensor field along with antisurveillance systems. How do we attack and still retain some element of surprise?"

"Trust me," suggested Nick, smiling tightly. "I have a plan."

The lion returned his attention to the troops. Xornakoff was giving orders. "All right, they're almost ready at the top. Mount up, everyone. And good luck."

The assault team sprang into action. Four at a time, they leaped over the railing, landed on the waiting saddles of high-powered skysticks docked in a neat row beneath the overhang of the porch. Vertical jets roared to life. The two dozen tiny vehicles spiraled lazily upward into Pocono's slate gray skies.

Almost in tandem, the twenty-four riders leaned forward, compressed their accelerators. Rocket tubes ignited, belched trails of white smoke. The skystick troopers streaked off into the brooding skies, disappearing into a patch of low-level clouds.

Their target was nearly eleven miles south of the hotel. The team would fly their sticks in a great arc: heading toward centersky, leveling off, then completing their parabola by diving toward the chalet at speeds approaching two hundred miles-per-hour. If the timing worked out as planned, the twenty-four riders would arrive at the house only seconds after Empedocles's Gillian/tway made the initial assault.

"I hope we don't lose too many," murmured Huromonus.

Empedocles chuckled.

A fresh roar reverberated across the porch as a small E-Tech Security craft sank from the clouds and banked for a landing. Seconds later, its vertical landing jets, expelling yellow flame, melted the ice and snow covering the Ballistic

Mystic Hotel's seldom-used helipad. Great clouds of steam blossomed around the craft.

Vilakoz, straining under the weight of the massive geo cannon, lumbered from the porch and ran toward the jet. Somehow, he managed to cover the forty yards in less than ten seconds. A ramp was lowered and the Costeau quickly squeezed inside. Shrieking rockets came to life. The jet ascended, momentarily hovered over the field, then blasted off in the direction of the skystick riders.

"What's the total strength of the second wave?" asked the lion.

"Eleven more jets like that one," replied Huromonus, "plus twenty-eight armored snowrovers and a force of twelve hundred and fifty ground troops."

"But will it be enough?" asked Empedocles, laughing wickedly. With blinding speed, the Susan/tway catapulted over the railing and landed on her own skystick. The saddled tube levitated until the rider was even with the lion, Huromonus, and Xornakoff.

"There is an old saying," uttered the monarch. "I learned it from the Czar." Empedocles pasted bright smiles across both his faces and uttered his final words in stereo. "If things don't work out . . . I'll see you in hell!"

The skystick rose, disappeared into the clouds.

"See you in hell!"

"I think you learned that one from me," said Nick.

"Not likely," replied Empedocles through his Gillian/tway.

The midget grunted and turned to the last E-Tech technician who remained in the shack. "Is the seeker set?"

"Yes, sir. Programmed, armed, and in the tube."

"Then leave us," ordered the monarch.

The technician glanced uneasily at Nick, then half-walked, half-floated out the door of Speed Slope Fourteen's launch hut. The metal seal slid shut.

The were in centersky, at the weightless starting gate of the nine-mile-long cable-suspended ice trough, which spiraled gradually outward from Pocono's central core, winding its way toward the inner living surface of the Colony, assuming greater and greater mass as the cylinder's spin-induced gravitation relentlessly increased.

Empedocles's Gillian/tway hung three feet off the floor, perched on his polished silver uniski, which was attached to the roof of the launch hut via six foldaway slipbars, making him look and feel like some weird inverted spider. His feet were fastened to the ski via rigid interlock boots, and his body was arched severely forward, in the traditional downhill pose. His head was encased in a long tapering Giger helmet, with the back of it spring-buckled to the heels of his boots. Fastened over top of the helmet was the jetpak, its twin thrusters oozing faint whiffs of evaporating coolant. Beneath him, the four-foot ski swam in a fog of low-tension polyfreeze, which the just-departed technician had sprayed across its underside.

"You're as ready as you're gonna be," said Nick. "Just remember: the seeker will be heading down the slope about a thousand feet in front of you—your ski is programmed to follow its course. When the seeker reaches the chalet—"

"We're wasting time."

The midget grimaced. "Yeah, well, tough shit. Maybe I like wasting time."

The monarch laughed. "You still think he's coming back, don't you?"

"I don't know what you're talking about."

"Gillian's gone for good. End of story."

"Watch that first step," warned Nick. "It's a doozie."

Another tech's voice flooded the hut. "We're ready in control. Launch countdown will commence upon your signal."

Empedocles gripped the ski's stubby sway bars. "Do it."

"Seeker is out of its hole," announced the tech. "Seeker is on the pike . . . telemetry green . . . autos engaging. . . . You'll be going in about four seconds . . .

" . . . three . . . two . . . one . . ."

Empedocles winked at the Czar. And then the sextet of slipbars ripped away and the floor beneath him disappeared. A maglev field came to life, yanked him straight down through the opening.

With a sharp bang, his ski landed on the twenty-foot-wide sloping ice trough. Jetpaks ignited. The ski leaped forward, accelerating rapidly, and then his Gillian/tway was heading down the linear section of the course—a full half-mile without curves—where the slope was still fully contained within its thirty-foot-diameter illuminated tube.

Sensors calculated his speed. Inner helmet gauges translated into miles-per-hour.

Thirty . . . forty-five . . . sixty-five . . . ninety . . .

He closed the eyes of his male tway, allowed himself to view the world discreetly through his female half. His Susan/tway's skystick had arrived at the top of its pre-calculated arc, was preparing to begin its final descent toward the chalet. All around her, white comet tails pierced the overcast skies as the rest of the skystick assault team fell into flanking positions.

When he reopened the Gillian/tway's eyes, the speed of his helmet gauge had climbed to one hundred and twenty miles per hour. A thousand feet in front of him, the low streamlined form of the seeker raced high up onto the banking of Speed Slope Fourteen's first curve. Target lights pulsed red on the back of the small robot: its lastrak measurement systems were continuously analyzing track conditions, scanning down the course for potentially deadly ice cracks, automatically re-adjusting its own position on the banks to compensate for such flaws, and then transmitting the latest trajectory data back into Empedocles's onboard computers.

His Gillian/tway was under full remote control. He was flying blind. He was traveling at one hundred and thirty miles per hour.

Entering the first curve, his ski soared high up onto the banking, precisely duplicating the seeker's path. Overhead, gray clouds abruptly burst into view; he had reached the end of the linear tube. From here on down, he would be racing in an open-top trough.

The banking tapered to nearly ninety degrees; he was literally on the side of a wall, so close to the top that the energized repellent fence—designed to prevent crashing skiers from leaving the course—hung a scant two feet away from the right edge of his ski. His speed indicator climbed to one hundred and forty.

He felt his body beginning to take on overall weight again

as Speed Slope Fourteen spiraled farther and farther outward
from Pocono's gravity-free core. Up ahead, he glimpsed the
seeker sailing into the first of a triple set of S-curves.

And then he was into the esses, high up on the bank . . .
down again . . . crossing centerline . . . roaring up the opposite wall . . .

Out of the esses . . . a short straightaway . . . and then into
this slope's most severe curve: a one-hundred-and-eighty-
degree arc that put his ski precariously close to the fence,
mere inches from the shimmering repellent screens . . .

And his Susan/tway slammed the skystick accelerators forward, felt the invigorating wind whip across her face as she
dive-bombed toward their target. . . .

The exhilaration of pure speed.

It soared through both his bodies, and he felt wildly alive,
lashed by rhythms of binary transcendence, knowing at long
last that his neuromuscular system had reached the arena of
its true potential.

And the world slowed down. And he arrived at a state of
consciousness he knew was as close to perfection as any
Paratwa could ever hope to come; the ultimate harmony of
interlaced tension, halves converging, racing into violence.

He screamed through both mouths—a deep-body expulsion of uncontrollable ecstasy—and he knew that he would
hit the target at the crest of this feeling, a rapture of mind/
body unity that nothing could withstand.

More curves . . . more withered skies . . . and both of his
bodies were traveling at speeds in excess of one hundred and
sixty miles per hour and still accelerating . . .

And it was time.

The countdown rang out in his Gillian/tway's helmet. He
performed slight readjustments to Susan/tway's skystick, re-
aligned his aerial approach velocity so that his tways would
arrive at the chalet only seconds apart.

"Eight . . ." said the mechvoice, "seven . . ."

Speed Slope Fourteen had now spiraled far from its origins
within centersky. He was nearing ground level. The smooth
curvature of the cylinder became visible at the top of the
trough, and he caught glimpses of houses and fields—speckles

of nonorganic creation littering Pocono's endless white landscape.

"Five seconds . . ."

And then the target came into view—a splotch on the side of a steep hill—three stories of teak-covered elegance, blessed with a huge picture window on its top floor, a mere sixty feet away from the rim of the ice trough.

". . . three . . ."

The Czar and the technicians had calculated precisely; the seeker's guidance system had been modified, fully armed. Up until the very last moments, everything would happen automatically.

". . . two . . ."

But no human could have attempted this stunt; only a creature endowed with escalated reaction times possessed the power to operate within the parameters of such blinding speed.

". . . one . . ."

A thousand feet in front of him, the seeker went crazy.

Brake spikes trailing plasticore bungis erupted from its stern, embedded themselves in the ice, high up on the trough. A brutal screeching noise filled Empedocles's helmet as the tiny robot, its linear motion retarded, lurched sideways, vaulted up the wall opposite the chalet, and then—as the bungis grabbed—flashed back down across the banking.

The seeker exploded.

It blew a massive hole in the chalet-side of the speed slope. Shards of debris—those few bits that had not been blown outward by the force of the blast—came flying across Empedocles's glide path.

And then his own brake spikes were firing, and there came a dizzying—but anticipated—moment of tremendous forward pressure as the bungis slowed him from one seventy-five to seventy-five in under a second.

His uniski pivoted to the right and raced up the side of the trough in a violently tight arc, missing the edge of the overhanging fence by less than a foot. Back down the banking he roared, heading straight toward the opposite wall, straight to-

ward the gaping hole that the exploded seeker had created in
the ice trough.

The bungis released. He bit down hard, felt the invisible
front and rear protective crescents shape themselves to his
compressed form. Airborne, he sailed through the jagged
opening in Speed Slope Fourteen, heading straight toward
the chalet's massive third-floor picture window . . .

Ghandi sat on the zephyr chair—perched on the invisible
fountain of bridled air—on the chalet's upper veranda.
Through the glass wall, Pocono's omnipresent overcast sky
peered in at him, its gray perfection marred only by the snak-
ing form of Speed Slope Fourteen, sixty feet away.

His hands rested serenely in his lap. His shoes lay on the
floor beside him. The zephyr's body-hugging streams of coagulated air produced a curious tickling sensation between his
bare toes.

He wiggled his feet and tried to empty his mind of all
thoughts, all feelings, all concerns.

But success in that regard continued to elude him.

Ghandi did not know how many hours he had been sitting
there. It did not really matter. There was no reason why he
should remain a prisoner of the zephyr's cradling security, yet
there was also no reason why he should get up. He supposed
that meant he had achieved a state of proper equilibrium,
trapped between opposing forces, intricately balanced. The
crushing apotheosis of gravity held him down; the leading
edge of disciplined air held him up. Neither force could be
seen, yet together they produced the appropriate neutralizing
effect. The symmetry of his prison pleased him.

He wiggled his toes and wondered what it would be like to
not remember.

Twenty-five years. And now she's dead.

From somewhere downstairs, another scream erupted. For
most of the day, the maniac's tways had been taking turns releasing gut-rending shrieks. Calvin had his own way of dealing with grief.

A faint odor of urine still filled the air. Earlier, during one
of the Ash Nar's nastier explosions of rage, the twins, Ky and

Jy, had run naked through the house, pissing on walls and floors. Ky had even managed to soak a few ceilings.

At one point, tway Calvin, his face bloated into a vicious smile, had leaped at Ghandi from behind and rammed the needle of the Cohe up under his chin.

"Go ahead," Ghandi had urged, and that had been that. The maniac lost interest, withdrew the weapon, and retreated to another room.

Later, during a brief period of sanity, when all three tways at least *appeared* serene, Ghandi had suggested that they should consider vacating the chalet. "Sooner or later," he urged, "E-Tech's going to find us here."

Ky, wearing a skintight rubberized suit splotched with twistik—the polarized adhesive paste that enabled him to adhere to walls and ceilings—whipped out his flash daggers and leaped over the railing of the second-floor balcony that overlooked the gym. His upward trajectory carried him back-first into the ceiling. The twistik grabbed and he stuck. Hanging upside down, the tway began to sing—a pre-Apocalyptic ballad about "cruising the seas for American gold." On the second stanza, tways Jy and Calvin had joined in. For the next half-hour, the chalet had echoed to the endless refrains of this ancient song as the Ash Nar assassin sang three-part harmony with himself.

Ghandi came to the conclusion that they would not be leaving.

After the musical interlude had ended, Ghandi had retreated to the sanctity of the zephyr. He told himself that he would remain there and wait for whatever was going to happen.

The growing wail of a jetpak skier suddenly grabbed his attention. He craned his neck and peered out at the suspended ice trough.

As the daredevil approached, the high-pitched whine grew more intense. But when the skier came into view, high up on the opposite bank of the trough, a sudden uneasiness gripped Ghandi. He had the feeling that something was terribly wrong.

A dull thud. A muffled explosion. And then there was a

hole in the side of the trough and an object was coming straight toward the picture window, straight toward Ghandi.

In that final instant, he realized that it was now in his best interests to overcome his lethargy and get the hell out of the zephyr chair. But he also realized that it was too late.

The gun on the front of Empedocles's uniski barked once— the reinforced picture window fractured into a spiderweb of tiny cracks. An instant before the Gillian/tway hit, the monarch fired his retros. When he slammed the window, the ski had decelerated to under thirty miles per hour.

Glass disintegrated, shattered across the enclosed veranda. The man that Empedocles recognized as the husband of Sappho's human tway sat inside, his body suspended on some sort of air chair, his mouth open wide, eyes frantic with disbelief. Corelli-Paul Ghandi threw his hands over his face as the glass rained across the room. The uniski passed right over his head, its underside missing him by less than a foot.

Ghandi screamed and rolled from the zephyr. With a tremendous crash, the crazed skier touched down, slid the length of the room on the right edge of his ski, then smashed into the far wall, beside the doorway leading to the stairs. Even before the uniski slammed to a halt, the madman was tearing off his helmet and jetpak, disengaging his legs from the interlock boots.

The skier straightened to his full height, and suddenly there was a three-tubed thruster in his left hand and a Cohe wand in his right. Comprehension came to Ghandi. He knew who the invader was.

Cold air whistled through the shattered window. The heavens erupted with new fury as a pack of screeching skysticks dove toward the chalet. From somewhere downstairs, Ghandi heard the unmistakable machine-gun roar of Jy's spray thruster coming to life. Explosions shook the house, and he knew that the skystick riders were blasting through the chalet's lower windows.

And then a skystick hurtled right through the veranda's disintegrated glass wall, touched down beside the wrecked uniski. With unnatural speed, a woman leaped from her saddle to land beside Gillian. Ghandi, on the floor, overwhelmed by astonishment, heard himself utter her name.

"Susan Quint!"

She smiled at him. They both smiled at him. And Ghandi knew. Somehow, against all reason, Sappho's traitorous breed-cousin had been restored.

The Ash Ock did not kill him. Instead, its tways leaped through the open doorway and vanished down the staircase.

More skystick riders poured through the shattered window, and then there were guns being aimed in Ghandi's face and he was being ordered not to move a muscle. He tried to comply. But from deep inside, the hated microbes—remarkably absent for these past few hours—began their feverish dance anew. His arms and shoulders started to twitch violently.

There was absolutely nothing humorous about his situation. But he could not help himself, and he began to giggle. Mild chuckling quickly expanded into full-blown shrieks. By the time the Security troops had gotten him to his feet, Ghandi was awash in hysterical laughter.

Get ready, warned Gillian. *There's great turmoil. We're in the middle of a battle. It's almost time.*

I can feel it! projected Susan, excited by the sharp images of movement, the heightened perceptions, penetrating the amalgam of her consciousness with newfound clarity. She sensed herself leaping down steps, sensed the body of Gillian racing in front of her.

We're going to make it! promised Gillian. *We're going to escape the monarchy—*

—and take back what was stolen from us! Susan yelled. But deep within, at the periphery of consciousness, shadows of doubt appeared, bleak forms cascading upward from the river of her being, jagged sirens of mortal dread.

I'm afraid, she whispered.

The shadows grew more ominous, coalesced into nightmarish proportions. An icy whorl of terror seemed to vault the length of what she imagined to be her spine.

Trust me, soothed Gillian. *It's the only way.*

The only way, she told herself.

* * *

Empedocles bounded down the stairway, Gillian/tway first, taking steps six at a time. He hit the second-floor landing, leaped through an open doorway, entered the chalet's large rectangular day room. His tways, back-to-back—crescent webs humming—danced into the unoccupied chamber. Gestalt awareness registered the arena in true 360-outline form, his interlaced monarchy creating a perfect internal icon of the room's dimensions and furnishings.

Chairs, sofas, ceiling-mounted kitchenette, pseudosheepskin hassocks. No windows. Walls covered in twenty-first century holo art, mostly naked male and female figures cast in erotic poses, with breasts, buttocks, penises, and vaginas prominently displayed within the multidimensional forms.

Empedocles knew with certainty that he was standing in a sanctum once used by Sappho.

In addition to the entrance he had just come through, the day room boasted three other doors—two along the opposite wall and a third leading toward the rear of the chalet. All three doors were closed.

The monarch whirled toward the center of the room, keeping his tways in constant motion, bodies pirouetting, like two rotating planets revolving around each other in a perfect closed system.

A tremendous din erupted beneath his feet; he felt the vibrations coming up through the floorboards. Down below, on the first floor, the main group of skystick troops were attempting to penetrate the chalet. From the plethora of noises, the monarch quickly distinguished individual sounds. He heard the muted bursts of small-weapons fire—mainly E-Tech Security thrusters—intermixed with desperate cries of rage and agony.

Death was being created down there, and the monarch knew its architect. High above the din, dominating the lesser sounds, came the relentless howl of the spray thruster. The first wave of attackers had run into the tway called Shooter.

Movement. To the Gillian/tway's left. The side door directly across from the stairwell slid open.

He pirouetted sideways, fired his triple-tubed thruster at

the figure in the center of the portal, squeezing off two quick blasts before realizing that he had been tricked, that he was firing on a full-sized target dummy emerging from the bathroom.

The back door melted in a roar of white-hot flame and Slasher came cartwheeling into the day room, a blur of violent motion, hurtling end over end, twin cartoon daggers lashing the air, defensive web glimmering as strands of flame clung to its front crescent.

Simultaneously—from overhead—a panel in the suspended kitchenette split open and a fierce orange light, as bright as an unfiltered sun, spilled down over Empedocles's tways.

His eye sets squinted. The intense liquid light seemed to whistle and crackle as it splashed across the monarch's crescent webs. Puffs of brown smoke filled the air. And Empedocles knew that his defensive screens had just been nullified.

But he had planned for this particular contingency, for the Czar had known about the tripartite's web-neutralizing weapon.

But wait for the right moment, he urged himself. *Wait until you can surprise him. Wait for an advantage.*

The monarch jerked both tways sideways, felt subtle tremors pass through his bodies as both halves slipped from the smoldering remains of his decomposing energy screens.

Slasher completed his final cartwheel, landed on a hassock within striking distance of the Susan/tway's back. Flash daggers blossomed in length, whipped outward, seeking her flakjak collar. But through the eyes of his Gillian/tway, Empedocles saw the blow coming. The monarch dove his female half toward the floor, felt the withering heat of the incinerating blade pass inches from her left shoulder.

He rolled forward with his Susan/tway, compressed her legs, then leaped up into a full-tilt attack posture, striding forward in great leaps, flash daggers held in front of her body like fiery lances.

Empedocles bit down hard with both mouths. And his *second* set of crescent webs ignited.

For a fraction of a second, Slasher seemed to pause, perhaps surprised by the appearance of backup defensive screens.

But the tway's hesitation passed too quickly for Empedocles to take advantage of it.

Slasher lunged forward, wielding one blade high and the other low. The monarch countered.

Four flash daggers came together with a violent hiss. The surrounding air burst into a rainbow of flames as each weapon's intricately modulated energy pattern was disrupted by an opposing field.

For a stark moment, the four daggers hung there, locked in a garish turmoil of heat and light. Empedocles's Gillian/tway lashed his Cohe toward the side of Slasher's web, but the assassin twisted his lower body, easily blocking the beam's entry.

Slasher grinned. Abruptly, the tway yanked his daggers away, breaking the stalemate. As he withdrew the weapons, he brought the heel of his boot upward, angling toward the Susan/tway's open side portal.

Empedocles saw the blow coming. But he could do nothing to prevent it. When Slasher withdrew his blades, a counterpoint recoil of energy sent his Susan/tway stumbling to the left.

Slasher's boot caught her in the side of the head, directly below the left ear. Stunned, the monarch's female half reeled. And then—like a gyroscope torn from its axis—the Susan/tway's feet buckled out from under her and she slammed into the floor.

Slasher, still grinning, changed targets, lunged at the monarch's Gillian/tway. Empedocles fought back with his Cohe—another side swipe, aimed at Slasher's right portal. But the tway again anticipated the beam's strike point, and he merely pivoted a few inches in that direction. The monarch's Cohe energy splayed harmlessly against the Ash Nar's web.

Slasher laughed. "You are weak, *Ash Ock*! The Gillian creature—it did better without you!" Suddenly the tway dropped to his knees.

Standing directly behind Slasher, in the melted doorway leading to the small balcony overlooking the gym, was Calvin.

In one coordinated blur of motion, the Ash Nar's namesake tway fired his thruster and whipped his Cohe beam in a long arc across the length of the room.

Empedocles twisted sideways—black light splattered harmlessly against the Gillian/tway's front crescent. But that sudden turning put his tway slightly off balance. And then multiple blasts from Calvin's thruster were compressing his web, and he was careening backward, arms flailing at the air in a desperate attempt to maintain equilibrium.

Slasher, screaming in triumph, made another lunge with his daggers.

The stairwell door exploded inward. Two E-Tech troopers charged into the room.

With a hiss of anger, Slasher turned away from Gillian to face the new threat.

Calvin came forward, thruster wailing. Empedocles, still off balance, got hit by one too many packets of condensed energy. Shoved backward by the concentrated blasts, his rear crescent nailed the edge of a hassock. He tripped, fell to the floor.

And then Calvin's Cohe was all over him, the black beam slashing across the width of his front crescent, the flickering spear of projected energy seeking a way through his side portals.

In complete desperation, Empedocles dragged his still-groggy Susan/tway to her feet. He threw her forward, directly into the path of the black light.

Her web blocked Calvin's first two slashes. But her equilibrium was still off. Calvin flicked his wrist a third time, and the black beam came in low, along the Susan/tway's left side. It slipped through the gap between her front and rear crescents.

Empedocles screamed through both mouths as the energy stream entered the side of her left knee, burning straight through the bone.

The black light exited cleanly, barely missing her other leg. His Susan/tway collapsed to the floor, her destroyed leg sweeping wildly back and forth, its sheared muscles caught in a furious spasm.

Intense pain rocked Empedocles to his core. A blast of emotions, rooted in bitterness, soared through him, the feelings swelling in power as the excruciating agony rose up to poison the interlace. And borne upon that pain and bitterness was a dense icon of pure logic—a rationality linking his multiplex turmoil into patterns of defeat . . .

Patterns of death.

The Susan/tway was too much the novice, her untrained body no match for an assassin boasting an uninterrupted lifetime of combat experience. The Gillian/tway was beyond my control for too long. I did not truly possess the power of monarchy that I imagined I did.

In that instant of clarifying candor, Empedocles realized that he had never really stood a chance.

A tremendous explosion rocked the chalet. From the corner of his Gillian/tway's eyes, Empedocles saw the entire front wall of the day room coming apart, disintegrating into huge threaded slabs of plastic and wire. Pocono's icy winds whipped in, lashed his faces with an almost comforting spray of fresh snow crystals.

And borne upon those winds, hurtling down out of the swirling white tempest of an unprompted storm, came a wave of skystick riders.

Now! shouted Gillian. *Now—before it's too late!*

Susan opened up to him.

She imagined her body, imagined its wholeness—the conglomeration of bone, tissue, and flesh, the entirety of balanced tensions which defined the creature Susan Quint.

She remembered Timmy's lessons, down on the Ontario beach, so long ago. She remembered the purity of her first awakening, remembered how it had felt when that buried spirit of her life had swollen beyond the artificial boundaries imposed by a lifetime of repressed pain. She remembered that majestic freedom, being able to soar into synchronicity with her very soul as physical/emotional/intellectual states melded into a unified perfection.

I am my body-thought.

And then Gillian was approaching, like an apparition of energies, a ghostly invader from some other space and time. She felt him touch her, drift into her—*through her*—penetrating the very amalgam of her consciousness as if she were not even there. She opened herself to him, felt his psyche slipping into her mind, into the iconic representation of her body-image. It was a feeling of intimacy far more profound than their love-making had been, beneath the waters of the Atlantic, in the cell of the Os/Ka/Loq.

But Gillian brought a host of brooding shadows with him. And those shadows brought terror.

Fear what is, she commanded herself sternly, *not what might be.*

She gazed into the depths of those shadows. And at last, she perceived their true nature.

I know what terrifies me! I know what it is!

Gillian knew too. He shaped her fear into his own words. *You're afraid that I'll become like the monarch. You're afraid that once I have you, once I'm controlling you, I won't ever surrender you.*

Yes, she whispered, feeling his calming spirit permeate the river of her life, his waters begin to merge with her own. And she felt the truth of him. And she knew that there was nothing more to fear.

They were together, two amalgamated consciousnesses, superimposed, and Gillian was taking her toward the place that she no longer possessed the power to enter alone—the realm of her own physical self.

As they soared upward, Gillian acknowledged a pang of loss, perceiving his own body from the outside, untouchable, the mnemonic cursors poised like ramparts, blocking all possible entry. But Susan's form boasted no such defenses.

He led them back. Together, the joined power of their superimposed psyches soared upward from the quarantine of amalgamation, wrenched Susan's body loose from the monarchial interlace, and reentered the world of sight, smell, and sound.

And pain.

Shards of white-hot agony lanced across Susan's left knee.

But there was no time for pain. Not now.

With iron will, Gillian ignored the burning flames that seemed to be racing up and down Susan's leg. He swept his head to the side, looked out from this new vantage point into a scene of incredible violence.

Slasher, at the stairwell, killed a pair of troopers with his daggers, then whirled to face the new threat flying in upon the winds of the sudden blizzard.

They soared down from the snowy heavens—skystick riders, half a dozen strong, white phantoms diving into the chalet through the rubble of the exploded wall.

Slasher vaulted over a sofa, somersaulted feet first up onto the day room ceiling. Twistik grabbed.

Upside down, maintaining one boot in contact at all times, the tway attacked. Cartoon daggers leaped left and right, slashing across the paths of the first two riders, decapitating one man and slicing straight through the engine housing of the other rider's stick. That second rider leaped from his crippled propulsion tube, hit the floor directly in front of tway Calvin. A quick thrust of the Cohe and the luckless trooper went down. His directionless skystick smashed through the back wall, disappeared over the balcony, and plunged down into the gym.

Slasher killed a third rider, but the fourth aimed his skystick directly at the tway and stayed on course, handlebar thrusters wailing away.

In a blur of motion, Slasher pivoted. The skystick missed the tway by inches. From the floor, Calvin unleashed his own thruster, blasting the underside of the fourth rider until the trooper's machine gave out. The skystick swerved to the right, slammed hard into the suspended kitchenette, impaling its rider on the spoke of a thermal tube.

Gillian glanced away from the carnage, locked gazes with his own body—the Gillian/tway, still occupied by Empedocles.

The monarch's face overflowed with emotions—surprise, regret, pain . . . and something Gillian took to be an acknowledgement of defeat.

And Gillian knew—impossible as it was to believe—that his monarch had lost hope. Empedocles was giving up.

"No, you bastard! Fight for that body!" Gillian, gritting his teeth, ignoring the pain lancing through his knee, picked Susan up off the floor and balanced himself on her one good leg. He scanned the immediate debris for the flash daggers that had been knocked from her hands. But the weapons were nowhere to be seen.

On the ceiling, Slasher caught his movement, pivoted. Gillian saw the tway wrench a twistik-coated boot sideways, ready to break its bond, ready to leap down at him—at Susan—from above.

The fifth skystick trooper nailed Slasher head-on.

Both of Calvin's tways screamed as the flying rider tore Slasher from his perch. The tway spun through the air like a rag doll, crash-landed in the corner of the room.

The skystick rider out of control—plowed into the floor, somersaulted over his saddle, and slammed down onto the cushions of a sofa.

The final skystick rider missed all the action on her first pass. She raced to the far end of the day room, banked hard, performed a sharp one-eighty, and then headed back out toward the front of the chalet, targeting tway Calvin.

Thrusters wailed, but Calvin leaned forward, took the hits across his front crescent, and waited calmly for the rider to get within range.

The Ash Nar lashed out with his Cohe.

But this rider was quick. The trooper turned sideways at the last instant, deflecting the black beam with her front crescent.

Calvin adapted. The tway leaped forward, reached through the rider's side portal, caught her arm, yanked her from the skystick, threw her halfway across the room. The saddled tube upended itself, dropped lightly to the floor, less than a yard away from Empedocles.

The monarch did not move.

Never before had Empedocles imagined such a state for himself. Never before had he even considered the possibility that an Ash Ock could be brought down, defeated.

With bitter contemplation, he realized that his unshakeable belief in the invulnerability of the royal Caste had always been at odds with the simple truth.

Codrus had died. Aristotle had died. . . .

And Sappho . . .

Now it was his turn.

"Fight!" screamed Gillian, wanting to throw something at

his unmoving monarch. But Empedocles refused to get up from the floor.

Gillian turned away and limped toward the rear of the chalet, desperately searching the rubble for a weapon.

Slasher was on his feet again, blood dripping down the side of his face, flash daggers extended to their full lengths, the cartoon blades carving the air with wicked strokes. The tway met Susan's eye, sneered. Howling like an animal, Slasher bounded forward—

—while Calvin picked up the downed skystick, hopped onto its saddle, and aimed it out into the swirling blizzard.

Gillian, weaponless, his leg crippled, body almost numbed by the incredible pain, steeled Susan's body to meet Slasher's charge.

Empedocles looked on, feeling as if the events that were occurring no longer mattered. It was all over. Ash Ock monarchy was about to pass forever beyond his reach. There was no reason for him to continue fighting.

But curiously, at the moment that last thought entered awareness, its diametrical opposite also took shape.

There was no reason to pursue the struggle. But there was also no reason to give up.

Empedocles roared to his feet, threw his Cohe wand to Susan, and then leaped onto the back of Calvin's skystick just as the Ash Nar rammed the accelerator.

The saddled propulsion tube lunged forward, sailed out through the shattered wall, its tiny rocket motor protesting at the sudden doubling of cargo. The skystick was not powerful enough to lift both riders. Calvin and Empedocles made it just past the boundary of the wall—into the fury of the storm—before the overworked skystick sputtered, died. Like a sinking ship, its bow turned skyward, pointed straight up into the blizzard. Both tways dropped from the saddle; Calvin, Empedocles, and the skystick fell from sight.

Gillian caught the Cohe in Susan's right hand. He pivoted sharply and squeezed the egg.

The black beam sliced through Slasher's raised daggers, shearing both barrels. Twin cartoon images—their sources destroyed—hung in the air for an extended moment before deenergizing into harmless streaks of multicolored vapor.

Enraged, Slasher dropped the weapons, squatted low, and rammed his arms through the side portal of Susan's web, grabbing for the injured knee. Gillian screamed with new agony as Slasher plunged a finger straight into the cauterized wound.

He managed to hang onto his Cohe, but the pain coming from his leg was now so intense that he could barely focus Susan's eyes, let alone perform the subtle hand pressures necessary to control the wand.

Gillian felt his borrowed body being lifted into the air, held over Slasher's head, and then the tway was bounding toward the jagged hole in the rear wall of the day room. Slasher hurled him through the opening and onto the balcony overlooking the gym.

For an instant, Gillian felt ethereal—a shape without form, uprooted from the world, cast into space. And then his rear crescent slammed against the railing, and he flipped half over it, dangling precariously.

Slasher careened into him, intending to send Gillian plunging over the edge. But the balusters gave way. The entire railing snapped from its supports, sending both of them tumbling down onto the gym floor.

And beneath them, waiting with his spray thruster, stood the Ash Nar's third tway, Shooter.

Empedocles fell through the storm, hearing the shriek of cold winds, feeling the smudge of ice crystals adhering to his bare face and hands, seeing the blurred forms of Calvin and the riderless skystick dropping with him.

His rear crescent struck something solid, and then he was rolling out-of-control down the steep slope in front of the chalet, red sparks leaping from his web as his tumbling body gouged great chunks of ice and snow from the virgin hillside. Nearby, Calvin and the skystick somersaulted with similar abandon.

The hill tapered. Empedocles slowed, came out of one final

flip to land on his back and slide to a grinding halt against something warm and metallic.

Quickly, he struggled to his feet. All around him, figures were moving through the thick curtain of snow. E-Tech Security troops. Dozens of them.

The warm metallic object he had butted against was the lower side panel of a small assault jet.

Calvin slammed into him.

Empedocles was knocked back to the ground. He caught one quick glimpse of Calvin's face, raging in triumph, and then the assassin's Cohe was slipping through Empedocles's side portal, skimming across the top of the monarch's shoulder, sliding up toward his neck.

Empedocles felt the sharp needle penetrate a fold of flesh beneath his chin.

He felt Calvin squeezing the wand.

Darkness exploded.

The black pain rose from his neck, filling his head, filling every cavity of his being, and Empedocles was hurled from the Gillian/tway's body, instantly reconstituted back into the abstract essence of an amalgam.

The living tissue of Gillian's body—the very form that enabled Empedocles to exist—began a rapid descent into death. When that body expired, the monarch would be without habitation. There would be no place left for him to go.

His last decision was an easy one. He would end life as it had begun, within the realm of the corporeal.

Empedocles plunged back into the turmoil of Gillian's body, back into the maelstrom of cellular disincorporation, back into the sanctifying purity of mortal pain.

And in those final moments of existence, the monarch looked out through Gillian's eyes, and he saw Calvin roar to his feet, firing his thruster at anything that moved, lashing his Cohe into the blistering sheets of white, seeking any and all targets.

But no one closed in on the tway. Instead, the assault troops scampered desperately toward Calvin's left and right flanks, clearing a wide path directly in front of the assassin.

And Empedocles knew that it was not cowardice that drove the troopers back.

Calvin realized his peril. The tway whirled, came face-to-face with the huge misshapen figure marching out of the storm directly behind him.

It was Vilakoz, wielding the massive geo cannon.

There was a crack of thunder.

For one spliced fragment of time, nothing seemed to happen. And then Calvin's front crescent exploded as the blast ripped through his web, pulverizing flesh and bone, lifting him off the ground. . . .

And he was gone, his shattered body hurtled out into the storm between the flanks of E-Tech troopers. All that remained to mark the spot where the tway had stood was a fading spiral of red snow.

Empedocles closed his eyes.

Inner vision gazed upon the image of a five-pointed circle. It was the Sphere of the royal Caste, the icon that had served to bind the Ash Ock into a symbolic whole. But even as the monarch watched, the Sphere started to decompose, crumbling into motes of dust, being swept downward, into an encroaching void.

Empedocles's final thoughts were of Theophrastus.

Now there is only one of us left.

Gillian hit the gym floor at a sharp angle, his crescent-protected shoulder slamming against the padded deck. He tucked Susan's body into a forward somersault and used her momentum to vault himself up onto her one usable leg.

Shooter instantly targeted Gillian with his spray thruster. But Slasher landed directly between them, blocking Shooter's line of fire.

The pain coursing through Gillian—arising from Susan's pierced leg—was now almost unbearable. It took all of his power just to raise the Cohe, squeeze out a spiraling shaft of black light. He tried to aim the beam, but a wave of dizziness nearly overwhelmed him. The wand deenergized. His hand fell to his side.

Concentrate! he commanded himself.

And then a strange feeling entered consciousness, and he felt as if something were being drawn out of him, extracted from the core of his being, pulled free from his very essence. It hung there beside him for a moment, like a ghostly apparition, before desolidifying, falling away, becoming a rainfall of dust, streaming into a yawning pit far below.

And Gillian knew that Empedocles was gone.

And that could only mean that his own physical body had perished.

Slasher leaped sideways, giving Shooter a clean shot at Gillian. But the tway did not fire his weapon.

Hideous screeching echoed across the gym as the Ash Nar went into a rage, four arms thrashing wildly at the air, two bodies spinning madly across the padded floor.

And Gillian knew that Empedocles had not been the only casualty.

Gillian's awareness of his own loss—the death of his actual body—should have felt devastating. Yet instead, a wonderful sensation coursed through Susan's physique, leaping from her head to her toes. It was a feeling of corporeal freedom—a freedom Gillian had never known before, not within the entire breadth of his life.

He was no longer a tway.

This is what it feels like to be a true individual. This is what it feels like to be human.

The binary interlace—a quintessential element of his being, a part of him since birth—was gone.

He was free.

But he no longer had a body. Even if he could have overcome those protective mnemonic cursors, there was no place left for him to go back to.

From the depths of the heretofore silent creature whose body he currently occupied, whose limbs he commanded, whose superimposed essence rode beneath him, shadowing his every move; from those depths, came the echoes of renewed turmoil.

I'm afraid, projected Susan.

Gillian allowed soothing feelings to cascade through her. *You have nothing to fear. I would never take away what is truly yours.*

His words did not calm her. And he realized that this time, he had misinterpreted the nature of her dread. Another feeling rose up from within her.

Sadness washed through Gillian, immaculate in its totality. He understood. She was not afraid that he would stay.

She was afraid that he would leave.

Slasher and Shooter suddenly froze in the middle of their mad gyrations. Two sets of eyes, crazed with the pain of tway/death, locked on Gillian. Two mouths, leaking spittle and blood, emitted low guttural noises.

Gillian raised Susan's arm high over her head, held the Cohe wand aloft, aimed its tiny needle up at the ceiling. This time, his hand remained steady. This time, that wondrous feeling of autonomy—that singularity of spirit—enabled him to hold Susan's turmoil in abeyance, momentarily overriding all tangents of her pain.

He flicked his wrist, created a rapidly oscillating coil of black light. The spiral rose upward until it nearly touched the ceiling. His skill with the wand condensed into one ephemeral flash of physical perfection.

His arm came down.

The black light leaped forward, punctured Shooter's upper neck, emerged out the other side, leaped twenty feet across the gym to burn through Slasher's head, directly above the right ear.

For one taut moment, the beam appeared to arc between the tways—a bolt of dark lightning, grounding itself on twin staffs. And then Gillian released pressure on the egg and the energy stream disappeared. He lowered his arm.

The tways did not fall. They just stood there, rock solid, blood streaming from their wounds, as if their monarchial consciousness refused to acknowledge that it was all over, that life had ended. And even though Gillian knew that the assassin had passed beyond the point where sounds could be heard, where thoughts could be interpreted, there were still words that needed to be said.

"That was for Martha," he whispered, "and for Buff."

The tways fell together, collapsing like ruptured airbags, two shapeless masses landing in heaps on the padded floor.

Gillian deenergized Susan's web. He sat her body down, leaned against a pommel horse. Noise erupted in the outer hallway as troopers poured into the chalet.

It was time to go.

From deep inside, he felt Susan protesting his decision.

It has to be this way, said Gillian, shaping her cheeks into a fresh countenance, leaving her with a smile.

He detached himself from her consciousness, slipped away. And then he was falling into a deep chasm, falling toward a place where nothing existed but a pure golden light, swaddled in darkness.

It was truly a contrast of the light and the dark.

The lion gazed out at the brilliant yellow crescent curving upward from the lower horizon of the shuttle's midcompartment window, dominating the bottom half of the vista. Above the glowing rim, the blackness began—a spacescape devoid of all other stellar objects, the distant stars etched from the scene, their minor lights unable to overcome the radiant effusion emanating from that glorious golden sphere.

With a little imagination, the lion could almost believe that he was looking at the sun instead of the earth.

"It's actually beautiful," murmured Huromonus.

Nick, standing between then, nodded. "Yeah, in a weird sort of way."

Speakers came to life. "Sir, we'll be entering primary orbit in five minutes."

The lion depressed the intercom switch. "Is the storage bay prepped?"

"Yes, sir. Cargo is ready for launch."

He released the switch and turned to the fourth figure in the weightless midcompartment. Meridian's friction boots were planted on the window wall itself; he hung perpendicular to everyone else. The Jeek was gazing downward, at the spacescape beneath his feet.

"You've not said much since we left Irrya," offered the lion.

Meridian shrugged. "I was thinking of the future."

Nick, with distinct rancor underlying his tone, said, "You're lucky to *have* a future."

A smile touched the assassin's face. "Then let us praise luck."

On the wall directly in front of Meridian—from the lion's perspective, the ceiling—lay his dog Lancelot, hanging in a zero-G net. The poodle and borzoi, sleeping back to back, convulsed in tandem, as if caught in the turbulence of some violent dream.

Huromonus cast an ironic eye at the Jeek. "Perhaps we should also praise your merciful masters?"

"Merciful, my ass," grunted Nick.

Meridian continued to gaze at the Earth, resplendent in its cloak of vivid gold. Physicists suspected that a temporary self-sustaining reaction—temporary at least until Van Ostrand's fleet of Ribonix destroyers arrived with their fresh payloads—accounted for the planet's fierce new tint. According to the latest theories, the thermonuclear bombing was believed to have ignited vast strands of biological toxins, which had also been introduced by the E-Tech/Costeau shuttle armada. Those upper-atmospheric strands, blasted by heavy radiation from above and below, had somehow achieved a photoluminescent state. The overall effect made it appear as if the very air was on fire.

"Mercy was not a consideration," agreed the Jeek. "The Os/Ka/Loq spared the human race because it was the logical thing to do."

True enough, thought the lion, *although Meridian still refuses to admit openly the real reason why the Os/Ka/Loq didn't massacre us, why their actions—on the surface—seem to denote a benign acceptance of defeat.*

Nick had figured it out. And from the Os/Ka/Loq perspective, allowing the Colonies to survive did indeed fit a logical paradigm.

Nevertheless, despite the invader's final machinations, there was no arguing with the simple fact that the Irryan Colonies would—for the foreseeable future—endure.

The Biodyysey's decision had come two days ago, less than sixteen hours after the battle at the chalet. Meridian had disclosed the actual details to Council, including the Os/Ka/Loq's surprise announcement regarding the human and human-type Paratwa who lived aboard their massive vessel. Meridian had recited the Os/Ka/Loq's official statement with a diplomatic flair worthy of the most outrageous of the pre-Apocalyptic politicians.

We, the Os/Ka/Loq, have chosen to cancel our plans leading toward the colonization of the Earth. The strident efforts on the part of the Irryan Colonies and their defensive units have convinced us that peaceful coexistence is not possible between our species.

Therefore, in the interest of preventing further loss of life, we have decided to nullify our viral threat and provide you with the locations of all skygene suitcases hidden within your cylinders.

Our vessel is currently reformulating navigational parameters. We will be leaving your solar system within a very short time. However, in light of our decision to abandon your planet as a viable place for colonization, we request in return that you accept into your Colonies the majority of our vessel's human and human/Paratwa population.

We essentially ask that you provide living space—in whatever capacity you judge appropriate—for approximately four thousand singular humans and nine hundred and fifty binary humans.

That had concluded the official statement, although Meridian had not been shy in adding what he thought would happen to those humans and human-type Paratwa should the Council reject that particular portion of the peace proposal: "Complete extermination of the Biodyysey's human and human/Paratwa populations would be a possibility."

Nick had immediately complained. "This is an old guerrilla warfare tactic. If you're forced to retreat, you saddle your enemy with refugees."

Despite the midget's objections, the fate of the so-called refugees had been decided quickly. Later, when the Council's acceptance of the Biodyysey's initiative was made public, fiery opposition had arisen. Although most of the intercolonial rioting had ended, many citizens were understandably outraged by the idea of having their former enemies welcomed into the cylinders.

But the Council had been unequivocal—and unanimous—in agreeing to accept the refugees from the Biodyysey. Ostensibly, the Council's reasoning was based on humanitarian principles. But they all knew that altruism was just a smokescreen to disguise a less noble incentive.

Even Van Ostrand, whom the lion thought would offer at least some token resistance to the plan, had quickly agreed, rationalizing *his* decision by suggesting that the refugees might provide a rich source of intelligence data on the inner workings of the Biodyysey.

That was a distinct possibility, of course. But like "altruism," "new sources of intelligence" was merely an excuse to make an unpopular decision more palatable.

It had been Meridian's casual mention of a certain fact—a detail smoothly inserted into the Council's discussions of the matter—that had truly swayed the five of them into voting to accept the refugees.

With that single fact, Meridian had guaranteed a place in the Colonies for himself and his compatriots.

Nick had been the only one to argue vehemently against the decision. "Nine hundred and fifty Paratwa being allowed to emigrate to the Colonies! Hell, these are the creatures who caused the Earth to be rendered uninhabitable in the first place! You can't be serious about letting these bastards in!"

Losef had thanked the midget for his concern, but had pointed out to him that he was not a voting member of the Irryan Council and was being permitted to take part in the discussions only at the Council's indulgence. "However," she noted, "your objections will be duly recorded."

At that point, Nick, shaking his head in disbelief, had stomped out of chambers.

"He is a warrior," offered Meridian, as the door had closed behind the midget. "But the war has ended. And now, he does not know what to do. I doubt if the Czar will ever truly know peace."

Silently, the lion had found himself agreeing wholeheartedly with Meridian's evaluation of Nick. But he also recalled Nick's oft-repeated appraisals of Meridian: *Never forget—this Jeek is a shrewd political animal.*

That too could not be disputed.

Within hours of the Council's decision, the refugees had begun their exodus, emerging from the bowels of the massive Biodyysey in the same Star-Edge vessels that had departed from the solar system over two-and-a-half centuries ago. Van Ostrand had sent transports out to rendezvous with the starships. The refugees would be placed aboard Guardian ships for the actual trip back to the cylinders.

The Council had initiated plans for an underutilized research Colony in the distant L5 group of cylinders to be converted into the refugees' new home. Meridian, his other tway, the nine hundred and fifty Paratwa, and the four thousand humans would be sent there. For the immediate future, the refugees would be quarantined within that Colony.

Extensive medical examinations would begin immediately upon their arrival.

The lion returned his attention to the midcompartment, to Meridian. "I'm still curious about Theophrastus and the other humans and Paratwa who will remain aboard the Biodyysey. Did they have a choice? Would they have been permitted to join the refugees?"

"They chose to stay."

"But did they actually have a choice?"

"The Ash Joella and their minions, as well as those several hundred humans, voluntarily elected to remain aboard the Biodyysey."

"And what about Theophrastus?" wondered the lion. "Did he have a choice?"

Meridian shrugged. "Theophrastus is most valued by the Os/Ka/Loq. His scientific prowess is not exaggerated—even by their standards, he is considered a genius. I suspect that the Os/Ka/Loq would not have permitted him to leave."

Huromonus asked, "Do many of the humans or Paratwa who chose to remain with the Os/Ka/Loq have extended life spans?"

Meridian smiled. "As I've explained to you several times

now, I do not know the exact number of humans and Paratwa who were given the infusions. The Biodyysey is huge. Many of us lived and worked in separate sections and had little or no contact with one another. For all I know, there could be entire sequestered populations of humans and Paratwa in other areas of the ship.

"Still, the infusion process was rather complex, and most of the original Star-Edge crew—both human and Paratwa—died natural deaths long ago. The Os/Ka/Loq provided the infusions only to those of us who they felt could be utilized over extended periods of time."

The infusions, thought the lion. Such a simple phrase, yet one that bore a semantic power, an intensity of meaning—far beyond its basic symbolic capacity.

The infusions. Here was the fact casually mentioned during the refugee discussions, which had led the Council toward their unanimous decisions.

The Os/Ka/Loq had been able to prolong Meridian's life by giving him periodic infusions of a genetic elixir. That was how the Jeek had been able to survive for so long. Colonial doctors had already confirmed his assertion.

Meridian was almost three hundred years old. Greatly extended life spans—once thought to be a unique Ash Ock attribute—had been granted not only to other Paratwa but to humans aboard the Biodyysey as well.

That had been the bait the Jeek had dangled in front of Council. And five men and women—none of whom were under the age of fifty—had leaped for the hook.

If the Council of Irrya accepted the refugees, it might be possible for Colonial science medically to reconstruct that genetic elixir. Meridian and the others who had received the infusions might well provide humanity with the mythical fountain of youth.

"You've sold your souls," Nick had accused them.

The lion did not think so.

But time would tell.

The intercom came to life again. "Orbit achieved, sir."

The lion turned to the others. "Does anyone wish to say anything?"

Huromonus shook his head. Meridian remained silent.

"Do it," muttered Nick.

The lion gave the order.

A bright flash came from the main cargo bay as the sarcophagus containing Gillian's body was launched toward the planet. With its retros firing at full capacity, the black coffin remained in view for only a few seconds.

And then it was gone, swallowed by the darkness, heading down into that vivid crescent, plunging toward its rendezvous with Earth's fiery cloak. Given the new atmospheric conditions, the incineration of the sarcophagus would occur even faster than normal. In a matter of minutes, Gillian would be consumed.

It was the traditional funeral ceremony of the Costeaus. Most of the clans called it the *élan vital*—the force that forever adapted.

It was the dive that began but never ended.

They were silent for a time. Finally, the lion looked away. "He won't be forgotten."

"Yeah," whispered Nick.

Meridian continued to gaze outward. At last, he turned to the midget. "I am curious. What will you do now that hostilities have ceased?"

"The war's not over, Jeek," said Nick calmly. "This is merely a break in the fighting."

"Perhaps. Does that mean that you will be returning to stasis once again?"

The lion and Huromonus both turned to the midget, waiting for his answer.

Nick sighed. "Frankly, no. I've had enough of this shit." He met the lion's gaze. "If it's all right with you, I'd just as soon live out my days in your era.

The lion smiled.

"May your days be long," proposed Meridian, with a hint of laughter in his words.

Nick's face blossomed into a sudden grin. "Ya know, maybe I'll become a freelancer. They're mostly a bunch of whackos, but they do have a way of cutting through the bullshit."

"Over the centuries," countered Meridian, directing his

words at the lion and Huromonus, "Sappho probably could have destroyed the Czar on a number of occasions. Yet she never truly made a concerted effort to do so, and she only regretted that indulgence during the final days of her life. Would you like to know why?"

"Even if they don't want to know," muttered Nick, "I got a feeling you're going to tell them."

"Sappho always thought of the Czar as her worthiest opponent, one of the few humans capable of actually challenging her reign."

Nick grunted. "She was a real noble bitch, that Sappho."

Meridian shook his head. "Nobility had nothing to do with it. You were very useful to her. You kept her on her toes, prevented her from getting sloppy. She spared you for functional reasons."

"That sounds more like 'competition of the fittest.' Still, I'm glad to have been of service."

The lion faced Meridian. "And what about you? What will you do with your new life?"

"Of course, quarantine may severely limit my choices," said the Jeek. "But I suppose I'll adjust to the rigors of that situation in short order." Meridian shrugged. "I'm sure I'll find something to occupy my time."

"Until your masters return," added Nick.

Meridian smiled serenely.

Nick continued to push. "How long till they come back, Jeek? What was the final calculation?"

"I am not aware of any return plans."

Nick chuckled. "Oh, hell, Meridian—we've already figured things out. We know why your masters chose to spare us."

"Then please enlighten me."

"Be glad to," said the midget. "You see, the Os/Ka/Loq know that we've already made the planet unlivable for a hundred years." Nick pointed through the window. "Hell, that ecosphere is so hot that we don't even dare send down a salvage crew to see about retrieving your masters' underwater vessel—Sappho's hidden cell. Too bad. I figure we could have learned plenty about the Os/Ka/Loq by examining that ship. Still, you can't win 'em all.

"At any rate, when those big Ribonix destroyers arrive with their nuclear missiles, the Earth's going to get a dose of hellfire that'll keep it contaminated for millennia to come."

"Your victory seems ensured," said Meridian.

"Not quite. You see, I figure that the Os/Ka/Loq have a pretty good handle on human psychology. I mean, they've had plenty of time to study us, under a variety of conditions: on the Earth, in the cylinders, in captivity aboard the Biodyysey. Over the years, I figure they've learned quite a bit about us.

"They know that we're one hell of a tenacious species. And they know that we're ultracompetitive—cooperation of the fittest is *not* standard operating procedure for the human race. Oh, we're cooperative all right, but it's a very limited form of cooperation and is usually based on the fact that an organization can achieve dominance better than an individual can."

The Jeek stared through the portal. "Among the Os/Ka/Loq, cynicism is very rare."

"Yeah, I'm a cynic all right. Maybe I've had good reason to become one. But my point is this. Your masters figure that those good old reliable human traits—humanity's twin demons, profit and progress—will be on the rise once again.

"The technological spiral which led to the first Apocalypse will begin anew. And a couple of hundred years from now, the Colonies will start to covet the Earth again. Oh, they won't forget about the Biodyysey, but they'll rationalize that the Os/Ka/Loq are just another problem that can be solved by the proper application of technology." Nick pointed a finger at the fiery planet. "And humanity will use its shiny new science to turn that burning hell back into a livable green world.

"The Os/Ka/Loq will watch this happen, secure in the knowledge that they won't have to wait millennia for their interrupted reseeding project finally to start.

"And then the Biodyysey will come back."

Meridian chuckled. "A most bizarre scenario."

"Yeah, it's bizarre all right. But it does account for why the human race is still alive. If the Os/Ka/Loq had released those skygene suitcases and wiped out most—if not all—of humanity, they would have had to wait thousands of years for the Earth to rejuvenate naturally. Either that, or mount a massive terraforming project themselves.

"But why bother doing things the hard way? Just let humanity go its merry way. We'll do all the work ourselves, and probably in record time. We'll restore the Earth. And then the Os/Ka/Loq can return to reap our harvest."

Meridian sighed. "You are truly a shortsighted and paranoid species. Perhaps longer life spans will help overcome these difficulties?"

It was the lion's turn to chuckle. He was actually beginning to like this Jeek, even though a part of him found the very idea revolting.

"Meridian," began the lion, "you are, without a doubt, a diplomat of the highest order."

"Among the Os/Ka/Loq," murmured Meridian, turning his gaze back out toward the golden world, "such a creature is known as a survivor."

EPILOGUE

"Downsiders—get ready!" ordered the hidden game matron, her swollen amplified voice filling the vast arena, her harsh words reverberating through the empty grandstands.

From his bench at left center field, Spigot leaned forward, permitted his feet to make contact with the circular skateboard. He heard the snap of the locks as his boots secured themselves to the board; he watched his helmet sensors turn from amber to green, offering proof positive that he was ready to play the game.

Spigot swiveled his head, glanced around the arena. The other five players were making similar preparations. Directly across from him, at the right center field starting position, was Wafer. The three corners were occupied by Guernsey, Special, and Plimsoll. Spigot did not know who the sixth player was. The man in the fourth corner was a novice, about to begin his first game, mere seconds away from losing his Downsider virginity.

"Linkages forming!" announced the matron.

Spigot felt the familiar vibration begin in his toes, spread into his lower legs as the powerful induction beams came to life, aligning his board with his Upside counterpart. Today, Spigot was lucky. He had drawn Blockbuster Giga-Quad as his champion. Blockbuster was a four-time grand winner and one of the best whirlers ever to play the game.

"Counting down!" began the matron. "Three . . . two . . . one . . .

"Fin Whirl!"

Spigot's board leaped forward as his mirror-image master opened his jetpak to full throttle and blasted straight toward center field. Spigot knew that he was in for one hell of a ride. To suggest that Blockbuster Giga-Quad was an aggressive player was to be guilty of gross understatement.

Spigot shot past Wafer and passed within inches of Guernsey—a definite near-miss. His board decelerated, pivoted ninety degrees, and began a long arc across the length of the field.

In front of him, Plimsoll and the novice headed straight toward each other—a head-on collision course. Upside, that meant that their champions were playing chicken. Spigot could almost envision the wild excitement rippling through the grandstands. Even without the intrinsic excitement of money wagered on both players, "chicken" was a surefire crowd pleaser.

At the last minute, the Upside masters controlling Plimsoll and the novice broke from their collision course. Unfortunately, both champions chose the same side of the field as their escape route.

Plimsoll and the novice slammed into each other; the force of the crash broke the induction-beam linkages, caused both Downside players to be wrenched loose from their Upside controllers. With a flurry of sparks, their metal boards skimmed over each other. Plimsoll, experienced at breaking a fall, allowed his padded body to go limp; he tumbled end-over-end several times, landed softly on his back. But the novice possessed no such game skills. The new man hit the ground hard.

Spigot's helmet lights went yellow, indicating a brief caution period. Spigot had no way of knowing precisely what had transpired beneath his feet, Upside. But statistically, he knew that over ninety-seven percent of Upside/Downside action was identical.

Plimsoll staggered to his feet, shook his head, picked up his unlatched board, and trotted quickly to the sidelines. The novice remained prone on the ground, unmoving. He was probably unconscious. Possibly dead. An ambulance sled raced out from the edge of the field, scooped the novice onto its flatbed, and whisked the player away.

Welcome to Fin Whirl, thought Spigot, tracking the ambulance sled as it raced through a portal beneath the vacant stands.

Today, the bleachers were completely empty; spectators only came here occasionally. Even the serious Downside bettors preferred to be on top of the action. Besides, Downside cameras fed their outputs to a plethora of Upside monitors. The perpetually curious could always watch the videos.

Spigot wondered if the notice would return. Stats indicated that most new players who suffered a violent collision during their first game did not come back. In fact, the majority of Downsiders lasted less than six months. Downside, after all, was not a goal of life; it was, more often than not, the result of an existence gone sour. Most of the men and women who ended up as counterpart players did so because they were running away from someone or something, although occasionally, underfinanced rookies deliberately competed Downside in an attempt to make a name for themselves. Those young hotshots hoped that their limited abilities to influence the outcome of a game might eventually draw the attention of an Upside sponsor. And once in a great while, such dreams came true. Once in a great while, a Downsider was promoted to Upside.

But most of the players here were like Spigot. Downside was the end of the line.

Spigot had been here for two years now. Before that, he did not know where he had been. The massive cribloc injections and neural restructuring had blotted out most of Spigot's memories.

Shortly after Spigot's mnemonic erasure, a smuggler—a man named Este Faquod—had offered Spigot a job, claiming that he had been a friend from the old days, when Spigot had gone by another name. Actually, Faquod had offered Spigot several good job opportunities within legitimate areas of his vast inter-colonial organization. But despite his age, Spigot had requested Downside. This had felt like the right place for him to be.

And in the two years since, he realized that Downside had been the proper choice. Spigot had made a name for himself as a sound, reliable player. In fact, most of the better Upside champions preferred Downsiders like Spigot beneath their feet. Spigot was a player who never tried to influence the outcome of the game. He did not introduce random changes, did not upset intricately crafted Upsider strategies. Spigot never tried to angle his torso to either achieve or prevent an Upsider hit; he never elbowed an opponent, or clipped one from behind when boards skimmed close. Spigot prided himself on being completely neutral. He was one Downsider who could be counted on to perform consistently. Spigot always took the path of least resistance.

My legacy, he thought, in a rare moment of self-analysis. Instantly, he regretted the introspection, for it brought to the surface vaguely unpleasant images from his former life. He had been told over and over again by his counsellors that cribloc injections and neural restructuring were never one hundred percent perfect. Sometimes, former memories would leak through.

This time, Spigot saw a beautiful golden-haired woman. She was sitting next to him, on a wide plush sofa. She was whispering in his ear.

Come to me, Corelli-Paul. I desire you.

Spigot had no idea who Corelli-Paul was. Perhaps that had once been his own name. But it remained a mere phonetic sound, detached from identity. In fact, none of the words meant anything to him. Even the golden-haired woman's obvious sexual advance produced no corresponding desire. Other injections had neutralized those sorts of longings.

Spigot squeezed his eyes shut—a technique that usually provided quick mnemonic relief. It worked. The images rapidly faded.

"Downsiders—get ready!" announced the matron.

Spigot—from his spot on the field where his board had stopped when the caution lights came on—leaned slightly forward. His helmet lights went green. His board leaped forward.

The game restarted.

"Thank you for seeing me," said Susan. She remained standing in the doorway, abruptly uncertain about her reasons for coming here. After all, this man was almost a complete stranger; their few meetings had occurred over two years ago, during those debriefing sessions following her recovery.

"Please," offered the lion, waving his arm toward one of the chairs in the center of his private office.

Susan forced a quick smile and sat down. She folded her hands tightly, squeezed them between her knees. The lion assumed a seat directly across from her. She swallowed, began tentatively.

"Your retreat . . . it's very beautiful. The woods . . . this house . . ."

"Thank you."

"It must have been completely rebuilt . . . following the . . . Paratwa." She hesitated. "A great deal of effort must have gone into its restoration."

"A great deal," said the lion. "Calvin's attack did horrendous damage to the A-frame."

"I saw the memorial," she blurted out. "On the lawn . . . the plaque listing the names of the dead. . . ."

"Thirty-two of them," murmured the lion, "fifteen from E-Tech and seventeen from the clans." His thoughts automatically returned to that terrible day, and he wondered again, *Why are you here?* He hoped Susan Quint had good reason for stirring up the past.

"It's good not to forget," she said, in a tone of voice suggesting just the opposite.

The lion frowned. "Costeaus have always prided themselves on having long memories. The recollection of injustice, of tragedy—these things are part of our heritage."

Susan dug her palms even deeper between her knees.

"Would you like . . . refreshment?" he asked.

She shook her head. "No. Thank you."

He waited. She said nothing, keeping her gaze locked on her bundled knees. Finally:

"I've been seeing a psych counselor for a while now. But recently, it's been . . . especially difficult for me. . . ."

"Gillian?" asked the lion.

She wagged her head, as if thankful he had been the first to utter the name.

"Yes, Gillian." Susan squirmed in the chair. "In the beginning . . . in the months after he went away, I used to have intense dreams about him. Almost every night. I could barely sleep. That phase eventually passed.

"For a while, things were all right again. I went back to work. I actually found a job without Aunt Inez's help." A hesitant smile crossed her face, then disappeared as quickly as it had appeared.

"But lately, the strangest thing has been happening to me. My psych counselor . . . she's a bit stymied. I mean, I'm a genuine one-of-a-kind. A human—a gencjob, actually—who briefly became the tway of a Paratwa. And as my psych counselor frequently points out, our current comprehension of T-psionic forces is little better than the pre-Apocalyptics' understanding of such phenomena.

"Still, my counselor has a theory. She believes that since my subconscious mind no longer dreams about Gillian, I may have undergone something called a mnemonic transposition. In other words, those tremendous feelings occasioned by my brief fusion with Gillian—the very power of that binary interlace which placed us in such extraordinarily intimate coalescence—those feelings may be coming back to haunt me. Since those emotions can no longer find release in my dream life, they're being expressed in another way."

"In what way?" the lion asked gently.

Susan drew a deep breath. "I guess you could call it . . . a mental affliction."

The lion frowned. "Your psych counselor . . . did she suggest that you come here?"

"Not exactly . . . not in so many words. But she did say that it might be a good idea if I sought out people from Gillian's past. People who knew him well."

"I see." He turned away to gaze at a permanent holo occupying the corner of his desk. The statue showed his wife Mela, posed beside a replica of a twentieth-century sailing ship. The surrealistic artwork had been created just last month, in the sea Colony of Aegean, during a glorious three-week vacation.

Mela looked happy; her smile was a composite of cool but vibrant colors, the most clearly discernible element of the 3D artist's juxtaposition of hue and form. Warmth infused the lion as he recalled the day of the holo's creation.

He turned back to Susan. "The truth is, I did not know Gillian very well. He was someone who had an extraordinary impact upon my life . . . someone whose actions altered the course of my existence. Yet, at a certain level, we were barely more than acquaintances."

She nodded. "From what I've read, I was sort of left with that impression. Still . . . I thought that you would be the easiest person to approach. Gillian did not have many friends. I was going to see Nick, but . . . well, I was watching some of his telecasts recently and . . . and he seems so . . . I'm not sure how to describe it. . . ."

"Utterly outrageous?" suggested the lion, chuckling.

Susan forced a smile. "I suppose so. I never paid much attention to the freelancers. I've seen Zork/Morgan a few times. But Nick . . . his presentation is even more . . . intense."

"Yes," murmured the lion, "he is intense. Did you know that his show has recently surpassed Zork/Morgan's in popularity? *Reckoning with the Czar* is now the top-rated daily freelancer report."

"I'm not surprised. At any rate, I decided to come here first. The only other real choice was . . . Meridian. Do you know him well?"

"I know him."

"Since he was released from quarantine last month, he's theoretically . . . accessible."

"Theoretically," agreed the lion. "But the doctors still keep him quite occupied." He paused. "The fountain of youth . . . it remains a zealous quest."

She nodded. "I suppose so."

The lion prodded. "So what is this . . . mental affliction of yours?"

Susan forced her knees apart, withdrew her fisted hands, laid them in her lap. "As I said, my counselor thinks that it might be merely old feelings being expressed in a new way. But . . . I'm not so sure."

The lion waited patiently.

"You see, I just can't figure out why my memories of Gillian would be continually expressed in this one specific way." She stopped again, feeling suddenly—inexplicably—flustered.

"Say what must be said," he advised.

"Yes, you're right. My counselor tells me the same thing—sometimes I don't come to the point."

She took another deep breath. "It's my hands. You see, every time I look at my hands, and then close my eyes, a certain phrase—a phrase endowed with strange feeling—comes into my mind."

Susan opened her fists, extended the fingers, stared down at her open palms.

"I see two hands. I see ten fingers. I see a broken nail. A couple of wrinkles. I see knuckles. Lines through the skin. I see fingerprints. Normal images, right?"

She closed her eyes.

"And now . . . I see something else. Now I see hands which could reach out to destroy the fabric of all that they touch. Now I see the hands of chaos."

The lion frowned.

Susan opened her eyes, swallowed hard. "I don't know what it means. I thought maybe . . . you might know. 'The hands of chaos?' Is that an expression . . . something Gillian used to say?"

The lion remembered. It had been the day of the massacre. Gillian's written message, delivered by Buff. He had kept the actual slip of paper, but there was no need to retrieve it.

He closed his eyes and quoted:

"The pressure never yields. Being more than one and less than one— simultaneously—is like living within a cracked sphere. And every day, fractures grow larger, threatening to shatter my life into fragments. I want to fight and destroy. I want to be fought, be destroyed. The hands of chaos cannot be denied."

He related the origins of the message.

Susan looked down at her palms. But with her eyes open, the word/feeling was gone. Her hands were merely hands again.

The lion shrugged. "That's the only reference I can recall."

For a long moment, she stared at him, and he was left with the impression that Susan Quint contained desires which transcended any hope for gratification.

Abruptly, she stood up. The lion rose with her.

"Thank you again for seeing me."

"It was my pleasure."

He walked her to the door. But as the portal opened, as she prepared to step through it, the lion placed an arm across her path.

She turned slowly back to him. Her eyes, brimming with expectation, met his.

"I have to know," she whispered.

"I understand," he said gently. "And I realize that you did not come here for advice . . . not really. But I'm going to give you some anyway.

"Learn to live with it, Susan. Keep it inside, no matter how awful that seems, no matter how hard it is for you. Especially, don't go to Nick or Meridian."

"But I have to know."

"They'll make your life hell."

She sighed. "One way or another, I have to answer the question. Is Gillian still inside me? Is he still a living amalgam within the deepest whirlpools of my subconscious? Or is 'the hands of chaos' just some mental trick I'm playing on myself, or some weird memory residue, a useless bit of flotsam from the days when we were together?"

"But that's not your real question, is it?"

Susan shook her head. "No. Not really. I suppose what I really want to know is . . .

"Is he coming back?"

BEST OF SF FROM TOR

☐ 53016-0 *THE SHATTERED SPHERE* $5.99
             Roger MacBride Allen $6.99 Canada

☐ 53022-5 *THE STARS ARE ALSO FIRE* $5.99
             Poul Anderson $6.99 Canada

☐ 52213-3 *TROUBLE AND HER FRIENDS* $4.99
             Melissa Scott $5.99 Canada

☐ 55255-5 *THE GOLDEN QUEEN* $5.99
             Dave Wolverton $6.99 Canada

☐ 52047-5 *EON* $6.99
             Greg Bear $7.99 Canada

Call toll-free 1-800-288-2131 to use your major credit card, buy them at your local bookstore, or clip and mail this page to order by mail.

Publishers Book and Audio Mailing Service
P.O. Box 120159, Staten Island, NY 10312-0004

Please send me the book(s) I have checked above. I am enclosing $ _____
(Please add $1.50 for the first book, and $.50 for each additional book to cover postage and handling. Send check or money order only—no CODs.)

Name_____
Address _____
City _____State / Zip_____

Please allow six weeks for delivery. Prices subject to change without notice.

THE BEST OF SF FROM TOR

☐ 53518-9   *THE VOICES OF HEAVEN* $5.99
                Frederik Pohl $6.99 Canada

☐ 51704-0   *THE PRICE OF THE STARS* $4.50
                Doyle/Macdonald $5.50 Canada

☐ 53415-8   *WILDLIFE* $4.99
                James Patrick Kelly $5.99 Canada

☐ 52433-0   *THE FORGE OF GOD* $5.99
                Greg Bear $6.99 Canada

☐ 53515-4   *NEPTUNE CROSSING* $5.99
                Jeffrey A. Carver $6.99 Canada

Call toll-free 1-800-288-2131 to use your major credit card, buy them at your local bookstore, or clip and mail this page to order by mail.

Publishers Book and Audio Mailing Service
P.O. Box 120159, Staten Island, NY 10312-0004

Please send me the book(s) I have checked above. I am enclosing $ _____
(Please add $1.50 for the first book, and $.50 for each additional book to cover postage and handling. Send check or money order only—no CODs.)

Name_____

Address _____

City _____ State / Zip_____

Please allow six weeks for delivery. Prices subject to change without notice.